PRAISE FOR THE EXPERIMENT IN TERROR SERIES

"Perry and Dex are two charismatic and slightly crazy characters that carry you in kicking and screaming along for the ride." – Naughty Between the Stacks

"I don't think, short of being completely ridiculous, I can encourage you more strongly to read this series. It has quickly moved to the top of my favorites list." – The Bookish Babes

"Halle continues to surprise readers with different twists and turns." – Living Life Through Books

"A ghost hunting adventure with original characters guaranteed to please!" – Romancing the Darkside

"Seductively entertaining…I'm convinced that it has some secret ingredient (like the sauce on a Big Mac or the coffee beans at Starbucks) that makes it immediately addictive." – Bitsy Bling Books

"Loved it, loved it, loved it. I can't say it enough. I've never related to a character as much as I did to Perry Palomino." – Pretty Opinionated

"Halle's first-person narrative is written in a breezy fashion that instantly made me feel like I could hang out with her protagonist." - Forever Young Adult

DEAD SKY MORNING

BOOK THREE IN THE EXPERIMENT IN TERROR SERIES

∞Karina Halle∞

\m/ Metal Blonde Books \m/

First edition published by Metal Blonde Books
October 2011

Publisher's Note: This is a work of fiction. Names, characters, places, and incidents either are the product of the author's imagination or are used fictitiously. Any resemblance to actual events, locales, or persons, living or dead, is entirely coincidental.

Copyright © 2011 by Karina Halle
All rights reserved, including the right to reproduce this book or portions thereof in any form.

Cover illustration by Crystal Chapman/KEAH
Design by Crystal Chapman
Author photo by Amanda Sanderson

ISBN-13: 9781466208179
ISBN-10: 1466208171

Metal Blonde Books
P.O. Box 845
Point Roberts, WA
98281 USA

Manufactured in the USA
For more information about the series
and author visit: www.experimentinterror.com

For my favourite M & M's from San Francisco, Mollie and Marc

"Red sky at morning, sailors take warning. Red sky at night, sailor's delight" – old proverb

From 1894 to 1924, D'Arcy Island was the site of a (primarily Chinese) leper colony run by the Canadian and British Columbian governments. Over the years, the lepers were left to fend for themselves, save for the supply ships that came in every three months to drop off food, opium and…coffins. On the virtually escape–proof island, at least forty souls lost their lives to Hansen's Disease. Though difficult to access, today it stands as a park as part of the Gulf Islands National Park Reserve. A commemorative plaque plus a few leftover ruins and makeshift graves are the only reminders of the travesties that occurred there.

MAP OF D'ARCY ISLAND

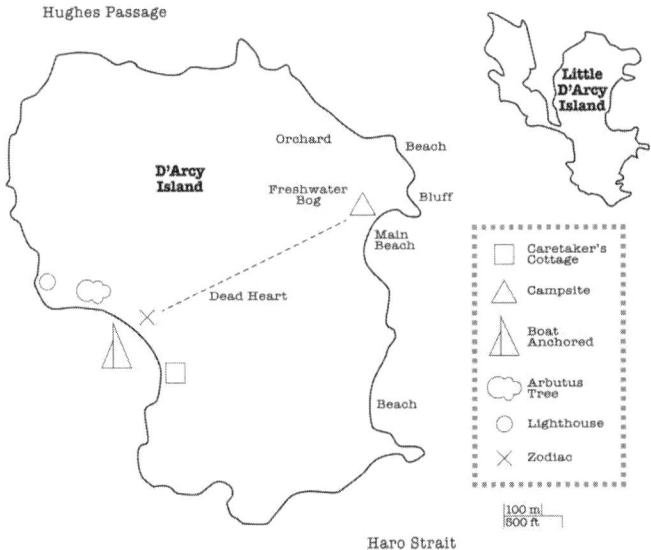

CHAPTER ONE

My mind reeled awake like the slow wind of undeveloped film. Everything was black. Very black. A shade of coal darker than anything behind closed eyes. But my eyes weren't closed at all. They were open and squinting against a light mist that burned them like salt.

Where was I?

I couldn't bring my mind around fast enough to remember anything concrete. But there were thoughtless flashes. The reel in my head spun wildly, more shady images skittering past the spokes. There was a forest. I was running. I was hunted down by hounds. Or humans on four legs. Their grotesque figures flickered in the woods like a waning pilot light.

Then nothing.

"My watery grave." The phrase floated around in my head.

I lay still. I was on my back, on top of something awkward and bony. I told my limbs to move but nothing happened. I concentrated, desperately finding some light my retinas could latch on to, to give some meaning to where I was and what was happening to me.

There were sounds, suddenly, like ear plugs were plucked out of my head. I heard muffled cries, like someone was yelling from far away and the sloshing sounds of water encompassing the space around me. I had the distinct feeling that I was floating as my inner ear rolled and swayed inside my heavy head.

All my senses were coming to me now. I could smell seawater and a putrid, decaying odor, like rotted fruit and mold. I felt dampness at my back and, bit by bit, the sensation that my hands were emerged in ice cold water.

I tried to move my arms again and this time they responded sluggishly. They had been in water all this time even though the rest of me was dry. I moved them out to the sides and they struck barriers with a force I barely felt through my numbed skin. The sound of the impact echoed around me. It told me I was in some sort of box or...or...

Panic swept through me. I moved again, feeling like I was balanced precipitously on top of something very peculiar. Whatever it was, it was smaller than the length of my body and I noticed my legs had dropped off below at an angle. I kicked them up. A spray of ice water fell up on top of my shins and my waterlogged boots thunked against something solid.

I felt all around me, wildly placing my hands and feet on whichever surface they could reach. I was in a box after all. The space above my head was only about half a foot before a damp wooden ceiling cut me off from the rest of the world.

I tried to catch my breath but the fright inside my chest was overpowering it. I was trapped, trapped in a box. A mime's worst nightmare.

Not only that, but a box that was filling with water. I felt the liquid fingers crawling up my legs and arms and saturating my back.

I started writhing and fighting. I couldn't keep it together any longer. I was in a box and I was going to drown in here.

I started pounding my hands against the top, hoping to break through. They were tired and without much feeling. I felt a gush of warmth flowing from them. It was my blood. It seeped freely from my tender knuckles and from the wounds at my both my wrists. I didn't care. I had to get out. If I didn't, I would die.

The water came in faster now and it wasn't long before I was slightly buoyant, rising above whatever was below me. In seconds it would come over the tops of my pants. My pants, where my front pocket felt tighter than usual.

I quickly slipped my hand into the pocket on a hunch. There was the lighter in there.

I pulled it out and started to flicker it. My fingers were cold and clumsy and I almost dropped it but after a few awkward attempts, the flame came alive, the spark catching hold. I held it up and away from me. The weak, orange light illuminated the space around me.

I was right. I was in a box.

It wasn't just a box though. No it wasn't. I knew what it was.

My watery grave.

I swallowed hard, feeling my world jar wildly with the incoming waves. I was in a coffin, set adrift in the sea.

"Your ship has come in." A man's voice echoed inside my head.

Amidst all the commotion, among all the confusion over what had happened – I knew where I was and why I was here. I wished I was alone. But I knew that wasn't true either. I knew that awkward, protruding, lumpy shape beneath me spared me of that luxury.

My left hand slipped into the water, gingerly feeling the bottom of the casket. Maybe the only way out was through the bottom. I was careful now to avoid what was directly beneath me.

The water was up to my chest now. I was running out of time and fast.

I placed my hand on the bottom and tried to stabilize one part of me while I planned to kick out with my legs, hoping that the splintery walls would give way.

Tiny, slimy fingers made their way around my submerged wrist.

I screamed but it escaped through my lips like a wordless gasp. The fingers tightened like a tiny clamp and held my wrist down, drowning it.

Something shot out from the water beside me and knocked the lighter out of my hands, enveloping the casket in darkness again. My arm was seized by another miniature grasp. It yanked me down into the water.

I tried to move, to yell, to fight, but the water's chill had seized me like poison. I was being held down; the water was rising and almost to my face.

Something moved beneath my head. It came up close to my submerged ear. Someone whispered into it.

The voice was distorted and muffled underwater. But it was unmistakable.

"Mother!" it cried out, cold child lips brushing my earlobe.

I opened my mouth to scream again but only found water. I took it in instead of air and let the liquid saturate the life out of me.

"Mother" it said again and again until we were floating together and the world closed its eyes.

~~

"Excuse me?" a strange voice said from behind me.

I took my change from the coffee shop barista, giving her a short smile in the process, and carefully turned around to see who was talking. It sounded more like a hesitant question and not a plea to get by.

A pleasant heavy–set man in a windbreaker, holding a coffee and pastry, was behind me off to the side of the line. He had that look in his squidgy eyes that said he recognized me. But for the life of me, I had no idea who he was.

I gave him an even shorter smile than the one I had imparted seconds earlier. I don't get picked up all that often but it happened enough that it made me leery anytime some strange man attempted to talk to me.

"Uh huh?" I said, trying to be polite but still seem uninterested.

His cheeks puffed up when he saw my face more clearly. He let out a little guffah that stood out against the coffee shop's irritating music.

"You're the ghost lady," he said, smiling, pointing at me with his pastry bag.

I frowned. Was I the ghost lady?

He took a step closer to me and jabbed the pastry in the air again, pink frosting falling off it and snowing onto the tiles below.

"You're the one on the internet," he exclaimed, just a bit too loud for comfort. I looked around awkwardly, feeling strangely embarrassed at what was happening. A girl in line was looking at me, obviously not impressed given her once–over, but no one else was paying attention. Typical hipsters.

I looked back at him and smiled again, despite the burning, tight sensation on my own cheeks.

"Oh. So you've seen *Experiment in Terror*?" I asked.

"Yes, of course," he said, chuckling to himself, the jowls in his throat waving back and forth. "I just stumbled upon it a few weeks ago. I love it. It's very *Blair Witch Project*. You know, it's real. We all know the *Blair Witch Project* wasn't real, but you know, this seems real. It is real, right?"

"Yeah, it's real," I said slowly, aware that every time I admitted the show was real it made either a believer or a disbeliever out of someone.

"I could tell. I knew that was real fear in your eyes. Sorry, it's Perry. Perry Palomino, right?"

"That's me," I said, feeling more comfortable with the situation. He was just a fan of the show. A fan of my show. A fan of me. My first fan!

"Well, I'll let you get your coffee," he said as he aimed the pastry over at the counter, where a barista was placing my latte down haphazardly, foamy milk spilling down the sides of the cup and seeping into the cardboard sleeve. "Keep up the good work!"

And just like that, he spun around and shuffled out of the coffee shop, munching away on his confection as he rounded the corner.

I wiped off the sides of the latte with a napkin and shook my head. Not so much about the sloppy coffee presentation but the fact that someone not only liked what I was doing, but had actually recognized me enough to stop and say hello. It was unnerving and exciting at the same time.

So much had changed over the last few weeks. The trip I took to the town of Red Fox in New Mexico had done a number on me. Having nearly died at the hands of two bitter and deranged ranchers/lovers turned skinwalkers, it really made me rethink my current situation. Mainly, did I want to be involved in hosting a "shitty" internet show about the supernatural when our very subject possessed the ability to not only hurt us, but kill us? I mean, despite my run–ins with Ol' Roddy at my Uncle Al's lighthouse, the possibility of death hadn't really been in the job description.

That's all I was able to think about on the flight home from Albuquerque. Dex had gone on his merry way back to Seattle and I was alone with only my thoughts and my iPod to accompany me on the way to Portland. Too much had happened on that weekend, aside from the fact that we were exposed to a type of danger that most people would never be in. My beliefs in what was possible in this world, in my reality, were ripped to shreds. My partner, who I still barely knew, had become the closest person to me (in more ways than one). And the show began to resemble nothing more than a vain attempt at notoriety through the most amateur of all mediums. After all, who wasn't famous on the internet these days?

On top of that, there was the fact that I was living a lie to my parents, pretending I had a job when in fact I had been fired from the advertising agency just before.

But within a matter of days of my return, when the nightmares of zombie coyotes and shape–shifting bears began to fade, everything seemed to right itself. It's almost as if it was my destiny to keep going, to keep our web show *Experiment in Terror* alive, and to keep Dex Foray in my life.

Dex sent me over the footage of what we managed to capture in Red Fox, and the results blew me away. So much so that I had to watch it with my younger sister Ada; otherwise I would have probably shit myself. Though not everything was captured on film, the fact is, everything really happened and it wasn't hard for me to mentally fill in the missing pieces we collected on digital film. Even Ada was scared by the whole ordeal. She had already known the whole story but seeing parts of it come alive must have throttled her.

It was hard to know what the public was going to do with the whole thing so I did the best I could and wrote up everything on the blog that would accompany the footage. I changed some people's names to protect the innocent (Dex had actually blurred out the face of Will Lancaster, the man who was tormented by the skinwalkers – I think that was a guilty reaction on his part) but I told the story exactly as it happened. I knew that a lot of people (probably 80% of viewers) wouldn't believe a word of it but it was truth, and to quote Fox Mulder, the truth was out there.

Luckily, whether people accepted the truth or not, *Experiment in Terror* got its proper (i.e. not a demo) debut on the Shownet website that following Sunday.

It was...amazing. OK, I know what you're thinking; of course, it was amazing because I was in it. No, not at all. In fact, I was barely in it (which I kind of liked – still not used to this whole "on camera" thing yet). But there was no denying that the show actually looked great. In combination with my blog and with the score Dex somehow whipped up in a week, "Red Fox" actually worked.

We had a show. Even my parents looked a tad more impressed about it (and they are the show's toughest critics). Dex would send me text messages throughout the week keeping me informed on hits to the website and if people were linking to it. That one episode was becoming a bit of a phenomenon, just as my original footage of my adventures in my uncle's lighthouse had been. Well, a small phenomenon, but that still surpassed any of the doubts I had earlier about the future of the show and my involvement in it.

The next step to ensure our success continued was for me to make Twitter and Facebook accounts for the show and manage them. I knew enough from my marketing programs at the university that we had to promote as much as possible. And since Dex was busy being a composer, a filmmaker, editor, and trying to arrange future filming opportunities, that all fell into my hands.

It had been a lot of fun, actually, even though all the "tweeting" became a bit of a crutch when I should have been applying for jobs. Then came Dex's brilliant idea to open the blog to comments. By the way, I say brilliant in the most sarcastic way. Opening the blog comments did increase a sort of communal feel on Shownet, and maybe attracted more attention overall, but unfortunately a lot of the comments were rather negative.

At first it was just people like ALEX64 saying things like, "This show is crap, what bullshit" and that sort of stuff, which is to be expected. I couldn't say I wouldn't want to say the same thing. Without a ghost (or whatever) coming up to you and slapping you in your own face, it was a hard thing to fathom and even now I had a hard time coming to terms with what happened. Honestly, it was easier to just pretend it was all a figment of your imagination than to accept that the world, as most people know it, is just an illusion, and predatory, evil, things really do lurk in the shadows. Lately, though, the comments were getting a bit personal.

Two weeks ago, Dex had come to Portland so we could do some filming. We ended up actually filming two different places that weekend – Portland has no shortage of haunted tales. The first place we hit up was The Benson Hotel, which always had a scary reputation. It's actually a really nice hotel with a spiffy doorman outside and everything, and most people have a very pleasant and lovely stay. Still, there was always someone, at least once a week, complaining to management about seeing a strange lady roaming the hallways and the grand staircase, or weird sounds and noises, or random stuff going missing. A lot of staff workers acknowledged that weird things did happen, but no one seemed very bothered by it, evidenced by a local "Ghost Walk" tour that poked around every weekend.

So when we showed up at the hotel, they didn't bat an eye. They said that we could roam freely in the hotel and poke around (without poking around in people's hotel rooms, of course).

We didn't really see anything too out of the ordinary. I was still scared out of my wits, as usual. It didn't seem to matter if I was getting attacked by animals in the fathomless New Mexico desert or if I'd seen a ghostly apparition in the elevator of a crowded hotel; I still got scared. But there was nothing wanting to kill us (a nice change) or anything really sending our minds packing. Just a load of things that "could be," which always becomes "is" in my own overworked mind. And thanks to Dex's clever work and bit of luck, we were able to convey the same thing on film. We caught a lot of weird floating orbs of light, and picked up weird heat shapes on the infrared camera.

Same thing happened the next day when we spent the entire night at a haunted pizza joint that used to house a brothel. Apparently the madam had been found at the bottom of the old elevator shaft with her neck broken; the verdict was murder. We often heard people walking around in the upper dining area (when we knew no one was up there) and we managed to get that on film. And the basement, the basement was something else. Hot and cold spots everywhere, more weird orbs and an incredibly creepy feeling at every turn. Even Dex, who is normally quite composed when he's filming, said he was happy to get out of there.

We had aimed to film something every weekend but as our series was just getting off the ground, and I had to keep up the illusion that I was still working for most of the week, that wasn't feasible. Luckily, filming both the hotel and the pizza parlor on one weekend allowed us to get two episodes out of it.

I'm getting a bit off track. Anyway, the hotel episode "The Benson" just aired and to as much applause as the "Red Fox" episode did. Unfortunately, that also meant the comments were coming in as well, and this time they were meaner. More personal, as I said. Someone "Anonymous" (aren't they always?) had started attacking me and the way I looked. Saying I was too fat to be on camera, that I was ugly, that I looked stupid and sounded stupid. You get the idea.

The worst part of it all was that I believed it. This anonymous coward was just reinstating everything I felt about myself already. I had always felt like I was too heavy to be on camera. I always felt ugly and I knew for sure I sounded stupid.

I know I should just shrug it all off. I know that the internet is a terrible place that attracts terrible people who wouldn't have the balls to say anything if they had to put a face to their name. But it was getting harder each day. Yes, some people said some nice things in defense of me (I wasn't fat, I had a pretty face, I sounded knowledgeable) but it was only the negative things I believed.

I wanted to tell Dex that perhaps we should switch off the comment section, or run it with a moderator, but I couldn't figure out how to bring it up without sounding totally insecure. Although I had been in daily texting contact with Dex, and sometimes it wasn't even work–related, I wasn't in that place where I could just tell him how I felt.

Back in New Mexico, after spending almost every waking (and sleeping...but just sleeping) moment with him, I had felt so connected to him. I know it makes me sound like some blathering girl, but I honestly felt like he and I were on the same page. We were finally communicating.

But since we got back, I only saw him for that weekend in Portland. Because it was my hometown, I just stayed at home and he got a cheap motel by the airport. I saw him when we did our filmmaking, and there were a few times I thought maybe something was going to happen (what, I don't know) but then he would go back to his motel and I would go back to my parents' house. All the intimacy I had felt in Red Fox was gone.

And the contact we had now was just in text messages and emails. I can't lie and pretend that I didn't get kind of giddy and stupidly smiley every time a message from him came in, even if it said something as simple as "liked what you wrote" or "I hate the new Muse album." But that was the extent of our "relationship" at the moment. It was like the kiss never happened.

Yeah. The kiss. It weighed on my mind. It's what my thoughts turned to whenever they drifted away for a few seconds. It's the feelings that were stirred up when the wind on the street caught my face just right, or when a certain song came on shuffle. Dex had kissed me, as we were perched up in a swaying pine tree, as we were certain we would meet our deaths below.

It seemed appropriate at the time. I thought I was going to die and I know he did too. But it couldn't have been just that, could it? Couldn't it have meant more, couldn't it have been something he had always wanted to do? I know it was something more to me. I'd been wanting to lay my lips on him ever since we first met.

There was Jennifer though, Dex's mega–babe girlfriend. The tiny, pathetic voice in my head, the one that so hopelessly wished that maybe they'd be through after our trip, was stifled. They hadn't broken up. The kiss meant nothing in the end. Dex was back with Jenn and back to his zany self.

Well, sorta. He had been off his medication in New Mexico (accidently) and though he had a few rough patches he was sort of normal, for lack of a better word, by the time we parted ways. Yet when I saw him again he seemed off. Bored, in a way. The playful banter we had shared was subdued and the bright, zealous light that sparked from his eyes had dimmed. He was obviously back on his medication again, or perhaps some new one, but whatever "illness" it was keeping at bay was also keeping the real Dex at bay as well. I didn't think it was a fair tradeoff. Yes, Dex was manic and often behaved like a wind–up toy but that was who he was. The last night in Red Fox I had told him I hoped he would always feel alive. I think my words fell on deaf ears.

But I was probably overthinking and overanalyzing everything as I always did. I wouldn't be surprised if I thought he'd changed just because of the circumstances. I mean, they *had* changed. I think I just had to accept that our relationship was going to change each time we were together. We were partners, we kept in touch and when we were together, we were at the mercy of something else. When we weren't, he went back to Jennifer and I went back to awaiting his texts like a naïve schoolgirl.

That dilemma aside, which was really just a need to keep my wandering feelings in check, everything really had fallen in place. Though last week's trip was canceled due to bad weather, we were supposed to embark on a trip to a haunted old leper colony in British Columbia, Canada, on the weekend. Our next episode, the pizza parlor one, would air when we were gone. And my 23rd birthday was the next week.

Everything had fallen into place, except the whole job thing. I was still looking, every day, for someplace to hire me, still lying daily to my parents about having a career. In fact, my 4 p.m. coffee ritual in the lobby of Portland's Ace Hotel signaled the end of my job search day. Another empty day of holing up in various internet cafes, writing worthless cover letters that would never be read and applying for jobs that companies wouldn't give more than a glance to.

I sighed and poured a packet of sugar–free sweetener in my coffee, watching the chemicals dissolve in the hot frothy liquid. It was frustrating, to say the least, having to spend so much effort in trying to get a job. It was almost like a job itself, but of course it didn't pay.

But as long as my parents didn't find out about it, I was going to be OK. Although, it was annoying and extremely stressful to keep on lying to them. So much so that I barely had an appetite (actually that boded quite well in one way; I'd lost a few pounds – take that, Anonymous!) and the guilt I had was tearing me up inside at night, clouding my dreams and filling me with shame when I was the most vulnerable. I had no choice but to deal with it though, and keep filling out stupid applications and whore my resume around town.

At least that guy had recognized me and looked pleased with himself for doing so. He was a fan of the show. That little encounter, as panicky as it made me feel, did a lot to raise my spirits.

I wanted to text Dex and tell him what happened. He'd probably get a kick out of it.

I brought out my phone but noticed I already had a text message. Before I got a chance to get excited, I noticed it was from Ada, not Dex.

–DO NOT COME HOME TODAY– it said. All caps, too.

A wave of nausea swept over me. I was simultaneously disturbed and puzzled.

I put the coffee back down on the condiments counter and texted her back.

–What do you mean?–

I sent it and decided to plunk myself at a table that was miraculously empty at this caffeine rush hour. Normally the 4 p.m. coffee break meant I took my latte back to my motorbike, Put–Put, which was parked a few blocks away, and finished it on the walk there. But if my sister was telling me not to come home, I wasn't in a huge rush.

I sat around for five minutes, fingers nervously picking at the rubber iPhone cover. Ada hadn't texted back.

What did it mean, don't come home? I looked back at my calls and texts from the day. There was a text from Dex earlier saying that the weather for the weekend looked like it was cooperating and there was a missed call from my father. I had called him back, though, and no one answered. I didn't think it was a big deal. He often called to ask me stupid questions (you know, "what's the name of that actor in that cop show, yadda yadda"), whereas my mother would call to make sure I was "fine."

Other than that, there were no clues, and Ada wasn't responding. I looked at the time the message was sent: A half hour ago. I keep my phone on silent but normally check it once an hour to see what had gone through. Though to be honest, I was checking it more and more lately in case someone had responded to one of my tweets, or Facebook postings, or if someone else had said something nasty on the blog.

Ada probably meant to send the text to someone else (it had happened before) or maybe she had a boy over or something. I didn't know, but what I did know was that I wasn't going to keep sitting in the coffee shop and pretending to drink my latte, which I had already downed.

I shrugged off the uneasy feeling, tossed the coffee in the trash and stepped out into the street. It was a mild pre–winter Wednesday in early November, less than a week before my birthday. I hated thinking about it. I had been fine with turning 22, but turning 23 took on a whole new meaning for me. It was closer to 25 than anything else and 25 had always been the age I figured I'd have my shit together.

That said, some stranger had just complimented me on my TV show (OK, fine, "internet" show) and that wasn't exactly something I had planned on achieving before I turned 25. Maybe this was just a sign of good things to come, all the things that I needed to acquire before I turned 25: A boyfriend, a condo in the city all my own and a job that showed people what I was really made of. Or maybe it would just help the last part. Either way, it wasn't anything to sneeze at.

That thought made me feel more confident as I walked over to the meter where I had parked Put–Put, and piloted him through the cold winds that ruffled my back and propelled me home.

CHAPTER TWO

I pulled Put–Put into my parents' driveway, amazed at how dark it was already. The clocks had gone back last week and I still hadn't adjusted to the perpetual gloominess. I hated knowing it would be a long time before the sun was bright and the days were long.

I eyed the house warily. The lights were on. The warm contrast against the darkness would have normally made me feel all cozy inside, but it made me feel strangely anxious instead, like the house was alive and waiting for me. I wasn't sure what that meant but I knew I probably had to trust my instincts. They were right most of the time.

I walked over to the front door, slowly fishing out my key. I paused on the bottom step. A strange wave of energy radiated towards me from the closed door. My anxious feeling intensified. I looked around me, wondering what it could be. A movement at my bedroom window on the second floor caught my eye.

It was Ada. Her small frame was barely visible against my room, which was lit only by my desk lamp. She was waving at me frantically, making the shooing motion.

I was about to step back and holler at her, hoping she would open the window and explain what was going on, when the front door flew open. My father was on the other side.

"Are you going to come inside?" he bellowed.

This was not the normal greeting from my father. Though it was hard to see his face since he was backlit by the foyer, I could tell he was scowling. Few things strike fear in my heart quite like my father does when he's angry. Ghosts and skinwalkers were one thing, but my dad was something else. Something I understood. Our tempers were unfortunately very similar.

I swallowed hard. "I was just looking for my keys."

He glanced down at the keys visible in my hand and walked back in the house. I didn't want to follow him but I had no choice.

I walked inside and closed the door gently behind me. He had disappeared. I shook off my boots, placing them neatly in the hall closet instead of leaving them lying on the floor like I usually did, and creeped forward down the hallway, hoping that I could get to the stairs and the safety of my room before anything happened.

"Perry?" I heard my mother call out from the living room.

I turned to my left and saw her and my father sitting on separate armchairs. They looked like a job–interviewing panel. In the light of the room, my dad was indeed scowling. He was sucking in his cheeks, something he did when he was keeping the verbal volcano on lockdown. Underneath his glasses, his eyes explored my mother's face and avoided my own.

My mother looked rather blank except for the lines of worry that always wiggled on her forehead. I didn't like this situation at all.

I heard a noise behind me and turned to see Ada standing awkwardly on the staircase, staring at me frightfully. Her eyes were red like she had been crying and her makeup was more smudged than normal, which said a lot.

"Go back to your room, Ada," my dad said forcefully without looking at her.

Ada's eyes met with mine and I could almost hear her saying, 'I told you to not come home' in my head. Then she ran up the stairs and I was left feeling very alone and very scared.

"I called you today, Perry," my father said thickly.

"Uh, I know. I called you back but no one answered."

"I wanted to know if you wanted to go out for lunch with me since I was heading into the city."

"Oh. Sorry," I stammered. My heart began to thump louder. This was not just about missing a lunch with my dad. I knew deep down inside what this was all about.

"So, I decided to surprise you and stop by your office," he said, his eyes focusing on me like a laser beam.

My heart must have stopped. It felt like it fell out from my chest and onto the floor, along with my lungs and nerves. It's exactly what I was afraid of. He knew. They knew. I was done for.

I couldn't say anything. What was there to say? The room swayed.

He continued, "Do you know what I found when I got to your office? I saw a strange receptionist. And when I asked if I could speak with you, I was told that you no longer worked for the company. Naturally, I got a little upset."

Oh God. I could just see my father blowing a gasket in the middle of my old work, disturbing the stuffy advertising suits just as I had done on more than a few occasions.

"And then your boss – sorry, your ex–boss – came out and explained to me what happened. She had told me they had to let you go. You took your promotion and then demanded you be allowed to work part–time."

My father continued on, trying very hard to keep his voice down and in control. I stopped listening. His voice wavered in and out of my ears without sinking past the first barrier. I looked at my mother but was unable to read her face. I knew she was disappointed in me too and that was probably an understatement.

"Are you listening to me?" my dad shouted, rising up out of his chair, his stocky body hovering over me. I had no choice but to listen. "Do you know how, how *fucking* humiliating it was to discover you had been fired?"

I winced and took a step backward. My dad was religious and never, ever swore. I couldn't remember the last time I had seen him that angry. Maybe back in high school when I was involved in that "accident."

I felt tears pricking the back of my eyes and a building feeling of hate and frustration flowing up through my throat. I was either going to vomit or yell back at him. The former would be a million times more preferable.

"We trusted you! You lied to us. For weeks!" he screamed, spittle flying off his lips and into my face.

"I had to!" I yelled back, unable to keep it down. "You wouldn't have understood at all!"

"Don't raise your voice at me!" he yelled even louder.

I bit my lip hard, hard enough so that I tasted the bitter salt of blood and clenched my fists until I felt all the energy getting choked in them.

"All of this for some stupid show. A show based on lies! A show that makes you look like a total idiot. Useless, meaningless and stupid."

The dam burst. Tears spilled out of my eyes, my fingers uncurled and picked up the nearest object, a lamp, and gripped it in my hands, ready to throw it across the room.

"Don't you fucking call me stupid!" I screamed. The scream came up like an overpowering wave of anger, like it was a cloud of pure hatred rising out of my body. My world blurred for a split second as the feelings drowned me.

Then...

All the paintings on the wall shook violently and fell to the ground in a simultaneous smash.

I froze. So did my father. I saw a flicker of fear behind his eyes. My mother covered her face in her hands and whimpered, "Not again" to herself.

I was panting heavily, trying to catch my breath as the fuzzy threads of unconsciousness began to fade in the corner of my mind. The living room carpet was bordered with glass fragments. Had my scream brought them down off their hooks? Was that possible?

My dad looked around him, dumbfounded, and back at me. He opened his mouth to say something but then thought better of it. He walked over to my mother and patted her on the back. She was crying softly.

"You see what you did. You're scaring your mother again," he said. His voice had quieted but the accusatory tone was still there.

I took in a deep breath and carefully placed the lamp back on the table. My emotions were coming back around. I didn't need to break the lamp in order to prove my point.

"I'm sorry," I said feebly. "I should have told you I got fired but I didn't want you to know. I was afraid you'd make me quit the show."

"Damn right you're going to quit the show," my dad said.

The urge to explode was rising again. I eyed the lamp.

"Perry, please don't start this," my mom whispered through her hands. I paused. She looked up at me, her eyes pleading. Not from concern but from fright. She was afraid of me.

I wanted to ask what she meant by "this" but I didn't. That seemed like a path I didn't need to go down at the moment.

"I'm not quitting," I managed to squeak out. There was no way that was happening. It wasn't an option. They should have known that.

"Perry," my father warned.

"No. No, I am not quitting. This job is all I have!" The panic in my voice was unmistakable.

He laughed. It was bitter, angry. "It's not a job. I have a job, Perry."

"It pays. I am making money. I signed a contract to be employed by ShowNet. So it is a job." I was losing my patience and afraid I was losing the war.

"I am not discussing this with you further. As long as you live in this house, you will not be doing that show."

"Oh yeah? Well, try and stop me," I said, crossing my arms, surprised at my own stubbornness and nerve.

He looked surprised too. He sat back down in his armchair with a heavy sigh and pinched the bridge of his nose.

My mother spoke up gently, "Perry, we're more concerned with the fact that you lied to us. I didn't think you would lie like that anymore."

"I said I was sorry," I mumbled but kept my stance. "And I am sorry. I feel terrible about it. I haven't been able to sleep, I haven't been able to eat. And I'm not lazing around doing nothing, I'm out every day looking for jobs. It's just hard. No one is hiring."

"This wouldn't be a problem if you hadn't messed everything up," dad said. "You had a chance for a great career and you threw it away. I mean, you actually had it in your hands, Perry. We were so proud of you. Why did you have to ruin it? Why do you have to make problems for yourself? You need to just...grow up."

The tears were coming again. Not from anger or frustration but because I truly did feel terrible. I hated lying to them and even more than that, I hated the fact that they thought less of me.

The tears spilled down my cheeks but I tried to hold it together.

"I'm so sorry," I said again, feeling utterly, destructively helpless.

"Just…go, Perry. Your mother and I have a lot to talk about," my father said, turning his attention away from me. It was like he couldn't even look in my direction anymore.

I sniffled, wiping my tears on my coat jacket and took off up the stairs, my vision blurring. I almost tripped on the last step but suddenly Ada was beside me and had me by the arm. We didn't say anything to each other; she just took me down the hall to her room and led me inside. I stumbled through my tears and flopped onto her bed.

I spent a few minutes heaving into the down comforter, my sobs choking my breath. Ada patted me on the back and I was thankful for the rare affection from my little sister.

"Parents just don't understand," I said into the blanket, my voice muffled.

"What?" she asked.

I rolled over and gave her a weak smile. "Will Smith was onto something."

She still looked puzzled at my old school rap reference. "Whatever. I'm sorry they found out."

"Did they figure out you knew?"

She nodded. No wonder it looked like she had been crying. They laid into her for lying for me, for trying to save my ass. I felt very guilty for bringing her into my mess, for having to cover up my lies. I told her that.

"It's OK," she said licking her finger and wiping away her mascara smudges on her cheeks. "They were mad, though. Dad said some pretty mean stuff."

"I bet Mom wasn't an angel either," I scoffed.

She tilted her head. "Actually…Mom was standing up for you."

I sat up a bit straighter. "Really?"

My mom and I weren't exactly close. We never had been. That feeling that I had earlier, that she was afraid of me…it didn't exactly come from nowhere. I always felt my mom treated me with kid gloves, more for her own concern than mine.

"Yeah. She thought maybe this would lead you to something better down the road. The show. Not the whole fake job thing. She even told Dad it wasn't that big of a deal if you didn't have a job at the moment since you were living at home anyway."

That didn't sound like my mom at all.

"You're sure?"

She shrugged and got off the bed. She peered in the mirror. "I don't know, it's just what she said. Then Dad ended up yelling at her. You know, the usual stupid shit. And I ran away while I could. And that's why I told your stupid ass not to come home."

Well, would it have killed you to text a little more information? I thought, but didn't say anything. She had done enough for me already.

She glanced at me. "So what are you going to do now? What are you going to say to Dex?"

Dex. Oh shit. For the first time in awhile, I had completely forgotten about him.

"You going to call him?" She came over to the bed and sat beside me.

"I can't deal with that now," I said, though I knew I would have to tell him something. I was supposed to meet him in Seattle on Friday.

It was just too much. My head began to spin wildly and I fell back into the covers, closing my eyes, wanting to shut everything out.

"Want me to text him?" she asked.

I sighed. "Could you?"

She reached into my coat pocket and pulled my phone out. "There's only one Dex in your contacts, right?"

I nodded.

"OK, well what do you want me to write? Sorry dude, I have to bail. Forever..." She trailed off dramatically.

"Oh, give it to me," I said impatiently, and snatched it from her hands. If I had to think about what to say, I might as well write it myself.

I typed the first thing that came to my head.

– Bad news. My parents are forbidding me to do the show. I'm so sorry. I'll try and talk them out of it but no promises. I am so sorry. –

I hesitated before pressing Send. It felt like a cop-out. But I did press it and threw the phone away from me. I covered my eyes with my hands.

"Ugh."

I waited a few seconds before I nervously eyed it. It was on silent after all.

Ada followed my gaze and peered at the phone.

"Nothing yet," she said. She looked back at me, "What are you more upset about? Losing the show or losing Dex?"

The question startled me. It was oddly accurate. "Who are you, my shrink now?"

"Well, since the old shrink quit, I –" she started with a smirk.

"Shut up," I cut her off.

"Hey," she smacked my leg. "You owe me, stupid head."

"I know." I just wanted to avoid the question. Finally I said, "It's both."

That was the truth. I was terrified of losing the show because it's all I had going for me. It's what kept me going, kept my confidence, kept a strange sense of importance and destiny in my soul. It's like I was meant to do this (do something) after years of searching blindly for anything that made me feel like I was as good enough as anyone else, or hell, even better, and I didn't want to let it go.

And Dex. I couldn't let Dex go. It was no secret I was in love with him, no matter how hard I tried to push my feelings down or rationalize it in some logical way. I just loved the guy. I know I didn't know him that well – but I loved what I did know. And what I didn't know drove me crazy like some book that you can't stop reading, just to see how it ends, just to see if your hunches were right. The thought of losing him, even as just his dorky little partner, pained me. Literally. The more I thought about it, the more my heart seized up in sharp little spasms. I put my hand on my chest in an effort to soothe it.

There was pity in Ada's big blue eyes. She knew. I didn't have to say anything. Silence enveloped us both as I got lost in my own thoughts, and she in hers.

"Things will work out," she eventually said.

I really wanted to believe that. "Must be nice to be young and optimistic."

"You're young too."

"Well, I'm not 15-years old anymore. When I was 15, I thought I was invincible. And don't say anything about how I was all fucked up back then; it's not part of my point."

She kept her snide remarks to herself and looked over at the phone. An apprehensive wave flashed across her brow. I knew the text had come through.

She handed it to me. I didn't want to look at it. I gave it back to her.

"You read it. Don't tell me what it says," I said.

She read it over. I studied her face carefully. The side of her mouth stretched slightly. It wasn't good. I felt sick.

"What does it say?" I asked.

"You told me not to tell you!"

"It's bad, isn't it? He's mad, isn't he?"

"Uh. I'd say so. He says 'Are you shitting me? You need to be an adult and learn to handle your parents better. This is fucking ridiculous'."

"Oh my God," I gasped and took the phone. She wasn't lying or sugar–coating it either. "Wha...what do I say? He hates me." I spat out the last words. The tears pinched behind my eyes, threatening to emerge again.

"What did you expect, Perry? I mean...he's kind of right."

I fastened my eyes on her, hoping her smug face would burst into a million flames. She flinched a little and that same look I saw in my mother's eyes passed over hers. All the anger and bitterness from earlier was rising up from my throat. It wanted to come out and get her.

I closed my eyes tightly and tried to keep calm. I felt so disjointed. It was hard to get control of my thoughts and to keep reality in check. She was just being Ada; I should have known better than that. And Dex had every right to be mad. If he hated me, I could only just accept it. I was the only one to blame here.

There was so much shame inside me. So much that it scared me. I felt like I was heading down a big, deep hole again. Who would pull me out this time? I couldn't even trust myself to do it. I was a miserable, pathetic mess. No job. No show. No Dex.

"Are you OK?" Ada asked. I realized I had been off in my head, boring holes in her Zac Efron poster with my eyes. I wasn't sure how much time had passed but my knuckles were blue from gripping my phone.

I wasn't OK. Not in the slightest. I needed to either pass out and push the world go away, or embrace it and put on the angriest music I had. Since almost all of my music was angry rock and heavy metal, that wouldn't be a problem. NIN might do the trick. Then I would systematically trash my bedroom and maybe put a hole in my wall. I'd done it before.

"You know what," she said getting up. "I'm going to go make you some tea. Then we'll think of what to do next and stuff."

I nodded bleakly and laid my head down on her pillow.

CHAPTER THREE

The sound of the doorbell's jarring ring entered my dreams and eased me awake. Something about water, darkness, a baby crying. Then the fragments of the dream were gone. Where was I? My eyes focused lazily on the silky ribbon tails that were sticking out of Ada's desk drawer. She had won those years ago when she was a promising ballerina. *She must be ashamed of them now,* I thought absently.

I raised my head up higher and looked at her alarm clock. It was 8 p.m. There was a full cup of tea on the bedside. I must have fallen asleep while she made it for me.

I heard a sharp giggle and flipped over to see her sitting on her window seat, on the phone with someone. She was listening intently and smiling broadly, her cheeks pink. I immediately knew it was a boy.

My phone was lying beside me in bed and everything came flooding back to me. The fight with my parents, what Dex had said. As disappointed as I was to realize that it wasn't a dream, I was too exhausted, emotionally and physically, to care as much as I did earlier. My heart and head were heavy and even when I tried to think about everything that had changed, I was numb.

There was also a tiny bit of relief washing over me. That was the one bright side to all of this: I didn't have to lie anymore. That weight was no longer on my shoulders.

I eased myself up on my elbows and rubbed my temples. Naps always made me feel more tired than before I went to sleep, and this was definitely no exception.

"Yeah, it's OK," Ada said into the phone, her voice a few octaves higher than normal. "I should stay home. I don't think my parents would let me out anyway. They're stupid."

She burst into a flurry of girlish giggles before saying, "OK hottie, see you tomorrow. Bye."

She hung up her cell, staring at it for a few moments with a goofy grin on her face before placing it down beside her.

"Hottie? Who was that?" I asked groggily, not meaning to intrude but insanely curious just the same. I knew Ada liked guys, but I didn't recall her ever calling any of them "hottie" before.

I fully expected her to tell me to mind my own business but instead she rushed over to me and held out her pinky finger.

"Pinky swear you won't tell Mom and Dad?"

I took her pinky in my own and promised. For once Ada looked and sounded like someone I could relate to.

"Okaaay," she grinned and went over to her designer bag and started rifling through it. She pulled out a high school yearbook photo, you know the terrible ones you got to hand out to your friends and sign the back of. Not that many people ever wanted mine with my double chin and blue hair and all.

I took it and looked it over. The cute, albeit older, face of a buzz–cut boy stared back at me. He looked like a jock with nary a spark of intelligence behind his dull eyes.

"That's Layton. He's my boyfriend." She pronounced 'boyfriend' like it was joke. I could see from her eyes she wasn't joking though. She was head over heels and trying to play it cool.

"How long have you guys been dating?" I asked, feeling just a tad protective. I remembered last month I had found a box of condoms in her drawer (I wasn't snooping if that's what you think) and prayed she wasn't using it with this guy. He looked too old for her.

"Oh, since the beginning of the school year," she said in a tone that was both casual and proud.

"And he's a good kid?"

"Yes," she sighed, and snatched the photo out of my hands. "Are you Mom now?"

"I'm just wondering."

"You don't trust my judgment."

"I..." I put my hands up in the air and ended up shrugging. "He looks cute. I'm glad he makes you happy."

"He does," she squealed. "He's more than cute, he's fucking hot. And he's on like every sports team there is."

I never pegged Ada to be the type to think dating a jock was cool, but if it was popular, then that explained a lot. Ada operated a successful fashion blog and who knows how many people she won over on a daily basis from just showing off her enviable body and insane wardrobe.

I wonder if she gets any hateful blog comments, I thought. I made a mental note to ask her later.

The image of the condom box flashed in my head again. I had to say, "I hope you're not sleeping with him."

"Perry!" she admonished. "That's none of your business."

"Maybe not...and I don't want it to be. I just want you to be careful. Things can turn ugly really fast and if you're not careful..." Fuzzy, angry memories drifted into my head. I waved them away.

"I am careful!"

"So you are having sex!" I exclaimed.

She leaped off the bed and crossed her arms. "For your information, no I'm not. And like you're a saint...you're sleeping with Dex."

Now it was my time to leap off the bed. "I am not!"

The accusation was ludicrous (though immensely appealing).

She raised her penciled brow at me. "Right," she said slowly. "You just spend all this time with this 'hot' older guy, you know, being chased by ghosts or whatever and jetting all over the place. Sure you're not fucking him."

My jaw dropped. It all sounded so vulgar coming from her mouth. Suddenly I felt ashamed that I had those feelings to begin with. And why did she use air quotes around "hot"?

"First of all, Missy," I said, sticking up my fingers and ticking them off, "I'm 23–"

"22."

"Whatever. I'm 22. Which means I'm old enough to be able to handle having sex with someone. Second of all, Dex has a girlfriend. Third of all, Dex is my partner. Yes, we spend a lot of time together, but it's on a purely professional level."

More images flitted into my head while I was saying that. The way he sometimes looked at me, like he was searching deep inside my skull to discover how I was really feeling. The times I found myself being comforted in his arms. The way I had fallen asleep with my head on his bare chest, hearing his heartbeat lull me to sleep. The way his lips felt on my mouth, the jolt of electricity that made dying almost seem like a fair tradeoff.

"Yeah, well you obviously want to sleep with him and it's only a matter of time," she said, stuffing the photo back into her purse like it was a secret document.

My ears pricked up at that comment but I brushed it away. "I doubt it, Ada. It won't happen."

"I hope you're right," she said as she walked over to the side table and picked up the cold mug of tea. "Do you want me to make you more tea since this went to waste?"

"Sure and what do you mean, you hope I'm right?"

"I'm sure you can figure it out," she said overconfidently and walked out of the room.

Figure it out? Figure what out?

I hopped off of her bed and followed her into the hallway like a curious cat. She had stopped halfway down the staircase and was just standing there, staring into the living room just as she had done earlier when I was fighting with my parents. A horrible feeling swept across me. What was she looking at? Were my parents both dead in the living room?

I didn't even let my mind dwell on that morbid thought. I walked down the stairs to join her and heard my dad's voice boom, "Just know I don't like this one bit," letting me know that they weren't dead after all.

I stopped beside my sister and followed her gaze.

My dad and mom were sitting in their armchairs. It was like they hadn't moved at all. The glass fragments and paintings were still on the floor.

They weren't alone. On the couch across from them was a man.

It took a few seconds to realize that I knew who the man was. I knew his slouchy position as he leaned forward on his cargo pants, his grey hoodie, his floppy, messy dark hair.

My nerves were on fire, gluing me to the spot. I wanted to look at Ada to see if she could see what I was seeing but I couldn't look away.

I closed my eyes tightly, thinking it was some fucked–up illusion. It wouldn't have been the first time.

When I opened them, the room had gone quiet and my parents were looking up at me. Dex slowly turned his head in my direction and our eyes met. Those eyes of his were unmistakable. Dex was in my living room, talking with my parents.

What. The. Fuck?

I was speechless. And thoughtless. I could only stand there, staring. I'm pretty sure my mouth was agape too.

"Perry, seems you have a visitor," my mother said.

I barely heard her. My eyes were still locked with Dex's. They were masked and offered no clues to what was going on. But the tiniest twitch of his upper lip said enough.

Out of the corner of my eye I became aware that Ada was watching me closely. Everyone was waiting for me to say something.

So I said the first thing that came to my mind. "Dex...what are you doing here?"

He pursed his lips and let it slide. He casually looked at my dad, who had stood up.

"Dex came all the way over here from Seattle to talk business. Your business," Dad said in that command respect sort of way. It was the professor in him coming out.

I finally looked at Ada. Her eyes were wide but she seemed to be enjoying the whole situation.

Dex was looking at us. He got up, easing himself off the couch, and sauntered over to the staircase, eyeing Ada with a bemused smirk. "This must be Little Fifteen."

"The name's Ada," she said in her angsty teen voice, the amusement disappearing from her face. "You must be Perry's crazy partner. You're a lot shorter than I thought you'd be."

I closed my eyes in embarrassment while Dex said, "Ah. I can already tell you guys are related. The Snarky Sisters."

I opened my eyes at that just in time to see Ada muster the evilest stink eye as she flounced down the stairs and went into the kitchen. I looked back down at Dex.

"Sorry to just show up unannounced. Can we talk?" he asked in that rich voice of his. I glanced over his head at my parents. They seemed to expect it. I don't know what they had been talking about but it was obvious Dex needed to bring me up to speed in private.

I nodded and looked up the stairs. My bedroom seemed like the most obvious place. I could almost feel Ada snickering in the kitchen at how absurd (and fitting) the situation had gotten in the last few minutes, from talking about how I hadn't slept with Dex, to leading him to my bedroom. It was insanity.

I walked up them with Dex coming up behind me. I felt shaky, nervous and pale. I wasn't prepared for this. I could almost feel the energy he radiated glowing at my back. Then vanity kicked in. Was my bedroom clean? Did I have underwear flung all over the place? I must have looked like absolute shit from crying my eyes out.

I opened my door. The desk lamp was already on but that light was a bit too romantic so I flipped on the overhead lights and ushered Dex inside. He stopped in the middle of the room and looked around, taking it all in. I closed the door behind us and did a quick scan to make sure nothing was out of the ordinary.

It was messy as usual but my underwear and embarrassing items were tucked away for once. Well, I guess the row of stuffed animals I had could have counted as embarrassing. Least they were when he laughed and lazed over to them, picking up my tattered monkey Tim.

He waved it in my direction. "How old is this poor guy? His fucking eye is hanging out." He flicked it with his finger and it waved back and forth like a pendulum.

I gasped and ran over, plucking Tim out of his destructive hands. "That's Tim and I've had him since I was two years old." I held Tim to my chest in protective instinct. Dex stared at me with utter amusement.

"So I have stuffed animals, so what?" I asked defensively. I thought my Alice in Chains and Melvins posters made up for that fact.

He smiled, shrugged. I put Tim back down in the pile with the rest of his friends.

"So?" I asked, turning around to face him, feeling all nervy again.

He was looking over my walls. "So what?" he repeated blankly.

I reached over and smacked him lightly on his shoulder so his focus was on me.

"Dex. What are you doing here?"

He frowned. "You're not happy to see me?"

My head craned back on my neck, caught off guard. "Well, yeah, but…I mean…"

"It's OK, I won't hold it against you. Unless you want me to."

I raised my brow.

He grinned, a very quick flash, before he wiped it off with the back of his hand. Then he was all serious, his lips in a tight line.

"I couldn't let you back out of the show," he admitted. "I knew if you talked to your parents you'd just fuck it all up even more."

I winced. That wasn't very nice. But Dex was nothing if not brutally honest at times.

"It's just a two–hour drive," he continued, oblivious. "I've done more for a lot less."

"You should have told me," I said.

"Yeah? And have you freaking out for the next two hours? Come on, kiddo, I think I know you by now. This way was easier. And it worked. You can thank me, by the way."

"What do you mean, it worked?"

He walked over to my bed, humming some song to himself. He lied down on it, putting his hands behind his head and kicked the mattress with the back of his heel. "Not bad, not bad. Could be a bit bigger, though. How do you fit your boyfriends on here?"

As annoying as he was being, it was a nice change to see him being a little more playful than the last time I saw him. Still, I didn't want him to get the wrong idea and I wanted to be a little bit serious about the situation. I went over to my chair, pulled it over to him and sat down.

"Dex. What did you talk about with my parents? What was the business?"

"Oh," he said as if he was surprised. "I just told your father that you'd be in some legal trouble if you broke your contract."

My jaw opened a little bit.

"Uh, you have some balls, you know that?"

"Oh, I know." He grinned to himself.

"I'm serious. That's like…that's like threatening my father. My father does not take threats well. Believe me."

Dex looked at me, turning his head to the side. "You give your parents too much credit. Your dad is just a dude. He may be your big, scary father but to me he's just a man who likes his wine, indulges in hypocrisy on a daily basis, and does what he can to be the main provider of the house. He responded just like I thought he would, like any man would. To reason. To logic. If you backed out of the contract, ShowNet would take action. You can't break it without just cause and the fact that you haven't figured out how to have a proper relationship with your parents is not just cause. Sometimes you need someone on the outside to point out common sense."

I mulled that over with a mix of emotions. I didn't like how Dex assumed he knew my parents better than I did, and I didn't appreciate his condescending opinion on our relationship. He knew nothing about me and my parents – he hadn't been here, growing up in this house, dealing with all the shit we had to deal with. But on the other hand...it worked.

I didn't feel like giving him credit though.

"And then..." I coaxed him.

"What? He agreed. He gave me some big long spiel about how disappointed he was in you and how he raised you better than that, which I tried not to laugh at, and how this show was not a proper career and blah, blah, blah–"

"Yeah, I've heard enough of that today, thank you."

"But then he came around and said it was only professional to do the right thing. Which is to keep doing the show. But you're going to have to start paying rent here. Sorry about that."

"What!?" I yelled, the loudness of my own voice surprising me. It didn't surprise Dex, though. He only looked mildly apologetic.

"You're 22. You probably *should* start paying rent. I have to pay my mortgage. It's called being an adult. Responsibility."

My fists began to clench again. I'd have a heart attack by the time this dreadful day was over.

"Thanks for the lecture, Dex. I turn 23 next week."

He chuckled. "That's not helping your case."

I sighed angrily and walked over to my dresser. I spotted a vial of this herbal remedy you sprayed in your mouth every time you were upset or about to have a panic attack. It was probably all a placebo effect but that didn't matter if it worked, did it? It was almost empty.

I sprayed it into my mouth as Dex got off of the bed and sauntered over to me, curiosity flickering in his eyes.

"Breath freshener?" he asked, taking it from my hands and reading the label over. He looked disbelieving and gave it back to me. "You've had quite the day, haven't you?"

"How can you tell?" I muttered sarcastically.

"It's written all over your face," he said pointing at my eyes. "Those bags belong in cargo hold."

I gave him my most withering look. "Did you come here to make things better or make things worse?"

I aimed the spray into my mouth but the nozzle was turned the other way.

I ended up squirting Dex right in the face.

He winced hard, grunted and turned away. I swear it was an accident but it was a perfect one. I burst into giggles.

He wiped his watering eyes and stepped backward.

"I guess I deserved that," he said, blinking rapidly at me. "What's in this, pure alcohol? No wonder it calms you down."

He came forward again and rested his hand on my shoulder. I felt that warm current flowing between us.

"Look, kiddo, I saved your ass," he grimaced, wiping away a tear.

"It's a pretty big ass."

The smile came easily to his lips, his eyes red but dancing. "We both know how I feel about your ass."

Ah, yes. He had grabbed it while we were slow dancing at the bar in Red Fox. It was the first time anyone had complimented my bubble butt. Well, anyone of importance, that is. And just like that I was starting to get inappropriate thoughts, images and feelings in my head, swimming around in a heady circle.

And the reality, that he was in my bedroom, standing close to me, his hand on my shoulder, wasn't helping matters either. I became aware that I hadn't said anything and the silence was getting awkward.

I cleared my throat. "I'm thankful you saved my ass. I really am."

He squeezed my shoulder. I stared up at his face, his strong jaw and expressively wide mouth flanked by his barely there 'stache, his low, dark brow that sheltered those all-knowing eyes that shined like polished coffee, the way his black hair flopped lazily across his handsome forehead. Wow. Thoughts like that weren't helping the awkwardness either.

He's your partner you idiot, I told myself. I broke my study of him and focused on the rescue spray in my hands. "So we're still on for this weekend?"

With his hand still on my shoulder he said, "How about right now?"

"What?"

"How fast can you pack?"

"Sorry, you didn't answer my 'what?'" I wasn't supposed to be ready until Friday.

Finally he took his hand off of me. My shoulder felt cold and exposed without his comforting palm. He walked over to my closet and flung it open.

"It's just as nineties as I thought," he said to himself, inspecting the haphazard contents. "Should I just start grabbing stuff? You kind of wear the same thing every day. Let's see, we need leggings, a band t-shirt and skirt. Maybe jeans."

I marched over to him and shut my closet door, facing him with my arms held against it like I was guarding some secret passage. "Seriously, where could we possibly be going tonight? Also, I wear my band shirts to sleep."

"I've seen you wear them at other times. Weren't you wearing a Kings of Leon shirt last week?"

"Dex!" I said through gritted teeth. I hated KOL with a passion. And also, he was pissing me off with his avoidance.

He yawned. Don't tell me he was bored?

"Here's the plan. I drove all the way down here to, uh, fix things. Now it makes perfect sense that you come up with me tonight to Vancouver. BC. Canada. Not the fake Vancouver across the river."

"Are you kidding me?" I said. "It's like nine o'clock at night!"

"OK, maybe we won't make it as far as Vancouver, but anyway, we'll get as far as we can. We have a hockey game to attend!"

"What?" I rubbed my temples again. None of this was making any sense.

"You said last time that it would be 'great' if we actually hung out in a normal setting and got to know each other as people instead of running around with ghosts and scaring our panties off each other."

It's true. I did say that. Not the panties part but I did mention, offhand by the way, that it would be nice if we could just hang out like normal people did. Like friends. But I didn't see where this was going.

He read the confusion on my face. It wasn't hard. "There's a Canucks hockey game against the Rangers tomorrow night. I got us tickets. We have to go to Vancouver anyway, to talk to someone about the filming. So you know, I was just trying to be a good guy and please you."

"Phhff," I sniffed. "Please me? What if I said I hated hockey?"

"I'd never speak to you again," he said, narrowing his eyes. It was hard to see how serious he was. He hadn't really mentioned hockey before, at least not when I was listening, but he also took the weirdest things very seriously. "Is it true?"

"No." I didn't have anything against the sport, I just didn't know anything about hockey. Understandable, since we had no NHL teams in Oregon, just the minor league Portland Winterhawks.

"Good," he said, still watching me carefully. "Then we can still be friends."

"So, we leave tonight…go to the island on Friday?"

"Correct–a–mundo. Then we come back on Sunday, just in time for your birthday on Monday."

"You know when my birthday is?" I was sorta touched by that. It was sad that I was so easily impressed.

He tapped his head. "I'm more observant than you think. Now, without any more jerking off from you, I suggest you get packing as fast as you can. I'll help. Where are your bras and underwear?"

I rolled my eyes, pulled out my overnight bag and started cramming crap in there.

~~

I don't think I've ever packed so fast in my life – I obviously needed to get out of that house more than I knew.

With Dex at my side it also kept any exchanges with my parents at a polite distance. My dad even helped us rummage through the garage to find me a sleeping bag. Staying on the island did not involve staying in any fancy cabins. We would be camping the entire time. Yeah, in November. In Canada. Fun times.

I could tell my parents were having a hard time coming to terms with the situation. They were still mad at my lies, disappointed in my choices but at the same time they understood where Dex was coming from. As much as they hated the idea that I had involved another person in my problem, they had no choice but to accept it. And having Dex there, an accomplished (sorta) and mature (again, sorta) man there probably helped.

And Ada…well, I knew how Ada felt about the whole thing. Just as we were coming out of the garage, she yanked me aside.

"You're totally going to sleep with him now," she hissed roughly in my ear.

I ignored her. There was no way I was going to get caught in that argument again, not with the subject slinking around in front of me.

Luckily we made it out of the house in record time and were soon cruising through the darkness on the I–5, heading north. Dex's black Highlander was packed with everything from filmmaking equipment to a tent and camping gear.

Dex is one of those people who prefers to blast the music loudly and keep chit–chat down to a minimum. This trip was no exception. I found a strange comfort in our shared silence now, just hearing the music and the sound of his toothpick as it flitted against his teeth. When we first met I was so nervous being alone with him, I just needed to blab about anything to fill the air. I felt just a teeny bit proud that I knew Dex enough now that if we needed to talk, he'd be the one bringing it up.

Which is what happened an hour into our journey. I was in the midst of checking my emails on my phone when I felt him give me a curious look. It sounds stupid but you can always tell when Dex is looking at you. At least I could, even from miles away. Something about those eyes…

"So I've seen you've got your fair share of haters on the blog already," he said. "Good job."

I sighed loudly. I had wanted to talk about this for so long.

"You're telling me," I said, giving him a pained and drawn–out look.

He seemed to think on that for a moment; a hint of gentleness graced his expression.

"Well, that's the nature of the internet," he mused matter–of–factly. "If you didn't have haters, then I'd worry."

"Yeah but they are really mean," I pointed out.

"The internet is full of meanies. Their opinion doesn't matter."

Yes, it does, I thought.

He picked up on that. "Okay, it shouldn't matter."

"Maybe we should close down the comment section... it reflects badly on the show, doesn't it?"

He chuckled to himself and shook his head. "No can do, kiddo. Don't underestimate the power of creating a community on the web. By having a place for people to voice their opinion, no matter how fucked it is, attracts more people to the site. The more people to the site, the more people to watch the show, the more people to watch the show, the more ads we get, the more ads we get, the more pay I get, and eventually you. It's a numbers game. You just have to buck up and ignore the haters. Everyone gets them, from the smallest blogs to the biggest websites."

"Besides," he said, slapping me on the leg. "I think it'll be good for you. Toughen you up a bit."

"I'm already tough enough," I muttered.

"If you were that tough, this wouldn't be bothering you. It should be water right off your back."

My eyes automatically narrowed into two little slits. He took his eyes off the road and smiled when he saw them. Not the response I was going for.

"Is that look supposed to scare me?" he asked, his lips twitching in amusement.

I wanted to explode on him, just start shooting the salvos and bring up a lot of crap about my past, so he had an actual idea what it was like to be me. But I couldn't. Because what he said actually had a point to it. I always considered myself tough...going through drugs and other problems while in high school, growing up with a family shrink (all my doing), the stunt woman classes I had taken for a defunct career. I had been through a lot – mentally and physically. So how was it that a few comments from people I didn't know were weighing on my mind so much?

I kept my mouth shut and looked out the window at the black rushes of roadside that flew past.

"Honestly," he spoke in a more serious tone. "It's not worth your time, Perry. You're better than that. And the more successful this gets, the more successful you get...it's only going to get worse. But you'll be OK."

At that last bit he reached over for me again, but instead of slapping my leg, he squeezed my knee. It was borderline ticklish. Any more pressure and I would have been squirming. He didn't remove it right away, either, and I could feel his eyes coaxing mine to meet them.

Too many feelings were running through me and my body was responding; my tongue felt dry and thick, the skin on my upper neck danced nervously, the hairs coming alive. I looked at him. He seemed concerned or interested in my response but there was something else lurking behind those brown eyes. Something I couldn't place my finger on. It was almost as if he was undecided. A restlessness.

"So where are we staying tonight? Your place?" I found myself saying.

At that his eyes flinched and he quickly withdrew his hand.

"No," he said, pursing his lips. I obviously said the wrong thing. I wanted to push it.

"Does Jenn object?"

If he flinched it was barely detectable. He did crunch down hard on his toothpick before saying, "No, no. She...it's just better if we get as close to Vancouver as possible. I think Bellingham is probably a safe bet, just find a Motel 6 there or something like that. If we went through the border now we'd cause too much of a fuss...especially with all the gear back there. I don't want to tell them we're there on work since we would need a visa and all that."

I nodded, not really convinced by his spiel but it did make sense. I wouldn't have blamed Jenn anyway if she didn't want me in their apartment. Still, the apprehension that Dex subtly gave off was enough to make me store the memory in my mind for future use. There was something else, and maybe one day I'd figure it out.

CHAPTER FOUR

"And where are you from?"

I leaned forward in the car and smiled up at the questioning border guard, who looked like he had taken on too many shifts in a row.

We were in the border lineup heading into British Columbia, a place I hadn't been to for at least five years. It used to be a popular jaunt for cheap shopping back in my high school days, but with their rising dollar and the visitor paranoia after 9/11, I hadn't been itching to come back. I was just glad I actually had a passport (thanks to various trips to Sweden to see my grandfather Karl over the years) since that whole regulation had changed too.

I understood why they were being thorough but it didn't stop me from feeling extremely guilty. And yeah, Dex and I were actually fudging the truth a teeny bit.

"I'm from Portland, Oregon," I said as confidently as possible. Even that felt like a lie.

He peered at us suspiciously, doing a once–over of the SUV with his eyes.

"How do you know each other?" he asked.

"We're a couple," Dex said smoothly, flashing him his joker grin. The guard did not find it as knee–shaking as I did.

"From different states?" the guy asked, trying to get a better look into the back.

"Yes," Dex said. I could tell he wanted to elaborate more but he obviously knew in these instances the less you said the better. We had decided that if we were a couple, it would attract less suspicion.

"What is your business in Canada?"

"A hockey game tonight and then a few days of camping afterward."

The guard locked eyes with Dex, trying to read him. *Good luck with that*, I thought while keeping the fake smile plastered on my own face.

Finally he said, "Go Canucks," and waved us through.

I gave him a short wave and once the car was a safe distance away, we both breathed a sigh of relief.

"Damn, he didn't even ask about what booze we had," Dex said, slapping the steering wheel lightly. We had stopped at the Duty Free store and he picked up a bottle of Jack Daniels and a carton of cigarettes. "I could have bought a few more bottles."

"What kind of weekend did you have in mind, Dex?" I asked teasingly.

The corner of his mouth lifted. "Oh, you'll see."

Last night we had finally found refuge in a motel a few miles south of Bellingham, Washington. We had gotten there pretty late, so we both retired to our (separate) rooms right away. It was nice to be back on the road and staying in strange motels I normally would have passed by. It made me feel like I was out there doing something.

Anyway, bet you thought this was going somewhere interesting. Nope. I slept in my room, he slept in his. We got up this morning fairly early and started on our way to the Great White North which, at this point in the year, was blindingly green in the faded morning light of autumn.

Our plan was to check–in to our motel in Vancouver in time to meet with some park ranger who Dex wanted to talk to. Then I guess there was this hockey game. The following day we would head out on a ferry to Vancouver Island, meet up with another friend of Dex's and borrow his boat to take us to the island. It sounded all very convoluted but I wasn't one to complain. I was just glad to be with Dex on another adventure, even though I was a bit in the dark about this one. Then again, all I had to do was ask.

"So," I said while watching the farmlands and bloated creeks roll past, "what exactly is at this island we are going to? I thought you'd have a stack of books all ready for my homework."

"I was hoping I would, but what little has been written about this island can only be found at the Vancouver Public Library and fuck if I have a library card. That's why we're meeting with Bill."

"Ranger Bill," I mused.

"Yes. Hopefully, he can bring us up to speed."

"So, you're saying that you, Declan Foray, isn't even that all sure of what we are investigating?" I asked mockingly.

"The island was a leper colony for many years at the turn of the century. A lot of men died there, Chinese mostly. That's enough for now."

"What is your middle name, by the way?" I asked.

"Why?"

"So when I use your name when I'm angry I can throw it in there."

He glanced at me and smirked. "Damned if you'll get it out of me."

"Can I see your passport?" I asked innocently.

He quickly snatched it from the cup holder he had stuck it in and slid it into the pocket of his grey cargo pants.

"Hell no."

"It can't be worse than Declan."

"Oh really, do you really want to get pulled into a discussion over who has the most ridiculous name here because that is a fight you can't win."

"I'm pretty sure I can take you on," I said smoothly.

He opened his mouth to say something, then sucked it back. Finally he eyed me playfully.

"You know, Perry, sometimes I get this uncanny impression that you are flirting with me."

It was true. I let myself feel awkward for exactly 2.5 seconds before I said, "You think the waitresses at Denny's flirt with you, Dex."

That was also true. And I didn't blame them.

"Because they do," he finally said. "Who can resist this handsome mug?" He stroked his broad jaw and I tried my hardest not to nod along.

"Complete with rapist facial hair," I added.

"Touche," he said. "Tomorrow can we make fun of you? I mean, if it won't make you cry and hole up in the bathroom for hours?"

"Ha," was my reply. I turned my attention to the landscape. Despite it being November it almost looked as fresh as a summer's day. Some of the trees still had leaves on them. Probably helped that, like all of the Pacific Northwest, it did nothing but rain up here. Yet on this gorgeous, clear day, rain was the furthest thing from my mind.

Dex flipped White Zombie's "Astro Creep 3000" on the mp3 player and by the time the album was over we were crossing a bridge and heading into Vancouver, the city rising around us like a kingdom of tall glass buildings, clear water and snowcapped peaks.

We ended up staying at a Best Western right on the entertainment strip of Granville St. For once it wasn't a motel but Dex justified the cost since we were only staying one night and we had a whole weekend of backwoods camping to do. It wasn't even that nice of a hotel but I was pretty excited nonetheless.

We quickly got settled in our rooms and headed out the door. Dex had been on the phone with the ranger and wanted us to meet him at a coffee shop on the corner of Stanley Park. Dex had been to the city a lot more than I so we opted to get there by taking the scenic route, the seawall that took us along False Creek before it opened up into English Bay.

It was a gorgeous day in the city. People were jogging past us in next to nothing, ignoring the temperature, which wasn't cold but it wasn't exactly balmy either. Families pushing strollers made up the other half of the population on the seawall.

At one point it seemed like Dex was going to overthrow a stroller in order to get past their ignorant monopoly of the path.

"No patience for the wee ones?" I asked as we scuttled past the offenders before they came after us with the baby launchers.

"No patience for their parents," he scowled, and kept walking at a fast pace. My fat little legs strained to keep up with him and the sun was overheating my yellow peacoat. When we got a safe distance in front of the stroller mob, he stuck his hands in his black jacket pockets and shot me a curious look.

"Like you'd have any patience for the 'wee ones' either," he said.

I couldn't disagree with him; the idea of babies and children always made me feel uncomfortable. It wasn't that I didn't want them for myself…I knew I would, some day. But that I was uneasy with them. They weren't like animals and they weren't like little short fat people. They were like another species altogether and one that I didn't understand at all. And they didn't seem to understand me either.

"I don't have patience for a lot of things," I said. "You and Jenn are not planning on having kids anytime soon, I take it."

I said it as a joke, not as an actual personal question. I mean, we weren't that close. But Dex didn't seem to take it that way. If I hadn't been watching his "handsome mug" as closely as I was I probably would have missed the whole thing. But I had been watching him as I always did and I saw the flicker of horror snake across his brow and burrow beneath his eyes. In a moment it was gone, but it had been there. It was a mixture of fear, disgust and shame and it matched the terror I had seen on his face many times before. Only those times he was actually in a life or death situation.

I wasn't surprised when he changed the subject. "I think I could live here," Dex noted.

He was staring out at the sparkling bay as we hurried along on the wall. I had to agree. The way the weak sun hit the water was hypnotic and spread out in front of us like a wavering welcome mat. The far off islands were dark lumps of green and on some of them was a light sugar dusting of snow. The sky was cloudless and cheery, bouncing off the mixture of high rises that bloomed to our right.

"Sure. If you don't mind being Canadian," I said.

"With our economy these days? No, I wouldn't mind."

"You'd probably have to marry a Canadian first."

"Mmmm," he grunted as we narrowly squeaked past another stroller army. "Too bad you're American."

I let out a shy laugh. Why did he have to say things like that?

We shuffled along in silence, his attention turned to the beauty around us. My attention was locked inside of me, where my confused emotions turned and churned like the waves that lapped to the side of us. I hated feeling like this. I hated how easily my feelings got involved in every single thing he did or said. I always thought maybe it intensified when we were apart, you know, like a celebrity you'd pine after from afar. But it only grew when we were together. Sometimes it felt like looking at his face and just accepting the way things were between us was the hardest thing in the world.

"You OK?" he asked as we rounded a corner where a large Inukshuk stood stoically over an expanse of beach. I must have been inside my head for the last five minutes.

I shot him a quick smile. "Yeah, I'm fine. Just taking it all in." I gestured at the gorgeous landscape for emphasis.

I could tell he wasn't satisfied with that answer but for once he just let it go. Maybe we both were hiding things.

It wasn't long before we came to a Starbucks on the corner of two busy streets.

"What does Bill look like?" I whispered to him as we walked inside. The shop was pretty much packed to the doors. The scent of coffee and sugar assaulted my nose.

"No idea," Dex said, and walked forward. Maybe he could sniff him out.

He walked straight over to where a middle–aged bearded dude was sitting, engrossed in a newspaper and sipping a tall coffee. We stopped in front of him.

"Are you Bill Ferguson?" Dex asked.

The man looked up, surprised. Maybe he did sniff him out after all.

"Yes. Are you Dex? Sorry I wasn't expecting you for another ten minutes," he said as he glanced at his heavy–duty watch.

"I walk fast." Dex smiled, all cheese and elbow grease.

I waited anxiously for my introduction but there was none to be had.

"Oh, OK," Bill said quickly, folding up his newspaper and getting out of his chair. "It's pretty crowded in here, did you want to take this out to the beach? It's a lovely day and I could bust some litterers while I'm at it."

"Just out there?" Dex nodded at the seawall we had just walked along. Bill nodded.

Dex turned to me. "Do you mind getting me a venti dark roast. Black? We'll be right out there somewhere."

Before I had a chance to object, Dex and Bill turned and headed out of the Starbucks.

What the hell was that? First there was no formal introduction and now Dex was ordering me to get his coffee. What was I, his gopher? He didn't even give me money.

I stood there for a beat, watching them wait outside at the intersection. It was almost like Dex needed to explain who I was in private, or had to discuss something else in private. I hated being clueless about something I had a part in, especially this time since I was making it my mission to appear more professional. No way was I giving those anonymous internet idiots another excuse to poke fun at me.

I sighed and ordered Dex's gigantic coffee as well as a skim latte for myself and went out to the beach.

It took me a minute to spot them – there were an awful lot of people walking about, considering it was mid–day during a workweek. But maybe they were all unemployed like I was.

I eventually found them sitting on a long and sturdy piece of dried up driftwood. Even with Dex's back to me, I recognized him anywhere.

I slogged across the beach, kicking up the sand, until I was standing right in front of them, catching them in the middle of some conversation.

Dex held his hand out for the coffee but I kept it at my side.

"Aren't you going to introduce us?" I asked, smiling at Bill.

"Bill, this is Perry, Perry this is Bill."

I handed the coffee to Dex and then stuck my hand out for Bill. We shook. His handshake was disappointingly weak.

"Dex was just filling me in about your project," Bill said. I thought I detected a hint of animosity in his voice or maybe I was just extremely paranoid. Probably the latter, though it did depend on what he and Dex had been talking about.

"Oh yeah, what do you think?" I asked, not letting on that I actually knew less than he did. I sat down beside Bill so he was sandwiched in the middle.

He turned to me, the sun glaring off of his balding peak and exhaled slowly.

"Frankly, I think it's a waste of your time," he said gruffly. "We've had film crews over on that island, archeologists. The heyday is over. There's a plaque now to commemorate the ones who died there so we've done what we can. I'd prefer if everyone just moved on so it could just be a park, just be a campsite that families go to for a nice holiday."

I could feel Dex staring at me intently but I didn't want to meet his eyes.

"So you'd rather we didn't tramp all over your island cuz it may scare off future campers, is that it?" I asked, which was somewhat ballsy.

"You're pretty direct." Bill chuckled unpleasantly.

"Only when I need to be." It was then when I shot Dex a look to tell him to shut up.

"Look," said Bill. "The park board has no problems with curiosity. But, personally, I'm uneasy about the island being exploited for a TV show–"

"Internet show," Dex interjected.

"That's even worse," Bill continued. "Internet show. You two aren't from here, you don't understand the history of the place. You just want to make things up in order to sensationalize it for a few viewers. You may end up doing more damage to the park than the government did back when it was a leper colony."

"That seems a bit unfair," I said. "We work history into our show, we don't ignore it. We plan to show it as it is. I mean, hell, I think a haunted island would draw more visitors to it, don't you think?"

"No," said Bill. "And D'Arcy Island doesn't need more visitors. It's fine the way it is. People go there to escape the crowds on other islands and nine times out of ten, nothing spooky or mysterious goes down. I'd like to keep it that way."

"When was the last time you were on the island?" I asked.

"Five years ago," he answered.

"So why all the concern if you have nothing to do with the place? You're what, working in the city parks now?"

"I have my reasons," he said grumpily, pulling his coat in closer around him as if he was suddenly cold.

"But you're not stopping us," Dex prodded.

Bill stared straight out at the water, watching the waves as if he was under their spell.

"No," he said finally. "I'm not stopping you. Only because I don't think you'll find what you're looking for."

Even I didn't know what we were looking for, but I nodded as if I understood.

"How are you getting to the island?" he asked Dex.

"I'm borrowing a friend's sailboat out of Victoria," he said. I raised my brows at him, which he ignored. Sailboat? Since when did Dex know how to sail? Ah, what did it matter – when did Dex know half the things he seemed to know.

"I hope your friend knows where you are going and will give you the proper coordinates and instructions when approaching the island."

"Such as?" I asked, just in case Dex's friend, whoever he was, wasn't so educated.

"Campsite is on the southeast side of the island but you're going to want to anchor off the northwest side and take your dingy ashore. There's some good anchoring spots near the lighthouse where the mud is a bit grabbier."

Lighthouse? Not again. I exchanged a quick look with Dex.

"You're not going to write this down?" Bill asked him suspiciously.

"I have a good memory," Dex said, tapping the side of his noggin.

"Anchor off the northwest then. It's only a short walk through the forest to the campsite. But if I were you, I'd think about staying on the boat the entire time. That island can play tricks on you–"

"What kind of tricks?" I shot in guiltily.

"Tricks... you know, like birdsong suddenly appearing or disappearing, or feisty raccoons. The bigger problem is that you'll be constantly worried about your boat swaying free of its anchor hold in the middle of the night. The west side is the best, but at this time of year, your boat is never completely safe in those rip tides. There's a reason why that island was chosen to house the people no one wanted. It was impossible for them to escape."

And it still is, I thought to myself. Dex looked at me sharply as if he shared that thought with me. I don't even know where it came from. It was like someone else put it in my head.

"Did you hear me?" Bill asked, getting slowly to his feet.

I stared up at him dumbfounded, not sure what he had just said.

"If you get in any trouble out there, you can phone me," he repeated testily. "Just know your reception will be useless most of the time and the boat's radio will be your only point of contact. In that case, I'd call the Coast Guard. If you can reach your boat, that is. It's not much good if it's out adrift in the middle of Haro Strait and yes, that does happen at least once every year."

"Can I use the Shining to contact you?" I asked. Dex smirked at that like I thought he would.

"Shining?" Bill repeated. "Oh, I get it. You're having a bit of fun, eh. Fair enough. But don't say I didn't warn you. Approach from the west, make sure your anchor is secure, tie up your dingy securely at night and try and keep most food on the boat. Like I said, feisty raccoons."

He looked over at a white "parks and recreation" truck parked nearby. "Now I better get on with the rest of the day. Good luck, you two. You'll need it."

Bill turned and walked off to his vehicle, leaving Dex and I sitting on the log with a wide distance between us.

"*The Shining* probably scared the hair off of him," Dex said, watching him go. He focused his eyes on me. "Now you've got a pair of balls today."

I rolled my eyes quickly. "I just like to know what's going on. What were you talking about while I was sent on a coffee run?"

"I was just getting the lowdown."

"Which is?"

Dex shrugged. "The history of the island."

"Which is?" I repeated.

"I'm going to call my friend in Victoria, Zach, see if he can pick up some books from the library there. We don't have time or the resources to get them here."

"So we're basically heading into this blind? Heading to an island that you can only approach from the west and stay on the boat and beware of killer raccoons."

"Ah, so they are killer raccoons now. You better watch that imagination of yours; the results might not be so pretty."

I didn't know what to say to that so I sipped on my latte, which had turned cold.

"Just tell me what you know, so we are on the same page," I said, my eyes imploring his.

He scooched over closer to me and faced me with his right leg lying across the log and leaned forward, diverting my attention away from my coffee.

"This is what I know," he said, giving me all of his attention. "It was a remote colony for Chinese lepers. They pretty much all died there. It's a provincial park now. It's hard to get to but people still camp there. Some people report strange occurrences. Most people don't stay overnight and when they do, they don't go back. Given that fact and the fact that so many unhappy people died there, I have no doubt that the island must be haunted. And despite what Bill said, we'll be staying overnight on the island so as to not miss a moment of it. There. We are on the same page."

Something was off. I wasn't sure what. There was nothing on Dex's face that told me he was lying but somehow I felt like he was. But to bring that up wouldn't do me any good. I didn't want him to think I didn't trust him. I did trust him. I just felt like he was holding something back, not out of spite or something, but because he wanted to protect me. It was almost like I was buying a house from him and he was telling me someone had died there, skirting over the fact that many people had died there from some massive brutal murder. Dex would be an excellent real estate agent.

I told him that.

"Okaaay," he said suspiciously. "You think I'm selling you something?"

"You know I'd buy whatever you were selling," I blurted without thinking.

He wagged his finger at me. "See, there you go, all flirting with me again."

"Don't flatter yourself."

"Why should I when I have you to do it for me?"

I grunted and stood up, tired of the conversation. He got up too and slapped me lightly on the arm.

"You know I'm kidding, kiddo. Ha. Kidding, kiddo."

"Let's go get this hockey game under way. I feel like punching someone." I started walking towards the seawall and the way back to the hotel, ready to take on the strollers and spastic joggers.

"See you're getting into the spirit already. That just warms my heart." He grinned at me before polishing off his giant cup of coffee and tossing it in the trash. Had he littered on the ground it probably would have caused Bill to come running out from behind a log, ready to slap a hefty fine on us. I knew that man really didn't want us going anywhere near his island, and I couldn't say I disagreed either.

CHAPTER FIVE

After the meeting with Ranger Bill on the beach, we went back to our hotel and I promptly passed out on my bed. The late night, the travels and the change of location did a number on my mind. Like usual, I had a bizarre dream that I couldn't quite remember as soon as I woke. Normally I was so good at remembering the details but lately I just couldn't. Though, perhaps that was a good thing. Some nightmares were best left forgotten.

The game was at 7 p.m., so I was putting the finishing touches of my makeup on and listening to the band Mini Mansions on my iPhone speaker when there was a knock at my door. It was Dex, who walked in wearing a ratty black and yellow Canucks jersey and holding a new, smaller blue one in his hands.

"Uh?" I asked, pointing at it.

"You listening to ELO?" he asked, peering at my phone.

"No. What is this?"

"Oh, I went for a walk, thought you should wear this."

He pushed the jersey into my hands. It was my size and not as hideously ugly as the one he was wearing. But still. Confusion.

"You bought me a Canucks jersey?" I asked. "I don't even know if I like the team. Or any team, for that matter. Or the game."

"You will. And you're welcome."

"I thought you were a Rangers fan. You grew up in New York, didn't you?"

"I was, now I'm not and I did, but I'm not in New York anymore. Either way, it's going to be an exciting game and I would be honored if you would slip that jersey over your pretty little head and wear it tonight."

I wondered if he ever tried to dress Jenn up, too, and drag her out to games. But there was no way I was bringing that up. I was getting the distinct impression that Jenn was a touchy subject this weekend, though I wasn't sure why. Maybe they had a fight or something. I can't say that didn't tickle the back of my head in a delightful way.

So I decided to be a good sport, be the anti–Jenn if you will, and put on the jersey. I was only wearing a thin, long–sleeved shirt at the moment anyway. I walked over to the mirror and peered at myself. It didn't look half bad. It was a bit tight around the boobs; Dex somehow had underestimated them, but it flowed loosely everywhere else.

"Really brings out your eyes," Dex said, standing behind me, meeting my gaze in the mirror's reflection. It was almost romantic. Then he said, "They aren't as angry as usual."

I mustered up the best glare I could, hoping it might shatter the glass in the mirror.

"Yes, that's the look," he remarked with a nod.

I tugged the jersey down further and walked over to my phone and switched off the music. Then I had to quickly check my emails to see what was being said on the blogosphere.

He followed me over to the bed and snatched the phone out of my hands.

"What are you doing?" I cried out.

"I hope you realize that I didn't pay extra for the wireless here and if you're using roaming on your phone, it's going to be retardedly expensive."

"I just need to check something," I explained, making a grab for it.

He held it high above his head, which was too far for me to reach. I was only 5'2" after all.

"What are you checking?"

"None of your business!"

"I think it is... if you're checking those blog comments, it's only going to bring down your whole weekend. We're here now, and there's nothing you can do about them. Haters gonna hate."

I *hated* that saying.

"I have to promote on Twitter," I stammered. That was the truth.

"I've seen your Twitter. You've got haters on there too."

That wasn't true. On Twitter I was amassing a range of followers who genuinely seemed interested in me and the show. Twitter had become something of an addiction for me. I probably checked it at least once an hour, which probably was racking up a huge bill while I was in another country.

"I have to text my sister."

"I'll text her for you," he said, and brought the phone up to his face.

I almost agreed to that until I remembered the last text Ada had sent me, about an hour ago. It said, "Are you guys humping like bunnies yet?"

Horror filled me with a jolt and I lunged for the phone while a "Nooooooo!" escaped from my mouth. I nearly knocked Dex backwards. He looked pretty shocked at my outburst and quickly tossed the phone back at me.

"OK, OK. No need to go apeshit here. Save that for the game."

I quickly stuffed the phone into my jean pocket for added security.

"Just promise that you'll just use your phone for texting and to stay in touch with your family."

"Why do you care?" I asked, grabbing my purse and coat.

"I just do," was his answer. I could tell he wanted to say more but he kept his mouth shut this time, for whatever reason.

Soon we were out on the streets and heading towards the game. It was a bit darker here than it was in Portland and people were out and about, milling on the streets, a mix of early–bird party brats, homeless people and all–around weirdos. It reminded me a lot of home.

The hockey games were housed at a large arena downtown and judging by the number of people in blue jerseys as we got closer, it was the place to be tonight. Without knowing much about the game or the team, I could see that hockey fever in this town was a very contagious and highly flamboyant disease. By the time we reached the steps that led us up into the building, I couldn't help but feel as excited as everyone else seemed to be.

We made our way up to the level where our seats were (I got a few random high fives from overzealous drunk boys) and Dex immediately made a beeline for the concession stand, where he was hell bent on getting us beers.

"As long as you're buying," I said, eyeing the prices. Eight bucks for a beer seemed like highway robbery but I figured it was all part of the experience. And since he was paying, I wasn't arguing. Dex and I never really got drunk around each other, so it was nice to actually just be real people and have a fun Friday night instead of worrying about ghosts showing up to spoil the show.

Dex handed me my beers – yeah, we got two each, stocking up you know – and walked up through the entrance until we were overlooking the arena.

He said he had gotten the tickets from his boss, Jimmy Kwan. Or should I say, our boss Jimmy Kwan. I'd only met Jimmy the one time when Dex was trying to sell him on the show and I hated him immediately, thanks to his terribly rude personality. He pretty much called me fat and ugly and laughed me out of the office. Well, I might be exaggerating but it was enough to reduce me to tears. But Jimmy also had a million connections and apparently hockey tickets were one of those perks. I probably shouldn't complain too much about the guy who is paying my meager hourly wage but, hey.

The seats were in the nosebleed section of the arena but luckily from the way the place was laid out, it seemed even the cheap seats got a pretty awesome view of the hockey rink. The seats were also on the aisle, which meant we didn't have to squeeze past the fans with our overflowing cups of beer in hand.

The tension and excitement in the air was thick and kinetic. The arena smelt like a mixture of ice, chemically cheesed nachos, and stale beer. The people around us were shit–talking the Rangers, which took precedence over the terrible anthem music blaring from the speakers.

"Good thing you're not a Rangers fan tonight," I told Dex as he flipped through the game leaflet some kids at the door were handing out.

He shook his head and placed the leaflet in my free hand. "You should probably read up on this, get to know the roster." He jabbed it with his finger.

I eyed it briefly. "Are you sure you weren't a teacher in another life?"

He laughed at that. It was nice to see it reach his eyes.

"We would all be doomed."

I shrugged. "We pretty much already are."

"Kiddo, I'm afraid you're the only person who actually listens to me," he said, peeling the lid off of his beer cup. I knew that wasn't true. Jimmy seemed to cave into whatever Dex asked of him, and my own parents were somehow shown the light within minutes of meeting him.

"And you barely listen to me at that," he added. "Not that I blame you."

"I'm listening now," I said, leaning in closer to him. We were already quite cozy in our seats and I couldn't help but want to make it cozier. He brought his eyes to mine and let them slide lazily down my face. "Tell me something," I said with a soft voice.

He grinned with a boy–like awkwardness that I rarely saw on him. "Yes, m'am."

And then he proceeded to explain the entire game to me, from what "icing" and "offside" meant, to who did what on the team, who were the best players and what constituted a penalty. If I were a hockey player, I know I'd be in the penalty box for most of the game. I'd wanna just hip–check the fuck out of everyone.

By the time we were at the intermission before the third period, I was heavily buzzed on four beers and trash–talking the Rangers with the couple next to me.

Dex was beside me being strangely silent. Not that he didn't lapse into his quiet spells from time to time but considering how enthusiastic he was (and damn loud) every time the Canucks scored, almost scored or made a save, it was a bit strange. When I wasn't talking to Jim and Trudy (the couple who were next to me) I was stealing glances at him. He was engrossed in his phone and from the way he was chewing on his lip instead of drinking beer, I knew it wasn't something good. I also knew enough to leave him alone.

I took my attention off of him and looked around at the large crowd. People seemed as lubricated as I was and the atmosphere was infectious.

"How are you liking the game so far?" Jim asked kindly, trying to keep me engaged while Dex was in texting land. He was an amiable looking man in his late 50s, with a shock of white hair and a leather jacket with the Canucks logo on it. He had been coming to games for almost as long as there had been a team.

"I think I'm hooked," I admitted. "It's fast, it's fun and aggressive. Almost makes me want to take up the game myself just so I can beat the crap out of some people and not get in trouble."

He laughed. "The small ones are the most dangerous. If you play against your friend here, I'd advise him to wear protection."

I giggled and looked at Dex. He had been telling me earlier that he used to play hockey when he was growing up in New York, and I had a sudden fantasy of tackling him while he was in full uniform. He'd look very sexy.

Dex finally realized that we had been talking about him and looked up from his phone with a sheepish look. What a hypocrite. Even though it was constantly gnawing at the back of my head, this itch that people somewhere out there were talking about me, I hadn't looked at my phone once this whole game.

"Sorry," he apologized, putting the phone back in his pocket and eyed Jim. "Are you trying to convince her to play hockey against me?"

"She obviously has a lot of aggression to get out," said Jim good–naturedly. "I'd be careful with her."

Dex smirked at me. "Oh, I am. She'd show no mercy against me. She's a tiny tiger."

Our eyes locked. A wave of tingles rushed through me. My head felt weighted with the beer and it seemed like there was more than face value to what Dex was saying. Then again, it always felt that way. With us sitting so close to each other it was taking a lot of strength to blot away the impulse to straddle him right there and show him how aggressive I really was.

"Hey!" Jim exclaimed loudly, tapping me hard on the shoulder. It snapped me out of my mini daydream with a jump. He was gesturing up at the screen above the rink. The "Kiss Kam" was on (you know, when they film couples in the crowd and try and convince them to kiss for the cameras) – and it was on us. Us.

There was Dex and I, our big, stupid faces splashed across the massive screen in high definition for the entire arena to see, with hearts drawn around us and a gum logo. I knew what people were expecting. Everyone – and I mean everyone – was looking at us. I suddenly wished the two seats in front of us were occupied so I could hide behind them.

In what felt like slow motion, my head turned to Dex. He was grinning at me, borderline sleazy. He lifted up his arm and put it around me. He took his other hand and touched my chin with his long fingers, tilting my face towards him.

This was happening. He was going to kiss me. In front of thousands of people.

Despite the mix of surprise and anxiousness flooding through me, I coaxed my wide eyes shut, parted my lips, leaned forward and…

SLURP.

He *licked* my face – from my chin, over my lips and nose, in between the eyes and ending at my forehead. I grimaced automatically, pulling back from the sloppy wet trail of spit he just left. My eyes flashed open to see him laughing like a 12-year old, while everyone else around us joined in too. I don't know why I thought for one second that Dex would have taken something like a Kiss Kam seriously. I couldn't have felt stupider.

But to show I was a good sport, I sucked it up and made an even more disgusted face for comic relief. I eyed the screen and luckily it just flashed on to another couple. To satisfy the giggles of the people around us, I took my hand and smacked Dex squarely in the forehead.

"Thanks a lot, you doofus," I said, rolling my eyes and trying not to sound as embarrassed as I felt. Oh, but he knew. He always knew. That's why he did it. That jerk.

Jim leaned over me to Dex and said, "You should sleep with one eye open tonight, sonny."

Dex nodded at him and wiped his mouth with the back of his hand. His eyes were devilish, enjoying himself immensely. I had the urge to smack him in the head again.

He took his arm off of me and leaned in closer. "Sorry, kiddo," he whispered in my ear.

I glared at him, hissing, "Would it have killed you to kiss me like a normal person?"

He smiled quickly. "Maybe if it was on a dare..."

I rolled my eyes again and sat up straight in my seat. I was relieved to see that the game was resuming in a few minutes, anything to save me from the awkwardness. On a dare? Or how about if we were about to die? Were those the only two reasons he had? That thought tugged at my heart a little bit, making me feel foolish all over again. I loathed this stupid school girl crush of mine.

He was watching me. I could see that out of the corner of my eye. I wanted him to get out of my head and go back to texting Jenn or whoever the hell he was so wrapped up in minutes earlier.

The players came out on the ice and all the attention was diverted their way. I needed to get wrapped up in the game again. And I did. I finished my beer, started cheering for a fight and slowly forgot about what had happened.

I didn't say much to Dex, either, and kept my questions directed to Jim instead. He was in the middle of explaining how even though some seats in the arena were empty (such as the ones below Dex and I) that Canucks games had sold out consecutively for many years, when Dex's phone went off. He snatched it out of his pocket and put it up to his ear.

Jim kept on talking but I didn't hear a word he was saying. My ears were tuned to Dex's conversation.

"I can't talk about this now," he said roughly into the phone, his voice trembling slightly.

He closed his eyes to whatever the person on the other end was saying. His brow furrowed, scrunching up his forehead in a landscape of expressive lines and the grip on the phone tightened. His other hand came up to his eyes, covering them. I could almost feel his breath seize. I had never seen him like this before. It was fascinating.

Finally, he took his hand away and looked up at nothing in particular. His eyes were red, but not watery. He looked plain scared. I wish I could have heard what the person on the other line was saying to make him look that way.

"I'm sorry, I can't," he said to the mystery party, his voice breaking. He looked around him wildly, his eyes catching mine for a second but they didn't "see" me. Dex could have been anywhere at that moment.

"I can't do this now," he cried out.

And then he got up, knocking over one of his beers and started hurrying down the stairs with the phone to his ear, shaking his head as he went. I leaned over and picked up the beer before the spillage reached my feet.

"Bad news?" Jim asked me. I jumped and looked at him, making an uncomfortable face.

"I have no idea," I said quietly.

"I'm sure it's nothing," he said sincerely and then turned his attention back to the game, hinting that I should too.

I tried. I really did, but now all I could think about was Dex. What was going on? Was he OK? As intriguing as it was, I also felt for him. Whatever was going on wasn't good.

I mulled over what it could be but my inebriated mind couldn't really come up with anything and the game's commotion kept distracting me.

Jim tapped me on the shoulder. I looked up to see him standing. A bunch of people on his end were trying to get out and needed me to stand up so that they could pass. I guessed even though there were 15 minutes left in the game, some people liked to beat the rush and leave early.

I flashed them a quick smile, trying not to look annoyed, and rose out of my seat to let them by. They blocked my view of the game momentarily and at what sounded like a very exciting moment.

As soon as they had passed I sat back down just in time to see the Canucks' goalie, Roberto Luongo, make a great save with his pad. The crowd chanted "Luuuuuuuu," as they always did when he made a good play (or any play) and I joined along too.

And then I noticed there was a woman sitting in front of me in the previously empty seat. She had probably sat down while I was letting the other people pass. I didn't know why anyone would catch the last half of the last period but people were fanatical here.

I looked back at the game but something strange brought my attention back to the person. I couldn't see her properly because a rail was between us and she seemed as short as I, but a feverish tickle at the back of my neck was letting me know something here was wrong. I knew not to ignore that feeling.

My breath slowed as my eyes locked on the back of her head. The hair was old–fashioned, like something Betty Grable would have worn with short, perfectly coiled curls. It was the shade of the palest smokey lavender. I had seen that hair color on someone before.

I wanted to lean forward to get a better look at what she was wearing but I already knew what I was going to see. The puffed taffeta collar at her neck was enough of a hint. As were the glimpses of pom pom appliqués through the rail.

I froze in my seat. My thoughts slowed. I only had one.

She was here.

The lady shifted, subtly, like she was receiving some incoming message from me, and turned around at an excruciatingly slow pace. She really was in slow motion – the rest of the world around me continued on at its regular go.

And then her eyes were peering up at me through the space in the railing. Blank pools of darkness rimmed by a shoddy makeup job. Below them her mouth was spread wide in a disturbing grin, her face cracked by the corners of her shellacked lips. It was a mask of pure and utter derangement and it was looking at me. Looking *into* me.

Every inch of my body was telling me to run; my nerves were sizzling at their endings from the build–up of dread. I wanted to look at Jim to see if he could see what I saw, to make me feel safe, to make me feel sane, but I couldn't. I couldn't do anything but watch.

Time seemed to lose all meaning and I wasn't sure if it was seconds or minutes that passed while I was under her spell, while we just stared at each other like two equally immovable corpses.

Then…

They look at you the way they looked at me.

Her lightly accented words formed in my head, much like they had on previous occasions. She had the ability to talk to me without opening her mouth.

I opened my mouth to say, "Who?" but caught myself. I don't think I could have formed the words if I'd tried. It didn't matter anyway because her voice continued resonating inside my skull like I was hearing someone yell underwater.

They'll always be afraid of you.

Who? I projected.

He'll fear you too.

Dex? I thought. He had already told me that on several occasions.

A different kind of fear.

What kind of fear?

I loved her so much but the fear drove her away. They put me away.

Who? Who did? Who is she?

It will happen all over again. They'll take you too. And I won't be able to help you. It will be too late.

Help me? I thought, while waves of dizziness pulled at my eyes. Despite the anguish in her words, her face remained caught in that same, creepy clown–faced expression. *How are you helping me? What do you want from me? Why are you here?*

I'm always here. I always have been. But you can't end up like me.

How the hell would I ever end up like you? I mustered.

It's easy. You let them talk to you, you talk to them. Everyone will pull away, all the ones that you love, and you'll realize they never loved you. Not enough. Blood runs thin. There are no ties. And they'll take you too.

Take me where?! Panic and frustration shivered up my spine. I didn't know what she was talking about and it was terrifying. She was talking inside my head. She was here. She had to know something.

You're not crazy. But I'm not here.

What the fuck?

Be there for him. He may be the only one there for you in the end. The end. When they come for you. That's the end. Then it's just you and me. Forever. Forever. Forever.

Her words grew louder and louder as they bounced around in my head until they were as loud as a jackhammer and as painful as a drill. I closed my eyes in pain and put my hands to my ears, vaguely aware that people were staring at me. I thought I heard Jim ask, "Are you all right?" but it was barely audible above the racket inside my brain.

Her face flashed before my closed eyes and she was inside of me. I was unable to escape her stretched, inhumane face. The darkness started to close around me like a cloak. There was no way out.

I screamed and jumped up, stumbling over my purse. The bright lights of the arena blinded my eyes but I kept them focused enough on the ground in front of me. I grabbed my purse and made a run for it, nearly tripping again over Dex's empty seat, and then flung myself awkwardly down the steps, almost taking out a young boy who was making his way into the stands.

"Sorry," I cried out, and I got a quick glimpse of where I had been sitting. The crowd around me was staring at me full of amusement and concern, while Creepy Clown Lady sat there, watching me. Always watching me.

I looked away before she could get in my head again, before I could hear her demonic chanting, and booked it down the hallway that lead into the rest of the building. I ran until I was out beside the concession stand we had been at earlier. It was now closed, which made me feel even more creeped out, but there were enough people milling about, leaving the game early, so that I wasn't entirely alone.

I leaned forward, my hands on my knees. I needed to catch my breath and to lasso my brain, which was running wildly all over the place. What had just happened? And did it actually happen?

I listened, half expecting her voice to resonate in my head again, but there was nothing but the sound of my heart pounding madly and the pulsing flow of blood. I wasn't as relieved as you would think. I was just worried. She said she wasn't there, but I had seen her. I had heard her. Rarely do your illusions tell you they are actually illusions. Just how fucking crazy was I?

As I pondered that, my mind running over what she said, what she could have meant, I realized that Dex was standing nearby. He was leaning against the wall near the entrance to the restrooms, his back to me, his head bent over. It didn't look like he was on the phone anymore. He looked so vulnerable in his ratty jersey, back to me, back to the things he was afraid of.

A different kind of fear.

I straightened up and walked over to him. Even if he wanted to be alone, I sure as hell didn't.

"Hey," I said. I still hadn't caught my breath yet so the word came out in a whisper.

He didn't move or flinch. I stopped in front of him. He kept his head down, staring at a spot on the floor. I followed his eyes. There was nothing there.

Did he just have the same experience as I had?

"Dex," I whispered. "Are you OK? Did you see her too?"

He blinked, a sign that he had heard me, and lifted his head. He looked horrible. His eyes were dull like they had given up seeing anything, his lips were raw and chewed on. His hair was messier than normal, as if he had been pulling it out. I forgot all about clown lady and immediately wanted to embrace him, to smooth down his hair with my hands, to make everything OK. If only I had that power.

"Oh," he said listlessly. "I'm fine."

"No, you're not."

"Neither are you. You look spooked."

"I am spooked. About you." And Creepy Clown Lady but for some reason I didn't feel like I should bring it up, lest the attention get diverted to me. I wanted to know what happened to him. I needed to know.

"Who was on the phone? Who called you?" I asked, carefully placing my hand on his shoulder. He stared at me. From that angle, with the way that his arched brows connected with the bone, he was as unnerving as she had been. I thought he was going to kill me.

I took my hand off of his shoulder. That action broke his concentration. The hate left his eyes, his forehead relaxed.

He came off of the wall and stretched his arms above his head. He groaned, holding the pose for a few seconds, then let his limbs flop to the side. He shook out his shoulders, pursed his lips and said, "You want to get out of here? Game's almost over. We have this one in the bag."

There was nothing I wanted more than to get the hell out of there, but I wasn't going without an answer of some kind.

I sighed and stood rigidly, hoping I conveyed business. It was hard to feel authoritative at my height.

"We'll go when you tell me what the hell is going on," I said sternly, keeping my eyes as hard as steel.

He gave me a wry look. "No offense Perry, but some things are a private matter."

Oh.

"I'm sorry," I said feebly. "I'm just worried about you."

He shrugged. "It's fine.

"Was it Jenn? Is she OK?"

"It's *fine*."

I could tell he didn't want to talk about it. And after all, why should he discuss personal problems with me? I didn't discuss personal things with him.

"Now, are *you* OK?" he asked, taking a step closer.

I quickly nodded. If that's how he was going to be, I didn't have to share my fears either. My fears that I might be going insane.

"Then we're all good," he stated. "Do you want to come with me to a strip club?"

"Say what?"

"Come on." He took my arm and led me towards the doors just as the buzzer from inside went off, signaling the end of the game. "Game's done. The rest of the night awaits."

~~

It probably won't come as much of a surprise to you but I had never been in a strip club before. I wasn't sure exactly what to expect, yet it still met my expectations. I've never blushed so hard before in my life.

After we left the hockey arena, beating the throngs of excited and drunk fans by milliseconds, we walked quickly through the brisk night air until we got to a strip club/hotel past our hotel, just at the foot of the Granville St. Bridge.

It was apparent that Dex had been here many times before. It wasn't like the barely-dressed waitresses knew him by name or anything, but he knew his way around the place all right. For a minute I was certain he was going to make us sit at the foot of the stage where the bare-breasted strippers danced but I think he could tell I was feeling as awkward as anything and led me to a dark, small booth in the corner. We still had a nice view of the stage anyway. Well, nice for him.

"Look at it this way," he said to me as the waitress gave us our drinks (he ordered us both Jack and Coke, big surprise). "You pay cover going into any other bar nowadays. Might as well get a show with it as well."

He raised his glass at me. I held up mine.

"Even though these drinks are probably $10 each?" I mused.

"Oh, it's worth it." And then we clinked glasses.

I looked around us warily. The place was half full. The creepier guys were as close to the dancers as possible, as were your usual Ed Hardy–wearing douchebags. On the stage the last stripper was just stepping off and another one was coming on. She was dressed in a flurry of sequins and sheer clothing. Having just seen the previous girl exit bare–ass naked, I knew it wouldn't be long before this one would be as well. She was tall, beautifully crafted (by God and her plastic surgeon) and had a thick wave of ravishingly red hair.

"I guess we'll find out soon if the carpet matches the drapes," I said underneath my breath.

"Ha," he remarked, leaning back in his seat. "There's not a carpet in this place. All hardwood."

The music came on and the stripper started her artful grinding.

"Marla always has the best moves here, doesn't she?" he said, his eyes enraptured with her, as if I'd know. I couldn't help but feel a twinge of jealousy at the way he was looking at her.

"You know her name?"

"You always remember the best ones. That's not saying much," he said. I never really took Dex for a stripper sort of guy. In fact, I never really thought of Dex as much of a guy in many respects. But why not? He played video games. He liked rock music. He probably watched a lot of porn as well. And like most guys, it didn't seem to matter that his own girlfriend was a million times hotter than any of these girls.

I remember finding out my boyfriend in college, Mason, had a nasty porn habit. It wasn't even that nasty; I was just so shocked. Why did he need porn when he had me? Looking back, I don't blame him one bit for it. Maybe it's because now that I was older, I kind of understood. And maybe it would have disappointed the old me to learn that Dex was a frequent customer of strip clubs, but now it didn't at all. If it hadn't made me feel deathly insecure about my own appearance, it would have been a turn on. Not that I needed another reason to find my partner attractive.

He shot me a sly look, and asked, "Is this making you uncomfortable?"

"You'd like that, wouldn't you?"

"You think less of me now."

I laughed at the mock hurt look on his face. "If anything I think more of you."

He smiled and reached over for my glass, lifting it up to my face for me to drink. "Good," he said. "You're learning."

I raised my brow but slurped back on the drink. I didn't need all that much encouragement, though my tiny voice of reason piped up that getting drunk around Dex, at a strip club, was not the best idea. It was only a matter of time before my insecurities starting spilling out of me, leaving me as exposed as Marla, who, at this point, had no hair down there to verify that she was a redhead. Dex was right. All hardwood.

"You need to relax a bit, kiddo," he said. "Enjoy it. Enjoy the naked ladies and the pervy weirdos and the free booze."

"I'm sitting with a pervy weirdo."

"So you should be used to it. And you know what? I need to relax too. This place helps. You just feel things. No need for thoughts here."

"Except perverted thoughts."

"That's not really thinking. That's instinct."

He waved over the waitress, this time a different one dressed in a simple black dress. Her hair was cut short, which showed off her cute, minxy face and pouty lips.

"Two more Jack and Coke doubles, sweetheart," he said to her. He was sleazy about it, which would have bothered me, but I detected that level of amusement that always sat beneath Dex's surface. In the end, everything was still a bit of a joke.

The waitress eyed me up and down. I had already taken off the Canucks jersey and was just wearing my black top from underneath. "This your girlfriend? She's cute."

I fidgeted while Dex said, "She is cute, isn't she."

I blushed at what Dex said (and at the fact that he didn't correct her – it's the little things). She eyed me again and came in closer to me, smelling like overtly flowery body lotion. "Honey, with your eyes and those breasts, you should be up there too." And like that, she left, leaving Dex and I saddled with that comment.

My cheeks grew hot, hotter than they had been all night, and I gave Dex an incredulous look.

"Guess it doesn't matter what sex you are," I squeaked.

"Don't be so modest," he said, turning his attention back to the next dancer, a black girl with a butt that rivaled mine. Maybe I could be a stripper...if I lost a million pounds and wore 10–inch heels.

"I'm not modest..." I trailed off. I really didn't need to get into it. Once again the booze was just begging for me to open up like a book.

"You know, kiddo...you're way better than any of these women," he said seriously, his eyes still on the stage. "You just need some confidence."

That I knew. And I was getting better. But confidence didn't come out of nowhere.

"You've got a beautiful face," he continued, his voice a register lower. The roughness of it made the hairs on my arms stand up. "Gorgeous eyes. I mean

I've rarely seen eyes like yours. Fuck. It's like looking out at the ocean, trying to read it as the weather's changing. Perfect lips. The most adorable freckles and the tiniest little nose. You're like a sexy…bunny."

I was so confused. Dex was laying on the compliments like I've never heard him do before, all the while watching a naked chick gyrate on a pole. The absurdity levels were overflowing tonight.

I didn't know what to say…did he just say I was gorgeous? Did he just compare me to a rabbit? But he ended up turning his face to meet mine, looking surprised at my dumb expression.

"Speechless? That's a start."

At that, the waitress came by and plunked our drinks down. Dex slipped her $25 bucks with a wink. In turn, she winked at me and sauntered off.

"Has no one ever complimented you before?" he asked honestly, once she had left. He pushed my drink into my hands even though I wasn't done with the other one.

I shook my head. I mean, I've heard I was cute. And I knew I wasn't as bad as my ego wanted me to believe. When I called myself fat, I knew I wasn't actually fat anymore (though I definitely was back in the day), I just knew I was miles from perfect. And if I wasn't perfect, like Jenn, like these girls stripping, like the women on TV, then what was the point? I might as well give up.

He was watching me closely. I focused my eyes on his.

"Can you see the ocean now?" I challenged.

The corner of his mouth twitched. "You don't believe me. But you want to. You still think you're fat. Or something. You think those fucktards on the internet are on to something."

That actually is what I was about to think next. His insightfulness was crazy. Was I really that easy to read?

"I really hate you sometimes," I blurted out.

He shrugged. "I don't blame you. I hate myself too sometimes. Often. Look, I brought my partner to a strip club while on assignment, and not a very good strip club at that. We might as well be at Hooters. I guess I am just a pervert with rapist facial hair."

"Well, you're my kind of pervert," I said. And then immediately regretted it. You're my kind of pervert? What the hell was that? So, I covered it up with, "And I probably don't need this drink."

"Yeah you do. So do I." He downed his drink and moved on to the next one. He stared down at the fizzy bubbles for a beat, taking in a deep breath.

"Honestly kiddo? You're beautiful. You use your weight as an excuse but you're just all woman. Not every woman has to look like a stripper. Or a model. Or Megan Fox. You're petite, have a tiny waist, a fantastic rack, a devastating ass...what the hell more do you want? You should know it. Everyone else knows it...that's why you're getting all these asinine comments. Can't you just see that it's just jealously that's ripping these people apart?"

I swallowed hard, my cheeks still burning, my heart pounding hard against my ribcage. I felt tingly, dizzy, awkward. The man I loved just told me how beautiful I was. I could barely explain it. How could he just say these things to me? Didn't he know?

"And now I've embarrassed you. Which was my plan."

I eyed him suspiciously. "So you didn't mean any of that?"

He grinned at me. His eyes looked a bit sloppy. He was feeling the bourbon as well.

"I'll be right back," he said, slapping the table with his palm and heading off towards what I assumed were the bathrooms. Probably to jerk off. Though at this point, I wasn't exactly sure who he would be jerking off about. I could pretty much guarantee it wasn't Jenn for once. I'd be lying if I didn't have a sick, twisted little thrill about that. That was fantasy fodder for later.

I sat back in the booth and carefully sipped my new drink. It was much stronger than the other one. Bartender probably poured me a triple. I didn't drink all that often and tonight I think I drank more than I had all year. But I did feel relaxed…despite everything that had been going on. Despite the comments and my parents and Creepy Clown Lady telling me people would be coming to take me away…

OK, I probably shouldn't have thought of that last one. Suddenly her face was all I saw. I shut my eyes hard, hoping to will it away, hoping her disembodied, foreign voice wouldn't infiltrate my senses and barge into a place I had protected. I was at a strip club with Dex. That alone was enough for me to focus on.

When I opened my eyes again I was shocked to see a woman standing in front of me. But it wasn't Creepy Clown Lady – far from it. It was Marla, the redhaired ravisher. She was clothed again, this time in tight club gear. She smiled at me with perfect teeth, which had me calculating how much they would have cost and how much she made a night.

I stared at her teeth for so long that she stepped forward and put her hand on the table, leaning forward.

"So, how about this?" she purred, her voice somewhere between cat and lion.

"Uhhh," I stuttered, not sure what she meant.

"It's your call. Want to do it here?"

"What?"

"Your boyfriend bought me, silly. For you."

I looked over her shoulder and saw Dex slowly making his way over, another drink in his hand. He stopped a yard away, leaned against the wall and just watched us. It was…weird. Unnerving. Perverted.

I gave the girl, Marla, an innocent look. "I don't think he meant to buy you…least not for me."

She chuckled, rich and throaty. "It's just a lap dance, sweetie."

She grabbed my arms and pulled me out so I was sitting at the edge of the booth. And she started moving, slowly, up and down like a silk–skinned snake. Ironically it was to a song called "Stripsearch."

I wanted to laugh. Badly. But I kept it in and watched it all unfold. After all, I didn't have to do anything. I just had to sit and watch.

Marla had some smooth moves (and smooth skin) with some intense eye contact action. It was enough that I had to look away half the time, especially when her clothes started coming off. Was that even part of the lap dance? Or did the rules not count because I was a girl?

I brought my eyes over to Dex, who still stood behind Marla, watching the whole thing go down with a strange look on his face. It was conflicted. Maybe he wasn't sure what he should be staring at. His quivering nervous partner or the quivering naked Marla with the excellent taste in music?

He took a few steps forward and finally met my own eyes. He was chewing away on his lip, ignoring the underwear that she just discarded on the floor, ignoring the fact that she was stroking my knees and bending over in front of him.

I don't think I ever felt so awkward in my life. Keeping my attention on Dex instead of Marla was only helping marginally. Both felt off.

There's something wrong with him.

The thought flashed through my brain, distracting me from Marla's buoyant bosom that was waving in my face. She noticed this look. She reached for my head and slipped her hands into my hair. She brought her lips up to mine and I thought she was going to kiss me. All I could think about was how her red lipstick was going to make a mess of my face.

But she just whispered, "Relax. This is really all for him. He wants to see you loosen up. Enjoy it." She pulled away and winked at me.

She danced for a few beats more to the driving guitar at the end of the tune. And then the song was over. She picked up a robe that had come from out of nowhere and walked past Dex without any acknowledgement. He followed her walk with his leering eyes. Then came back to the booth and plopped down in his seat.

I stared at him, not amused. I know Dex was just being like any other guy, getting off on the idea of two chicks getting it on, or something close to that. But there was something off about him tonight. When I thought there was something wrong with him, there was a reason. He was being strange; I could see it in his eyes when he didn't know I was looking. I wondered if it had anything to do with the phone call from earlier.

Then another thought flashed through my head. One that made me perk up a bit and then feel guilty for doing so. What if Jenn broke up with him? Or visa versa? What if Dex was a single man now? I mean, the strip club is usually the first place they go after a breakup…

"What?" he asked lazily.

"Nothing," I said. I pulled out my phone and looked at the time. It was getting late and we did have a ferry to catch in the morning. I could do well on little sleep, but not when combined with a hangover.

"You want to go?"

I nodded. "I had fun though." I didn't want him to think I was ungrateful. It was my own idea that we hang out outside of work...although I didn't in a million years expect that we'd go to a hockey game and a strip club in another country. "Obviously you had more fun than me. Though you weren't in the bathroom all that long."

I expected him to laugh at that or protest. He was watching me closely instead. I took my sight off him and watched the stripper on the stage. I didn't want him to read me anymore. It didn't seem fair.

"I hope you remember what I've said," he said earnestly. He finished the rest of his drink in a few gulps, got out of his seat and walked around to my end. He held out his hand for me.

"Everytime I think of strip clubs, I will think of you," I joked, taking his hand and letting him pull me up.

He pulled me up so I was right up into his chest. I was expecting him to take a step back but he didn't. I could feel the bottom of his scruffy chin grazing the top of my head. He put his hands on my shoulders and pushed me back just enough to get a better look at me.

"I hope next time you feel – well, retarded – about yourself, you'll remember that I think you're..."

I looked up into his eyes. They were drunk, yes, but still absolutely mesmerizing.

He didn't finish his sentence. Instead he said, "Sorry I licked your face."

He turned and started to make his way out of the club. I followed in a hurry, feeling the eyes of the patrons and waitresses staring at me. We must have seemed like quite an odd pair.

We went back to the hotel but I didn't fall asleep for at least two hours. My mind kept going over the events of the night. Creepy Clown Lady was a definite cause for alarm (or panic, or madness) but it was Dex's words that kept resonating throughout, digging deeper at my heart and causing it to flutter with random palpitations. Did he really mean what he said? And if he did...what were we doing? I didn't want him to go back to his hotel room, I wanted him in this big empty bed, beside me. I wanted to put more dirty and obscene thoughts in his head. I wanted to *feel* that he wanted me, not to just hear it.

Did I see a glimpse of the real Dex tonight? Or was that someone else, just a mask to cover up what was really going on, what he really wanted to hide.

I didn't even think about checking my phone once.

CHAPTER SIX

"Oh, by the way, if Jimmy asks about those porn charges, just say it was you," Dex said with a sly grin while sticking a cigarette in his mouth.

I shook my head, not willing to go to bat for him over that and not at all surprised that he had racked up quite the adult movie bill after last night.

It was 10 a.m. and we were on the upper deck of the ferry that was taking us from the mainland to Vancouver Island, where we had to pick up the boat.

The morning had started out in a perpetual raincloud. I eventually fell asleep last night and woke up to a wake–up call and the overall fuzziness of "what the hell did I do last night?" Of course, I didn't do much of anything. It was more of what I saw and that all came flooding back to me in a haze of stale Jack Daniels and Coke. I think I saw enough boobs to last me a lifetime.

We got in his car and headed south out of the raincloud. As soon as we reached the farmlands that led to the ferry terminal, the clouds broke open and a fairy tale ray of sunshine flowed down from above and enveloped the ocean. I took it as a good omen.

We had gone straight up to the upper deck of the nearly–empty boat because he wanted to have a cigarette. At least I thought it was just one. He leaned against the railing, looking down at the waves that flowed past the ferry in a foam–filled rage and lit up one cigarette after the other.

The wind cleared the cobwebs from my face and messed the hair off of his head. He was only wearing a black hoodie with his camouflage pants below, but he didn't seem the slightest bit cold even though the breeze was a lot sharper than I had expected. Actually,

I was borderline freezing and knew my nose was an acute shade of red.

But I stayed up there with him, soaking in the ocean air and enjoying the glaring sunshine and his quiet company. Dex did seem a little more pensive than usual but that was coupled with bags under his eyes and an ashy complexion. I kept it to myself, but it was obvious he hadn't slept all that much. Perhaps the stripper giving me a lap dance was a powerful stimulant. At least, I kind of hoped it was. Still, there was something off about him last night too.

"How's your new medication doing?" I asked. I was probably overstepping my boundaries but I was curious.

He didn't bite. He just shrugged. "It works."

He took a long drag of his cigarette, the ashes flying off into the wind and flowing down the length of the ferry deck. His hands were shaking slightly.

"I didn't see you smoke a single cigarette yesterday," I said, eyeing his trembling fingers.

He shrugged, again. "It comes and goes."

I wanted to say that constantly eating Nicorette like it was candy wasn't helping his quitting case but who was he kidding? He wasn't trying to quit; this was just what he did. Sometimes there really was no reason – it was a hard concept for me to accept.

Maybe he knew what I was thinking because his eyes darted over to me. "What now?"

"Nothing," I said quickly and turned my attention to the sharp mountains of Vancouver Island that rose in the incoming distance. "At least the day is turning out nice."

"Are you worried about me?" he asked, his voice noncommittal. It caught me a bit off guard, enough so that I had to look at him.

The line between his brows deepened, from thought and from the glare. We both were without sunglasses.

It was one of those things you forgot about needing in the Pacific Northwest. He didn't seem angry or upset, or even really curious. I had to think about whether I wanted to tell the truth or not. The truth was so…iffy.

"Well," I said, drawing it out. "I think I always worry about you. And I think you know that by now."

"No, I mean, are you worried about *being* with me," he said, straightening up and flicking the cigarette overboard, even though there was a cigarette disposal unit behind us. "On this island. Alone. With me."

"Why would that worry me? Also, it's a park, there will be people there." I wasn't sure what he was getting at.

He shook his head with a small smile. "You've seen how empty this ferry is. You really think people go camping in November? In Canada? To some hostile island? The place is barely occupied during the summer."

I hadn't thought about that. In my head I was expecting a full campground with other people there to keep us company. I didn't think we'd actually be the only ones on the island.

"Isn't there a ranger on the island or something?"

"No. That's why Bill said to call him up on the damn radio if something went wrong. It's just going to be you and me, kiddo."

It didn't seem like a big deal, really, but I guess it was the first time we would be *alone* alone…with no Maximus or Uncle Al meddling in our business. But still…

"I don't know why you think I'd have a problem being alone with you. I trust you more than anyone," I said truthfully. Honestly, the only thing that worried me now was the damn inappropriate ideas I kept getting in my head, all thanks to Ada's incessant texting about Dex and I possibly having sex. Maybe these thoughts ran in the family.

He watched me for a few beats like he was trying to pick out exactly what I was thinking. I knew I was probably blushing but hoped the chilly wind was doing a good job of disguising that.

"I don't know. Figured you probably thought I was a...what was it? A pervy weirdo, after last night." He said it so sincerely that I had to laugh.

"I liked that side of you." Oh dear. That totally came out wrong. "Or...I mean, I liked–"

"No, don't cover it up," he said, placing his finger on my lips. His smile was sweet, almost sad.

I waited for him to take his tobacco-scented finger away before I said, "I had fun last night. You're just a man, Dex, that's what I got out of it, and it was a bit of a relief, to be honest."

"Good," he said, fishing out his pack. "This morning I couldn't really remember what happened, thought maybe I scared you more than I wanted to."

I reached over and put my hand over his, closing it over the pack. "Ease up, OK? You've had like five in a row. If I have any reason to be worried about you, it's because of that. Not because you got a stripper to give me a lap dance."

He sucked on his lip and thought it over. Then he put the pack away in his jacket pocket.

"You did enjoy that lap dance, didn't you?"

"It was eye–opening."

"You've never been with a woman before?"

I burst into nervous giggles. "What? No, of course not. Have you been with a man? No wait, I don't want to know. Don't answer that." Nothing would have surprised me but I definitely did not need that mental image.

He raised his brows. "Are you sure?"

"Yes," I said. "Do you want to go inside? I'm freezing my ass off."

He opened his mouth to say something with that familiar glint in his eye, so I added teasingly, "Don't you dare say anything about my ass."

"Wow. No cigarettes and no compliments. You run a tight ship, Perry Palomino."

Dex knew he was the chief operator in our whole operation, but I just nodded. I had to take what I could get, while I could get it.

After the ferry docked, we drove off onto the long, tree–filled expanse of Vancouver Island and down the winding road towards the city of Victoria. As we neared the town of Saanich, we had glimpses of various islands floating out in Haro Strait. I couldn't figure out which one was D'Arcy Island but we'd know soon enough.

Dex was actually more talkative than he had been on the ferry, which I took as a good sign. Only now I was feeling a bit sullen and moody. I wasn't sure why, except I got this terrible feeling that I had forgotten something or was going into this situation ill–prepared.

I know Dex had asked if I was worried about being alone with him, and at first I really wasn't, but the more I examined the weekend, the more I started to fret. Not about him in any way. I mean, I'd love nothing more than for him to make a few moves on me. But I knew that wasn't going to happen anytime soon. Or anytime. Ever. Sigh.

No, I was worried about myself. I was going to be sharing a tent with him for two nights. Sure, we had our own sleeping bags and everything (thank goodness), but the isolation plus our proximity, with no prying eyes to see…it made me nervous. What if I did something stupid, like jump his bones in the middle of the night? I'd be mortified and I'd scare him off. Probably ruin everything we had.

And yeah, I know it seems pretty unlikely that insecure little Perry would do anything like that but the more I was around him, the more I wanted to do terrible x–rated, nasty things to him. Only a few moments ago he had leaned over to take something out of the glovebox and during the instant where he turned to look up at me, I was so afraid I was actually going to lean forward and kiss him. I just thought, what happens if I just kiss him right here? What if I just grab his hair with my hands and pull him towards me and just kiss those irresistible lips of his? It was getting pretty ridiculous. I have never wanted someone so badly before, mentally and physically, that I was afraid my body might act without any instructions from me.

Finally, vague thoughts of Creepy Clown Lady kept drifting into my headspace. She acted like she knew me in some way. But I still wasn't sure if I had seen a figment of my imagination or a ghost. Or an actual cracked–out clown lady who just followed me around from place to place like a lost carnie. Er, speaking telepathically in my head and all of that. I've heard carnies can do that.

I kind of wanted to bring it up with Dex just to see what he thought, to see if he had seen her too, lately, and was keeping it from me as I had been from him, and I was seconds (well, minutes, maybe days) away from doing so when we pulled up to a modest blue, one–level house in a leafy suburban neighborhood of Victoria. He parked the car on the street and flipped it into park.

"This is Zach's," he said.

I gave him an expectant look. "And how do you know this Zach?"

"He's a documentary filmmaker, did some projects with him over the years. He's a nice guy, no appetite for bullshit, which I appreciate. Has a kid, Amanda, who is six, I think, or something like that. Anyway old enough to talk intelligently with you, young enough to not have a fucking attitude. Buddy just got divorced though, so...try not to bring that up."

Noted. We got out of the car and walked to the house. For a single guy, his garden was very neat and tidy, even with the approach of winter. Christmas lights were already on the hedges and lining the roof. The grass was cut short and rimmed with dew.

A little girl answered the door.

She was pretty with long blonde hair that was in the chokehold of a rat's nest. The dress she wore was ruffley and light pink but overwhelmed by a Picasso-like mess of dirty smears. Either this was a tomboy in a princess's body or dad wasn't used to having a young girl around.

"I'm Amanda," she stated forcefully as she blocked the entrance with her tiny body.

"You remember me, Amanda," Dex said, leaning over to get a better look at her, hands on his knees. I felt a rare pang under my ribcage. "It's Dex."

"You smell," she said. I couldn't help but laugh. Amanda shot me a look.

"Sorry, Amanda. I agree with you," I said in my most child-like voice. I never knew how to act around children, regardless of their age. Luckily Amanda grinned at that, showing off a wide gap in her teeth. She then skipped away, leaving the door open. Success!

A bearded man came around the corner, wiping his hands on a dish towel. His eyes lit up when he saw Dex.

"How are you, my man?" he exclaimed.

Dex went up and embraced him heartily. It was charming to see from someone who didn't seem too affectionate with anyone.

"Good, good. I like the beard, Zach," Dex noted as he pulled away and gave him the once-over. "You look like the singer of Clutch."

It was true. He did look like Neil Fallon of the band Clutch. Zach had a receding hairline coupled with a bushy mountain–man beard. He had a proud beer belly poking forward through his navy tee–shirt, though he seemed in otherwise good shape.

"And I like the moustache. You look like a rapist," Zach shot back with a wink.

Dex looked at me. "I guess you aren't the only one who thinks so."

I smiled at Zach and extended my hand, "Hi, I'm Dex's partner, Perry. I also think he looks like a rapist."

He shook it firmly and said, "Nice to meet you, Perry. I can tell I like you already. Come on in. Don't mind Amanda. She's here for the weekend. School had a professional day or something."

"I'm in Grade One," she said suddenly, poking her head out from the kitchen in front of us and then quickly disappearing again.

Dex and I laughed nervously. I mean, what do you say to that? Good for you? That's nice?

Zach looked back at us, saying, "I know, who the fuck cares."

"Dad!" she yelled from around the corner.

He rolled his eyes. "Right. Sorry, Amanda."

He leaned towards us, voice lowered, "She's the swear police now. Her mother...well, anyway, come in, come in."

Zach led us into the living room, where he served us coffee and Twinkies. His house was small but had a homey feel, wood-paneled walls and lots of thick moody–colored rugs thrown about on a dark hardwood floor.

"Sorry, I'm not very good at hosting people," he said, shoving a Twinkie in his mouth.

I eyed the spongy creation in my hands. I already had breakfast on the ferry but decided to nibble at it just to be polite. At least the coffee was strong and good. Seemed like the type of coffee a sailor would make.

"So, D'Arcy Island, eh?" Zach mused with a hard gleam in his eyes.

"Yup. Nothing says a fun time like an old leper colony," Dex said.

"And the park board is letting you do this?"

"Yeah. They're letting us. Not stopping us at any rate. Though that Bill dude definitely had a tent pole up his ass."

"I'm pretty sure they've been approached by TV shows before…all that ghosthunting crap. Sorry. I just don't believe in it."

"You don't believe in ghosts?" I asked. Even though it seemed like most people didn't, it was still fascinating to me to find out why.

"Oh, no, I believe in ghosts. Very much so. But I think those TV shows are crap. That's probably why they said yes to you guys. What I think anyway."

"Cuz we aren't crap?" I asked, carefully slurping on my coffee.

"No, because there's really no chance of being exploited through…you know, the internet. What I mean is, it's not on the A&E channel. There's no moron leading the charge."

He paused and gave Dex a funny look. "Well, except for this guy of course."

"Actually I'm the moron of the show," I offered with a smile.

Dex grinned at me. "Can we get that on tape?"

Zach carefully watched the exchange between us before saying asking, "You still with Jennifer, Dex?"

The coffee cup rattled loudly in Dex's hands. They were shaking again, albeit for just a quick moment. He swallowed hard and put it down.

"Yes, of course," he said matter–of–factly.

Damn it. Obviously I had been hoping that the phone call meant they'd broken up. Guess not. I tried not to look annoyed, especially since Zach was looking at me now. I don't know why it was but I always got the feeling that people were tiptoeing around the relationship question with him. It was like they couldn't quite believe that Dex and I were just partners. I flashed him a bright smile, anyway. Didn't want to let on how I was feeling or what I was thinking.

"Gotta love *Wine Babes*," Zach remarked rather awkwardly.

"Oh, yes. Who doesn't?" I added. I could tell Dex eyed me suspiciously but I didn't want to acknowledge it.

"Indeed," Zach mused with a smile and got out of his armchair. He took his and Dex's empty cups into the kitchen. I looked around the room, at the expansive library of books and the hominess of the place and decided that whatever happened between him and his ex–wife (which I was not supposed to mention) left him pretty well off. I think I'd be happy with a house like this albeit probably not with a daughter.

At that, I turned my head and saw Amanda standing in the doorway to the front hall, peering at us with her large eyes. She smiled shyly but didn't move. It was like her need to know overcame her instincts to run away from strange company. I knew that feeling all too well.

"Hey Amanda," Dex said, his voice animated. "When was the last time I saw you?"

Amanda smiled broadly at him in a girlish way and put her finger to her mouth, pondering.

"I don't know. It wasn't this year because you never got me a birthday present," she said teasingly.

"That's true. But what if I said I had your present right here?" he said, his voice raised along with his eyebrows. I watched him, more fascinated than I should have been.

She eyed him like he was the Easter Bunny. "What is it?"

"You'll have to come over here and see."

I briefly wondered if children her age were taught to fear the rapist moustache because that's one thing that would have had me running the other way (that and a white Chevy Astro van with no windows). But she skid towards us on the hardwood floors, using her socks in a *Risky Business* type manner.

She stopped in front of Dex and looked at him expectantly.

"Where is the present? What is it?" she demanded.

I wanted to know too. I looked at him with as much expectancy, hoping he wasn't so cruel and stupid as to actually fool a child with promises of gifts. That shit never worked on me.

He didn't miss a beat. He reached down into his cargo pants pocket and paused. He leaned forward to Amanda and whispered.

"Close your eyes."

Amanda stood up straight, hands clasped behind her back and closed her wide eyes with a silly grin splashed across her face.

"Open your hands."

She displayed her hands forward, palms up. I watched Dex fish a few rubber bands out of his pocket and place them in hers. They were in the shape of a boat, a rose and a heart. They were Silly Bandz, a trend that was slowly taking even adults by storm, though I didn't have the foggiest idea why. I mean, I liked the look and music of the '90s but something like Silly Bandz was way beyond my appeal.

But Amanda liked them and as soon as she opened her eyes, she was exclaiming loudly and dancing around the house in some frantic child boogie. Zach came back out of the kitchen with another cup of coffee and a couple of books under his arm, shaking his head at his daughter who was running upstairs to put the other bands she already had on. I figured a Silly Bandz fashion show was in order.

As much as I didn't hate the idea of humoring a child, I just wanted to get to the island and get the whole project going. Zach must have too, because the books he brought in were about D'Arcy Island. He plopped them on Dex's lap and handed him the coffee.

"Thanks, bud," Dex said, taking the cup in his hand, "but the books are for her."

He jerked his head in my direction, spilling a drop of coffee at the same time.

"Ah," said Zach, and handed me the books instead. There were only two and both were thin and unscholarly.

"Is this it?" I asked.

"Yeah that's it. Afraid there's just not much written about the place."

"Why?"

He shrugged. "There just isn't much to go on. The island was kind of run below the surface. Those books report everything that is traceable but a lot of it is just speculation. There's really not a lot of records about it."

"But...Dex told me people had died there."

"Oh, yeah. At least 40–something people died there. But they were lepers. And Chinese lepers at that, so you have to understand they weren't really considered people. If it was a white man's leper colony, there'd be tons of books about it. But those are the breaks."

I looked down at the books in my hand. They seemed to be poor consolation for what happened.

Zach must have been reading my face because he said, "It gets worse as you get into it. The fact that the government at the turn of the century barely kept any records, any real insight, anyway, is just the tip of the iceberg. These people were left there to die. That's why they call it the Island of Death."

A marked shiver ran up behind me. "Are you serious?"

Zach nodded grimly and looked over at Dex. "You haven't briefed her?"

"He never briefs me," I said. "It's like he wants me to look totally unprofessional."

Dex looked at me with a quizzical expression. "I got you the books, didn't I? You'll have plenty of time to read up on the sail over. Just relax, kiddo."

He turned back to Zach. "It's still supposed to be fair, right?"

Zach pulled out his Blackberry and entered in a few keys. "Yeah, it should be. There's a chance of strong northwesterlies tonight but as long as you stay on the boat you should be OK."

"Stay on the boat?" I repeated. I could feel Dex tense up beside me.

"The anchoring is very poor over there," Zach said. "It's fine when the weather is calm, but this time of year, you're better off on the boat."

It wasn't a suggestion, it was a demand, and it was one I took to heart. I had no problems with being on the boat overnight. The more I learned about the "Island of Death" the more that staying on the boat seemed like a perfectly sane and enjoyable option. Besides, it was Zach's boat.

"But we'll have no problems getting there?" I asked.

He shook his head. "Weather is at least holding nicely for today. You might get some fog tomorrow morning but hopefully that's it. The patterns change really quickly out in Haro Strait. It looks like it's really close by, and it is, but believe me, that place can get rough."

"Bill said they chose that island for a reason...you couldn't escape," I said, my voice feeling heavier.

"He's right. People tried. They drowned. Some days the supply ships couldn't even come in because of the winds. When it hits just right, you get a nasty rip that prevents any boats from coming to the shore. And will take any desperate soul out to the Pacific to die."

My shoulders sank a little at that. The more I heard about this island, the more I wanted to just throw in the towel and call it a day. Yeah, maybe I was chickenshit when I shouldn't have been, maybe I was feeling unprepared when I really needed to feel like I could own the whole thing and prove I wasn't some idiot, maybe I was afraid of being alone with Dex. Even beyond the worry that I would molest him at some point (which I knew wouldn't happen) – it was the idea that we would be alone on the "Island of Death" together. What if something went wrong? Sure we handled skinwalkers, but there were still people there to aid us. In this case, we would be utterly, entirely alone with only each other to depend on.

But there I was, sitting with a few library books on my lap, sipping a lukewarm cup of coffee in some stranger's house. I had come this far and from Dex's determined expression, there was no turning back. And so far, in all of our experiences together, there always was that moment that I could have turned back and I never ever did. Even if it scared me to the core, to my very soul and fiber of my being, I still went forward into the unknown. Some may call that brave. I don't think I'd call it that. Stubborn beyond repair seemed more fitting.

It wasn't long before Dex gulped down the rest of his coffee and we were off towards the marina. I was sure that Zach would have come with us and shown Dex the ropes again in how to manage a sailboat but he seemed to think Dex could it handle himself. He had more faith than I had. Even if Dex was suddenly an expert sailor, I don't think I'd trust him with a boat.

On the other hand, I trusted Dex with my life. Go figure.

~~

The boat was actually a lot scruffier than I had expected, considering how neat Zach's house was. This was a good thing though – it made me feel a lot better about having Dex at the wheel knowing he wasn't going to be scratching a multi–million dollar yacht.

I didn't know much about sailboats (the only sailboat I had really been on had been my grandfather's yacht in Sweden, but I was quite young and the memories of that were vague), but it was a C&C 38, which is kind of your standard boat. At least that's what Dex told me as we drove over.

After a few trips back and forth to the car to get all of our stuff, it was time to go aboard. I handed Dex the cameras, extra careful not to drop them in the space between the boat and the dock. That would have been the worst thing ever.

He took them and disappeared down into the cabin. I felt more comfortable standing on the creaking, moving dock than going on board. I was in no rush. On the dock I still felt attached to the land, attached to the smiling sailors who were going about the area tending to their own boats and taking advantage of the mild autumn day before the winter rains set in. It was pleasant and familiar. The boat, with its fading aqua color, peeling wood trim and crackled paint job on the name "Mary Contrary" (apparently his ex–wife's name) was not.

Dex popped his head up inquisitively, and asked, "What are you doing, skipper?"

"I'm skipper now?" I asked, hesitating before lifting my foot onto the first wrung of the boat ladder. I stared down at the dark depths beneath me.

"You will be if you come aboard. You need help to get up, shorty?"

Who was he calling shorty? I grabbed the railing for balance and stepped up onto the slanted, grainy surface of the deck and carefully made my way over to the cockpit, staying bent over for balance and thankful for the smooth grip on my Chucks.

"You'll get your sea legs soon enough," Dex said, climbing up from inside and standing beside me. He had a book of nautical charts with him. He poked around the area beside the wheel, lifting up a few panels. "Thank fuck Zach was smart enough to put in sonar and GPS."

I stepped over to him and peered down at the instrument panel beside the wheel, which had a moldy, damp cover on it. "Would we have been screwed otherwise?"

Dex laughed. "I'll say."

Well that was encouraging to hear. What did he think would happen if he hadn't? Would he have just winged it with someone's boat? Probably.

"Do you want me to do anything?" I asked, hoping he'd say no. I just wanted to sit in the corner of the bench and hide.

He pulled out a key and a cigarette from his pants pocket. He lit the cigarette, took a large puff and stuck the key in the slot, giving it a hard turn. The boat roared to life, a sound much louder than I had expected, and we were vibrating from the motion.

"Dex?" I asked.

"Right," he said, and pointed up at the deck. "I'll need you to take in the bumpers once we get moving.

And I might need you to help me cast off." He looked around him at the surrounding boats. "I don't want to bug anyone here for a sendoff."

That might be better though, I thought.

He rubbed his chin. "Don't worry, I'm not going to ask you to jump aboard while the ship is moving. Last thing I want is for you to take a dip."

"Good."

"I'll just get you to steer."

"Uh…"

"You ride a motorbike, Perry. You can steer this boat in a straight line for a few seconds. I believe in you." He smacked me hard on the back.

I had my doubts about handling the long ocean beast, but it wasn't that hard. The way the marina was laid out and the position of the boat among the berths meant all I really had to do was shove the gearshift forward, keep the pace and hold the boat straight. The calm seas made this easy to do and soon Dex had thrown all the lines on deck and had leaped on board the slowly moving ship with ease. He sure was sprightly for someone who wasn't that tall. The casual, streamlined manner of which he did it in was a surprise too.

I guess I was doing a good enough job that he walked to the bow and back, taking up all the bumpers as he went.

"Thanks, skipper, I'll take it from here," he said after he finished, flashing me an appreciative smile and squeezing in beside me. He put his hands on top of mine, which were on top of the wheel.

I stared up at him stupidly, torn between wanting to move my hands and get out of the way or just keep them there.

He eyed my hands underneath his and gave them a quick squeeze. "Unless you want to steer? I don't want to cause a mutiny on board."

I quickly took them out from under his. "No, you're the captain here. Where did you learn to sail anyway?"

He turned forward, eyes searching the horizon of islands. "I went to sailing school when I was young."

"In New York?"

"Yes. New York has a long island."

"Ha, I know that. How old were you?"

He glanced at me quickly and frowned. "You really like to know everything, don't you?"

"Yeah. I do," I said crossing my arms. I didn't get why he was such a stickler with details about his life, especially his life in New York. What's the harm in talking about where he learned to sail or where he learned to play hockey?

The breeze was starting to pick up as we motored to the edge of the small harbor. It ruffled his hair around his eyes so I could only catch glimpses of them.

"I was 11. My father was a sailor and I was on the boat a lot as a child. He thought I should learn how to do it properly, in case I ever inherited the boat one day. So he put me in sailing classes at the yacht club. I did them once a week…for about a year. Mainly little skip boats but sometimes we would do races and gay shit like that."

He was telling me so much, I almost felt like I should be writing it down. "Why did you stop? Was it because you were playing hockey?"

"No. I was doing both for a while. The years before I was also doing archery, competitive swimming and playing tennis at the same time."

All very pricey sports to be involved in. His range was impressing me more and more. I always felt with Dex that one day he was going to reveal that he was a CIA agent or something like that. He seemed to have all these skills hidden up his sleeves to the point where nothing was starting to surprise me. Though picturing him doing archery and tennis was pushing it.

"So why did you stop?" I didn't mean to bug him but he had just tried to avoid the question. "Didn't you like sailing? You seem like a natural." And with the wind in his face, his scruffy facial hair, the new cigarette hanging from his lips, and his dominating stance behind the wheel, that statement was all true.

"I loved sailing. I loved hockey too. Tennis was a lot of fun, even though I hated the people I competed with. Rich snobby fuckers. And I was probably the best at swimming. You wouldn't know it from looking at me now."

His shoulders were rather on the broad side and he did have a nice V–shape going for him, especially leading down to his hipbones and... (stay on track, Perry) but he wasn't your typical swimmer type. And he was still avoiding the question. I kept staring at him expectantly.

He sighed.

"My dad left and he was the one with the money. So, no more sports for Dex," he said in a flat, robot-like voice.

I was shocked at that. I don't know why, it wasn't that unusual to have a broken home. I just didn't see it coming. I felt bad for him, which is probably the last thing he wanted, so I nodded and asked as nonchalantly as possible, "Where did he go?"

Dex shrugged. "Beats the fuck out of me. Who fucking cares where that asshole went? No skin off my back."

"Did you ever see him again?" I felt like I was pressing my luck a bit.

He took a large inhale of his cigarette. Pause. "No. I didn't. Didn't even see him at my mother's funeral."

"I'm sorry," I whispered, wanting to put my hands on top of his. They were starting to go a bit blue in the wind.

He adjusted his shoulders and his stance, keeping his eyes focused straight ahead. "That's life."

There was so much more I wanted to talk about. This was the first time I really felt like I knew the real Dex. He had mentioned before that his parents were dead, but I had no idea one of them was metaphorically dead, which was worse in some way. To know they were still out there, but that you were dead to them and visa versa.

He finally turned his head to me. His eyes were dull, as if he had put up a shield to prevent me from learning anything more from them. "You got everything you needed to know?"

I shook my head. I wanted to know when his mother died and how she died. I wanted to know what it was like for him after his dad left. How it felt to give up all the privileges he had grown accustomed to. I wanted to know if he had any siblings. I wanted to know what high school was like for him. I wanted to know how all these things had affected the man who was standing beside me, piloting a boat towards the "Island of Death."

"Tough tits, then," he smirked. "Maybe we should do a session with you and your past. You know, find out why you seemed to be the subject of so many family therapy sessions when you were young. Unless your cousins were pulling my leg when they brought that up. Although, judging from the way your parents were talking to me about you, I can see that's still a major issue in your family."

My ears perked up and my heart slowed. "What did they say?"

The last thing I wanted was for them to say anything detrimental about me to Dex. Not in that way anyway. That shit was personal.

He enjoyed watching me squirm. "They didn't say anything. Not really. Just that they worried about you. And they had hoped you had put all this ghost business in the past."

"I don't know what they are talking about it," I said. That was the truth.

"That makes two of us, kiddo. And I didn't ask either."

Just then I felt my phone vibrate in my pocket. Saved by the bell... or silent mode.

I brought my phone out and looked at it. It was Ada.

– You on the island yet? Bumping uglies yet? –

I sighed and put it back in my pocket. Dex peered at me inquisitively.

"Don't tell me you're getting tweets and Facebook messages sent straight to your phone."

I gave him a haughty look. "No. I am not. And not that it's any of your business, but I haven't checked the blog more than once today."

He looked at the clock on the instrument panel. "More than once? That would probably mean something if it wasn't early in the day. Anything new from Miss Anonymous?"

"Yeah. How do you know it's a girl?"

He quickly ashed his cigarette into the wind and said, "I don't know. I assume. Chicks do that stupid stuff. Jealousy, remember. What did it say?"

I didn't want to get into it so I gave him the Cliff Notes version. "The usual. I look stupid, don't have what it takes to be a good host, don't even belong on the internet." I left out the part where they said I only got the job because I was sleeping with the cameraman. That was too embarrassing to mention and I didn't want things to get awkward. Why they would assume that, I don't know. It's not like Dex was really ever on any footage. Even Ada was off and running with that assumption. Was I so obvious?

The wind turned sharp as the boat rounded a rocky barrier and we headed in a northeasterly direction, with small waves rising up from nowhere. I shivered, realizing that the clothes I had brought with me probably weren't going to cut it during this trip.

"There are some jackets below in one of the cabins," Dex said, noticing.

I nodded and I told him I was going to go down and start reading the books. I didn't feel like getting into a conversation about "Miss Anonymous" and he obviously was done talking about himself. Only problem was once I made my way across the rolling ship and down the stairs, I started to feel sick and claustrophobic.

Inside was nice enough and did have a nautical and homey feel but it was quite small. The galley was tiny, as were the two back cabins and the living area. The double bed at the front (head) of the boat was larger and cozy. It didn't seem to matter where I sat, the up and down movement from the waves and the overpowering roar of the engine (mixed with the smell of diesel fuel) gave me the largest headache and tickled my nausea bone, especially when I opened the books on D'Arcy Island.

I did manage to get some reading done before I had to shut them and lie down on the couch. What I read didn't help to make me feel any better either.

Basically, at the turn of the century or just a bit before, Chinese lepers were gathered off the streets of Victoria, Vancouver and other places in B.C., and shipped to the island, where they were left to fend for themselves with no medical treatment. They had rudimentary housing and the only outside contact was from a supply ship that came every three months to drop off food, water, opium and...coffins. Turns out that when one of them died on the island, it was up to the lepers to bury them. They really were just left on the small island to rot away.

And some of them did rot away. The leprosy not only caused huge bumpy lesions on their bodies and faces, they also disrupted their nerve endings. On the eyes it would cause them to go blind. On their feet it would cause them to walk around with glass and other sharp objects embedded in them. They couldn't feel any pain, so they didn't notice, even if the wounds had been worn down to the bone. And their hands would often curl up and get burnt to a crisp – it was easy to burn your hand in the fire if you couldn't feel it. Not to mention the fact that rats would come in the middle of the night and nibble away at their fingers until they fell off. Imagine waking up in the morning to find your fingers on the floor, breakfast for vermin.

It was absolutely disgusting. Not just the disease but the way they were treated. I couldn't imagine the lives they lived, knowing that no one cared, knowing that they were going to die there to a terrible disease. One of the books had mentioned that after awhile, people had taken pity on them and a reverend from San Francisco had lived on the island for a few years, taking care of them or at least observing them. But even with that comfort, too many men had already died.

"Perry!" I heard Dex bellow from the upper deck. I opened my eyes and gingerly raised my head, careful not to disturb the pukey feeling that was rustling around in my stomach. "Come up here! Whales!"

That got my attention. I walked unsteadily to the stairs and made my way up. Dex was at the wheel, trying to take a picture with his iPhone. He saw me and told me to get one of the video cameras from downstairs.

I did so, picking the smallest one, and brought it up. It was cold and bright up top, a change from the feeling below. I handed him the camera and followed his gaze. Off in the distance, a pod of killer whales were gliding through the water, their dorsal fins puncturing the waves like wet knives. I had never seen whales in the wild before. It was pretty amazing.

Dex brought the camera to his face and started to film them. "Can you take the wheel, skipper?" he asked.

I went behind it, feeling every bit like a pioneer.

"Just keep it on the same path. They have a law here that we can't get too close."

As much as I would have loved to see them closer, I had also heard horror stories about killer whales overturning boats. No thank you.

I kept the boat heading in the same direction while Dex filmed them. We didn't say anything, just enjoyed watching them move through the water, the sunlight gleaming off their black heads, the misty spouts of air as they exhaled, the hazy green islands in the background. It erased the creepy, sick feeling I had below. I decided, even as the distance between us and the whales was steadily increasing, that I'd be staying on the upper deck for the rest of the journey. Cold air be damned.

When they were too far away to see clearly, Dex put the camera down and smiled at me. He looked genuinely happy and enthused, his eyes round and childlike. It suited him.

"How cool was that?" he exclaimed.

"Very cool," I agreed, moving over so he could take over the wheel again.

"I've seen a lot of dolphins out here but never a pod of killer whales. I'm so glad I got that on film. That was amazing. What great fucking luck."

"Hoping to make this episode part nature documentary?"

"Nah. Hoping to lull people in with something beautiful so they'll be shocked when everything starts going horribly wrong later."

I shivered again, this time from what he said. "I don't think we should plan on things going horribly wrong."

"They always do, don't they?" he commented.

"I guess." Though we always did make it out alive, so I guess it never really went *that* wrong. That said, there was no way I would ever want to experience what happened to me in the lighthouse when Old Roddy had his kelp hands around my throat, nor when I thought I was going to be raped by local rednecks slash human hawks while in Red Fox.

"I'm just kidding you know." He was staring at me with a frown of concern. I must have looked worried.

I gave him a weak smile. "I didn't know but that helps. I don't want to push our luck out here. And not on the Island of Death."

"You've been doing some reading?"

"Yes. I really wish you had told me more about what went on back then…"

"Why? Would you have changed your mind about it?"

It was a possibility. Had I known I was going to an isolated island where 40 forgotten, miserable, rotted souls had died, I might have said no.

"I don't know. Guess it doesn't matter, does it? Too late now."

"You're right about that. There she is."

I looked up and followed his gaze. A rather flat looking island comprised of rocky shoreline and dense forest was fast approaching the bow of the ship.

This was it. I knew it. There seemed to be an invisible wall of angry fog washing over the boat. Dex and I both shivered simultaneously.

I turned and looked behind me. The landmass of Vancouver Island seemed so close yet oh so far.

CHAPTER SEVEN

Now that D'Arcy Island was close enough to make out the little details, the nausea I was feeling down below was starting to creep up my throat again.

It looked like any other island that you'd see in the Pacific Northwest. But the strange part was, you knew it wasn't. Even if no one had told me what had gone on there, the feeling of dread that washed over me, the animosity that just reeked out of the island's pores, was unmistakable.

"I'm getting a bad feeling about this place," I said to Dex while pulling my coat in closer. "You?"

"I will if you can't keep your mouth shut for the next few minutes," he answered, peering off the bow with intensity. I opened my mouth to say something back but decided not to. Dex was only that rude when he really had something to be worried about and I could see this was one of those times. So I shut my mouth, stepped away from the wheel by a few inches and followed his gaze.

From what I could see it didn't look like much was out there. We were close to the island but not close enough to be hitting any rocks. But the water was rippling like a few opposing currents were working the surface.

"Hand me the maps," he said, pointing at a bench where the charts that were flapping in the breeze were anchored under a couple of sailing books.

I leaned over and pulled them out, asking, "Want me to look at them?"

"Would you know what you were looking at?" he scoffed, eyes still on the water.

I brushed his attitude off my shoulders and picked up the first book, which was Cruising Guide. I flipped to the index and quickly looked up D'Arcy Island before Dex had the chance to bark at me to do so.

I found the passage on it and looked over at him. He put the boat into the lowest gear and we slowed down considerably. He squinted at the spread-out maps, which glared white in the sunshine, then examined the water between us and the island.

"What does the book say?" he asked.

"It says there are no good anchorages, only acceptable ones in the right weather. It recommends the cove south of the light, on the west side, and that we should use a stern anchor or something to restrict swing. It also says to be on the lookout for the kelp reefs and submerged rocks."

"Yeah, got that right here," he said, jabbing at the sonar. It looked like a bunch of dark spots on the screen but I trusted that Dex was reading it properly.

"So what, we can't get to the island?" I asked. Maybe a bit too hopefully.

He eyed me carefully before saying, "Oh, we can get there. Just a few things to be mindful of, that's all. Don't get your panties all in a bunch."

I glared at him and looked back at the book. It showed a happy photo of bright kayaks on a beach. It couldn't be that bad, could it?

I looked up at the island again as we started heading further west and rounding a point. The lighthouse slowly but surely came into view.

Thankfully it wasn't a lighthouse like the one me and Dex had met in, the one with Old Roddy on my uncle's farm. It was just a tall white post with a light at the top. Below it, the cliffs sloped to the churning waters. Bill was certainly right about the riptides. Aside from the currents I could see squirming in the water around us, the ocean's swell seemed to build around the island, creating frothy breaks and sprays as they met against rocks and pebbly beaches.

"Well, I'm just going to sit over here," I said, gesturing to the bench. "If you need help, you know where to find me."

I sat down and tried not to watch the progress of the boat with an eagle eye. I was freaked that we were going to run into some hidden reefs or get tangled in a kelp forest. I looked behind me at the Zodiac we were towing and thought if anything was going to get stuck, it was going to be that thing.

Dex was absorbed into complete concentration and rightfully so. As he watched for rocks on the radar and spied telltale currents up ahead, I looked over at the island. We were pretty much in the slight cove and the shore wasn't too far away. I could make out the individual branches of the fir trees, the glowing green of the ferns nestled at the bottom sparkling in golden rays of sunlight, the smooth shapes of the rocks that made up the shoreline. Seagulls darted to and fro and with the sound of the motor at a minimum, I could hear the waves rolling the rocks in a rhythmic manner. It seemed so peaceful, so idyllic but...

Someone was watching us.

A face hidden in the leafy foliage. The grotesque rotting face of a leper, with rough, lesioned skin that matched the bark of the pine next to it. The eyes were narrow and black, the mouth open and fathomless. It was an expression frozen in terror.

I gasped, afraid to blink in case I lost sight of the monstrosity. I wanted to look away from the creepy, mask–like face but I couldn't for fear of losing it.

"Dex," I slowly squeaked out, not taking my eyes away.

He grunted, not wanting to be bothered. "Kinda busy right now."

"There's a creepy face in the woods, staring at us."

He looked at me and then looked in the direction of my gaze. For the amount of time he stared at it, I was sure he could pick it out.

But he eventually turned back to me and said, "I don't see anything."

That was impossible. I could still see it.

"No, there's someone there. Right in the ferns, where the trees start to come down further to the beach. Straight ahead, then to the right a bit."

He looked again and I could see him shaking his head out of the corner of my eye. Annoyed and scared at the idea that it was only something I could see, I narrowed my eyes and tried to make sure that I was really seeing what I thought I was. It was a face wasn't it? I looked below it and saw the outline of dark shoulders fading into the forest shade. It had to be a person. But it wasn't moving either.

Dex put his hand on my shoulder and I jumped in my seat, eyeing him wildly.

"Hey, kiddo, there's nothing there," he said calmly, looking down at me. He removed his hand and went back to navigating. My eyes flitted over to the forest and now I couldn't see it anymore. The face was gone and only the trees remained.

"OK! This spot should work, hopefully," Dex announced loudly and thrust the boat into neutral. He poked me in the shoulder to make sure I was paying attention to him. "Can you hold the wheel steady and press this button here when I tell you to? It will be stop and go and you'll have to hold your finger down to make it run."

I nodded and got up, scooching over behind the wheel and making sure I could reach the black button that stuck out on a low panel on the boat's side. The creepy feeling hadn't left me yet but I was glad to be concentrating on something else.

Dex made his way to the front of the boat. I quickly stole a glance at the forest. It was entirely plausible that I imagined the whole thing. After all, it didn't move even once and the lines and shadows of the forest could be molded into any figure of your imagination, like a Magic Eye painting.

"OK go," Dex cried out from the bow, amongst the sound of clanking chains. I pressed the button, holding it down while the anchor lowered into the water. It didn't seem like that hard of a job until the current began to tug at the wheel, making it shake underneath my hands. I tightened my grip and held it steady, while holding the button down with my other hand.

The wheel began to move even more under my hands, almost violently, like someone down below was pulling the rudder left and right. I put the weight of my boobs against the wheel for extra leverage, not able to let go of the button yet. But it was getting tedious. I was close to having to take my hand away.

"Let go!" Dex yelled, and I gladly did so, putting my other hand on the wheel to steady it. He ran along the deck towards me, not even bothering to hold onto the lifelines as he did so.

"The wheel is going crazy," I explained.

"The currents are fucked here." He put his hand on the anchor button.

"Are you getting hold of anything?"

He frowned. "I should be. It's a really sharp slope so I have to be sure."

After a few moments of hearing the anchor motor purr, he let go with satisfaction and turned the boat off. He looked at my white knuckles at the wheel and smiled wryly.

"You can let go now," he said. "We aren't going anywhere."

I did so. And the boat swung quickly to the left, away from the island. It was almost as if the island was giving it one huge push to stay away.

I almost fell over but Dex grabbed my arm quickly.

"You were saying?" I glared.

He sucked in his lip and looked back at the shore while the boat continued to spin like the second hand on a clock. He grabbed hold of the wheel and kept it steady. He glanced down behind him.

"There's no stern anchor to keep us from swinging all weekend."

"Does it matter if we aren't on the boat?"

"Hell yes it does. The anchor is barely holding up front and this is a fucking calm day, for this place anyway. Another hour of this and the boat will wiggle itself free. If we left, it wouldn't be here when we return."

So what he was saying is that we were fucked. Oh well, time to call it day and go back to the marina. Nice try but not in the cards. I understood.

Oh, but no.

"Doesn't matter, there's an easy fix," he said while my shoulders deflated. "Here, take the wheel."

I did so, shoving my weight against it. It was even harder now to keep steady than before. Just what the hell was going on in the water? It looked like a lot of commotion on the surface, but not enough to make steering as difficult as it was.

The image of sunken coffins slowly rising to the surface entered my head. I pictured fingerless hands coming out of the rotted caskets, skin peeling, bloated white flesh, reaching for the rudder underneath in the dark, green depths.

"Perry!" Dex barked. I snapped out of it and gave him my attention. He had lifted up one of the benches and was pulling out a long yellow rope out of a hidden storage area. "You hear me? Keep that wheel as still as you can, we're in a good position now."

The boat had done a 180 around the anchor and the bow was facing the way we had come in. I nodded and did as he said.

He came beside me and tied the rope around a metal hook thing, finishing it off in a fancy sailor knot, then opened the lifelines behind me and started to pull in the Zodiac.

"Where are you going?" I asked anxiously. I didn't want him to leave me on this thing.

He kicked over a metal ladder and stepped down towards the Zodiac, jumping the rest of the way. He landed with a thud, the boat shuddering beneath him, but managed to stay upright and inside. He pointed to the cliff area. There was a lone arbutus tree that was jutting out of one of the rocks.

"I've got to tie us to that tree there," he said, starting the small engine on the Zodiac like a finicky lawnmower. After a few attempts it roared, blueish smoke emanating from the tank, the propellers whirring violently.

"Do you have enough rope?" I asked. He nodded and adjusted himself on one of the pontoons.

He looked up at me. "Just hold it as steady as you can; otherwise, you'll be leading me around. Make sure the rope doesn't tangle. I'll be right back."

How many times had I heard that?

And off he went. The little boat straggled a bit at first and I could see Dex jerking the engine around, fighting off the current, but as soon as the boat picked up speed, it was smooth sailing.

I watched him, aware that the wheel was trying hard to be free of my grasp. There was no way in hell I was letting go for anything. The rope trailed out from behind the Zodiac and it looked like the spool of it at my feet was going to unwind sooner rather than later.

Just when the rope's length was almost all used, Dex reached the rocky outcrop beneath the cliff. He killed the engine, leaped on land, climbed up over a few wet boulders and reached the tree. It made me nervous. It was obvious that he knew what he was doing and Dex could certainly be a little monkey at times, but seeing him scamper over those wet boulders, crashing waves beneath him, I knew it just took one wrong step for him to lose his footing and tumble backward into the sea.

This seemed like an awful lot of trouble just to visit this island. Why the government decided to make it a park was beyond me. How the hell did most campers get here anyway? No wonder there was rarely anyone here – half the people probably gave up. There was another island only a few miles away that had a dock and everything. The smart boaters went there; the crazy ones came to this hostile place.

Hostile was the most apt term. From the moment we saw this place, this feeling of GET OUT was running through my bones. I didn't like it at all and all this trouble with the currents and the boat weren't helping.

Dex got the job done though. He had tied the line around the tree as much as he could before there was no more slack and got back into the Zodiac. He started the engine, motored along loudly and within a minute he was back at the boat and climbing aboard.

He breathlessly tied the Zodiac back to the boat and said, "Now let go."

I did so and braced myself for the swing. The boat moved over but stopped after a couple of feet, the rope straining tightly against the tree. I could hear the anchor chains from the bow rattling. But we weren't going anywhere.

We breathed out a sigh of relief in unison.

"You're not a bad skipper," he said to me. "Maybe you should take up sailing after this."

"We'll see," I said.

Now that that was all done, we climbed below and started organizing everything for our pilgrimage to the campsite on the opposite side of the island. We had two large backpacks each full of our personal crap, a small cooler that Dex had stuffed with food we had purchased on the way to the marina, a small cooking stove with propane, a long duffel containing the tent, pegs, mattresses and a tarp, two sleeping bags, two pillows, the large professional camera, the handheld camcorder, a strange old camera case I hadn't seen before, an SLR camera, two large golf umbrellas, lighting boards, a small pack full of our ghost–hunting equipment and the like, Dex's laptop…and a bunch of other crap.

"Uh, don't you think it'll be easier if we just left everything on the boat?" I pointed at all the junk. "It's going to take several trips to the island just to take everything."

"So it will," he mused, gathering up his backpack. "Can't forget the jackets either."

He went to the forward cabin and pulled them out. They were real, proper sailing jackets. I knew they would come down to the knees on me. He placed them in my hands then noticed the look on my face. "What?"

"I'm just saying, maybe I should stay on the boat? That will at least cut down on bringing some stuff."

"Are you getting cold feet?"

"I've had cold feet this whole time."

"So you're scared?"

"Yeah! It's called Island of Death for a reason and it obviously doesn't want us here."

"Don't be so dramatic."

I felt like throwing the jackets in his face but just held his gaze steadily and with a stern eye. I could see the wheels working behind his brow.

"Fine," he said, "if you want to stay on the boat tonight, that's fine. Do whatever you got to do. But you know you still have to come on the island, bringing the rest of the stuff, and do all the damn filming we have planned."

I nodded; of course I knew that. He did not look impressed with my decision though.

"Well, I'll go do the first run. You stay here. Try not to wet yourself."

He turned, gathering up as much stuff as he could and climbed on the upper deck. I sat down and opened the cooler looking for something to eat. It was way past lunch by now and the nausea that had killed my appetite earlier was gone.

I heard the sound of the Zodiac starting and through one of the portholes, saw Dex on it as he passed briefly outside, heading for the shore.

There was just enough food in the cooler for the weekend. We erred on the side of being cheap and having less to carry. As long as we had coffee, I was good. In fact, the two of us could live off coffee.

There was a strange poking feeling in the back of my conscious that was starting to make me reconsider though. Now that I was here, going to the island with minimal rations didn't seem like the smartest idea.

I walked over to the galley and opened the tiny fridge and freezer. Empty, obviously.

I pulled open the cupboards up above and found a few boxes of half eaten cereal, several cans of soup, some canned vegetables, pasta sauce and an unopened box of Triscuits. That made me feel a bit better knowing there was food on board. No one said we couldn't come back to the boat.

I grabbed the Triscuits and opened them. I doubted Zach would miss it and it was better than me nibbling at the food we were bringing to the island. I shoved a few in my mouth and walked over to the table.

A movement out of the corner of my eye made me stop. I slowly turned my head to the wall.

There was a hand on the outside of the porthole glass. A hand reaching up from the depths.

I screamed like hell, dropped the box and made a frantic dash for the stairs, pulling myself up them in a ragged, scrambling hurry.

I fell on the deck, scraping my knees on the pebbly surface, and scampered for the wheel, pulling myself behind it as if that was going to offer me some protection.

Dex had finished dropping the gear high on the beach and was walking back to the Zodiac. I couldn't tell if he had heard my scream or not; it didn't seem like it. I looked back at the cabin and let the sticky, eerie feeling wash over me. The cabin wasn't the problem. The hand had been on the outside of the boat. Someone had to have been in the water, like they were trying to climb on board.

That thought made me want to vomit and having my back to the open sea was now becoming a problem. I stepped out from around the wheel and stood as in the middle of the cockpit as I could. I didn't want to look on the sides of the boat; I was too afraid of what I might see.

I waited, standing as still as possible, hand on my chest, trying to hear anything besides the whoosh of blood in my head and the sweet, sweet sound of the Zodiac motoring back to me.

Well, that settled it. No way in hell was I staying alone on the boat tonight.

Within a minute, Dex was back and climbing back on board. He re–tied the rope, giving me a funny look.

"Are you OK?" he asked, coming over to me. "You look like you've seen..."

He didn't finish the sentence.

"Can you do me a favor and look on the sides of the boat?" I squeaked. "The left side in particular."

He appeared confused but did what I asked. He glanced over the left side. "What am I looking for?"

"There's no one there?"

"No," he said slowly. He walked over to the other side and did the same. "No one or nothing there either."

He stopped in front of me and folded his arms. "What's this about then? Saw another face?"

I could tell he wasn't going to be very supportive, no matter what I said. "No, I didn't see a face. But I'm definitely not staying on the boat tonight."

He smiled wryly. "Decided you would miss me too much?"

"Something like that," I answered.

A wave of suspicion clouded his eyes. I wasn't sure if he was judging my sanity or what, but he didn't say anything. Had it been the other way around I would have been bugging him to death but I guess that is where we differed. Well, that and the fact that I wasn't a medicated nutter.

He let it go and I decided to as well. I probably just *thought* I saw a hand. Maybe it was a gull or something flying past, I don't know.

We climbed back down and my eyes immediately went to the window. He was right in that he didn't see anything. Whatever it was wasn't there anymore.

Yet I couldn't get the image out of my head. I know I saw a hand. I had seen it clearly. It was a greenish white, bloated and scabby. The palm had been open and pressed firmly against the glass, the wrist and arm leading down below out of sight, belonging to some... body.

Dex gathered the rest of the stuff. I supposed I should have helped but something was bothering me. I walked over to the window, heart in my throat, and peered closer at it. I moved my head around, trying to lose the glare from inside the boat and then I saw it.

There was a very faint impression on the glass, like half a handprint. I could make out the lines where they would have snaked across at the top of the palm. It was fading quickly.

"Come look at this," I commanded, no time to explain or ask nicely. To his credit Dex came right over, his head right beside mine, smelling like cigarettes and aftershave. I pointed at the mark on the glass, careful not to touch it myself. Not that it mattered, since the impression was on the other side.

"Look," I whispered and looked at him to make sure he saw it, before the impression faded before our eyes. His eyes were locked like lasers. He saw it.

"It looks like an oil or heat smudge," he said. "What is it?"

"It's a handprint," I said incredulously.

He frowned. It was all but gone now. "Are you sure? Did I touch the side of the boat?"

"No, not you. While you were on shore, I saw a hand come on the glass, on the other side, like this," I put my hand on it to demonstrate. When I lifted it off, I too left a mark, albeit a full one.

"You saw a hand?" Now it was his turn to sound disbelieving.

"Yes," I hissed. "I didn't tell you because you wouldn't believe me and then you said you didn't see anything so then I didn't believe me, but here it is."

"Here it was," he conceded. He rubbed his chin as we both watched the mark I left disappear, at a much quicker rate than the other one. I prayed that he believed me. I wasn't crazy and I wasn't making it up. There was proof and he saw it.

"I don't know if that was a handprint," he finally said. He looked at me carefully, obviously afraid that I was going to blow a gasket at him. He was on the right track but I managed to suck the explosion inside.

"It was a handprint," I stressed through my teeth. "You could have given it a palm reading. Now what kind of fucking ghost leaves a handprint?'

"The same kind that leaves a mark..." he said invitingly and reached over with his hand and stroked his finger slowly down the length of my neck, "... here."

I shivered internally. Partly because I was remembering when Old Roddy had left bruises on my neck after our little altercation, partly because his soft touch was borderline sensual. That and the serious, almost seductive look in his eyes as he stared at my neck, like a vampire before its first meal.

"So what do we do?" I whispered, trying to not break the moment.

His eyes met mine. I wasn't sure if he was thinking about ghosts. I was thinking about him running his wide tongue down my neck. Maybe that's what he was thinking too. A weird heady tension was building inside of me and spilling out into the air.

"We keep doing what we're doing," he said, his voice low and gravely. "And try and keep a camera on us at all times."

He held my eyes for a few extra beats before straightening up and going back to the stuff. I eyed the glass again, feeling the tension dissipate.

"You believe me though, right?" I asked him, coming over to his side and bringing my backpack on to my shoulders. Please say you do believe me.

"I do, kiddo. If you say that was a handprint, then that's what it was."

"Thank you," I said softly.

"Of course, it would be better if I had seen it too, or if you got it on tape but since we just got here, I'm going to take this as a sign of things to come. I'm sure this is only the beginning."

He scooped up most of his gear, gesturing for me to take the cooler and the ghost equipment bag, and headed up the stairs. His words were not encouraging. This was only the beginning. We weren't even on the island yet.

CHAPTER EIGHT

I guess when you expect the worst it's always a pleasant surprise if everything ends up going smoothly. I totally expected some dead soul to rise up from the waves and overturn the Zodiac as Dex and I motored towards shore, or perhaps we might have run into some hidden rocks and sank (then get pulled down by that...hand).

But we didn't. We arrived in one piece and, loaded down with stuff, pulled the Zodiac up along the pebbly beach until it was far away from any rebellious tides. Dex even tied it to a tree to be safe.

The fact that we had to carry so much shit in a half–hour trek across the island was also distracting me from the ghostly dangers that lurked about. I had the backpack on, my sleeping bag under one arm, the cooler under the other, a camera case and the ghost equipment bag hanging off of each shoulder, and the lighting boards in my hand. The weight was nearly unbearable and made it hard to walk on the stones.

Dex was no better off, but at least he had the frame to carry everything on him like some sexy, overloaded pack mule. And he somehow managed to fish out a camera out of the old–looking case.

He shoved it in my free hand.

"You film our walk," he said. I looked down at it. I hadn't seen one of these in years but it was a totally vintage Super 8 camera. Luckily that meant it was easy for me to carry (it's kind of shaped like a gun), but still. If I fell over at any point, and that was very likely, the camera would be the thing breaking my fall.

"OK," I said slowly.

He reached over and flicked it on. "But don't film anything unless you have to. You've only got three minutes and 20 seconds of film before we have to refill and we won't have the time to do that yet. Or, I won't have the patience."

I wanted to ask him why he didn't film it but he did have both his hands full. What a little opportunist he was.

Dex walked into the forest and I followed. We broke through the bushes, taking our time since both of us weren't very agile, and came across a small trail heading up and down with the coast.

We walked along the path in silence, listening to the cry of far–away ravens, the crunch of dead leaves and broken twigs beneath our feet, and the sound of waves against the shore, stirring the pebbles. From the glimpses between the heavy trees I could see that Mary Contrary was still anchored out on the water. Whether she was tied up or not, I was still going to worry about her. What if we came back to the boat tomorrow to charge our phones and she was gone? I had a mini heart attack just thinking about it.

After we trudged along for a few minutes, another faint trail looked like it broke off into the depths of the forest, marked by a red and white plastic disc on a tree.

"Straight or turn?" I asked Dex as he stood at the intersection. "Is this even a path?"

He pointed south where our path continued. "If we go south for a bit we can see the ruins of the caretakers' cottage."

That sounded creepy. "Uh, how about we come back and do that. Let's just get all this crap off of us."

He nodded and we started on the path heading inland. It wasn't as well trampled as the perimeter trail and with each step we took over the jumbled roots and overgrown ferns, I felt more and more uneasy. Sometimes the path wasn't even obvious anymore, especially when the spaces between the trees opened up. It took Dex's vigilant eye on spotting the discs on the trees to keep us going in the same direction.

It was when we reached this strange little glade that I told Dex we had to stop. My shoulders were killing me and the cooler was slowly but surely working its way out from under my arm.

I probably could have picked a better place. All the trees around us were dead and decaying, weighed down by old moss that dripped with stringy moisture from their branches. They looked like crippled, hunched–over people being enveloped by killer slime, frozen forever in agonizing positions.

Even when Dex said, "Are you sure you want to stop? It can't be that much longer to the campsite," I heard more fear in his voice than the annoyance that I was slowing things down.

I put the cooler down as gently as possible and then flung my backpack off through that one arm. Even with the weight off, I felt as broken as the rotting trees.

Dex saw the pain in my face and relented. He took his bag off as well and put everything else down on the ground. He walked over me and passed me a bottle of water from the cooler.

"Thanks" I said, taking a swig of it.

"Shoulders hurt?" he asked.

I nodded. He walked behind me, reached over and placed both of his strong hands on my shoulders and started massaging them very slowly. It was a beautiful pain.

"Did you take massage classes as well?" I asked lightly, trying to keep him from knowing how much I was enjoying it.

He grunted a no. I expected him to make a remark about giving Jenn massages but he didn't. And I was glad. That would have been too much. I liked to live in this weird fantasy world of mine where mentions of Jenn were jarring and inappropriate. Though, you know, half the time I was bringing her up.

Dex continued to massage but I could tell his attention was elsewhere. Had we been anywhere else, I might have felt a bit rejected. But I could feel he was scanning the dank, dark forest around us, taking everything in. I started to pick up an uncomfortable vibe, one that was miles away from the massage or Jenn.

"What is it?" I asked.

"I don't know. I don't like it here."

"I don't like it anywhere here," I admitted. But for Dex to say the same thing was saying a lot.

He slowly brought his hands to a stop and paused. We held our breaths in unison. There was something weird here. A feeling in the air, like the atmosphere was dragged down with the heavy, overgrown moss.

We heard a crunch behind us.

We whipped around, my upper body aching from the sudden movement, and saw a family of raccoons creep out from behind an old rotted stump.

We had a lot of raccoons in the Pacific Northwest and it was a nightly occurrence in the area around my parents' house. I still didn't feel any easier around them.

There were two babies and four adults. They stopped about five feet away from us and even though we were larger, I felt outnumbered, like we couldn't win in a fight.

They would have been cute if they were on another side of a fence, with their human–like paws, black eyes and twitchy little noses. But here they seemed like vicious predators wanting to attack. I had hoped the last of our "animal" encounters were behind us in Red Fox.

The raccoons made funny little noises and a few of them leaned back on their hindquarters to get a better look at us. Or perhaps to intimidate us. They stood like that for a bit, not moving forward or backward. They weren't exactly in our way but gathering up our stuff with them there didn't seem like a smart idea.

"Start filming," Dex said softly through the corner of his mouth. I looked down at the Super 8, which was beside my backpack.

"Uh..."

"Just do it," he hissed.

I eyed the raccoons and then made my way over to the backpack, lifting up my legs carefully, not wanting to scare or startle them. It was at that moment, when I sighted my backpack as I picked up the Super 8, that I realized we had no weapons with us. As far as I knew, we had no guns, no pepper spray, and probably nothing bigger than a kitchen knife. Even a baseball bat would have been something.

I picked up the Super 8 and pressed record. I didn't know what to shoot, but I just aimed it at the raccoons and heard the film spinning around the reel inside. I knew it was going to quickly run out.

"So we film them and then?" I asked, my voice low. "This is just more nature documentary?"

"Could be," he whispered, his voice low and his eyes focused on them.

At that, the closest and largest raccoon opened its mouth, teeth bared, eyes white, and hissed at us. It was a loud, unearthly sound like nails on a chalkboard over growling. It took a step closer and we took an instinctive step back.

"Or, it could be the part where everything starts to go horribly wrong," he quickly whispered.

I kept filming but wasn't sure what to do next. I looked at Dex. He had on his cargo jacket and hoodie underneath and his boots and long pants added protection. If the raccoon did make a leap for him, it would take a lot to bite through the fabric and by then

I was sure I would be beating the off rabid beast with the Super 8.

But then all the other raccoons – including the babies – started hissing at once. We were looking into six open jaws filled with sharp white teeth and black gums. The noise was terrifying.

I was pretty close to either peeing my pants or throwing the Super 8 into the forest as a distraction but as quickly as they had appeared, they suddenly dropped to their haunches and scrambled off into the woods. It reminded me of a pack of dogs responding to their owner calling them home.

I hit the off button and let out yet another sigh of relief. "What the fuck was that?"

Dex looked a bit shaken. "Guess they aren't used to humans intruding on their property. This is probably their little territory here."

"Well they can have their fucking territory," I said and quickly gathered up my stuff. I was getting the fuck out of there, pain or no pain.

Dex did the same and within minutes we were leaving the dead area, our legs moving faster than they had all day.

It only took about ten minutes before the claustrophobic tangles and damp undergrowth were forgotten and the foliage was replaced with waist–high, green salal bushes that allowed for uninterrupted views of the water and the beach. Though I didn't feel 100% welcome here, this area was at least bright and the traces of the campsite brought in an air of civilization. I was even comforted by a sign for the drop toilet.

The trees around this area were quite bare around the bottom; their branches didn't start until quite high up, which gave an open, airy feel to the campground. Judging from the breeze that was steadily picking up from the water ahead, it was probably due to the continuous bashing from coastal weather.

We walked down the path that led us past the seven campsites, each site marked with a square gravel plot and a picnic table, and stopped among the dry knee–high grass that led down onto the wide, expansive curve of beach. With the smaller "Little D'Arcy" Island just across a tumultuous stretch of water, and the lumps of the Unit Rocks just south of it, it could have made a beautiful postcard.

To my relief, Little D'Arcy had a fairly large house on it, nestled amongst the trees. It was the house a rich recluse would have owned.

"Do you think anyone lives on it?" I asked hopefully. Though I knew the short stretch of ocean between the two islands was notoriously turbulent and impossible to swim across, it would be comforting to know help was just a stone's throw away.

But Dex just shook his head before heading back up the trail towards the campsites. "I doubt it. Not now. Maybe in the summer."

Discouraged at that, I sighed inside and followed him back to the sites. We decided on the one closest to the beach. It had the best view and I was happy to be as far out of the forest as possible. The only problem was that if the weather turned, our tent was going to take more of a beating. But since everything seemed OK for the moment, we would just deal with that when and if it happened.

It felt good to have the backpacks off of us, but we didn't have time to relax and enjoy it. A quick glance to my phone told me it was already 2 p.m. and the sun would be setting in about two hours or so. I sent off a quick text to Ada and my dad to let them know I was OK and had made it safely (no point in telling them about any of the hassle we had). Then we made quick work of the tent.

I couldn't remember the last time I had been camping but, as usual, with Dex it was like second nature.

Also, it was his tent after all. I helped him when I could, holding down the pegs, fishing the poles through the tent legs and keeping everything together. He even went so far as to put a wide tarp on top of the tent, strung between nearby trees, to shelter us from any rain.

"Well done, sir," I said, admiring his handwork when he was done.

He wiped his hands on his pants and gave me a tense smile.

I stooped over and entered the tent. It was a four person tent so it was just big enough that I could stand up, albeit hunched over with my neck at a crazy angle. We laid out the large foamy mattress on the bottom and put the sleeping bags and pillows on top. I took the right side and put down my backpack, bringing the books out and other essentials I didn't want to go digging for later.

Dex pointed at the books. "You better get your script ready. We don't have much time if we want to shoot some stuff before the sun goes down."

"What kind of stuff?" I asked, stiffening. For some reason I didn't think we'd be shooting anything with me on camera today but, like I said earlier, he was an opportunist.

"Just the intro, you know the drill. There's that little grassy hill to the left out there that looks over the beach. Would be a perfect shot. You go whip something up, I'll get everything here ready. Then we'll shoot it, come back here and we'll figure out what to do for dinner."

Dinner sounded good. The Triscuits were barely holding out inside of me. I scooped up the books, as well as a notepad and pen, and got out of the tent. He obviously needed some time alone to get his shit together. Probably wanted some privacy to talk to Jenn on the phone or something like that. I looked down at the beach and the dried, reddish logs sprawled out along its length. It looked like the least scary place for me to do some work.

I walked further down the beach than I initially planned. Picking what log to sit on was a bit like trying on underwear. Some had bird poop on it, some were too small for my ass to rest comfortably on. Eventually I found a nice broad one and took a seat.

I was at the very end of the beach and had a wonderful view of our blue tarp poking up amongst the trees and leafy bushes, the grassy knoll that Dex had been talking about and the short distance to Little D'Arcy across the way. Gulls flew about in the sky, letting out an occasional cry, while other birds floated among the waves.

I wasn't sure where to start with my reading and what I should incorporate into my quick introduction script, but it didn't take long for me to feel completely creeped out again.

It turns out that where the lepers' housing had been was where the campsite now was and that the graves where they were haphazardly buried were all over the place. Apparently they were never marked either, except by a small mound, or by the placing of a boulder or two. I had already seen a few places like that around the tent and that realization turned my spine to custard.

I twirled around on the log, suddenly afraid with my back to the dark bushes and had this mounting urge to flee. I know I had read that they were all buried here, but I figured maybe a place like the dead mossy glade would have been the area. Or, you know, an actual cemetery. Not where I was, where we would be sleeping tonight and where so many other people had slept. To think that the next suspicious looking rock might house a rotting casket underneath...

I shivered violently.

I didn't need to read anymore. I didn't feel like I needed a script either. The history of this place already felt ingrained inside of me. I wanted to enjoy the casual scene of the beach, the glittery waves and the open space as the sun made the shadows long. The beauty of D'Arcy Island was so misleading.

I closed the books and gazed over the scenery. I did this for a few blissful minutes before I felt a little itch in my head. Surfing the internet seemed like a better, more distracting use of my time. I pulled out my phone and noticed the battery was already half used and the reception bar was nonexistent. Uh oh.

I opened the browser and it spun around for what seemed like forever until it latched on to a page. The bar wavered and then disappeared again. I had a feeling staying in touch wasn't going to be easy here. Then again, nothing had been easy so far.

Still, it at least allowed me to check my Twitter and Facebook accounts. There wasn't anything too interesting there. I was still new to the whole Twitter thing so I didn't have many followers but occasionally someone would "tweet" me and say something nice about the show. Today someone had said they really liked the concept of the show and asked where we were going next. I replied back and told him he'd have to wait and see. Dex and I had decided it was probably best if we never gave anyone straight answers – keep people in suspense, something Dex did very well.

It was nice that I never got any nasty comments on my Twitter (so far). I think people reserved that for actual famous people and stuff like that since Twitter accounts weren't anonymous; well, not really. You were still held accountable, plus it was easy to block people on Twitter. One click and you didn't need to look at them anymore.

The blog, of course, was another story. Every single nasty comment was left by someone anonymous who didn't provide a name or an email address. I suppose there was some way I could try and figure out who they were by finding out their IP address but that involved doing something in the back end of the blog and Dex would have to do that himself. I knew if I asked him to look into it, he'd respond with a flat–out no and then chide me for caring what other people thought.

I couldn't help it though. Every time I thought about checking the blog out of some strange torturous compulsion, I felt so nervous I was almost sick about it. I hated not knowing when these comments were going to come and what they were going to be about. They went straight to my email, too, which didn't help. Even if I avoided looking at the blog, I still had to check my emails at some point, and that's where they were, waiting for me.

Like this time. It's not like I got a lot of emails from people but sometimes it was from my cousin Jonas in Sweden, sometimes it was a concert announcement, sometimes it was catching up with my friend Gemma who lived down in Eugene. To be honest, I didn't get enough email to warrant being an obsessive checker but there I was, checking anyway. It seemed I got comments more than anything else.

Case in point, as the browser slowly logged me into my email account, I could see four messages from the blog comments. Three of them had names assigned to them, which usually meant they were benign or spam. I always checked those last to raise my spirits. The final message was by Anonymous.

That sick feeling returned and my heart started to pound loudly in my chest. It was a different kind of fear than the one I was experiencing on the island. It was almost more upsetting in a way, which was really ridiculous. It was just words, silly stupid words from people I didn't know. It shouldn't have been as terrifying as camping on a ghostly leper island, yet it was.

I took a deep breath and clicked the name. I closed my eyes as the internet was found among the spotty reception and waited. On the plus side, my fear of the island was subsiding.

I opened them slowly and looked down. The comment was short and read: "I can tell from looking at your face that you've never accomplished anything in your life. It's sad that this probably is the high point. Thank god you're too fat to have an ego."

Ouch. Major fucking ouch.

I felt tears pricking hotly at the nerves behind my eyes. It wasn't so much the fat thing; I was kind of used to that by now and it was such the typical cheap shot to take on a female who had a little meat on her bones. It was the other thing. It hit a little too close to home, to be honest. This actually was the most I had accomplished; at least it felt that way. And they were right. That really was sad.

"What the hell are you doing?"

I looked up and saw Dex storming towards me like a gruff freight train, the pebbles kicking up behind him. I must have totally been in my own little world to not have heard him coming.

He stopped in front of me, spied the phone, and yanked it out of my hands.

"Hey!" I yelled at him.

He looked at the phone and read over the email with disgust. "Another comment? Nice. Way to play the fat card again, you bitch."

He stuck my phone in his pocket, shaking his head at me. "I gave you a simple task, read the bloody books and work on the fucking script and instead you're back to checking the blog again. Do you like to torture yourself?"

If I wasn't close to crying before, I definitely was now. Those hot prickles came faster. But I couldn't cry in front of him and not over that. So I channeled the tears into anger and gave him my most potent glare.

"I can check whatever the fuck I want to check, especially when it's on my own phone."

"You're technically on the clock right now."

"Oh, whatever, Dex, since when is it any of your business? And why do you care so much? I don't believe you have that much concern for my well–being."

"It is my business. You know I have to keep you in check here and that's hard to do when you keep getting sucked into this shit."

"You don't think much of me, do you?"

He sighed loudly and rolled his eyes to the heavens. He plopped down beside me on the log, leaned forward with his elbows propped up on his knees and folded his hands into a steeple.

"I'm going to say this only once, kiddo," he said slowly, his voice bordering on fatherly and fed up. "You know I think the world of you."

Actually, that was news to me. He could see the skepticism on my face.

"I do. All those things I said last night about...you, I meant them all."

Ugh. Why did he have throw that in there? Butterflies at the pit of my chest were beginning to stir. They did not need the encouragement.

"But again, it doesn't and shouldn't matter what I think. It's all about what you think. What you think about yourself. Obviously this crap is getting to you; otherwise, you wouldn't bother checking and you wouldn't be getting upset."

"I'm not upset," I said and opened my eyes wider.

He gave me a sad smile. "You looked pretty miserable as I was coming over. You think you're pretty good at hiding those eyes of yours. But you're not."

"Well, I'm sorry I'm not as deceptive as you are."

"It's a learned art. You're better off learning how to not give a shit about what other people think of you. Whether it's what some strangers on the internet think, whether it's what your old classmates think, or what I think or what your parents think, in the end, no one's opinion should matter but your own."

"So you're saying I shouldn't be listening to you right now?"

"You're not getting out of this that easily. And I'm not giving you back your phone either."

I stared at him, dumbfounded. He had to be joking but his eyes said he wasn't.

"You're confiscating my phone!?"

He got up off the log. "For now. We're all ready to shoot. I've got the camera up on the tripod, lighting is perfect. We are ready to go and I need you in the moment. Need you to be here and ready to tell the island's tale."

I was barely listening to him. My eyes flitted to the water, finding the rhythmic waves a less aggravating sight than Dex lording over me with a stupid smug look on his face. Sometimes I felt like we were total equals with each other and other times it felt like we were in some bizarre teacher–student situation. Or doctor–patient, as it seemed to be now.

"Aw, now you're mad," he said mockingly, bringing a cigarette to his mouth and lighting it.

I avoided his face and sucked in through my teeth. Stupid jerk. I had half a mind to pick up one of the stones and throw it at him. The anger inside me was astonishing enough that I was almost afraid I'd do it. He twitched a little too, as if he could feel the energy rolling towards him in an invisible wave.

But I just got to my feet, grabbed my books and walked off towards the grassy knoll, my feet sliding awkwardly on the stones as I went.

"Where are you going?" he asked.

I didn't answer. It should have been pretty obvious. I could see the camera already set up on the hill, all he needed was me. Might as well get this part over with. I wasn't exactly in the camera host mood but by God I was going to have to fake it.

I made a quick stop in the tent. I zipped the door behind me so he'd have the common sense not to come in after me, and attempted to make myself camera-ready.

I changed into a flattering v–neck, long-sleeved shirt and swiped on a coat of cherry lipstick that was the same vivid red. Yeah, this was obviously not my usual on–camera attire but you know, fuck that. I was going to prove I did deserve to be out there. I knew the top made my breasts look great. I mean hey, Jenn shows hers off on freaking *Wine Babes* and she has nothing on me in that department, plus the red coloring and lipstick suited my skin tone and hair. I didn't care if I was going to freeze my ass off, I was a professional and this is what was going to happen.

I decided to keep my black jeans and Chucks on and applied a few eye–opening strokes of mascara. I was ready to go.

I stepped out of the tent and immediately was struck into submission by the cold wind.

Mind over matter, I thought to myself, though I suddenly wished I had worn a more padded bra. Oh well, I'd just make the headlights work for me. Keeping my chattering teeth quiet, I strode up the path over to the hill, where Dex was now fiddling with the camera settings.

The hill was grassy and undulating, with rocky mounds here and there. I didn't let my mind think about whether they could be graves or not. The view was gorgeous, especially in the fading sunlight. The beached curved out to our right, while a rocky shoreline and smaller beach spread to the left. Across the way sat the stoic Little D'Arcy Island and its lone house.

"Jesus Christ," Dex exclaimed. He had looked up from the camera and was staring at me all bug–eyed. Not ogling me, unfortunately, just surprised.

"Is there a problem?" I asked testily and crossed my arms. Naturally this made my cleavage even more impressive. I was doing it out of anger, though, I swear.

"Uhhh." He blinked hard and tried to focus.

"You are such a guy," I remarked, shaking my head at him.

He let out a small laugh, but kept his eyes on my chest. "Yeah, I guess I am. Sorry, I...you just surprised me...you're normally not...aren't you freezing?"

I shrugged as casually as possible. "I'm fine. Are we going to do this or what? We don't have that much use of the light and we're wasting time talking."

He hesitated. He wasn't used to me telling him what to do.

"OK," he said quickly. "Let's go then. Stand a bit over to the right, maybe back up a foot so you don't, uh, overwhelm the camera."

I did as he said, holding my shoulders back and tried to calm my nerves. I may have looked confident but I didn't feel it all. I was just going to have to fake the whole thing. I'd show everyone just how professional I could be.

Dex fiddled a bit with a bounceboard on the ground, propping it up against a rock (grave?) and gave the camera the final once–over.

"Rolling," he said. He pointed at me. "Go."

I took a deep breath, readied myself, and went into a lengthy intro about the island's history and a detailed, dramatic description of what it would be like to have been one of the lepers. I don't know where it was all coming from. I had been going over in my head earlier some key points to focus on and what order to do them in, but the description about the Chinese lepers just came out of nowhere.

By the time I was done, I was shaking at the knees from the overload of nerves (and the cold) and I was out of breath from trying to sound clear, concise and confident.

"Cut," Dex said slowly and a bit unsurely. He looked up from the camera, not looking impressed like I had thought he would. He looked utterly confused.

"What the hell was that? Better yet, who the hell was that?"

I felt a bit defensive. I thought I did an awesome job and I rarely thought that about myself.

"I was trying to be professional."

"Yeah, well, you were, kiddo. You were. But that's not why people love you. The world expects a pose from everyone these days. You have to loosen the fuck up. That wasn't *you*."

"Yes, Dex, it was me. That was me being professional and apparently people want that."

"No, they don't. They want you being you. They want your personality."

"I'm a goof. I don't know what the hell I'm doing half the time."

He stepped out from behind the camera and took a step closer to me. "I know you don't. That's what makes you...charming. That's why you're doing this with me."

I sighed, all confidence rolling out of me. Even when I try to change, I fail.

"See," he said, walking forward until he was right in front of me. He pushed a piece of hair back behind my ear. I flinched slightly at his touch. I couldn't help it. My nerves were jumping all over the place. "This is exactly why I don't want you to give a shit about those comments. I know what they say. But that's the opinion of a few people, and most likely, just one person. They're just a jackfuck who doesn't know what they are talking about. Everyone else, Jimmy included, they want you. Just as you, as Perry Palomino. And that's why we're going to have to do that all over again."

"Are you fucking kidding me?" I cried out. I was so ready to throw in the towel.

He cocked his head at me. "Just once. The information, it's all great. I liked what you did with the lepers and everything. That's perfect. But, come on, baby."

Baby? He reached for my shoulders and shook them around, my boobs jostling up and down. He tried, with little success, not to notice.

"Relax. Get jiggy with it. Have fun. I know you're a fun person. Let's let everyone see that."

Though I was appreciating how close he was to me and the fact that he was still holding my shoulders with his strong grip, I had to say, "This is still a ghost story, right? It's not *Girls Gone Wild.*"

"Hey, you're the one who put on that shirt." He leered and walked back to the camera. "It's just you and me here. Tell me about the island. I was barely listening the first time anyway. Things were, uh, distracting me. Tell *me* what you know. And go."

And so I pretended that Dex hadn't heard anything I said, and described everything as if it was for an audience of one. He asked the question, I responded, simple as that.

When I was done, Dex broke into that genuine, wide smile that so rarely stretched across his face.

"See how much better that was! Did you feel how much better that was?"

Not really, though I was more relaxed. I messed up a few times regardless of whether I was just supposed to be talking to Dex.

He could see I wasn't convinced. "It was much better. And just one take. Now that that part is done, we don't have to worry about it, and it's right on time. Look at that fucking sunset."

I turned around and saw the golden sun heading down for the horizon where a far-off freighter was making a nautical silhouette. My arms and chest glowed golden. And suddenly I was freezing, almost unbearably cold. The adrenaline of being on camera was gone and my goose bumps were out in full force.

I shivered and made a beeline for the tent. "OK, it's time for a sweater," I said through chattering teeth.

"Aww, don't be so modest now," I heard Dex call out from behind me.

I put on a Fu Manchu sweatshirt and my yellow coat on top and helped Dex put away the camera equipment before the darkness came. Then we got our lanterns and flashlights out and started setting out the small cooking stove on the picnic table adjacent to the tent. I heated up two cans of ravioli for us (yeah, totally gourmet) while Dex fixed another tarp across the table. It didn't look like it was going to rain, but if it did, it would be nice to have a dry place to sit.

By the time the tarp was up and we were all organized for the night, it was pitch dark. We sat across each other at the table and spooned ourselves our dinner into our paper bowls. The lantern sat at the end of the table, providing just enough light to see by (and dare I say, the glow was pretty romantic). The Super 8 camera and the night camcorder were beside Dex on his bench, while the books and a heavy-duty flashlight were on mine. As far as I knew, we didn't have any plans to go exploring tonight which suited me just fine.

But you never knew what might come exploring our way.

"There are no bears on the island, right?" I asked. I knew there probably weren't – it was way too small for them – and I hadn't read about it, but I figured it would be good to know since we had food out and all. Or at least the smell of food. I finished all of my ravioli in seconds flat.

Dex shook his head while he placed our empty bowls in the garbage bag hanging off the table. "No, but I wouldn't count out those raccoons. I'll put the garbage and the food away from the tent in case those little turds pay us a visit in the night."

I didn't like the idea of those nasty little creatures lurking somewhere in the forest, waiting for us to fall asleep. Beyond us and the tent, we could only see blackness. It was giving me the major creeps, not knowing what was out there beyond where the weak light fell.

I shook it off and noticed Dex was staring at me.

"What?" I asked.

"You OK?" he said.

"Yeah. Yeah, it's just fucking creepy here at night." That was starting to become an understatement and fast. The bad vibes and feelings that first washed over me when the Mary Contrary pulled into the cove were coming back, poking at me in different places. My mind wanted to think about the graves we could have been sitting on top of. It wanted to think about the coffins being delivered. It wanted to think about the hand coming up from behind and...

I turned around quickly, sure that something was coming. But only the salal bushes and the nearest trees glowed in the light.

I faced Dex with a sheepish grin.

"I've got your back," he said, leaning over and fishing something out of the cooler that was on the ground behind him. "I'll let you know if something is coming to get you."

He produced the bottle of Jack Daniels he had bought at duty free and placed it triumphantly on the middle of the table. "I think this will cure what ails us tonight."

"I might need the whole bottle," I joked.

"We'll see. You're at least getting half of it." He unscrewed the top and took a swig from the bottle, wincing hard before passing it to me.

"No glasses?" I said, taking it from him and eyeing it warily. The amber color looked pretty in the light but I knew it didn't go down the same way.

"We're roughing it now," he said and nodded at the bottle. "Go ahead. I'm trying to get you drunk."

I narrowed my eyes at him, sussing him out. He raised his eyebrow in a cheeky way. That fucker, I never knew when he was joking or not.

I sighed, closed my eyes and took a gulp. It burned my chapped lips and then my throat as it went down but luckily it wasn't bad enough to come back up again. The distinctive taste of bourbon was conjuring up the memory of drinking it with Coke last night. A belated hair of the dog.

By the time the liquid reached my stomach and produced a pleasant warmth, Dex was taking another swig of it.

"Does that mix well with your new medication?"

He paused in mid-sip. I was vaguely aware that my question might have been a bit too personal. But he shrugged and finished swallowing.

"They're all the same. I'm used to it by now."

Then it was my turn to drink again. I took the bottle from him, our fingers brushing each other. It was one of those instances that had he been any other person, I wouldn't have noticed every touch, every contact.

I was already starting to feel it. This was not a good sign. "Maybe I don't need the whole bottle after all."

"Whatever makes you feel good."

"I should be feeling good very soon." I took another swig, this one a bit smaller. It burned less. I felt floatier and the shadows around me danced in a non-threatening way. The heat in my belly was passing up through my nerves until it settled somewhere on my brain like a warm blanket.

"I wish we had music," I said lazily, passing the bottle back to him.

"I have our phones," he said.

That's right. He still had my freaking phone.

"Am I allowed to have it back?" I asked, annoyed. I put my hand across the table, palm up. He took my hand in his and held it. An electrical charge I was sure I could only feel sparked from his fingers to mine. Once again I was torn between enjoying the butterflies flying around in my boozy insides and actually wanting my phone back. Gotta say though, at the moment, holding his hand was taking precedence. I was such a girl.

"Not yet," he said, still not letting go. His hand was nice and warm against the cold.

"What if my sister texts me?" I implored him, not wanting to be swayed. "Or my parents? They'll worry."

"Oh, your sister already has and I said you were fine," he said breezily. "She agreed with the idea of you taking an internet break."

My heart skidded to a halt.

"W–what?" I stammered. "What...you can't read my texts, those are personal! Oh God, what did they say? No wait, don't tell me." I started mentally going over every single text that would have shown up in the last 24 hours. The idea of him reading those was mortifying. My pride was dying a slow death inside.

He squeezed my hand and grinned. "You should see your face right now."

"What?"

He let go of my hand and casually reached for the bottle. "You are so gullible. You are so gullible, to me," he sang in an incredibly baritone voice before taking another sip.

"You're joking?"

He finished and wiped his lips with the back of his hand. "You really think I'd go reading your texts? Wow, Perry, I've got to say...that hurts. That hurts big time"

I could see it didn't actually hurt and he knew exactly why it wouldn't have surprised me if he had read my texts.

"Whatever, give me that." I swiped the bottle from him and took another shot. This time it burned away the annoyance that was furrowed up on my forehead.

"That a girl. Though I must say, I'm incredibly curious as to see what texts you might be getting. Are you talking about me? Nice things I hope. You can get pretty mean."

"Shut up." I waved at him. "Just play some music from your phone."

"Done and done." He brought it out from his front coat pocket and laid it on the table. He made quick work of it, flicking through the screens until Queens of the Stone Age came on. It was energizing enough to go along with the increasing drunkenness I was feeling, but not eerie enough to make me feel more afraid. Not that I actually was afraid now that I was pleasantly drunk. Dex was right; it was curing what ailed me.

We talked about music for the next little bit, a usual topic between the two of us since we had very similar music tastes, until the booze made me sway a little. With his handsome face expertly lit in half glow, half shadow, I became more aware of how much, uh, looser I was feeling. The warmth was everywhere now and I leaned further across the table at every word he said. I felt like some stupid adoring fan but there was no way around it. I felt playful. I felt frisky. This was bad, bad news.

It wasn't just me though. He had a bit more swagger in his movements. Plus he was giving me the eyes (it at least looked that way) and acting more flirty than usual.

Maybe this wasn't the best idea. Or maybe it was the best idea ever. I wanted to find out, something sober Perry would never dare do.

"Let's play a game," I said after we discussed who was the better drummer, Dave Lombardo or Neil Peart.

He raised his brow and his bottom lip twitched. He was intrigued. "OK...what kind of game? Strip poker?"

Again, I couldn't tell if he was taking the piss or not but I acted like he wasn't. "Do you have cards?"

"No..."

"How about 'I Have Never?' "

It was the good old drinking game where you take a sip if "never" is a lie. I was a champion in college. Mainly because the game got sexual really fast and then I never got drunk accordingly. It was a great way to get to know people better though.

"Now you're trying to get me drunk..." he mused with a smile.

"You're already drunk."

"So are you."

"Then this should be interesting."

He pursed his lips and thought things over. Then he said, "We'll see what you've got. I'm going first. I have never...shoplifted."

He didn't drink. But I did. God, it burned.

"Perry! I am appalled!" he said, slamming his fist down on the table in mock fury.

I wasn't proud of it, but I told him I had shoplifted numerous times in high school. Makeup from the local drug store, actually. Not cuz I needed it or couldn't afford it but because of the thrill. I guess, anyway. Young Perry did a lot of stupid things.

It was my turn. I racked my brain for things I could get out of Dex.

"I have never...been arrested," I said.

He didn't drink. That surprised me. Yet, I had been arrested, so I had to. I took another timid swig.

His jaw literally dropped open. "What the fuck? What for?"

"For the shoplifting! I got caught one time. They arrested me, called my parents...anyway."

"What? Don't 'anyway' me. That's huge. Even I haven't been arrested."

"I know! That's why I'm surprised." I pointed at him.

"Wow, I have got to step up my game. You are out...bad–assing me right now."

I gotta admit I was loving the look of astonishment in his eyes. It felt pretty freaking good. "Your turn," I said.

He thought about it for a moment. I caught a wicked glint in his eye before he said, "Fine. I've never had a threesome."

Wow. And he was just jumping straight to the point. Of course I never had a threesome before. I've barely had twosomes. He probably did though. He was just looking for an excuse to show off.

But he didn't drink either.

"Huh," I said. "Did you think I'd actually drink?"

"I don't know, I didn't think you were a shoplifting criminal either."

"Oh, whatever. OK, I've never kissed a guy." I couldn't help but smile as I drank to that one. I watched Dex carefully. I could see the workings of his mind behind his heavy, drunk eyes. Finally he drank.

"Are you serious?" I asked incredulously.

He shrugged. "Does kissing your bandmate on stage count? He was a guy. And for the record, I didn't like it. Much."

I shook my head. "No. It doesn't count."

"Ah, rats then. OK, I've never had sex in public."

And he drank to that right away, naturally. I didn't though. No explanation needed.

Still, I had to ask him, "Where?"

"Where haven't I?"

"OK, that's enough," I said quickly, not wanting to get the mental image of Jenn and him in the sweaty throws of passion in a public restroom somewhere. "I have never....told someone I loved them when I knew I didn't."

It was a fairly heavy question considering the brevity of the scene. I wasn't sure why I asked it but I did.

There was a pause. Then he reached for the bottle and took a small swig, wincing.

He cleared his throat and said, "Well, that was certainly, uh, poignant. I'll bring it back around again. I've never been skinny dipping."

We both didn't drink.

"Interesting. Too bad the water is freezing here," he said with a wink.

"Ha. All righty. Next one I hope we don't both suck at. Let's see... I've never been cheated on."

And I said it before I even realized what I said. This question is normally standard, I mean it's a common occurrence these days, sadly. It's just that in Red Fox, Dex's old college friend Maximus had brought up the fact that Dex's ex–girlfriend, Abby, had been cheating on him. He found out. They fought. And she died later that night from driving drunk. In Maximus's opinion, Dex had a hell of a time trying to recover from it. He still didn't know if he had.

Dex had never known what Maximus had told me, so my reaction to asking the question (which was a face full of 'oh, shit, shouldn't have said that') probably told him all he needed to know. His face was pained. Almost angry. He knew now.

I quickly covered it up by reaching for the bottle and taking the biggest gulp possible. I wasn't lying either.

The flash of animosity and regret quickly disappeared from his eyes as he saw what I was doing and curiosity took over. I noticed he didn't drink. I didn't blame him, though he probably felt like it.

"Who cheated on you?" he asked.

"My boyfriend in college. Mason. He was a dick."

"What happened?"

I sighed and felt like drinking again, just to get through answering the question. I wasn't still hurt; I mean, it had been a few years now, but the feelings could sometimes feel fresh. I didn't want to get into them here and now, when I was feeling vulnerable. Dex had the right idea by lying.

"Uh...I don't know. I guess I wasn't attractive enough for him."

"That's never it," he said quietly. "It was something else."

"OK, it was something else then. Whatever, who cares. He didn't love me enough. He didn't want me, I don't know. He's an asshole, that's all I know."

"You never found out why?"

I gave him a stupid look. "Don't you think I fucking asked?"

"OK, OK, no need to get mad here. It was your question."

I rolled my shoulders, trying to get the building tension out and stared at the wavering light of the lantern. "He said it just happened. It was a study partner of his. He just didn't have the balls to tell me he wasn't in love with me anymore. He broke my heart and I'll never forgive him for that. It really fucked me over."

I glanced over at Dex. He was looking into the forest with a strange look on his face. Maybe he was relating.

"Should we play something else?" I asked. "This took a turn for the suck."

Dex looked down at the phone to check the time. "Sure. I was having fun."

I gave him a small smile. "Sorry. I know I brought it on myself."

"Hey, it's all good. I learned something new about you. Might explain why Perry Palomino is perpetually single."

It might. It still smarted to hear him say that though.

"I had wondered, you know," he said softly. "I was sure you'd just have to show your face at a concert in Portland and have a crop of guys in studded vests to choose from. I went to an Anthrax show at the Memorial Coliseum, way, way back in the day. I saw many Perry 'types' over there."

The truth of that was I rarely went to concerts, even to my favorite bands, because more often than not I had to go alone. But I didn't tell him that.

Dex reached into his pocket and brought out his pack of cigarettes. He offered one to me.

"Why would I want that?" I said asked while shaking my head and pushing the pack back towards him.

"I dunno. We're camping, drinking whisky out of the bottle, seems like the time when everyone smokes."

He lit it, taking a puff and blowing the smoke to the side of him. The light breeze carried it away into the darkness. "How about Truth or Dare?"

That game was no better than the one before, but at least you had the dare element, which could get pretty exciting, or at least funny. Frivolity is what we needed. I agreed and we were off and running.

We stuck to dares for the first few rounds to put enough distance between us and I Have Never. I dared him to take a large shot, he dared me to sing along with the next song on his playlist, I dared him to run around the picnic table, while he dared me to take a large shot and squawk like a chicken.

Then it was my turn again.

"Truth or dare?" I asked, leaning forward on my elbows, swaying slightly.

"Dare," he said without thinking about it.

"I dare you to kiss me," I said. I don't know why I said it. OK, I knew why, but it still surprised me to hear it coming out of my mouth, especially when we were just talking about cheating and all that. And, you know, it wasn't like me to be so blunt.

Dex, too, was taken aback. He barely showed it but I could tell he did not see that one coming. Good. It was about time I saw him shocked at something I said, though I guess the arrest and shoplifting story did a good job of that.

I watched him carefully, keeping a drunk, breezy smile on my face in case he was too freaked out about it. I took on the role of the teasing temptress. All in good fun, nothing on the line here, no one's feelings at stake. I was breezy.

He was trying to figure me out. His eyes were flickering, taking it all in. He wasn't sure whether to smile or not but in the end, the corner of his mouth won.

"I can't do that," he teased.

"But you have to," I pleaded in my lightest tone of voice. "You said during the hockey game...if you were dared. This is your dare."

"It's kind of inappropriate."

Actually it was perfectly appropriate when you took in everything I had just said.

"Whatever," I said. "You have to take truth then."

I tried not to look as rejected and pathetic as I felt with him turning me down, and kept that flirty smile on my face. He leaned in a little closer. Our eyes locked but I didn't want to give anything away. I hoped that being drunk was preventing him from reading me.

I think it worked because he leaned back slightly and said, "OK, give me truth then."

I wanted the truth to be something he couldn't back out of. Something he had to answer, inappropriate or not, something I really wanted to know. I had just the question.

"What was that phone call about? The one you got at the hockey game that you freaked out on and ran away. Who called you? What did they say?"

From the way his shoulders sunk like I had placed some giant, invisible weight on them, to the way his eyes went blank, I knew I had asked the right question. It was something he would have never answered in a million years and now he had to. Or at least, I hoped he had to. I couldn't force Dex to do anything but I hoped this time I wouldn't have to.

I let him bide his time, let him suck on his full lower lip, let his eyes try and to stay hidden by blasé and the shadows. I let him feel the booze work through his veins, hoping that it would take his guard down a few notches like it had done with me. I let him decide what to do next.

He answered. He tried to appear casual about it but he said, "Jennifer is pregnant."

And with those words, my whole world came crashing down.

CHAPTER NINE

I couldn't believe what he had come out of Dex's mouth. Jennifer was pregnant?

"Jennifer is what?" I squeaked. "Pregnant? Your Jennifer?"

He nodded somberly, his face as blank as possible.

Mine wasn't. I was unable to hide my emotions, even though I wasn't really sure what my emotions were. This hit me like a pile of bricks had dropped off the top of a building. I was floored. I was flattened. Jennifer was pregnant. *His* girlfriend was pregnant with *his* baby.

Wait, maybe it wasn't his baby. The thought relieved me for a second.

"With your baby?" I asked to make sure.

"Yeah. My...mine," he said awkwardly.

Fuck. Shit. Obviously this was all about Dex, this was Dex's problem (or not problem), but I couldn't wrap my head around it, about the way it was affecting me. He might has as well have told me they were getting married. My heart lurched again at that thought, more horrifying and defeating than the one before. It felt like I had a fish hook through my guts.

I needed to pull it together. I needed to stop staring at him with what I was sure was a pained expression. There he was, telling me something he didn't want me to know, something life–altering, life–halting (to me, anyway) and I was so engrossed in my own feelings I couldn't take a moment to ask what this meant to him.

What did I say? I'm sorry? I looked at his face and got nothing from it. He was as serious as he ever was, but I couldn't gather whether this was a joyous occasion or not.

So I just said, "Oh. Wow."

"Yeah," he said with a sigh and reached for the Jack Daniels.

"When did you find out?" I asked.

"Just last night. During the hockey game. Actually she had been suspecting she was. Missed her period last week. We thought maybe it was just stress because she travels so much for the show. That can fuck women up or something. She's on birth control, so it didn't seem possible. I mean, how the fuck is that fucking possible?"

"So...she thought she was pregnant...and she told you this?"

"Yeah, a few days ago."

"And you still came out here to the island?"

He didn't look vaguely bothered by that. "Yeah. It's work. Like I said, we thought it was just stress. She took a test yesterday. It was positive. That's when she called me."

No wonder he was so upset during the game. Wait a minute....

"So, she calls you and tells you she's pregnant. And then you celebrate by dragging me off to a bloody strip club?!"

He did look sheepish at that. He tried to shrug but it seemed the weight on his shoulders was too much.

"I didn't know what to do," he said feebly.

"I know what you don't do," I said, pointing at him. "You don't go to a fucking strip club and buy your girl partner a lap dance when you know your girlfriend just found out she's pregnant!"

As much as I hated Jenn, Dex was acting like a royal douchebag. My mind kept rolling back the reel of last night, looking for signs that Dex was dealing adversely with something so huge as finding out his girlfriend was pregnant. I couldn't find anything except his damn perversions and borderline sleaziness.

"Yuck, Dex. Yuck," I said again for emphasis, leaning back in my seat and staring him down like some disapproving mother figure.

Dex didn't say anything. He looked chagrined but it was wearing off as he gazed at the bottle, like he was trying to Jean Grey it into a ball of fire or something. I didn't even know if he was listening to me. I guess it didn't matter. He must have known he didn't handle it very well.

Not that I would have handled it well, had I been in his situation. Only I wouldn't have been able to drink the problem away.

He wasn't saying anything so I reached across the table and put my hand lightly on top of his. Just for a moment. He jumped and slowly moved his eyes over to meet mine.

"So, is this good news or bad news?" I asked as compassionately as possible. I wanted to be supportive for him, no matter what my own feelings were. It was no small thing to ask of myself but Dex, despite his actions the night before, deserved it. At least, I was going to try.

He chuckled wryly, shaking his head. "What do you think?"

"I don't know, Dex. I really don't."

He sighed and reached for the bottle. He took a gulp that was big enough for him to choke on. When he regained control of his throat, he gave me a frank look.

"This is bad news."

"For you or for Jenn?"

"I think for both of us. Definitely for me. And I thought definitely for her."

"You thought? Did she change her mind?"

He shrugged and pulled out another cigarette. I hoped he wouldn't hesitate too much longer. He was drunk, he was open and this was the only time I was going to get him to talk.

"I don't know," he said, lighting his cigarette, the stick bobbing up and down between his lips. "I guess she got thinking."

"Didn't you? I mean, when you found out?"

"Yeah. I got thinking. I got thinking about a lot of things."

"Such as?" Oh please Dex, don't make this as difficult as pulling teeth.

He didn't say anything for a beat or two, just took a couple of drags on his cigarette. The alcohol allowed me to be more patient than usual. I waited, hands folded across the table, making sure I never lost the expectant look on my face.

Finally he said, "I got thinking about how I'm not ready to be a dad. How I'll never be ready to be a dad. How...retarded the word dad sounds. How can I be a dad? I'd be the worst dad in the world. I'd fuck up that kid, whatever kid, so badly...I wouldn't wish that on anyone. So there's that. That's the unselfish part. And then there is the selfish part. The part that says, I don't want to fucking deal with that shit. If I had a kid...my life would change so much."

"Maybe for the better?" I said, playing the Devil's Advocate.

He shook his head. "No. Not with us."

"But...your life *is* going to change so much."

My words seemed to hit him like the pile of bricks I felt earlier. He cringed, just for a moment, and sucked back on that cigarette like it was the only thing keeping him sane. It might have been.

"I know. And I thought...I thought maybe it wouldn't have to."

"She was going to have an abortion?"

He nodded uneasily, maybe unsure of how I would react. It was a hard topic to talk about in this divided country.

"We had decided that if she was pregnant, she could just take the...abortion pill, I guess. I don't know the name. Or we would just go to a clinic. She didn't want a kid screwing up her career, or her body, I should say. As much as I didn't want one screwing up our relationship."

Huh. He was more worried about a baby screwing up their relationship than anything else. That was interesting. I wasn't sure in what way yet.

"And then..."

"I don't know," he shrugged with effort. "Something happened. She told me last night when she found out that she wanted to keep it. And that if I didn't want to have any part in it, I didn't have to. She didn't need me. If I'm not 100% in it, then I am not needed."

We both seemed to mull that part over.

"And you told her you still wanted the abortion?"

"Well. Yeah. I mean, I'm not pressuring her. It's her body, she can do what she wants. I will support her no matter what she chooses. But you know...I just don't know why she changed her mind. I would have thought finding out for sure would have, you know, cemented her fears even more. But then she just...switched. Just like that. One extreme to the other."

"An abortion isn't an easy thing to deal with," I offered quietly. "It can ruin you in ways you never thought."

"Mmhmmm, and how would you know?" he said asked, pursing his lips defensively.

I wasn't sure if I should say the truth right now or not, but I had nothing to lose. Dex had everything to lose here.

"Because I had one."

The truth felt like it was laden with iron. And it was something I had never told anyone else. I never told Ada, had never told my friends, never told my boyfriend, never told my parents. It had been inside me all this time, tucked away deep.

Dex's eyes widened, and then softened at the vulnerability I knew I couldn't help but exude. There was no hiding it now.

"I'm sorry," he said. "I didn't know."

"No one knows."

He swallowed hard and put out the cigarette on the table. We watched the ash spew out from the twisting butt.

"When was this? Sorry if I'm being too..."

"No, it's fine. I think...I think it would be good for me to talk about it. It was with Mason, ironically."

"The jackfuck who cheated on you?" he asked, holding out the bottle for me.

"Yeah," I said grabbing it and taking a sip. I coughed. "The one. And only."

"Only guy as in only jackfuck who fucked you over, only love or only guy you slept with?"

"All three."

"Sorry."

"Anyway...I was careless. I was on the pill too but it was during a time my stomach was acting up...I was throwing up sometimes because of this and that and you know. I guess one day it didn't stick in time."

I felt weird to talk about it because to talk about it was to remember it. I told him about the day I found out. This was before I found out Mason was cheating on me, as if that made a difference in the long run. I had missed my period, which was abnormal since I was on the pill, and it came as regularly as a clock. To the hour even. Naturally, my first thought was to freak out. I didn't tell Mason, even after I took three at–home pregnancy tests, different brands. I hid the used sticks with their stupid plus signs deep in the toilet paper rolls in the wastebasket so no one would know. I didn't want to tell him in case he thought I planned it or blamed me somehow.

It was just too big of an issue for my life to handle. Already I could barely handle going to class, I could barely handle living in a dorm, away from home, even with my roommate Gemma. I had dreams, the same dreams I still had. To have a baby would fuck everything up. I had plans. And deep down inside, as much as I knew I was in love with Mason, part of me knew that we weren't going to be together forever. It's like I already knew he was going to cheat on me. I wasn't going to be like one of those girls who has a baby just to keep the guy. I knew enough of those girls in high school.

I guess that was one reason to find Jenn's decision commendable. She was going to go through with it no matter what Dex said or felt.

I told Dex about booking the appointment by myself and being so scared to death about it. I mean, so scared. I didn't for a moment doubt my decision, as drastic as it was. I didn't think that what I was doing was wrong. I knew where my morals were. That wasn't the problem. I just didn't want to go through such a scary, painful procedure alone. The fact that I was alone said so much. Even though I could have brought a number of people to come with me, I needed to keep this to myself. I was too afraid of what others might think.

It was horrible, to say the least. I've blocked out most of it, or maybe time has gotten rid of the feeling. It's like when you break your arm or something. You know you were in pain and you remember the feeling of being in pain but that actual feeling is gone. This was the same kind of thing. I know it was painful beyond words and kept me doubled up in the bathroom for a week straight after. Gemma just thought it was my stomach, so she didn't suspect anything. If she had asked, I was pretty sure I would have caved in and told her, just to get it off my chest. But she didn't and then it became a thing of the past. Another ghost to be locked away, along with the drugs, and the accident and the family psychologist.

And then the dreams would come. I dreamed about the baby, what it would have and could have been. About maybe finding some essence of happiness in my life, about having something there to love unconditionally, something that may have validated myself. I wondered what he or she would have looked like and what they would have done with their life.

There was a lot of guilt. Sometimes it would sneak up on me. I didn't feel like God was judging me but that I was judging myself without even realizing it. That my subconscious, my soul, was tallying this act up for some future retribution. Maybe I'd fail a test, maybe I'd get cheated on, maybe I'd feel alone for the rest of my life all because deep down inside, I thought I should be punished.

I babbled on to Dex about this for who knows how long. He didn't say anything. He didn't light another cigarette or touch the Jack Daniels. He just stared at me. Not intrusively, just...involved.

When I was done, he said asked, "Do you regret it?"

I shook my head. "No. I don't. Because I think everything happens for a reason and I think we need to go through shit sometimes to strengthen ourselves for whatever happens down the line. I think it made me stronger. It at least made me realize a lot of things."

"Like what?"

"Like...it's OK to depend on people. That I don't have to go alone through everything. That keeping people at a distance and hiding everything can hurt more than letting them in."

The words hung in the air like the tiny bugs that flitted above the lantern's glow. Dex could have been wincing; the way his brow had come together looked furtive and uncomfortable.

"Are you glad you told me?" he asked, his voice lower, gruffer. His eyes darted the expanse of mine in rapid twitches.

"Yes," I said strongly. Honestly. "Are you glad you told me?"

He seemed to think about that. "Yeah. I am."

That warmed my chest more than the Jack Daniels ever could. This heat radiated from my heart.

"So, what are you going to do?"

"What the fuck can I do?"

"Are you going to marry her?" I asked softly. I had only a second of pure, blissful ignorance before he answered. Was I ready for the truth?

He locked his eyes on mine. "I don't know. I will *if* I have to."

A wave of relief. It was better than a yes. But still...

"Do you want to?"

He rubbed his chin scruff with his hand, more of a nervous gesture than one to signify he was thinking deeply about it.

"I'd rather not."

I almost laughed at that, at the glib way he said it, as if he would rather not have sushi for dinner instead of pizza.

"Why are you with her then? Do you even love her?"

This would have been another question for truth or dare had the bigger one not preyed on my thoughts in the last past 24 hours. I thought I had dug at it earlier with the "I Have Never" game but we both skirted the issue on that. From day one, from the moment I heard Dex talk about Jenn, I always picked up on something. Something that was off about their relationship. I know it's wrong to speculate on something you have no business in. How can we really know what goes on behind closed doors? It reminded me of a line in *Rear Window*, "That's a secret private world you're looking into there." People do a lot of things in private that they couldn't possibly explain in public.

But, I just didn't get their relationship, at least not from the end I was looking in from. He never really seemed to care that much about her and it didn't seem she cared that much about him. I had never met Jenn, but other than being a hot babe (Robo Babe, Baberaham Lincoln, etc) there just didn't seem to be enough to keep someone as complex and neurotic as Dex interested. And therefore, I had to ask. It had been picking at me for too long.

He looked put off by the question. I didn't blame him. I was almost being rude by asking that. But I had to know. I didn't care if he thought it was none of my business.

He took his time. Making me wait while he scratched slowly at his sideburns and let his eyes roam the dark forest in a wayward manner, as if he thought he might find an answer lying out there, or at least something to distract him from one.

"I think we should probably turn in," he finally said in his most simple tone.

I just stared at him in response, coaxing him with my eyes. He was avoiding them still. If I could just look into him, I would know. Even if he hid it all, I would know. I was looking that hard.

"I don't get it," I said, feeling a bit defeated despite the revelations at hand. All of this thanks to a spooky island forest and a bottle of whisky.

"Neither do I. But some things in life are safe, kiddo. And sometimes, when you've had a life in the falling rock zone, you just want something that's out of harm's way."

I sighed, out of understanding, not annoyance (I was trying to shove that way below) and gave him a quick smile and nod. I got up out of my seat, steadying myself on the table so I didn't keel over and picked up the books and flashlight. It was late and from the way his eyes were glazing over, I knew that storytime was over and the book cover was slowly closing shut.

I walked over to the tent, grateful that it was only a few feet away, and stopped as I unzipped the flap. I looked behind me at Dex, whose shoulders were moving lightly back and forth. The music had been turned off a while ago. He was swaying to some imaginary beat, as he often did, his outline black against the glow. I could see his fingers wrapped around the bottle, holding it like it was a lifeline.

"Looks like you're going to have to find something else safe," I said. He stopped moving but didn't say anything.

I put my books inside and was about to go in myself but the realization that I hadn't peed in half a bottle of Jack Daniels made the urge overpowering.

The outhouse was up the path a bit and in the open, just beyond the hill. It was probably the least scary place to have an outdoor toilet, and having used it earlier, I can vouch that there's nothing remotely terrifying or even all that gross about it. That was in the daylight though. The thought of using it at night was starting to make my heart race.

I grabbed the flashlight and straightened up.

"I'm going to use to the toilet. If I'm not back in five minutes, send help. And by send help, I mean, come and get me."

I walked past the table and glanced behind me to see if he'd heard me. He looked up from his daze.

"Do you want me to come with you?"

He had somehow gotten drunker in the last five minutes and was slurring. Maybe the conversation finally did his head in.

I actually did want him to come with me, but having him wait outside the bathroom would only make things worse for me. Performance anxiety or something like that.

"I'm good. Just...remember where I've gone."

He smiled. "To the shitter. Don't fall down the hole!"

That would be the least of my problems.

I aimed the flashlight at the ground and quickly picked my way over the path and across the rocky headland where the outhouse stood. Once I was out of the forest, the wind was cutting a sharp path through the air and reaching into my many layers. The waves roared and crashed onto the surrounding rocks but all I could see was blackness beyond the grainy flashlight. The sky was heavy with clouds that had suddenly rolled in, though in some patches there were faint twinkles from the heavens. It was unfortunate that it wasn't clear because I bet this place would be a gorgeous example of a fathomless, star-studded night sky. The nearest lights were emanating from the Victoria area, and though they caused the clouds above them to glow a sickly orange color, they weren't powerful enough to intrude celestially over here.

The thought of stars and the infinite universe put everything into perspective. At least it was enough for me to temporarily forget the horrors of the island and the potency of what Dex and I had been discussing. Even if Jenn was pregnant, even if I had an abortion, even if they ended up getting married, even if lepers had died here, none of that meant anything to a universe that treated our existence like a blink of an eye. In the grand scheme of things, our problems meant nothing.

And yet they meant everything. Good old drunk thoughts.

I used the bathroom as quickly as possible. I barely sat on the seat. This had little to do with germs but this fear I had of using outhouses at night. I always imagined something coming up and grabbing me. Maybe that hand I saw on the side of the boat...

Stop it! I yelled in my head and finished up as quickly as possible. I stepped out of the outhouse, put the flashlight between my legs and brought out a small vial of hand sanitizer from my pocket. It would have to do in lieu of a sink. Dex and I would be brushing our teeth with bottled water and my makeup would be coming off with wet wipes later.

As I quickly rubbed the acidic-smelling gel on my hands, I kept my eyes focused on the light coming from the forest. Dex had enough sense to keep the lantern lit until I got back. It was just a tiny illumination, but it made the island seem like less of a bottomless chasm of trees and unknown creatures.

"Don't listen to him."

A tiny, timid voice called out from behind me. I gasped and spun around, the flashlight dropping to the ground from between my legs, my lungs seizing from fright. I rapidly picked it back up, choosing to drop the hand sanitizer instead, and flashed it around me in a panic.

Someone did say something, right? I wasn't imagining things. It had been a woman's voice, a suggestion.

That was impossible. Wasn't it?

"Hello?" I said just as quietly. I wasn't exactly the picture of courage but I didn't want to feel like a loon either.

I held my breath and kept the flashlight searching around the outhouse and the surrounding rocks. I waited a few more seconds before my knees started to shake from the cold and the fright. I bent over to pick up the hand sanitizer. And then I heard it again.

"He lied to me."

It was a woman's voice. My first thought was that it could have been Creepy Clown Lady's but this voice was accent–free and spoke with the quavering uncertainty of youth. It sounded as if she wasn't sure she should be saying anything at all. I wasn't going nuts, I clearly heard it, which then made the situation more absurdly terrifying.

I slowly panned the light around, afraid of what I might illuminate. I only picked up the black of night, the far–off waves, the rocks and grass and stoic pines that lined the shore.

"Who lied?" I asked, still keeping my voice at a minimum so Dex wouldn't hear me.

The only sound was the waves and my rapid breathing. No response.

I waited for a minute, maybe two.

"Perry!"

I almost shit myself. Would have been embarrassing so close to the toilet.

It was Dex, yelling from the trees.

"Coming!" I yelled back, my voice shaking. I hesitated before returning, thinking if I waited a tiny bit longer, the voice might come back and tell me who was lying.

But there was nothing again. Nothing but the increasing cold, which was starting to win out over my curiosity.

I scampered back to the campsite as fast as I could, grateful to see Dex still sitting at the picnic table with two bottles of water out and a vial of painkillers. Before the light of our small civilization engulfed me completely, I turned one last time to look at the darkness I felt nipping at my heels.

There was nothing there but I had no doubt that whatever was out there would be back.

I tried to push that thought out of my head and quickly prepared to hunker down for the night. As Dex went into the tent to get changed, I wiped the makeup off my face and did a fast brushing of my teeth, spitting out the frothy excess onto the ground. I paused, thinking I might have heard something coming from the bushes. But it was only the sound of Dex shuffling around in the tent, the flashlight bobbing around from the inside.

I grabbed the lantern off of the table and brought it over to the front of the tent, choosing not to turn it off until I absolutely had to.

"Are you decent?" I yelled at Dex, tapping on the tent flap.

He mumbled something in response. I was going to have to take my chances.

I unzipped the flap and crawled inside. He was already in his sleeping bag, a heavy zip sweatshirt over his pajamas, aiming the flashlight at a torn copy of Stephen King's *Carrie*. How he could read while drunk was a mystery to me.

"Sorry, you're going to have to get out while I get changed," I told him.

He gave me a funny look and went back to reading. "I don't think so."

"Dex!"

He smirked and shrugged. "Whatever, it's nothing I haven't seen before."

"Excuse me?"

He didn't say anything else so I smacked him on the leg. "What do you mean?"

He sighed and put the book down on his chest. "I'm the one who undressed you after you were attacked by that birdman hick in Red Fox."

"You said you didn't look!"

He chuckled, "Of course I looked. I had to take your clothes off and bathe you. I had to look."

"Oh my God," I groaned, my hands flying up to my face. The utter humiliation was boiling up inside of me. At the time I had other things to worry about, so the chain of events that happened after I was clawed up and nearly raped totally took over from worrying about something as silly as him seeing me naked. But now that there was enough distance between then and now…ugh.

"Oh, grow up. We're adults here. I liked what I saw, if that makes you feel any better."

You'd think it would have but it didn't.

"This is so mortifying," I said to myself, my words muffled and hidden by my hands.

"Well, would you have rather it been Bird or Maximus, cuz those were your options."

Honestly, I would have rather it have been Maximus. Though I thought he was a sexy beast, I wasn't in love with Maximus and I didn't have to work with him every weekend.

"Oh come on, don't say you would have rather had the Ginger see you all nekkid."

I looked at him and shrugged.

He shook his head at me, saying, "You're breaking my heart here."

"You don't have a heart to break," I said. It came out in a light, joking way but I would have been lying if I didn't feel there was an ounce of truth to that.

From the way his eyes twitched, I wasn't sure if he took it as a joke either. So I smiled bashfully and said, "OK, fine. Just keep reading your book and don't look at me."

"Done and done," he said and went back to reading.

I wasn't sure if I trusted that or not but anyway, I got my pajamas out of the backpack, turned my back to him and sat down. I pulled off my jeans and shoved the bottoms on as quickly as I could. It was so fucking cold in the tent, the air hit my bare legs like someone was emptying a bag of ice cubes on them. Then came my tops, pulling them off of me as fast I could and struggling to do undo my bra. I shoved on my pajama top, the hoodie, and shivering like hell, climbed into my sleeping bag.

I looked over at Dex. He was still reading but the more I stared at him, the more his lips twisted until he was grinning and finally laughing quietly to himself.

I couldn't help but laugh too. It felt good.

"You totally looked, didn't you?"

"Just a bit," he said, closing his book and giving me a cheeky wink. It was the last thing I saw before he turned the flashlight off. I hoped the image would give me good dreams.

CHAPTER TEN

I woke up with the feeling that something was wrong, that horrible feeling of extreme uneasiness. I was on my back looking up at the ceiling of the tent. It was dark but I could see my breath rise in the air like a frozen cloud. The tent was moving slightly, like the wind was rocking it back and forth. I strained my ears but couldn't hear any wind at all.

I did hear Dex's breath in a sharp withdrawal next to me. I slowly rolled my head to the side and looked at him. His eyes were open which gave me a terrible fright. He had been looking over my head at the opposite side of the tent. Something in his eyes, the way they seemed stuck in an unblinking, concentrating position, told me that I shouldn't follow his gaze. That it was safer to stare at him instead.

So I did, until he looked at me. His eyes seemed to be asking, "Do you hear that too?" I listened hard. There still wasn't any sign of a breeze yet the tent was ruffling and flapping lightly. That was producing one sound. The other sound was coming from the area where Dex had been looking, where our bags and gear were. It was a scratching, shuffling noise. My first thought was that there were rodents in the tent with us, going through our bags. Rats that were waiting until we fell asleep before they chewed our fingers off.

I had to look. If it was rats I would be out of the tent like a shot. I gave Dex a weak nod and eased my head over to the other side.

In the dark I couldn't make out what was going on with our bags, they just looked like dark lumps. But the bags weren't the issue. The side of the tent was being raked from the outside. That was the easiest way to describe it. Something was outside of the tent and pushing inwards, in many places. It was almost as if a dozen fingers were running down the outsides.

My body went cold, colder than the air that nipped at my nose and cheeks. I watched in fear, unable to move myself, unable to decipher what was going on and what to do next. Something was out there, and as frightening as the idea that it was people (or aliens!) outside running their fingers up and down our tent, the strange scratching noise and the even placement of the trails said otherwise.

I felt Dex shift beside me, propping himself up slowly, as silently as the nylon sleeping bag would allow. He reached down for my face and gently turned it his way. He looked frightened, for sure, but determined. I knew he wouldn't stay in the tent and wait to see what happened next. He would make what happened next happen. He was making sure I knew that. He was also telling me, somehow, without saying a word, that he had my back. At least, I hoped that's what he was trying to get across.

He raised his finger to lips and then pointed at the video camera closest to us. It was the one with night vision and it was no coincidence that it was out. He had been prepared for something just like this. I wondered if he knew something about the island that I didn't.

I moved as quietly as I could and leaned over to pick it up. As I did, I looked up at the side of the tent. I couldn't make out what was out there, but I was right in thinking they weren't fingers. They were too pointy for that. It was almost like a couple of trees had come alive in the night and were prodding at us with their branches, their scaly bark creating this raspy noise that was getting louder by the minute.

Feeling too close to it, I pulled back and gave Dex the video camera. He flicked it on and started filming. I sat up and moved further back so I was out of the way, and for a minute we watched the trails do their vertical dance. Each second that we filmed, I felt more calm and relaxed. There was something, at least this time, about having it all on film that made me feel like nothing bad could really happen. If I was looking through the lens like Dex was, I would be even more removed. No wonder he wasn't as scared as me half the time.

At that thought, the camera pointed in my direction. I gave up on vanity and just gave the camera the most incredulous look. No acting needed. I had no fucking idea what was going on either.

Dex handed me the camera and motioned for me to keep it on the tent wall while he squirmed out of his sleeping bag and stood up. He was ready to go outside. And as I handed the camera back to him, I could see he expected me to go as well. Going outside to where those...things were was a horrifying prospect but the idea of him leaving me alone in the tent wasn't any better.

I got up and stood beside him, our eyes shifting between the tent flap and the phantom raking motion that was still going on. I could barely see him in the shadows but I knew he was trying to plan an ambush. He put his hand on my shoulder and gave it a light squeeze. His reassurance before shit got crazy.

In one stealthy motion he reached over and unzipped the tent flap and leaped awkwardly outside. I did the same, following right behind him, the flap smacking me in the face.

I barely noticed the cold damp air or the rough pebbles beneath my socks. I grabbed onto Dex's arm and we looked over at five large deer that were poking and prodding our tent with mechanical simplicity, as if in a trance. Their antlers scraped up the sides and didn't stop when even we had emerged. Any other deer would have gone bounding skittishly into the forest but these ones...they didn't move an inch. They didn't even look at us.

"What the hell," I whispered, my voice higher than I hoped. The deer didn't seem too bothered. I gripped Dex's arm harder while he aimed the camera at them.

He swallowed hard and said, "Five against two."

That wasn't comforting at all. Those five deer could do more than enough damage to us. Where did they come from? What were they doing?

I looked over towards the picnic table and through the fuzzy haze of the barely lit sky I could make out strange shapes amongst the trees and bushes. I gasped. There was something there too.

Dex looked at me and then in the direction of my wide eyes. He brought the camera over and I peered over his shoulder at the lit night vision screen, which presented everything to us in a green wash of grain and blur.

There were at least a dozen deer waiting in the bushes. Some were on the path. Some were at the picnic table just feet away from us. They all waited, frozen on the spot, staring at us, eyes glowing like white/green orbs. Five against two? More like twenty against two.

I thought my nails were going to dig clear through Dex's sweater. If he felt it, he didn't show it. He switched the camera up between the two herds, between the creepy, ogling eyes and the robotic, thoughtless bucks. We didn't know where to look.

"Should I turn on the lantern?" I whispered, my voice coming out in throaty rags. I knew it was just at the side of my feet. For better or for worse, maybe that would get their attention.

"Yeah," he said through a sharp breath.

I quickly picked it up and turned the knob until it flashed on. The light was so bright I had to shield my eyes with my free hand. When they recovered enough, I looked back and saw... nothing.

Nothing at all but the trees, the bushes, the table and the tent. And Dex standing in front of me with a dumbfounded expression, the camera shakily pointing at nothing. No deer.

"What happened?" I cried out. How could they have just disappeared like that?

"I have no fucking idea," he said, and anxiously started the playback on the screen. He stopped it after a few seconds and we watched together as the footage showed the bucks with their antlers against the tent. In one second they were there. Then a flash of light that overwhelmed the night vision. When that faded, the deer were gone. They just vanished. All of them.

"How is that even possible?" I asked, unable to grasp the reality of it.

He shook his head and walked around to the side of the tent where they had been poking and prodding.

"Bring the light over here," he said, gesturing to it.

I raised the lantern and walked over beside him. The side of the tent was marked with dark trails.

"Dirt?" I asked.

Dex squatted and ran his finger over one of them. He sniffed it then held it out for me in the light.

"It's blood."

That was too much. I looked around me, scared, my heart thumping around irregularly. The forest and the shadows began to spin. I realized I still might have been drunk. What time was it anyway? I didn't even have my phone to check.

"This is great. I'm not fucking sleeping tonight. What if they come back?"

"I don't think they will," he said absently, searching the ground around the area like a bloodhound picking up the scent.

"What if they do?"

"We will deal with it when it happens."

He bent over and gently placed his fingers on the earth. He looked up at me. "They left hoof prints. We didn't imagine them."

"And we got them on film too. So, no we didn't."

"Just making sure. I think it's good if we start questioning our sanity more often."

"Easy for you to say," I mumbled under my breath. I was too tired, too cold and too woozy to deal with any of this. I knew that if I gave it an ounce more thought, I'd have to give it my all and I'd be up for the rest of the night. All I wanted now was that warm sleeping bag and that blissful oblivion of my rested head.

"Go back to sleep," Dex said. "I'll finish up here."

"OK. Don't be too long or I'll worry," I replied. I stepped back into the tent.

He called from behind me, "Just look on the bright side. We got all of that on film."

I stuck my head out of the flap looked at him wryly. "Huzzah."

I stuffed my shivering soul back into my comfy, slightly damp sleeping bag and attempted to drift off to sleep. It didn't happen until the lantern's light went off and Dex was safely back in bed beside me.

~~

My sleep wasn't as solid as I had hoped. Dex got up at dawn to go take a whiz and considering the circumstances of the hours before, I automatically woke up too. Luckily the light of day was creeping over the top of the tent. Dawn always brought a sense of comfort and relief, an end to the night and the horrors it hid. As he climbed back in, I glimpsed a bit of the sunrise and a hit of the cold wind that had picked up in the last few hours. Everything was outside was red. Blood red.

"Some sunrise," he said through chattering teeth as he slipped back into his sleeping bag.

"Is it the apocalypse?" I croaked, half-joking. I leaned over and pushed the flap an inch to get a better look. The trees were swaying in the breeze, the sky was a textural mixture of thick, fast-moving clouds and a muddy red color.

"Red sky morning, sailors take warning," he muttered, rolling over so his back was to me.

Red sky night, sailors delight, I thought.

"What does that mean for us?" I asked. But Dex was already asleep and I was left to answer that question on my own.

~~

It had only been a couple of hours but the weather had changed radically in that time. When I finally woke up again, the tent was shuddering from blasts of wind and whips of rain that slashed the sides with a rat-a-tat sound. This time I knew it wasn't because maniacal deer were outside. A storm had come. The nautical adage was right.

Everything inside was this grey-blue color from the tent walls. I wanted to keep on sleeping. Being all cozy and warm in my sleeping bag, I didn't have any desire to leave my snug cocoon for wet and windy weather. That was the thing about camping. Outside of your tent, you had to be outside.

I rolled over and saw Dex's bag was empty. He was out there, somewhere, braving the elements. I kind of hoped if I stayed huddling in bed all morning that maybe he wouldn't notice. Also, my head didn't exactly feel like moving all that much, thanks to the copious amounts of Jack Daniels we had shared. I don't know how it was but sleeping in those extra hours had only made me feel even more hung over. I probably would have been better off if I had gotten up in those wee hours of the red dawn.

"OK, lazy bones," I heard Dex call from outside.

I groaned and pulled the sleeping bag further up over my head. I heard the front flap unzip and felt my leg being grabbed and shaken.

"You can't possibly feel as bad I do."

I peeked my head out and looked at him. He looked fine, maybe a bit pale, and had a noticeable five o'clock shadow spreading between his chin scruff and his sideburns.

"Why are you up then?" I moaned.

"Shit, shower and shave," he answered. "But I could only do one of those. Come on, I have breakfast going. There's coffee."

I normally didn't crave coffee when I was hung over but I needed something to wake and warm me up. And the idea of Dex making breakfast was intriguing.

"Is there a storm coming?" I asked.

"Oh, it's here. Come on."

He squeezed my calf and took his head back out of the tent.

I tried to take my time getting ready but the chilly air seeped through the fabric with each frightening wind gust, turning me into turbo mode. It would be Doc boots today, jeans again and several layers. Even with the giant jacket from the boat, I knew I was going to be soggy and miserable.

I stepped out of the tent and was immediately met with a misting of water. The sky was dark and grey, and the trees and bushes waved sporadically in the gusts that came off the water, which was mounted by a light fog that completely covered Little D'Arcy and made our island seem like it was the only one in the world, floating on the edge of misty space.

The tide was up and the waves crashed loudly on the shore, tickling at the driftwood. There were no birds flying about and there was no sound except the wind and the water. Everything was wet, cold and angry.

Dex had set up the stove on the picnic table, which was occasionally getting sprayed with a lashing of sideways rain. The tarp above that and the tent swayed with each gust but was holding together for the most part, giving us at least a partially dry place to huddle in.

I quickly zipped the tent flap shut, my fingers already feeling hard and icy, and scampered over to Dex, peering over his shoulder. He was actually in the midst of frying up some eggs to go with the bacon he had laid out on a greasy paper plate. The wind must have carried the aromatic wafts away earlier, because if there was anything that got me out of bed, it was the smell of bacon.

He gave me a quick glance and then pulled out a cup that he had kept down on the seat, handing it to me.

I thanked him and took a quick sip. It was instant coffee with the right amount of cream and sugar. He knew what I liked and considering it was instant, it wasn't half bad.

Once the eggs were done, we sat down and tucked into our food. Dex was a surprisingly good cook. OK, it was just bacon and eggs and maybe I was easily impressed but I'm pretty sure if I tried to make breakfast, I would have burned the bacon into the ground. I can make pie and that's about it.

He leaned back, looking full, and pushed his empty plate back from him.

"Hope you don't mind bacon for the next couple of days. I made a bunch in advance in case it went bad in the cooler."

I shook my head no just as the wind swooped in and picked up his plate, flinging it into the forest. We watched it go, flying through the air like a paper UFO. I raised my brows at him. "What do we do if it's like this the whole time?"

"Clearly we're going to go insane," he answered.

I eyed the tarp flapping above us. "What if that doesn't hold? What if our tent gets wet?"

"Then we get wet."

"What if our cameras get wet? Your computer?" I asked, pushing at the point.

He pondered that for a second. "Maybe I should take the footage that we shot last night and bring it back on the boat. I could do some uploading there too."

"If the boat is even there," I pointed out. I hoped by bringing it up, I would be insuring it would actually be there.

"It's there," he said, though he didn't look as confident as he sounded.

And within five minutes he was ready to go out on a mission to make sure.

He had the cameras gathered in their cases and nodded at the tent.

"I left you the Super 8…in case you happened to capture anything while I'm gone."

"I hope I don't have to!" I said. Even though I was the one reminding him about the boat, I didn't actually want him to leave me alone at the campsite. Yes, it was daytime and, even with the mist obscuring the nearest point of civilization, there was a harmless vibe to the air. But being apart from him wouldn't do us any good. Hell, I didn't want him to trek across the island all by his lonesome, going through that creepy place with the dead trees and rabid raccoons.

He adjusted the pack on his back and gave me a dry look. "Look, I'll be gone for an hour. Two at the most. I'll be fine. You'll be fine."

I loved that he assumed I was more worried about him than myself. It was kind of true though.

I sighed and shrugged. "If you're not back in two hours, I'm coming after you."

He gave me a wink. "Perry to the rescue again."

And then he was off walking into the waving, wet branches of the forest. I watched him until his bright red boat jacket disappeared into the bushes and then I felt utterly alone.

I wasn't sure at first what to do. There wasn't much exploring to be done in this weather and though there was probably more shelter in the forest, there was no way I was stepping foot in there. I thought about checking my emails (not for comments) and browsing the internet but of course Dex still had my damn phone. I couldn't even check what time in the morning it was.

I decided to crawl back into the tent. At least it was warmer in there and most definitely drier. Plus if the urge struck and I got really bored, I could always go back to bed. There was no one here to prod me awake.

But even though I was lying down comfortably on top of the sleeping bag, my mind kept reeling around to thoughts about the island. There was so much more to learn about this place and I knew so little.

I brought out the books I was reading yesterday and started flipping through one of them, looking for a chapter or a phrase that was eye–catching. And I found it in the heading "The Woman."

It seemed that when the Reverend John Barrett from Northern California had come up to D'Arcy Island, he hadn't come alone. He brought up a 19–year–

old missionary with him by the name of Mary Stewart. Mary was one of the youngest missionaries at a San Francisco mission, but had expressed an overwhelming desire to help the lepers. Even though the attorney general in Canada had denied their first request for them to work on the island, their second request went through. The book speculated that bribery may have been the cause. The government wasn't going to spend any money on these forgotten people, but had Rev. Barrett paid them, they would have easily made amends. The author didn't know why the Reverend and Stewart would have wanted to be on the island so badly, and didn't make any attempts to explain it.

Weird thing was, for me, as I was reading, I could almost *feel* why. As weird as it sounded, there was something very uneasy about the whole thing, as if I was picking up on some vibe that had died a very long time ago. There was duplicity at the root. Questionable motives.

It didn't help that the further I read, the more disturbing the story got. Mary died seven months into her island mission. The earliest records from the supply ships had noted her as a short and weak woman who barely spoke, so it wasn't much of a surprise when the Reverend informed them during one of their runs that she died due to pneumonia. The island was like it was today, a wet, inhospitable place. Mary would have died during the three–month lag where no contact was had. She would have been buried where the rest of the lepers were, buried by them or the Reverend in one of those delivered coffins.

My heart felt funny, as if I had some strange affinity towards Mary and her plight. All she must have wanted to do was help these poor, forsaken souls and, in the end, she died like one of them. And at only 19-years old. She basically sacrificed herself.

I shivered at that and tucked part of the sleeping bag over my legs for extra warmth.

"Hee hee hee."

I froze in mid page.

A child's giggle from somewhere outside the tent.

Did I really hear that?

Was it the wind?

I listened hard, trying not to breathe or make any sort of noise that would compromise my ears.

Nothing.

My mind was on overdrive and I was spooking myself out for no reason.

I carefully turned the page in the book and tried to get back into it, to find out what happened to the Reverend after Mary had died.

I heard it again.

"Hee hee hee."

That innocent, yet inherently creepy giggle plus the sound of scattering stones from the ground in front of the tent. Someone was outside.

I sat up as quickly as I could, body poised, my heart pounding painfully, flooding my head with blood and pressure. My eyes searched wildly around the walls of the tent, looking for signs of anything abnormal. The walls ebbed and flowed with the wind but there wasn't anything peculiar.

The giggles came again, this time from right behind my head. I spun around expecting to see a child there in the tent with me. But I was alone.

Then I heard it again. I quickly turned to the sound and caught a glimpse of a small shadow running back from the tent flap.

I stood up and unzipped it as quickly as I could and burst out of the tent. The giggling had stopped but I could hear delicate footfalls over the wind. I ran a few steps and stopped in the middle of the path. The rain had led up for the moment but the ground was already muddy, like brown soup. I looked down towards the beach area and then up to where the path led either into the woods or the outhouse.

There was nothing.

A terrible, skin–crawling feeling washed over my arms and legs, as if I were being watched by something I couldn't quite see. I wanted nothing more than to see Dex coming around the corner.

The giggle again, this time from behind me in the direction of the beach.

I turned and saw a little girl running along the sliding wet pebbles, skirting the incoming waves and dodging the hulking driftwood. She was wearing only a long men's shirt that covered her whole body. It was pressed against her tiny form in a bluish transparency, soaked from the rain.

I wasn't sure what to do. Why was there a kid here on the island, running around in the storm? Why was she wearing just a men's shirt? Where were her parents?

I looked around me and started off after her. I didn't have much of a maternal instinct but I still couldn't let some young girl run around in this weather dressed like that. As I reached the beach, I could see she didn't even have shoes on.

I stopped and watched her run excitedly down the beach until she stopped halfway, her back to me. She couldn't have been more than three or four years old. I started to take off my jacket, wanting to put it on her while I figured out what was going on. It was totally possible that she was the child of someone visiting. Maybe boaters or kayakers on the other side of the island. Or maybe there were people on the island all along. We were at the one campsite but that didn't mean people weren't camping on other areas of the island. For all Dex and I knew, there could have been a whole group of people on the south end. Maybe that was even the voice I heard last night, carried from a far-away bonfire.

The girl slowly turned around and made eye contact with me. She looked afraid. I held out my jacket for her to see.

"You're going to catch a cold," I said, raising my voice forcibly and trying to keep it from shaking. Couldn't say the same thing about my arms though. "Where are your parents?"

The girl didn't say anything but her face grew increasingly concerned like she was about to cry. I didn't want to scare the poor thing.

"I won't hurt you. I'm not angry," I yelled. "You look cold. Your parents must be worried about you."

The girl shook her head. "She hates me."

I was startled at how strange the girl sounded. Her voice was almost accented and a bit stunted. She might have even had a lisp.

I looked around me, thinking that at any minute some distraught hippie couple would come out of the woods and run towards her, while giving me a dirty look for scaring their kid or something like that. But there was nothing but the wind and the cold spray it whipped up from the waves.

I couldn't let the girl be out here like this. I didn't care if she was scared of me or if her parents were going to get mad at me over my parenting. She was a little kid and a lot colder than I was.

I started walking towards her, confidently, but not forcefully so I didn't scare her.

"Here, wear my jacket. It's warm, you'll like it."

I was ten feet away from her. She looked a lot worse off than I thought. Her legs were all scratched up, her hair was long and a total mess. Her skin was dirty and there was a strange dullness to her blue eyes, almost like they were clouded over by that same fog that sat a few yards off shore.

She watched me approach, but didn't seem to take me in. She looked afraid but I knew it wasn't because of me, as hard as that was to explain. She was afraid of something else. I might as well have not been there.

She looked at the waves.

And ran into the ocean.

I was stunned. I watched her splash through the grey water until the waves broke on top of her. And finally I was able to snap out it.

I dropped the jacket and ran after her, my boots sliding around on the pebbles as I tried to gain traction. After a few paces I headed into the water as well.

I could barely make out a flail of her small arm or a glimpse of her head as the waves crashed over and over again but she was out there and that was enough for me to keep going.

I was annihilated by the sheer coldness, as my legs sank into the water and the ocean crept into my boots and splashed violently up the front of my jeans. In seconds my feet and legs were unfeeling blocks of ice and I thought my whole internal system would collapse on me, even with the water just below my knees.

But that didn't stop me. I kept pushing through until the waves reached me and started to crash into my stomach.

The first hit took my breath away. I couldn't even inhale if I tried, it was that cold. It took over everything and spread through my limbs and to my brain, where it erased all thought and reason. The only thing left outside of the numbness was the instinct that some little girl was drowning in the waves, somewhere near me.

I kept going until the water was at my waist. At this depth, the waves continued to break on me, the current wrapping itself around my thighs like a thick noose carved out of an ice block. The grey hues in the water and sky started to fizz darker and details began to blur. I felt nothing. There was a girl out there but my movements were becoming too sluggish to look for her.

I had to turn around. I had to head back, to get out of the water. But my will to return, my will to live was no stronger than the will to find the girl, who must have drowned somewhere in front of me.

I thought I heard someone call my name from far off but it was ragged and phantom–like against the roar of waves and the hiss of wind and scattered foam.

With the little strength I had, I turned and looked. Dex was running along the beach towards me. I couldn't do anything except get jostled by the breaking waves.

He was swearing his head off, his face pale, eyes flashing. He started coming in after me, which was up to his mid thigh, and grabbed me by the arm. He pulled me roughly towards the beach. I was too numb to feel any of it. I let him take me, looking back at the water in a daze. There was something out there, right?

He dragged me over to a piece of driftwood and sat me down. He was yelling, his arms raised, gesturing. I couldn't look at him. My eyes were locked on the waves, looking for some sign of the girl. She had been there…I know she had. Why else would I have gone in there?

I felt a sting at my right cheek. He had slapped me. I think.

I brought my eyes up to look at him. It felt like it took all the effort in the world.

"Perry. Perry Palomino. Look at me. Focus. Please."

I tried.

"What the fuck happened?" he asked, his voice high and breaking. His eyes were wild like the waves.

I felt drunk. Stupid. Unable to articulate anything.

I tried to speak but everything came out in a chatter of schizophrenic teeth and a convulsing spasms. I was in ice–cold, wet clothing from my breasts down and my body was finally kicking into survival mode.

Dex decided that slapping and yelling at me wasn't a priority anymore. He literally picked me up in his arms. The vague recollection that this was becoming a common occurrence crossed my mind, but I put my arms around his neck and held on tightly as he took me up the beach and to the campsite.

He put me in the tent, in my sleeping bag, and then lay his sleeping bag on top. My head rolled back and I looked at the tent ceiling, which was shaking in the constant wind. I heard zippers open and clasps and a furious shuffling sound. It seemed like a pile of clothes were was being place on me. They didn't stay on for long as my out–of–control convulsions rocked them off.

I shivered violently for awhile, feeling an unbearable pain as the cold numbness left me and the hot pricks of pins and needles came wheeling through like I was bring dragged through a swath of prickle bushes.

It seemed to go on forever. My thoughts were more or less empty but the one that stood out was the one of me wondering when this would end.

It eventually did end, though. The spasms stopped, the shivers slowed, my teeth were able to rest against each other without clicking. My breath was coming back hot, deep and normal. My heart rate felt reassuring. My brain was starting to work over what had just happened.

I turned my head to the side and saw Dex sitting in the corner of the tent, his wet legs pulled up to his chest. He was staring at me. There were so many intense looks flowing across his eyes and lips, waxing and waning with each passing second. He looked deep into my eyes, trying to get something out of me. I hoped he could. I hoped I wouldn't have to explain it.

But I knew nothing was that easy.

He looked down at his boots that squeaked with the water that had pooled inside of them. I wasn't sure why he wasn't trying to warm up. His feet must have been dead inside.

"Your feet are wet," I said thickly.

"What the fuck, Perry?" He took in a deep breath and looked up at me. "What the hell were you doing? Going for a swim?"

"There was a little girl…"

"A little girl?" he repeated, his eyes wide and disbelieving.

"I…I was in the tent. I was in here. I was reading and I heard a kid laughing." It was taking a lot out of me. I paused and tried to regain my breath. He waited, the furrow in his forehead never leaving.

"A girl. I heard a girl laughing," I continued. "I got up and went outside and saw a girl on the beach. She was maybe three years old? She was just wearing a long white shirt. I asked her where her parents were but there was no answer. There was something…wrong with her, or something. I don't know but she was cold and already wet and there was no one else there. I tried to go near her, to give her my jacket and she just…she just ran off into the ocean. The waves broke…and…and I could still see her, though; I thought I could still save her. Then you came. And I couldn't."

Dex's expression never changed, though I knew he was trying to comprehend my story as quickly as he could. Finally he said, "Perry. I never saw a child. I was watching you. I saw you run into the water. I was just about to put my bag down in the tent. I saw you on the beach just staring at nothing with your coat held out. And then a second later, you ran into the water. I didn't see a little girl."

I felt sick at what he said. I brought my hand up to my mouth. Of course there was a child.

"Maybe you couldn't see her," I said as another wave of cold went through me. "Maybe I was covering her from...from that angle. You don't know. I know what I saw. I saw her well. Blue eyes. Ashy hair, messy, long, weird old shirt, like Victorian era or something. No shoes."

"There's no one else on the island, Perry."

"You don't know that. Have you looked?"

"No, but I was just at the boat. It's still there and it's still alone. Unless someone came by kayak, there is nowhere else to anchor your boat. If they aren't at that beach, or at this beach, they aren't here."

"Maybe they came by kayak then."

"Kiddo. Listen. Listen to yourself. There is no one here. If anyone came in this weather by kayak, they would die. You almost died out there and you were only at your waist. No one can come here in this weather. You know no one can come here in practically any weather."

"They could have been here before, they–"

"There is no one else on this island Perry, except you and me and bunch of psycho raccoons and flash mob deer." He said that with as much conviction and force as I had heard so far.

I thought it over. "Then what did I see? Are you calling me crazy?"

He sighed and slumped his head down, shaking it at the ground.

"What?" I asked defensively. "It's a fair question. I say I saw someone. I know what I saw. You say it's not possible. Then what did I see?

"I don't know."

"A ghost then," I told him.

"A ghost of what?" he asked, finally looking up at me. "There were no kids on this fucking island."

"There was a woman."

"Yeah, and?"

"She died," I said softly, almost feeling inexplicably sorry for her at that second, like I was talking about someone I knew.

"I know," he said. "I read about it. She died of pneumonia or whatever, like less than a year after being on the island. There was no kid. There were only lepers and coffins and opium and some religious idiot who thought he could ease their suffering when all he did was add to it."

I didn't get far enough into the reading about the Reverend to know what Dex was talking about but I didn't want to ask either. That wasn't the point anyway. I know what I saw. Whether it was an actual ghost or a child, something had just drowned itself off the beach outside our tent and that realization was slowly working its way through my body. I felt the tears coming, and I was tired, sad and very confused.

Dex saw this too, because he let out a much softer sigh and moved on over to me. He put his cold hand on my forehead and held it there, his eyes looking into mine.

"Just rest for a bit. I'm going to get warm and dry. I'll fix something to eat. Get some more coffee going. Have a bit of a nap, get warm. Then we'll get you dry and we'll talk about all of this. OK?"

I couldn't bring myself to agree. He lowered his face to mine. I could see the yellow and red pin pricks of color that snaked across the brown in his eyes.

"There is no one else here. OK? If you saw anything, Perry, you saw a ghost. I know that's still not an awesome thing but just please don't think you saw an actual child drown out there because I know you didn't. And I think you know it too."

He tenderly brushed a piece of hair off of my forehead and gave me a fleeting, close–lipped smile. Then he gathered up some clothes of his, left the tent and left me alone with my thoughts, which evolved from poignant to abstract to nothing at all.

CHAPTER ELEVEN

"Are you sure you don't think I'm crazy?" I asked Dex. "Because you're kind of looking at me like I am."

We were at the picnic table slurping our way through Mr. Noodles and more coffee. I had slept for an hour or so. The exhaustion from my emotions and from the near hypothermia had knocked me right out. I felt better now that I was dressed in warm and dry clothes but going over the incident with Dex again wasn't helping. There was something disbelieving in his expression, buried in deep, no matter how clearly I tried to describe what I had seen.

"As I said, I don't think you're crazy. I'm just trying to figure out what's going on."

"The books don't say anything about there being a kid on the island, but who knows? I mean can kids get leprosy? Maybe one was banished here and they didn't tell anyone."

"Did the kid look Chinese?"

"No. I guess not." She had been fair and her blue eyes were wide. Wide and fearful.

"Well," I pondered, "what if she had died at some other time?"

"Maybe," he said. "Maybe."

"I'll Google it. Give me my phone." I held my hand out for it.

A flash of fear passed over Dex. He fidgeted. "Sorry. I, uh, left it on the boat."

"What!?" I yelled, nearly spilling the Mr. Noodles everywhere. "Why the fuck is it on the boat?!"

"Whoa, calm down."

"Calm down?! What the hell, Dex?!"

My body felt like it was about to go all Hulk in a couple of seconds. My heart was racing and my bones were tense with anger and frustration.

"I thought it would be for the best if you–" he started. I didn't need to let him finish.

"Fuck!" I screamed and got up, the picnic table rocking. I threw the Mr. Noodles cup against the nearest tree. It smashed into it with a wet thunk. A firework of hot broth and steaming noodles flew everywhere and landed on the bushes below.

I looked at Dex. He was sitting as still as a statue. His eyes wide, his lower lip sucked in. The fingers on his right hand were shaking slightly.

I was torn between wanting to calm down and wanting to let myself be absolutely livid over this.

"Where the fuck do you fucking get off making those decisions for me?! I already have one fucking father! I don't need this, this pseudo–parenting from some hypocrite like you!"

"Hypocrite?" he asked softly.

"You had no right!"I said, ignoring him. "You are taking me back to the boat and I am getting my damn phone back, you got it?" I leaned across the table and jabbed my finger at him, my eyes fixed with blackness, my heart pounding in my throat.

He swallowed carefully and nodded, quick and swift.

"OK."

He got up and started up the path. Obviously, he meant now.

"Good," I said, my voice wavering the tiniest bit. I noticed my hands were cramped up into heated little fists. I didn't really know what had come over me. But at least it worked. Maybe Dex would get the point of all of this. I didn't want to be babysat or policed by someone who didn't know which way was up half the time. That was one of the most aggravating things about him, his assumption that because he was older or that I was a fuckup, he knew what was best. Sometimes he did. But that wasn't the point.

I walked behind him for most of the way through the forest. I was too irate to feel creeped out by the feeling of nothingness at my heels, or the shadows that the creaking and swaying trees left on the forest floor.

Dex smoked the entire time, one cigarette after the other, flicking the butts into the bushes. I made a mental note to come back later and pick them up, but I knew that wouldn't happen. At least the chance of a forest fire was nil in this weather.

It wasn't until we reached the creepy glade, that I found myself moving a little bit faster until I was right at Dex's back.

"Did you see the raccoons when you came through earlier?" I asked, my voice startling him a bit in the strange stillness around us. The wind didn't seem to reach here. It was like being in another world of dripping moss, slimy bark and decaying leaves.

He shook his head. "No I didn't but I got my ass through here pretty fast."

I didn't blame him. I was still scared and I had someone with me.

We went back to walking in silence as we left the glade behind us. The closer we got to the other side of the island, the more the wind and chill picked up again. My hair was still wet from the water, which only added to the cold. I started to wonder if maybe I would die of pneumonia at this rate. I shoved my hands deep in the jacket pockets and hunched up my shoulders to keep my neck warm.

We turned right when we came to the well–trampled trail that ran up the east coast. I looked through the waving branches, seeing glimpses of the roaring waves between them. I couldn't see the boat at first. That made my heart lurch uncomfortably.

But as we got off the path and the beach opened up, I saw her. She was shuddering with each upward thrust of the colorless, foaming swells, her anchors at both ends straining.

"She looks like she's going to break away," I said to Dex as we carefully made our way down a tangled trail and onto the slick pebbles of the beach. The wind here was razor sharp and relentless. It blew our jacket hoods straight back and messed up my hair within seconds.

"I know. I double–checked the rope though, and the anchor. She should be OK."

With the choppy surf and increment bursts of spray, I was started to second guess my desire to get my phone back. Getting on the Zodiac was going to be a bit of a challenge. Dex had stopped in front of me, staring at it. He was probably thinking the same thing.

I looked again at the Zodiac sitting high on the beach. And realized why he was staring. It was half the height it was before, the pontoons seriously deflated like a squished loaf of bread.

"Oh fuck no! No, no, no, no," Dex cried out and started running towards it. I followed.

He reached the Zodiac and pushed his hands down on the wet pontoons. They sank even deeper under his weight, a puff and hissing noise coming out from somewhere.

"We can still use it, right?" I asked hopefully, trying to squelch the panic that was bubbling up inside.

He didn't say anything. He stood in the boat and bent over, inspecting the bottom while pushing down with his other hand. He didn't have to say anything. I could see we were fucked. The Zodiac would sink like a stone.

And now the panic was coming in, rising fast. I put my hand to my temples and tried to keep calm, keep focused. Everything started to sway and the world became as rough and tumble as the never–ending waves that crashed so close. I closed my eyes and breathed in through my nose as deep as I could, knowing a panic attack would not do us any good here.

Still if anyone needed a reason to panic, being stranded on a haunted island during a storm was as good of a reason as any.

"Fuck, no."

I opened my eyes, staggering a bit off balance, and looked at Dex. He was looking up at me incredulously.

"We've been sabotaged," he said darkly.

"What?!"

He pointed at the left and right pontoons near the back of the craft. I stepped in the boat with him and kneeled down. There were identical slash marks on each one, about half a foot long.

"Could...could this have happened some other way?"

"No. I was just using this boat. Those were not there."

"Maybe the equipment...?"

"Perry, no," he glared at me if I was asking the stupidest question in the world. "It was not the equipment. After I dropped the gear off on the boat and uploaded some footage, I came back on here. I drove it to shore. The boat was fine. If the boat was like this when I was on the water – I wouldn't have made it back alive."

I ran my fingers along the slit. The fabric was very tough and very thick. The edges of the tear were serrated like someone had used a knife. I told Dex that.

"I know. But who the fuck would do this? Who the fuck is here?"

I turned my head to his. Our faces were only a few inches apart. He looked closer to losing it than I was. I wanted to say something about how adamant he had been earlier that there was no one else on the island but knew I shouldn't press my luck. I was snapping easily today and he was too.

I stood up and looked at the Mary Contrary, rocking and rolling in the waves. She might have been a short Zodiac jaunt away but there was no way she was in swimming distance.

"What do we do?" I asked myself out loud.

"We have to comb the island," he said, standing up beside me in a determined stance.

"Comb the island? Are you crazy?"

"We have to find the people who did this."

"Find the people who did this? Who are you, Charles Bronson?" I asked.

He gave me a dismissive look and stepped on to the beach, marching off towards the woods.

"Where the hell are you going?!" I screamed after him.

He didn't answer or stop so I ran after him. I nearly bailed on the rocks when a gust of icy wind knocked me forward. I grabbed on to his arm just in time and pulled back with all my force.

"Dex, please. Stop. Just talk to me..."

He rolled his eyes and tried to get out of my grasp. I held on tight, two hands on his bicep now.

"There's no point standing around here and thinking this through," he said.

"No point? Dex, look, we can't...I mean, say we do find the people who did this...then what? What's your plan? Confront them? They slashed our Zodiac...they obviously have a knife."

"We have a knife. And a flare gun."

I let go of his arm and put my hands at the side of my head, trying to absorb what he was saying.

"OK, this is just getting retarded. This is madness. Look, we can't get into some *Lord of the Flies*–type war here. Don't you know how that book ends? We can't go into this shooting flare guns at people!"

"So what do you suppose we do since you seem to have all the answers?" he sneered.

"I didn't say I had answers! I just want you, us, to think about this. Just for a minute. Give me a minute."

"We can walk and talk."

"No. We'll talk here where it's open and we can see things clearly."

He didn't say anything to that. I turned away from him and walked vacantly in the direction of the shoreline.

Our only way of getting to the boat was gone. We had to focus on getting back there instead of focusing on what was on the island. Screw the show, we were in danger here. I don't know what kind of people go around attempting to strand people on an island, but I gathered they probably didn't mean us well.

I looked behind me at Dex, who was deep in thought too.

"Call Bill. Call the coast guard. We need help," I ordered. "You do have at least your phone, right?"

He nodded and brought it out with a sigh. He shook his head and let out an exasperated breath of air.

"No reception."

"Are you fucking kidding me?!"

I walked over to him and brought the phone over to my face. It said No Service across the top. Well, thank you, AT&T.

"We'll just keep trying it. There's got to be reception somewhere. It worked fine near the campsite."

He shook his head. "I never got a signal this whole time."

"You haven't tried to call Jenn or anything?"

You know, to check up on the baby, I thought rather viciously.

"I *tried*. I said never got a signal."

"Oh, well I am so glad you put the only working phone on that fucking boat over there!" I said, throwing my arm in the sailboat's direction.

"Hey, this is not my fault!" he yelled right back at me. "I wouldn't have to put the phone over there if you could get your damn little head out of the clouds and start focusing on what's really important."

My jaw dropped. "Excuse me?! You think I don't know what's important? I thought having a phone, a connection to the outside world, was a pretty fucking important thing! Looks like I was right!"

He gave me a dismissive wave. "I can't stand here arguing about this. I'm going to find the pontoon-slashing motherfuckers who did this to us and then we'll figure out what to do."

He walked off into the forest. I felt like picking up the nearest rock and chucking it at him, much like I chucked that container of Mr. Noodles.

I looked behind me at the boat and made a silent prayer that the ropes and anchor would hold out. The clanking of the chains could be heard amongst the weather's roar and made me think some decrepit sea creature was deep below it, holding on with a lazy grasp. That boat was our only way out. If the weather calmed down and if we made it through till the next day without being ambushed or starting a knife party, maybe one of us could swim out. Though, knowing firsthand how cold that water was, it would be the last resort.

Dex was already way down the trail and nearing the turn off that went across the island when I caught up with him. The asswipe didn't even bother slowing down or waiting for me. Good to know when there were potential crazies on the island with us.

I followed behind him, not bothering to say anything. We made it through the dead part (the dead heart) without incident, though I could tell we were both extra paranoid knowing we had more than animals to worry about.

Back at the campsite Dex worked quickly to find the flare gun and the hunting knife. I thought that the knife was purely for kitchen use but Dex was a bit more prepared than I was. He had grabbed the flare gun from the boat's emergency kit as well when we first left the boat.

"So you thought we'd need it?" I asked him as he gave it the once–over and stuck it in his pocket.

"You never know," he said matter–of–factly and placed the hunting knife in my hand. "This is for you. I suggest we split up."

I was speechless. I looked down at the knife in my hand, the glinty steel which that matched the glinty ocean that crashed around us. There was seriously something wrong with Dex. There was no way in hell we were splitting up on this island. Didn't he care at all about my wellbeing? Didn't he see what happened the last time he had left me? I nearly drowned.

"I think you've lost your mind," I said quietly. "I can't even begin to explain why I think that."

"I'd give you the gun if I thought you knew how to use it."

"Actually, I do know how," I said through gritted teeth. "I've taken shooting lessons. With real guns too. And I'm a good shot. It doesn't matter. We aren't splitting up. Even if you try to lose me, I'm going to be right behind you. And if you don't like that, you can just waste that flare on me!"

I spat out those last words like it was crushed up Aspirin.

His eyes softened for a moment. Maybe he was starting to get it. "Don't be like that."

"Don't be like what?" I growled. "I'm pissed off that you would even suggest I go off there alone with a knife to protect me from who knows what. Pissed off and actually a bit hurt. Because it's nice to know you give a shit about my life. Seriously!"

There was something weird happening between us. I didn't know what it was. I felt like it had been building up for the last past couple of days, some strange animosity or an overload of tension or something. Being here on the island was only making it worse. I know I felt angrier and more uncontrollable than usual these last past few days and he was acting a bit more callous as well.

I wanted to keep staring at him with fire and intensity, but I had to relent and relax. The minute I did so, he did too. Maybe it was a girl thing, but I knew when I felt vulnerable, he often stepped up as the protector. Sometimes it didn't work but at least this time it seemed to.

He took a step towards me and pulled me into him. He wrapped his arms around me, the scratchy fabric of our jackets creating a vibrating sound as they rubbed against each other. I put my arms around his waist, careful with the knife in my hand, and rested my cheek against his chest. He put his chin on top of my head and sighed, long and controlled.

"Sorry," he mumbled, his voice gruff but sincere.

"It's OK."

He still held me against him. I listened to his heart rate, which was slowing down from a frantic dance.

"I don't mean to be such a dick. I don't know what it is. I just...this place. It's everything. It's Jenn. It's this weather. This island. Whatever the fuck is going on. It's you..."

"Me?" I asked, keeping my head on him, enjoying the comfort and the warmth.

"Yeah," he said after a moment of silence. "There's something about you...I don't know what. You're acting out a bit. But it's not you. It's hard to explain."

I pulled back and looked up at him. His lips were so close to mine. I was afraid of what I might to do to them if we continued to stand like this.

He took my face in his comforting hands and gazed at me, closer, deeper. My heart started to jump around sporadically, my nerves were on fire. I loved and hated it at the same time. I hated what he was doing to me, but I loved him. I hated my feelings, but...I loved him. I hated that he could just look at me like that and I couldn't think of anything else.

"I'm still me," I said heavily.

"I know. But you know you're acting...spazzier than normal."

"Can you blame me?" I whispered, too aware of how close our mouths were.

"No. I can't," he said. The pressure of his fingers was firm on my cheeks. "I'm worried that it's this place. That there is something here. Like there's been something everywhere we go. You went for a bloody swim earlier. Now we don't know what it was out there – what you saw – but it almost killed you and I can't let that...situation...happen again."

"So you wanted us to split up..." I leaned in closer.

"I'm sorry. I'm not thinking properly. No. Of course I don't want us to split up. If we had, I would have come running after you within seconds. I'm not like that. I'm really not. I have your back, OK? Don't forget that. I won't let you."

I nodded slightly. But for some reason I wasn't entirely convinced.

With his thumbs he wiped off smudges of mascara underneath my eyes and gave me a small, almost pained smile. "I won't do anything crazy, don't worry. I just want us to be armed if anything happens. We won't go all Kato on these people, if we even find them. I just want to know what we are dealing with."

I nodded. My cheeks felt so warm in his hands. It made me realize how my exposed skin was continuously frozen for the past 24 hours.

He stared at me for a bit longer. His eyes were fathomless, a mix of too many things I wanted – needed – to read into. It was unbearable. Our distance hadn't changed. I didn't know what he wanted. If he was going to kiss me, then god damn it, just kiss me. Do it before I do it. I was too impulsive.

Maybe he read that thought because his face came an inch closer to mine. The space between us was disappearing, and fast. Heat radiated from his lips and neck. My eyes drooped lustily, ready to close, and my insides pulsed vibrantly.

And then there was a flinch in his eyes. A hesitation. He pulled back and took his arms off of me. The spell was broken.

"Shall we get going?" he asked casually, as if nothing had just happened.

Nothing had just happened but something *almost* happened and that spoke volumes, but he pretended not to notice. Maybe it was all in my head.

I flashed him a quick, brave smile that I willed to be as nonchalant as he was feeling and we walked off into the woods once more. I tried to leave the awkwardness behind.

CHAPTER TWELVE

Dex had decided the best way to search the island would be to walk around the entire coastline, even though there were no trails that skirted the coast, aside from the one on the northwest side. This meant a lot of bushwalking, which in inclement weather and without proper equipment would be difficult to do.

We started off with the remaining campsites that sat inland from the ones we were staying at. On a normal, sunny day the little clearing would have been an ideal spot for a small group. There were three gravel sites, two picnic tables and a grassy, mossy bottom.

But on this day, it looked like the creepiest place to be, let alone camp. The picnic tables seemed rotted through and covered with black slime and moss. The grass beneath our feet was saturated and sinking, and all around us were clumps of piled rocks. We knew those were graves. It amazed me that people could actually be camping beside the sad, makeshift tombstones and not know about it. Or perhaps not even care.

After the campsite we headed inland for a bit. There was a small bog with year–round groundwater that used to be the only source of water for the lepers. I guess Dex and I were lucky in the fact that we were able to collect the deluge of rainwater that was falling every other hour; otherwise we'd probably have to drink the bog water. With the drooping, brown weeds that sprouted from the dingy murk and the broken, hanging grey limbs that surrounded it like a cage, the bog seemed like the kind of place where you were more likely to drink poison than water.

We were glad to get out of there and back onto the coast again, even though navigating was becoming more and more challenging the further we hiked away from the campsite. I had my stupid knife I had to contend with while I was struggling to break through the salal bushes. At first I tried slashing through like it was a machete and I was on some jungle expedition, but after a few futile attempts and one sharp cut to my finger, I gave up on that.

When we weren't dealing with tangled undergrowth, we were out in the open, climbing over large boulders and rocks that made up the craggy shoreline. With my lack of balance and agility, plus the knife in my hand, I was definitely slowing us up.

Dex stopped on top of one boulder that was covered in reddish moss and bird shit and gave me an impatient look.

"Are you going to make it?" he asked. His tone said he wouldn't care either way.

I narrowed my eyes at him and waved the knife. "You try this with a knife in your hand."

He sat down on the rock and held his hand out for the knife. I gave it to him and he grabbed my hand and helped pull me up, the slickness of the rain–soaked rocks falling away from my straining boots.

Once on top of the rock, I lay there for a minute and let the rain fall on my face, taking in a deep breath. I was soaked to the bone, freezing cold and absolutely miserable. We had only been on the move for about a half an hour and with the thick fog settled just a few yards off shore, it was hard to tell what direction we were facing. Any sign of the nearby Sidney Island, or even the closer Little D'Arcy, was obscured. It was disorienting.

What sucked the most was that I couldn't just give up and go back to the campsite. We had to keep going.

Dex moved over and peered down at me, his head blocking the rain from my eyes. It made a pleasant pitter patter sound on the back of his hood.

"Catch your breath. Then we'll keep going. I don't want it to get dark while we're out here."

I nodded and breathed in deeply. We did have flashlights with us, but he was right. There was no way I wanted to be in the forest during nightfall, looking for people who may or may not be waiting for us.

He got to his feet and grabbed hold of my hand. He started to pull me up as my Docs slid around a bit. Just as I got to my feet in an awkward, hunched–over manner, his left foot shot out from under him and he went flying over backwards off of the rock.

I screamed and reached for him as he went but I fell too, only onto my stomach, still on the rock.

"Dex!" I cried and pulled myself forward and peered over the edge of the rock face. He had fallen about eight feet and was lying below the other side, looking all bent up and battered. *Fuck, I hope he hasn't broken anything,* I thought wildly. If he had, we were screwed to high heaven.

He groaned and looked up at me. "I'm OK."

"How? Are you sure?"

He nodded then stopped himself. He held his head. "Ow."

"You're not OK, oh shit."

I carefully pulled my body around so I was facing the other way and tried to let myself drop to the rocky ground beside him as carefully as possible.

"Wait!" he screamed.

I paused, hanging off of the boulder, feet dangling, my arms barely gripping the slippery surface.

"Move to your left more."

I sidled over to the left as much as I could and then my hands and arms gave away.

I landed on my feet but immediately fell backward and pointy, crusty rocks went into my ass, elbows and back.

Now it was my turn to swear my head off and moan. Why was I so clumsy all the time?

I looked at Dex, who was staring at the space right beside me. The hunting knife was there and for some reason it was lodged in the ground with the sharp blade facing straight up. Had he not told me to move to the left I would have landed right on top of it.

I shivered, feeling nauseous at the close call.

"You OK?" he grunted, trying to sit up.

"I came down here to ask you that." I looked at my hands, which were lightly scratched with blood and dirt but nothing seemed too gruesome.

"We've both been worse," he said and moved to get up. He paused and lowered his head a bit, dark eyes fixated on something at the base of the boulder.

"What is it?" I asked, trying to see.

He got to his feet slowly, trying to hide the wincing, and took a few steps before squatting in front of the rock, where a small depression made a short and shallow, dark cave. He reached in, his disappearing hands out of my view.

When he brought them out, in them was a very old, dripping shoe. A man's shoe, quite small, brown and decrepit. We exchanged a curious glance. I guess finding a shoe wasn't that strange but…

He turned it over in his hands.

His eyes bugged out and he gasped in outright horror, dropping the shoe in disgust and stumbling backward away from it in a wild panic.

Instinctively I jumped up, scrambling to get to my feet and stumbled over to where he was. I grabbed onto his coat.

His hands were at his mouth, looking like he was about to vomit.

"What?! What is it?" I cried, not wanting to go any closer to it.

He closed his eyes and tried to compose himself. I put my arm around him to let him know I was there. After a few breaths he opened them, shaking his head very slowly, eyes focused on the shoe in horrid disbelief, skin transparently pale. The stubble on his cheeks stood out like dark cacti on a white sand beach.

"There's a foot in that shoe," he said blankly.

"Excuse me?" My hands flew up to my mouth as well. He had to have been kidding.

"There's a human foot in that shoe."

"Oh my God," I said, turning away and trying to remain calm. "What the? How? Why would there be a foot. Did someone cut off someone's foot?"

"I don't know. It might have fallen off."

"Jesus, Dex," I exclaimed. I looked at him with disgust. He gave me a barely perceptible shrug, his complexion still ashen.

"Leprosy," he said matter–of–factly.

"OK, for one thing their feet didn't just fall off like that. They lost feeling in their feet and hands and whatever, but that was totally different. And for another, that foot couldn't possibly be a hundred years old!"

"Did you see the foot?" he asked, looking at me wryly.

I did not want to see the foot. Sure, there was a part of me that wanted to look, the same part of me that slows down at car accidents in some sick hope that I'd see a dead body, but I also knew that if the sight caused Dex to nearly puke, it would do something much worse to me. In fact, I felt like spewing right here on the rocks just from the thought of it.

"I hate to say this, but I really think we should get going," I said, eyeing the moving fog that seemed to creep in closer. I wanted to be as far away from the foot as possible, even if the only other option was to continue on our pointless trek around the island.

Dex agreed and, after he scooped up the knife from its deadly resting place, we were back on our way, scrambling over the rest of the rocky coast in silence, mulling over the damn foot in the shoe. I didn't know what Dex was thinking but at least he was the one to have seen it, to have seen something for once. The shoe could have been a hundred years old, it could have been a few years old – the sea and climate ravaged things out here like nothing else. It could have been a leper's foot, it could have be the foot of someone murdered, or it could have just been the only remains of a drowned kayaker, washed up to shore. Apparently finding feet on the coast was a common occurrence in B.C. I didn't want to think about it anymore than I had to.

We had other things to contend with, including making our way through the forest again, choosing the cover of dark pine and twisting arbutus trees with their scaling red bark that reminded me of dead, sunburned skin. We rounded the head of the island and started down the other coast with the wild waves now crashing turbulently on our right side. After a while of exhaustive bushwhacking, my fingers cold, numbed and scratched to bits from pushing back scathing branches, we came back to the a familiar area where a trail opened up and the Mary Contrary could be seen rollicking off the coast.

She was a sight for sore eyes, all right. There was nothing I wanted more than to just toss everything aside and make a swim for it. We paused near the beach and watched her ride the waves. Dex could tell what I was thinking.

"Tomorrow," he said, "if the weather is better, I'll try and make a go for her."

I didn't like that idea but knew we might not have the choice. If we were even given the choice. The good news, though, was that if someone had actually sabotaged the Zodiac and meant to strand us here, they would have just taken the boat. With the sailboat still here, that seemed more unlikely.

We continued down the path until we reached the turnoff for the dead heart and the campsite. Instead of turning left, we kept going down the coast. This was all new to me. The path was almost wider at points and took on the appearance of a well–worn stroll through a city park.

"Did you come down here earlier?" I asked Dex. He said he hadn't.

It wasn't long at all before the trees around us began to clear. If there was a view to be had through the encumbering fog, it would have been quite the sight. With the sea falling below the low cliffs to our right, you could have probably seen for miles.

The first surprise came in the form of what was supposed to be the old caretaker's woodshop. There was nothing left of the building except low cement fixtures that would have held together the foundation and a single cement staircase that led to nowhere. The building was now home to spindly trees that twisted sideways from the wind.

The area around the cottage was strange, with a weird, thick feeling in the air, like the fog from offshore was choking us with an invisible hand. All I could think about was the history behind the ruins, how the coldness that was constantly seeping through my supposedly waterproof jacket and throttling my bones and joints was just a daily fact of life for the poor people who were left here.

Dex surveyed the area with one glance. Either he didn't care or it spooked him out as much as it did me.

We walked for a bit longer until we came across another ruin.

It was half a house, still standing. There were no floors or rooms, but two walls of vertical cement that met together in a tangled mess of vines and overgrown weeds that declared residency on the skeleton.

An arbutus tree shot up from the middle of the building, nature's triumph over mankind. Flanking the remains of the ruins were large toppled stones and boulders that were covered in a thick layer of dark green moss. Civilization still had its grasp on the place with the numerous tags of graffiti that sprawled against the walls. Some lovebird's initials, some racist slang, some innocuous cheers for Grad 2000.

Standing there with Dex, looking the eerie relic over, I think we were both glad to see something so trivial and modern as moronic graffiti. In any other situation I probably would have made some remark about punk kids ruining a historical artifact but all I could think about was how soothing the vandalism was. There was another world out there, another world of modern people who were going on about their lives. A world that occasionally brought over teenage kids to this godforsaken island so they could have sex away from prying eyes, get drunk and tag decrepit old structures that no one cared about.

"What do you think?" Dex asked. We had paused in front of the crippled cottage, both of us looking it over in silence.

"It's creepy and comforting. At the same time."

He looked out to where the lack of trees gave us a clear view of the briny waves and the vanilla cotton candy mist. "Would have been a hell of a view for the caretaker. You can't buy this location back at home."

True. But it would still be a hard sell. Sure you get a view, you just have to share an island with a bunch of lepers.

"Wish I had brought the Super 8," he lamented to himself and walked along one side of the ruins. I stayed put, not wanting to explore it any further. Like the previous ruin, there was something unsettling here. Then again after a day of almost drowning, finding our Zodiac slashed and discovering a foot on the beach, it didn't seem all that strange to find every single thing we came across just a tad creepy.

He went around the corner to the upright slabs and vanished out of my sight. I knew he was there, just a couple of yards away, but a wash of prickly cold came over me, almost as if I had an icy breeze inside of my body.

"Hee hee hee."

The girl's giggle.

I spun around and looked behind me at the forest.

The sound of leaves being crushed, branches cracking, light footsteps. But there was nothing there. Nothing I could see.

I listened hard. I couldn't hear anything else. Not even Dex. I was about to open my mouth to call from him when I heard a SNAP.

I looked around me again and saw a glimpse of a white shirt disappearing behind the concrete where Dex had gone.

"Dex!" I yelled and ran over. I went around the corner and saw nothing. Where was he?

I kept running and was about to round the next one, the area where the dying vines overwhelmed the cracked and pebbly walls, when Dex appeared. I put on the brakes, almost running right into him. He reached out and steadied me with his hand.

"What is it?" he asked.

"Did you hear that?" I asked breathlessly.

"Hear what?"

"The laugh. The girl laughed and then I saw her, I saw her, she would have run right into you."

I could see the hesitation in his face, followed by a tinge of concern across his brow. He kept his hand on me, tightening his grip.

"I didn't see or hear anything, Perry."

Of course he didn't. I gave him a wary smile.

"Guess I'm going nuts then!" I felt small and simple. Maybe I was going nuts. Though if I wasn't, I was a bit relieved to know that the girl, whether she was dead or alive, was still alive...if that made any sense.

I knew Dex was looking me over like some clinical scientist so I just brushed it off. "Well anyway, maybe you aren't very observant. Can we finish this stakeout up? I'm getting colder by the minute."

We took off down the path, leaving the ruins behind. The only problem now was the path deteriorated back into bush territory and we were back to slogging through mud and crisscrossed roots for the rest of the way. Sometimes we would come across a pretty curve of beach or a scenic outlook but with that constant armor of fog at our doorstep, nothing was as pretty as it could have been. Yesterday would have been the better day to go exploring. But then again, yesterday felt like a whole different life all together. Even the hockey game we went to – the strip club, God damn it – felt like something that happened years ago and to other people other than us. It had only been 30 hours or something but it felt like my whole life was rain, cold and fog, with the occasional foot thrown in there.

The south end of the island came up and we were soon making our way up the bottom, tripping up the east coast. Aside from the little girl, we hadn't come across anyone else. Dex pointed out that just because the perimeter was clean it didn't mean people weren't hiding out in the middle.

I started to doubt it though. We hadn't seen signs of anyone. The boat was still there the last we looked, and as we struggled through the brush until we saw our own tent again, shining in its blue plastic glory like a beacon, it only solidified the fact that if there was someone else here wanting to make trouble for us, they would have done something else, right? The boat would have been gone, our campsite would have been destroyed. It would have been more.

Unfortunately, this didn't mean the end of our journey. Dex was so determined to still find those "pontoon–slashing motherfuckers" that he made us keep going and hit up the one place we had missed... the dead heart of the island.

It really was starting to get dark. From the way the clouds grew blacker near their tops, it must have been at least 3:30 or 4 p.m. We maybe had an hour before the sun would set in a place unseen.

But Dex was insistent and as much as my feet hurt in my boots, as much as my bones and hands throbbed subtly from the fall, I still wasn't brave enough to wait it out alone at the campsite. So we kept going, heading deep inside to where the ferns grew to prehistoric heights and the only light seemed choked out by grasping limbs.

Though it was his idea, I could see Dex was apprehensive about heading into the middle. At one point in the path he stopped and quickly handed me back the knife for "safe keeping."

We reached the end of the path and started back again. There was nothing there. No raccoons, no saboteurs, no giggling girls. Just the hanging moss, rotted stumps, a floor of grey, wet leaves and the stench of dying vegetation.

As we walked along, our pace quickening with the relief that we were leaving, Dex looked at me and smiled. "At least this has taken your mind off of all the blog comments."

He was right about that. I wasn't quite in the place to smile about it yet but it all seemed very frivolous when compared to a real–life dangerous situation.

He looked up at the marker on the tree as we passed it and frowned.

"I don't remember seeing that tree before."

We stopped and I looked behind me. The tree looked like any other tree in this area. Slimy, scaly bark flanked with beaded moss and the drip of rainwater. There was a tiny nick in the side of it though, where the inner bark was clean and white. Almost like someone took a few whacks of an axe to it and then gave up. He was right. I hadn't seen that before. But I wasn't sure that meant anything.

I looked at him unsure of what to say. "I don't know."

He sucked in his lips and reached into his pocket. He brought out the pack of cigarettes. It was empty. He crumpled up the package in frustration and threw it on the ground.

"Really, Dex? Littering?" I bent over to pick it up but he grabbed my arm.

"Just leave it for now, trust me."

He brought out a pack of Nicorette gum and popped a few pieces in his mouth instead. Then he shrugged. "Almost there."

I gave him an odd look and we continued on our way. He pointed off to the side and started in that direction. It wasn't on the marked trail anymore but I went with it. I wasn't sure why he felt littering was of any importance at the moment unless he was just finding another way of being stubborn. Still, I–

"Shit!" Dex cried out. I turned my head in time to see him take off, booking it up the path like a racehorse out of the gate.

There was a two–second lag where I wasn't sure what was going on but I was quickly running after him, trying to follow his form through the mud and thick trees.

"Where are you going?!" I yelled after him, losing my breath already.

"There's someone here. I just saw them running!" he yelled over his shoulder, part of his words muffled by the trees he was darting in front of.

I gripped the handle of my knife tighter and struggled to catch up with him but with his comparatively long and agile legs, it was a losing game. It wasn't long before I lost sight of him and the sound of his breathing and strides were hidden by the density of the forest.

I stopped running and felt utterly lost.

"Dex!" I yelled. And waited.

I yelled again. Same deal.

I was alone in the forest, in the very worst part of the island. If it was a movie, I would have kept looking for Dex and gotten more lost. After all, I did have a knife on me. I was armed. But I still had a tiny rational part of my brain that functioned despite being waterlogged and hungry.

I remember seeing a film when I was in grade school. It was one of those PSA–type shows, akin to why you shouldn't play with fireworks and that sort of thing. They did a video in a local Portland area forest about a young boy who got lost. The best course of action for him was to stay put and curl up for warmth. The kid also had a package of some granola–like treats that kept him sustained. I remember really wanting those granola treats; I can see the pink packaging clearly in my head, even till to this day.

I also remembered the way he huddled inside a hollowed up log until the rescuers found him the next day. Now, I had no treats and though there were many creepy logs here I could certainly crawl under, I wasn't having any of that. If Dex even came back there was no guarantee that he would come back this way. There was, of course, no search party.

So I turned around and decided to get back to the main path as quickly as I could. I knew that would take me to the campsite and the campsite was the one place we both knew we could find each other. It was our constant. If I could get back there, there was no doubt he would eventually show up there.

I hurried down the path, fully aware that Dex was out there chasing something and that there might be other somethings around, watching me from the dead trees. I quickly passed by the cigarette package and picked it up. Even stuffed into a crack in a tree, it was better than leaving it on the forest floor.

I looked up at the tree we passed earlier and noticed again the nicks in the bark.

Only the marker wasn't there.

I stopped. Walked back to the tree. A few minutes ago the red and white glowing disc of the trail marker was on the tree. Now it wasn't. And it wasn't on the ground or on any part of the tree. It had just disappeared behind our backs, like someone was going around and plucking them off of the trees.

My breath came in short and shallow. My head felt heavy and my vision began to swim. After everything that happened today, I knew the panic attack was long overdue. But fuck, I didn't want to go through it alone and in this dead place.

"Think, Perry, think," I said to myself. My voice cut clearly across the glade. It almost made me feel embarrassed, which was a nice change of emotion given the circumstances.

This tree did have a marker on it earlier, which meant this was the path. But where was the next marker? Where did the path go? The ground was muddy and debris–covered in every direction, whether we had walked on it earlier or not, and with the way the trees were spaced out, it was easy to imagine a million paths were running in a million different directions. Without the markers, you really were lost and for the first time, I couldn't see a single one anywhere.

"Shit," I swore under my breath. If going forward was impossible, maybe going backward wasn't. The shoreline and the Mary Contrary were only ten minutes away at the most. It wasn't the campsite but it was something and in the worst case scenario, I could probably turn over the Zodiac and use it as shelter.

Part of me wanted to sit down on the nearest stump and cry my eyes out. I was lost, Dex was gone somewhere, chasing something, and we were stranded here. Not only that but my parents and my sister had no idea what was going on with me and were probably sick with worry. There was this constant irrational fear deep down in my chest that I might not see them again.

Maybe Dex would shoot off his flare gun and let me know where he was. That thought cheered me up enough to carry on back to the west shore and the boat.

I took in a deep breath and walked off in that direction.

And I stopped. I heard the sound of twigs snapping and feet shuffling slowly, not wanting to be heard in the quiet forest.

There was someone behind me.

I knew it wasn't Dex.

CHAPTER THIRTEEN

My arms and legs were frozen in fright. There was someone behind me. Someone who wasn't Dex. Someone who was either alive or dead.

I slowly turned my head, expecting to see lepers or a homicidal maniac with an axe and Dex's head in his hand.

There was nothing there. Just stillness. Just the forest.

Maybe the sound was a delayed reaction of–
SNAP.
Again.

I turned all the way around and tensed up, ready to fight or flee, my knife shaking in my firm grasp.

A burst of movement appeared between trees in front of me.

I took a step forward, keeping my eyes locked on the trunks they must have gone behind. If they were running away from me and not towards me, that was at least one good thing I had going.

"Who is there?" I yelled, my voice warbling.

A flash of a person. They left the tree and were running to my right. Between the trees I could make out long hair and a dress of some sort. She was tall, taller than me, a girl, but not a child.

I didn't know what to do but start running after them.

For once, I was the faster one and I was able to come closer in a short amount of time, all the while jumping over small logs, leaping over mud puddles, ducking between fallen limbs and slapping past reaching branches. I kept my eyes on the person, trying to suck in all the details I could. The girl's hair was very long, messy and dark, either from dirt or the natural color. The dress was black and old, patched in some lucky places with huge gaping tears in others. It was a very modest outfit with long sleeves, high collar and an ankle–grazing length. As I watched the girl run, as I started to catch up with her, I noticed the girth of the dress wasn't hampering her ability to jump over stumps or launch over streams. It was like she knew the landscape internally.

At one point I was close enough to reach out for her, but she darted around a heavy fallen tree and had let a thick branch swing back into my face. I put my hands up to protect myself just in time but ended up dropping the knife and was nearly flung backward.

I picked up the knife again and went past the branch but she was gone. There was no one there and the only sound was the ragged, raspy ones that my lungs were making.

A fine mist slowly trailed past my throbbing face as I tried to catch my breath. It was lighter here and the mist meant I was somewhere near the coast. I followed the direction of the airy fingers and saw that I was by a smaller eastern cove that Dex and I had passed by earlier.

I knew all I had to do was walk up and I'd be back at the campsite. If I could get there, maybe everything would be OK.

I was about to head in the direction when something inside made me look back at the cove.

On the tiny beach, there was someone sitting on a log. It was the girl, sitting like a statue, staring at the roaring waves, the wind ruffling her hair. I blinked a few times, trying to make sure she really was there. By the last blink she was looking up at me, or at least in my direction, but she made no effort to move nor made any indication that I was someone to run from.

I didn't feel like yelling at her. The only thing to do was find out what the fuck was going on. I held my knife up as much as I could, steadied my flaming, fiery nerves and made my way down the steep and crumbling cliffside until I was on the beach with her.

She still didn't move. She went back to looking at the ocean.

I approached her slowly, carefully, trying to make sure I was at least in her peripheral vision the whole time, kind of like how you would approach a horse. I kept walking, painfully aware of how loud the pebbles were beneath my shoes.

I stopped five feet off of her left and stood there. My knife was ready but I tried to look non–threatening. There was something so mousy and downtrodden about this person that any threat I had previously felt was gone. This was all just curiosity. Who was she? Where had she come from?

It felt like I stood there for a really long time before she finally turned her head towards me.

She had wire–rim glasses on, something I hadn't noticed earlier. One of the lenses had a giant crack in it. It was the really old kind, the type that modern hipsters would wear out of irony. Her eyes were dusty blue and seemed to pulse in a twitchy way. Her skin was dry, pale and ruddy, her lips chapped and peeling, her hair black. The dress she wore was as plain looking as she was and looked like something out of the turn of the century. That realization alone brought a fling of apprehension across my chest. She was non–threatening if she was alive. Dead, that was always a different story.

"Who are you?" I asked. I tried to sound authoritative and confident but given we were about the same age and she was taller, I didn't know if I had a lot of clout.

"Mary," she said simply. "He switched the markers on you."

"Who did?"

"What's your name?" she asked. Her voice was clipped, reminded me of the way high society types talked in classic films.

"Perry," I said.

"I knew that," she said. "It's a funny name for a girl. I prefer Madeleine."

"What are you doing here? Are you visiting?"

"I live here," she said looking back at the ocean. I looked down at her hands. They looked like they were caked in blood. The rain was falling steadily on us but they weren't diluting the red mess on her hands.

I took a step backward. She didn't notice. I tried to keep focused, keep calm. Act like all of this wasn't a big deal at all.

"Who switched the markers?" I asked again.

"John did."

"Who is he?"

"He's my...friend. He was my friend."

"Do you both live on the island?"

She looked at me and smiled. Her teeth were yellow, and a few bottom teeth were gone.

"We both live here. We are here to help people. Do the work of the Lord."

And then it clicked. She couldn't have been Mary Stewart, the missionary?

"John, is that the Reverend John Barrett?"

"You've heard of him?"

How did I answer that? Yes, I've heard of both of you. In a book. A book that was written a hundred years after your death.

I swallowed hard. The fear was pricking at my skin and at the back of my head. Maybe I was crazy. It didn't matter how many times I had seen the impossible; the impossible still wasn't acceptable.

As redundant as it was to say, I couldn't help but squeak out, "You're dead."

Mary locked her eye on mine through that one good lens. To have her look at me so poignantly, so real, it made what I said seem stupid and crazy.

But she casually said, "I died on my 23rd birthday."

My hands started shaking, the knife was coming loose in my fingers. She eyed it warily.

"Were you hunting something out there? Deer?"

"Uh," I tried to say, my voice thick and trapped. "It's for protection."

"You're a wise woman," she said. She patted the space beside her on the log. "Come sit down. You look tired."

I hesitated. It was the most absurd invitation.

"I won't harm you, if that is what you are pondering," she said.

I gave her a quick smile and gingerly took my seat on the log, careful not to sit too close to her. Now that I was sitting right beside her, I could get a better look at her. She was a good couple of inches taller than me, maybe 5'8", and looked like she'd be quite frail under her dirty, billowing dress. She smelled, too, which I found remarkable. It was the stench of body odor and mold and made my eyes water slightly.

"You must forgive my appearance. I haven't had a bath for awhile. Sometimes the bog seems more dirty than clean."

Being beside her, being able to see the dirty pores on her face, the rusted frames of her glasses and the wide, large white forehead with a smattering of freckles, there was no way I was talking to a dead person. It just didn't make any sense. I know what I had seen in the lighthouse, what happened with Ol' Roddy, but I still questioned things. Maybe my mind made up some of it. How could a ghost, someone dead, be as solid and physical as she was?

Before I knew what I was doing I was pointing at her shoulder, ready to jab her.

"What are you doing?" she asked, eyeing my finger suspiciously.

I paused. How did I explain that I wanted to make sure she was real and not a figment of my imagination?

"Just wanted to make sure you were real," I said uneasily. I slowly pressed my finger into her shoulder. The material of the dress was scratchy and wet. Her shoulder underneath was bony. I hoped she wasn't an actual rotting skeleton. But she was as solid as the log we were sitting on.

I withdrew my hand. She followed it with her eyes.

"That's peculiar. Why wouldn't I be real?" she asked, looking worried.

"You said you were dead. And sometimes I think I see things."

A strange look came over her face. "What kind of things do you see?"

I wasn't sure where to start with that one. Plus it was still entirely possible that I was talking to myself here.

"I see...ghosts."

"Like me?"

"I guess." I didn't mean to come across so blasé about it.

"John would tell me I saw things too. He said I was mentally unstable. Does your friend tell you that?"

"My friend?"

"The man you are with. He's the reason why John switched the markers on you. He's jealous. He was jealous of San and he'll be jealous of your friend."

Whoa. My head started to spin. I leaned forward on my elbows and held my head in my hands trying to regain equilibrium. I focused on the ground. Focused on Mary's feet beside me. She was barefoot. Her feet were cut open, oozing blood and white fluid. I quickly shut my eyes at the sight.

She put her hand on my shoulder and I jumped.

"Are you feeling ill? It's the pneumonia. It killed most of them in the end. I'm sure it got San too."

I slowly straightened up and blinked at the mist that was flying into my face. It was getting darker out and the wind was picking up again, moving parts of the offshore fog around. I could occasionally see the round grey lumps of the Unit Rocks in the distance. It was much easier for me to sit here and think about the weather.

Finally I had to say to her, "You died of pneumonia eight months after you arrived here."

She laughed, a sharp little giggle not unlike the ones I had heard earlier. "I did not. That's what John told everyone. I was alive. Maybe not well, but alive. He kept me hidden for years. He would tie me to a tree in the woods whenever the boats would come in. Tie me and leave me there for hours, with the baby right beside me."

"The baby?"

"He didn't want anyone to know about Madeleine. Can you imagine the scandal if the church had found out that their dear Reverend, the holy selfless soul, was intimate with his missionary? Out of wedlock?"

"That...wasn't in the book," I said stupidly.

"What book?"

I waved my hand at her dismissively. "So you had a baby? All alone here?"

"John was here but he wasn't much help. San was more of a father than John was. They both loved Madeleine though. More than they loved me."

"Who is San?"

"San was my lover. He was a leper. He was the healthiest, youngest, smartest Chinese you'd ever meet. If it wasn't for San at the beginning, I probably would have died. I took care of him, then he took care of me. Then he took care of Madeleine."

It was too much for me to comprehend. I stood up and took in a deep breath.

"You saw her the other day," Mary said plainly. "Madeleine. She was playing with you. She told me about you. I admit I was almost jealous. I thought Maddy had found a new mother."

"She ran into the ocean. I thought she drowned. I tried to save her."

"I tried to save her too."

"Your daughter drowned?"

"They killed both of us."

"Who are they?" I asked, feeling the horror slink through my veins.

She looked at me as if I was stupid. "John. San. And the rest of the lepers."

She got off of the log and took a few steps towards the waves. I couldn't help but watch her broken, bloody feet as they stood on the rocks.

"You better go back to your friend," she said looking at the ocean. She raised her arms above her head and stretched. "He's coming, and he's looking for you."

"Dex?"

She gave me a sharp look. "You better watch out for him. And watch out for John and San. They know you're here and they'll do what they can to keep you here."

"Why should I watch out for Dex?" I asked in a panic.

She chuckled, this one cut with dark tones. "Because he's a man. He's starting to think you're sick. Sick in the head. It's not your fault. It's this island. It's too isolated. There is too much death here. It makes you think. It makes you think too much. You do not want to end up like me."

She bent over and picked up a stone and threw it far into the churn of the waves. "I have to go now. He's here."

"Who is here?" I asked, taking a step toward her, wanting to grab her and keep her from leaving me. I needed to know more, so much more.

She nodded at the distance behind my shoulder. "Your friend."

I spun around and saw Dex standing in the forest, his dark figure half–hidden by the trees, watching me. It had been awhile since Dex had given me the creeps like that.

I turned back to look at Mary but she was gone. I was alone on the beach.

I looked back at Dex and walked toward him, mulling over what had just happened and what he had seen. Had he seen Mary? Or had he seen me talking to myself like I had feared? No wonder Mary said he thought I was sick in the head.

I stopped a few yards away from him, trying to suss him out. Technically I should have been rightly pissed off at him leaving me in the woods like that, so I went with that emotion.

"What the hell, man? Way to leave me alone in the woods like that," I said, crossing my arms.

He frowned and stayed suspiciously silent.

"Why are you just standing there like a creeper, huh? What's your problem?" I asked.

He seemed to snap out of whatever it was clouding over him and looked apologetic.

"Sorry. I thought I saw something."

"Thought you saw something? Dex you took off, didn't even bother to check if I was behind you. You know I can't keep up with you!" My voice was shrill as the indignation I felt earlier came back. "What happened to all that shit you said about having my back, huh?"

He puffed air out of the corner of his mouth and threw his hands up in the air. "I'm sorry, OK? I thought you were able to follow. I didn't go that far but by the time I came back you were gone. Look, I'm really sorry."

I didn't like this at all. And I was starting to lose my trust in him. Sure, Mary's words were floating around in my head, which didn't help, but the fact was he had just promised to never leave my side and then went against his word only an hour later.

He came out of the trees and walked up to me. I stood my ground.

"What the hell were you chasing anyway?" I growled.

"It was a deer," he said, chagrined. He rubbed his chin and looked away. "I know, I'm an idiot. If it makes you feel any better, I got totally lost trying to get back to the campsite."

"That's because someone switched the markers," I said. "How did you know to find me here?"

"I heard your voice. What do you mean someone switched the markers?"

"I mean what it means. Someone switched the markers. If it wasn't for where you threw the cigarette package, I wouldn't have noticed."

"So that's where that went," he mused. "I was trying to do a Hansel and Gretel trail."

I looked up at the sky and the waving tree tops treetops. The night was coming in fast.

"We'll get going," he said, taking my arm. I flinched a bit. "What, you hate me now?"

I didn't hate him. I was just annoyed. I felt like he totally interrupted my time with Mary, as silly as that sounds. And I wanted to talk about it with him but knew he probably wouldn't believe me anyway.

I shrugged him off and began the slog up the coast, back to the campsite. We didn't say much to each other, except near the end.

"Who were you talking to on the beach?" he asked hesitantly. I could tell he had wanted to ask me the entire journey. I gave him a quick look. He seemed more curious than concerned. Still, I didn't want to give him any reason to worry.

"I was talking to someone?" I repeated casually.

"Yeah. But I didn't see anyone else. I was watching you for a couple of minutes."

"Watching me? That's creepy."

"No, you're creepy."

I stopped in my tracks and raised my brow incredulously. "I beg your pardon?"

He stopped too and started fishing around for his gum, avoiding my eyes. "Sorry."

I narrowed my eyes at him, daring for him to meet them. He didn't. He popped the Nicorette in his mouth, three pieces at a time, and slowly chewed them, keeping his eyes on the space above my head.

I let out an angry sigh, not wanting to deal with him or what he thought of me. We got back on our way, easing into the campsite just as the clouds turned black and the light of day was gone.

CHAPTER FOURTEEN

Dinner was another lazy mess of a meal. Dex threw some of the bacon he had made earlier into some penne pasta and called it a day. That was fine with me. I should have been absolutely starving from the day's events, not to mention the constant battering from the weather but by the time the dish was in front of me, I could barely bring myself to eat it.

He also made some coffee to keep ourselves us warm; of course, we mixed the coffee with Jack Daniels and creamer. Sounds disgusting but it took the edge off while sharpening my mind at the same time.

We sat in relative silence, one more uncomfortable than usual. Dex flipped through the books about the island, though I could see from his ADD eyes that he wasn't really absorbing anything in. His mind was elsewhere.

So was mine. It was Mary I kept thinking about. And why not? Whether Dex saw me talking to myself or not, the fact was Mary had been there. I had felt her. I could hear her voice in my head. The details of her skin. The cracks in her one lens.

If Mary and John had a child together, why did John tie her up in the woods? Sure, I could understand the scandal. But so would Mary. Why would John do something like that to the mother of his child? Then again, Mary had called him her "friend." Not her boyfriend or husband or partner. There was so much more to this that I needed to know.

Especially if John and this San person were here on the island. If John could switch markers around, couldn't he harm me or Dex? If he was as solid as Mary and really meant to keep us here, what could we do to stop him? He could be watching us right now, hidden in the shadows of the trees, away from the light of our lantern.

A shiver violently rocked my body at the thought.

"What's wrong?" Dex asked quietly. He had put the book down and was looking at me intently.

"Can't seem to get warm," I mumbled, pulling my jacket in tighter around me. I had changed two times already and it just seemed to be a revolving closet of dampness.

"No. What's really wrong?" he asked, his tone serious. "You look scared to death."

Did I? I shrugged, trying to play it off. "That's nothing new."

"What aren't you telling me?"

"What aren't you telling *me*?" I turned it around.

He leaned forward across the table and clasped his hands, fire burned somewhere behind his pupils. "What do you want to know?"

I pursed my lips and thought about it. What did I want to know? How did I explain a feeling?

"I want to know what you're thinking about me. I feel like you're making all these assumptions about me in your head. It's like you're afraid to talk me about them."

"I feel the same way."

I gave him a look. "Come on."

He leaned back and took a straight shot of Jack Daniels out of the bottle. "Maybe we should play truth or dare again."

"Maybe you just give me the truth. You saw me talking to myself on the beach and now you think I'm nuts, is that it?"

"That's part of it. Also the fact that you rushed into the ocean this morning to save a little girl who wasn't there."

"Fine then. I'm nuts. That should be the least of your concerns."

He squinted at me, thinking. "I care about you. I care about you an awful lot."

His voice was gentle and sincere. His words made my heart thump, made a rush of pins and needles appear at my finger tips.

He reached out and grabbed my hand. I watched him, wide eyed.

"And because I care about you, I care about you. I don't… like I said earlier, I'm worried about what this island is doing to you."

"It's not about me. It's about you too. There are people here, sabotaging us, right?"

"Flipping markers, slashing the Zodiac?"

"Sure."

"You don't believe that. You know something that I don't and it's driving me crazy." He squeezed my hand hard, till I felt the blood run out.

"Ow," I squeaked and tried to take my hand away from his. He held on and leaned even further forward, his head blocking the light of the lantern.

"What are you hiding from me?" he whispered, his dark eyes roaming all over my face in crazed search for answers. "Who were you talking to? What did you see?"

I wanted to tell him. I wanted to let him know about Mary and what she said but I was too afraid. I couldn't let him in. I felt like it was my secret and one he wouldn't understand even if he let himself believe it. I don't know why I was seeing these things and he wasn't, but without him seeing Mary and Madeleine himself, I just couldn't trust what he was going to do with the information.

"Please, just tell me what you're thinking, Perry. What is going on in that head of yours?" He reached over and tenderly caressed my head with his other hand. It felt nice. But it wasn't nice enough. Funny how things had changed. It was only a month or two ago that I had met Dex for the first time and had asked him the exact same things about himself.

My eyes felt dead. I gave him the corresponding look.

"I'm cold. I think I'm turning in." I yanked my hand out from his and started to get up.

He actually looked hurt. Hurt and frightened. It only last lasted a second but it was enough for me to see. A twinge of guilt flashed on my conscience but I brushed it aside. He was a big boy. Time for him to wonder about some things for a change.

"Perry," he called after me as I rounded the table. "We are leaving first thing in the morning."

Good luck with that, I thought, and got in the tent.

I didn't bother brushing my teeth or taking off my makeup. I just wanted to go straight into the bed and put the day behind me. I quickly changed into my pajamas, which were, thankfully, still quite dry, and attempted to get in my sleeping bag.

It was wet. Soaked through with dampness.

"Ugh," I cried out. I had spread it out hoping it would have dried but I guess being put in the sleeping bag earlier when I was soaking wet was too much for it.

Dex poked his head in the tent, bringing the lantern inside with him.

"What's wrong?"

"The sleeping bag is soaked." I felt deflated. Now what? Was I going to sleep on the picnic table?

"Get in my sleeping bag," he said, coming in and zipping the tent shut behind him.

"Where are you going to sleep then?"

"In my sleeping bag?" he asked, putting the lantern down and taking off his jacket. "It's big enough for two."

Amazingly, the idea of sharing a sleeping bag with Dex sounded like a terrible idea. There was a weird distance between us that I wanted to keep. I didn't want to be up close and personal with him. I didn't want to cave in.

He started to take off his pants. I wasn't sure what to do. I looked away.

"Oh geez, kiddo. When did you become such a prude?" he joked. I looked back at him. He was already in his pajama pants and slipping a shirt over his head. "We'll be warmer this way anyway. I think it's going to get really cold tonight and you've had a rough day."

I nodded absently and made my way into his sleeping bag. Once I was all settled in, he crawled over, grinning.

"What's so funny?" I asked, already feeling the shivers from the cold. He was right about that at least.

"You're funny," he said coming in beside me. The sleeping bag was barely big enough for two. We definitely couldn't both lie on our backs beside each other. So he climbed on top of me, propped up on his elbows on either side of my shoulders.

I thought I was going to die from awkwardness. He was literally on top of me, holding the sides of my face in his hands, grinning at me with that stretched joker smile of his, only inches away from my face. He smelled like minty gum and smoke.

"Relax," he whispered. "You're as stiff as a board."

No, I thought, *you're as stiff as a board*. Which was true, I could feel that against my legs. I almost laughed at the thought. It was enough for a smile to creep on my lips.

"There you go," he said lazily. He brought his face closer to mine. "Getting warmer?"

"Don't you think this is a little inappropriate?" I asked, my words coming out like poured concrete.

He raised his brow, lowered his voice, "Would you rather be in a wet sleeping bag? Because you can trade inappropriateness for that."

"You are such a tease," I whispered, wishing he would stop looking at me like he was, all languidly, like a sun–soaked lizard or a playful cat.

"Takes one to know one," he shot back.

"That's mature."

His smile started to fade. I don't think it was over what I said. His expression became more serious. He brushed the hair off of my forehead with his hand, slowly bringing it across, grazing my skin. I wondered if he could feel my heart against his. It was pounding away like a marching band.

I had to stay strong. I didn't know what his game was, but I couldn't let myself give into it.

"Good night, Dex," I said, sounding more throatily than I had hoped.

He kept staring at me in that strange way. Determined yet seductive. Confused and concerned. Then he said, "Good night, Perry" and rolled off of me. We both had to sleep in a spooning position. But with my back to him and his arm draped over my waist, his breath tickling the nape of my neck, this was fine with me.

~~

I first woke up to my body being shook from behind and then by this horrible wailing sound that was filling the dark tent like a psychotic banshee.

"What? What's going on?" I cried out, trying to get my bearings in the dark, hazy corners of consciousness.

Dex was the one shaking me, trying to get me to wake up. I rolled on my back and looked up at him in fear. The white of his eyes glowed brighter as I adjusted to my night vision.

The wail wasn't coming from inside the tent but from somewhere outside. It was unlike anything I had ever heard before. It was definitely from a person, a person not in pain but in maddening personal anguish.

"What the hell is that?" I asked, panicking.

"I don't know. It just started. I think it's the nut," he said, his voice low and creaky.

"The nut?"

"There was a nutty leper on the island. He went crazy. Apparently he would roam the forest screaming and laughing and crying."

"Jesus," I swore under my breath. This is just what we needed.

"We have to get this on film," he said as he unzipped the sleeping bag in a hurry and climbed out, fumbling across the tent for the Super 8.

"What? No!" I cried out, making a grab for him but missing. "You can't go out there."

"Yes, I can, I have to." He grabbed his shoes and was about to put them on.

"No!" I yelled, my voice scaring me. It scared Dex too because he put the shoes down and gave me an unbelieving look. "You can't go out there; there are things out there that want to hurt you!"

"What things, what are you talking about!?"

"Please Dex, just trust me."

He shook his head. "No way, I'm not missing this. You stay here."

He started to unzip the tent, the wailing continuing outside, echoing through the forest like a deranged siren. My insides were iced with fear. The corners of my vision started to go black. If he left me alone, I felt like I would die. If he left, he would die. I was sure of it.

I reached out with my hand lurching further forward, coming out of the bag, latching on to his arm with all of my strength. I wanted to cry. I wanted to scream. The feelings that were coming up in me were overwhelming, overpowering. My heart was slowing, dropping in my chest, my lungs were tensing, the air was leaving me, replaced with terror.

I couldn't let him go.

"Don't leave me!" I whimpered pathetically.

He stopped and fell a bit into my grasp. I pulled him even closer to me.

"I need you," I said, heartbeats in my words.

He lowered the camera. His eyes softened into dark puddles. The air inside the tent was changing, becoming charged like the atmosphere before a lightning storm. In the dizzying array of emotions and feelings that were swirling around in my stomach and coursing up and down the hairs on my body, I realized we were about to pass the point of no return. Something was going to happen.

"You need me?" he asked huskily, hesitating, lips twitching.

I tightened my grip and swallowed the fear in my throat. I nodded, slowly, deliberately, not taking my eyes off of his. "I need you."

A wash of concentrated passion came across his face and settled in the darkness between his eyes and brows. I'd seen the look before but never like this, never in this feverish vibrancy that seemed to sizzle out of him.

I pulled him closer, close enough to feel the heat and electricity of his chest and neck. I kept my grip tight and started to shake lightly, my body convulsing with hot, nervous spasms, my breath heavy and labored.

"I need you," I said again with utmost poignancy, making them the most important words I had ever said.

I thought I saw a smile at the edge of Dex's lips.

And then they were on mine, kissing me. Dex lunged forward and grabbed my face with his hands, holding it in a tight squeeze, his wet, warm lips frantically pursuing my mouth, tongue dancing with mine in a vibrant frenzy.

I was caught off guard but didn't waste any time in getting caught up. I pawed back at him as we both fell backward onto the sleeping bag. The days of wanting him, needing him, were over and he was in my hands. He was the soft skin I felt beneath his shirt as I gripped him around his waist and pulled him forward. He was the hot tongue on my neck, licking and sucking beneath my jawbone. He was the tingly rush I felt between my legs, the heat on my limbs, the intoxicating lust that swam around in my head and made all fears dull. I only felt pleasure. Even the wails of the night were unheard.

I pulled his shirt off over his head and threw it somewhere across the tent. I raked my nails over his chest and tattoo and brought his mouth up to meet mine. Our kisses weren't neat or sweet, they were messy and dripping and with a deluge of pent–up lust and buried emotions. His hands found the slice of bare skin between my pajama top and bottom and my nerves leaped with the contact of his fingers. With one hand he pulled down at my pants. A quick calculation of what underwear I was wearing flashed through my mind but I was distracted by his other hand, which was disappearing under my shirt.

He alternated between being gentle and rough on my breasts. It sent shivers through my body and caused my leaden head to fall back on the sleeping bag. It had been awhile since I was with a man; it was almost like I was experiencing this all for the first time. I decided to help him out by pulling my shirt off myself.

There was that slightly awkward pause when I discarded my top beside me and he had leaned back. There was no denying it or hiding it. I was pretty much naked beneath him and he was taking his sweet time taking it all in. Part of me wanted to squirm with insecurity and embarrassment, part of me wanted to enjoy it. All I could do was blush furiously.

He, on the other hand, wasn't blushing. He looked like a madman possessed by desire and sheer want. Watching him was a turn on. His eyes were heavy, his breath raspy, his lips in a relaxed leer. And he was looking at me. At all of me.

He came back down and started ravishing my neck, from the earlobe all the way to my collarbones, tickling, biting and blowing hits of hot steam from his lips. I moaned despite myself, feeling the hairs at the back my neck rise along with my chest that was coming up to meet his wet mouth.

While he made work of me, my hands flew down to his pants and tugged them down with my hands and then slid the rest off with my feet. If I was going to be in my underwear, he was too. I couldn't see what he was wearing in the darkness or between the flashes of skin, but it felt like a soft pair of boxer briefs, and from the feel I got at the front, it would have been a very complimentary sight indeed. I groped him firmly with my hand, which brought out a moan from both of us. I wanted him, every inch.

He had other plans. He scooted back, leaving my upper body exposed to the cold air that felt like a gentle caress against my sweaty skin, and brought his head down to my legs, spreading them wider with his hands. With one hand he teased the soft underside of my knee with his finger, and then bent his head down and did the same with a flicker of his tongue. It was enough to make my eyes roll back in my head. He took his tongue and let it wash up the inside of my thighs until it skirted the sides of my underwear. He teased the area for awhile until he decided he had enough and pushed it aside.

And then he got right into it, his tongue going at me, soft and hard, fast and slow. He moaned and panted, the vibrations causing my back to arch and my hands to grip the hair on the top of his head. I joined in, losing all self–consciousness, losing all sense of reality. I was vaguely aware that my sighs and cries were competing with the wails outside of the tent but neither one of us cared. It was just us in the tent, it was all we needed, all that mattered.

Just before I was about to be pushed over the edge, he slowed and then came up, his sweaty, heaving chest sticking against mine, the weight of his body sending a feeling of deliciousness over me. He brought his hands down and brought a few fingers inside, while holding back my hair with the other hand, tugging on it roughly. He kissed me, both of us breathing hard and trying to express more than we could before.

He looked at me with so much intensity it was unnerving. He pulled at my hair again and stroked me with his other hand, determined to see me give in to him. His eyes were as rapturously intrusive as his fingers were.

I wanted to give in. I wanted to let go. I was so close. What I wanted even more was to have him inside of me, filling me. I wanted him to feel like I was feeling. I reached down for him clumsily, but he pressed himself harder against my leg, as if he was playing hard to get.

He went back at my neck, obviously knowing a sweet spot when he saw one. Within seconds I was a blurry mess of his soft, slick hands, nibbling teeth and something like starlight. I closed my eyes, unable to stop it from happening.

My world was blown wide open. There was heat and sweat and cries and whimpers and spasms and shivers and thirst and a fuzziness that obliterated everything around me. I was floating far away, above our bodies, above the tent, above the island. I was above the clouds, above the earth, above the moon. I was safe. I was whole. I was a million things I had never felt before.

And when I came to, I was back in the tent, with Dex's steaming body half on top of me, his fingers trailing up my stomach and resting there. I rolled my head over towards his and tried to focus my eyes, tried to push through the drunkenness I felt. He was watching me intently with a quizzical, almost frightened expression on his face. I wanted nothing more than to pull him closer into him, to kiss him, to hold him. But he was keeping his distance.

Now that he had gotten me off, I felt reality returning to me in small batches. What the hell just happened? What did it mean?

I stared at him, trying to catch my breath, unable to come up with words. I reached up for his face and stroked his sideburn with my finger. I was this close to thanking him, as stupid as that would sound.

He closed his eyes at my touch. I wanted nothing more than to get him off right there. I tried to lead his face to mine but he pulled back and slowly shook his head.

"I'm sorry," he said. "I can't."

"You can't what?" I whispered.

His eyes flew open. They shined with something I hoped wasn't remorse.

"I don't want to hurt you. And I will," he admitted.

"Maybe I want to be hurt," I teased quietly.

"No. Not like this. I...care about you too much to do that to you. This whole thing with Jenn. I can't. I shouldn't have done this."

Oh great. He really was remorseful. I thought this was the best thing that ever happened to me and he completely regretted it.

He saw my face fall and quickly put his hand on my cheek, bringing his face in closer.

"This has nothing to do with you," he said, his eyes like lasers, imploring sincerity. "I take that back. I don't regret this. It's strange to be needed for once. I just wish things were different."

"You can make them different," I said, putting my hand behind his neck and pulling him into me until I was kissing him. He returned it slowly, sweetly. His kisses were made of diluted fire, his tongue so soft and warm against mine.

"I still need you," I murmured. He rested his forehead against mine and closed his eyes, his breathing irregular. Then his lips found mine again. It made my heart ache, made my soul ache. I loved him far too much. I needed him to know.

But he pulled back again and ran his finger along my mouth. I could see the frustration in his forehead, which hid the struggle he must have felt below.

"If things were different," he said slowly. "If I was a different person."

"If you were a different person, I wouldn't be...I wouldn't want you," I said, trying to get him to see.

"You shouldn't want me," he sighed. "And I shouldn't be pawing at you like this. Not when we are partners. Not when I have Jenn. And not now when I have a child."

He was fucking right. Damn Jenn. Damn this unborn child and their stupid loveless relationship. The thought tore me up inside, erasing the moments of ecstasy I had been feeling only minutes before. I wanted to cry. My emotions were too high to handle. I should have just let him run off into the woods.

"Hey," he whispered roughly, stroking my hair off of my face. "We're OK. You know I'd do anything for you. You mean…so much to me."

"But it's not enough," I choked out, avoiding his eyes in case the tears decided to come.

"Kiddo… Perry. We're going to be OK. You still have me in every other way. You…you really have me more than she does. I'm here and I'm going to be here for you. We're going to get through this. And tomorrow we're going to leave this crazy place. For good."

He had so much sincerity in his eyes that I had no choice but to believe him, or at least relent. I nodded, though I didn't know what any of it meant. He smiled sweetly and kissed me on the forehead, keeping his warm lips there for a beat or two.

Then he got up, quickly put on his pants and tossed my pajamas at me. I gave him a shy smile and covered up my indecency.

He climbed back into the sleeping bag and patted the spot beside him. "Come here, please."

I did as he said with my back to him. He held me tightly against him, our head sharing the pillow, his lips at my ear. "Things will be better tomorrow. You'll see."

I nodded.

"Good night, kiddo," he said. He kissed the back of my head. It was only then I noticed the mad wailing had stopped and the only thing I could hear was my heart thumping slowly. It hurt just a little bit.

CHAPTER FIFTEEN

The next morning was Groundhog Day redux. Same whistling wind, flapping tarps, rat–a–tat sprays of rain against the tent, a gloomy blue glow and the ever–present damp nip in the air. If I had woken up to "I Got You Babe" on an AM radio, then it really would have been complete.

I was alone in the sleeping bag. I kind of preferred it that way. It gave me a chance to breathe and go over what the hell had happened last night. It was all coming back to me in the hazy light of day. The sound of his moans. The feel of his lips on me, like he wanted to eat me alive. The image of his head between my legs. Had Dex seriously gone down on me? Did he really run his mouth all over my body? Dex? My Dex? It seemed like a fabrication of my mind. I mean, I saw ghosts, why couldn't I imagine a heated sexual experience with the man I was hung up on?

But then the feelings came back. Dex's reluctance to go any further. His so–called allegiance to Jenn and her baby. Their baby. Ugh, the whole thing made me feel sick. Strangely enough, I didn't feel any guilt for having been the other woman, even though I had been in Jenn's position before. I just felt bad for Dex.

Although, I really shouldn't have. After all, I didn't force him to do anything. He kissed me first.

I put my hand to my forehead and scrunched it up. What a mess. In some ways it was amazing and some others…wow. Did I really do that? Even the fact that he saw me completely naked, the fact that he gave me an orgasm…I couldn't have been more vulnerable than that.

And then to say he couldn't go on. What a load of crap. I wasn't complaining but...how was that fair at all? It's like he just wanted to be in control of everything, even down to sex. He knew how I felt about him. Sure, I'm the one who got off in the end, but he wanted that to happen. He got at me. He won. And I was unable to get at him.

Suddenly, I was less embarrassed and more ticked off. It was a more manageable and face–saving emotion anyway. It was like he used me in the most backward way possible. All he did was bring my emotions and feelings for him to an absolute boil, and then walk away clean, as if he didn't do anything wrong. Walk away back to his stupid hot girlfriend and love child.

OK. Now I was mad. I shoved on my clothes, which were still damp since I had officially run out of anything clean, and headed out into the storm.

Dex was nowhere around the tent or picnic table. A quick glance at the beach told me he wasn't there either. Unless he was really asking for it and decided to go on a walk somewhere, the only other place he could be was the shitter.

The weather was the exact same as it was yesterday. In fact, in some ways the fog seemed thicker and the waves were steeper, angrier. They seemed to call to me, to echo my mood, which was rapidly going sour. The damp clothing and the overall feeling of grossness didn't help either.

I had decided that I should probably make some coffee, since he hadn't seemed to do that either, when I felt a presence watching me. The goosebumps rose on my arms.

I looked up and got the crap scared out of me. It was Mary standing in the trees, observing me silently in her dark swath of a dress and her pale, weird face. How long had she been there for?

I was about to call out after her but she put her finger to her mouth to motion me to be quiet. Then she turned and walked off, her figure disappearing behind the trees.

I got up and went after her. I knew it wasn't right for me to leave the campsite without telling Dex first but I didn't really care what he thought at this point. Mary held the answers.

I followed her into the woods, towards the inner campsite and past the bog, to an area I hadn't been to yet. It was another clearing like the other campsite but had rows of stunted fruit trees and some foreign–looking bushes deliberately placed throughout. It looked like a long forgotten garden.

Mary headed across the soggy grass and walked along a narrow, pebbly path that cut through the center of some rustic rose bushes. I followed carefully, not wanting to get caught on the spiny thorns and overgrown brambles.

On the other side of the bushes was a patch of weeds and a low stone bench surrounded by small stacks of chopped wood. She sat down on the bench and clasped her hands in her lap. I paused, ripping my sleeve on a greedy branch and looked down at her. I wasn't sure whether it was safe to talk to her yet or not.

Finally she looked up at me in surprise, exclaiming, "Oh, you're here. How nice to have your company."

She wasn't being sarcastic. It's like she didn't realize I followed her. I gave her a small smile. "Where are we?"

"This is my rose garden in the orchard. I had brought the seeds with me from California. I thought the flowers would cheer the poor souls up."

"Did it?"

She shook her head, "It was a waste of money to come here. A waste of life."

"Money?" I repeated. I remembered the bit in the book that mentioned the rumors of how the Reverend paid the Canadian government to let him and Mary come here. "You paid them to let you come, why?"

"John did. He paid them so he could be alone with me. My mentor, my Reverend, he was more sweet on me than he was on the Lord. He brought me here to be alone, away from the church and everyone else. He knew I had no one else, that I would do whatever he said."

I know what I wanted to ask next but I wasn't sure how to say it. "Did you love John? Did you want to have a child?"

Mary started picking at her hands, peeling off dead skin in long scaly layers and flicking them on the grass below. I tried to hide my grimace.

"I loved John. Yes. But not in that...way. It was sinful. Perhaps I would have if I was given the chance. But I wasn't. He brought me here. He...had his way with me. And then I was with child. I think the child was all he wanted. I know I didn't want it."

Oh, geez, Mary was raped by the very person she trusted. I felt increasingly bad for the mousy woman with her twitchy eyes and sad complexion.

"I'm sorry," I said.

"That's kind of you to say that," she said. "But it doesn't change anything. I was stupid and naïve. He had me by the scruff of my neck and we both knew it. Then of course I found San. That was wrong too, I knew that. But what did it matter. I was already having a child out of wedlock. I was already on the wrong side of the Lord."

"Why are you telling me all of this?" I asked. I didn't mean to, it just sort of slipped out.

She took a quick glance at me before diverting her attention back to her hands. "I don't have many other people to talk to."

"What about your daughter?"

"She's three years old. And she's dead."

"So are you."

"She's dead to me. There is a difference. How could I love something like Maddy when all she did was bring me pain and bring me death?"

I took in a deep breath. I didn't like where the conversation was going.

"Yesterday you said that people here could harm me and Dex…"

"When was yesterday? Who is Dex?"

"Dex…the man I am with."

"Your husband?"

"No." I didn't want to embellish.

She shrugged. "Forgive me, I forget details. You trust this man?"

I nodded. She shook her head. "No you don't. He had his way with you, too."

I ignored that. She obviously had no idea what she was talking about. I took a step toward her. She eyed me up and down, her delicate frame tensing.

"Mary," I reasoned. "Mary, Dex and I seem to be in a bit of a predicament and we were hoping you could help us out."

"We? He doesn't know about me. You haven't told him."

"No, you're right. I haven't."

"This is because you are unable to trust him."

Who was she, a ghost shrink?

"If you tell him about me, it's only going to make him angry," she continued. "And when he gets angry, you'll be in a lot of trouble. More trouble than you are in now. Believe me."

"Why? Why would he be angry?"

"He doesn't like secrets. And he's jealous of you."

The second part didn't make any sense whatsoever. Why on earth would Dex be jealous of me?

I let it pass, for now. I crossed my arms and said, "Tell me more about this trouble we are in."

She shrugged again and started to hum a song to herself in a lilting tune.

"Mary?" I repeated.

She looked at me and smiled brightly. "Oh, you again. So glad you could join me."

Oh my God. She was a fucking nutter. Maybe she was the loon roaming the forest last night.

"I'm really grateful you are talking to me," she said in her singsongy voice. "No one ever stops and chats with me. I can't remember the last time someone acknowledged my existence. You must be a special person, Perry."

"I've heard that before," I scoffed.

"That's why he's jealous of you. Right now, he's out there, walking up the beach looking for you and cursing you."

"Dex?"

"You have something he wants. You also have something John wants and something San will want. I've seen them watching you. You can see them if you look harder."

The hairs on the back of my neck tickled unpleasantly.

"What does Dex want?"

"You'll have to ask him that."

I sighed, trying to compose myself. My brain felt sluggish and lazy. Too lazy to really understand what was going on.

"What do John and San want? Did they slash the Zodiac? Are there other people on the island?"

Mary started to sing to herself again.

"Mary!" I yelled, exasperated, and reached for her. I shook her bony shoulder, feeling the bones crack and crush underneath my hand. I gasped and recoiled in horror.

She looked down at her collapsed shoulder with all the breeziness in the world. "They won't be so easy to break. The sea, it does peculiar things to your bones."

I wanted to tell her that I was sorry but I couldn't form the words. I felt like vomiting.

"Look," I said, sucking the feeling down. "I know this is a strange situation and all. For me, anyway. I mean, I think I might actually be mental. Maybe you're not real at all. Maybe this whole place isn't real. But still, if you could somehow help me out in any way, help me get off this island, I'd really appreciate it."

She laughed. "I can't leave this island. What makes you think you can?"

"Because I'm not dead."

"You will be soon," she said simply, her little–girl voice gone. The frankness cut me to the core.

"Will you help me, Mary?" I tried. "Can you just…just tell John and this San person to leave us alone? To let us leave. We don't have anything to do with whatever this all is. As soon as the weather clears, we will be out of here. We will never come back."

"I can't. I hope I never see them again. I've been moving around this island for God knows how long, trying to stay one step ahead of them. Perhaps you need to borrow a lesson from me. You're much easier to catch than I am."

I felt breathless. "Where are we?"

"This is the Island of Death. This is purgatory. This place has a dark soul of its own. And it will drown you in its depths."

And at that Mary got to her feet, her bloody, pussing feet. "I have to keep moving. My advice for you is to do the same. Don't trust anyone. Anyone. He does not have your best interests in mind. No one does. Not even me. But I recommend you take my advice to be safe."

And then she was off and running. I looked behind me, expecting to see Dex, or God forbid, the Reverend, but there was no one there. And of course she was long gone.

I tried to shake some sense into my head as I carefully slipped past the rose bush's prying thorns, and down the orchard trees, dead and grey from the cold winter or a hundred years of neglect. I didn't know what to make of anything anymore. Reality seemed to be losing its grip on me, sliding off like the chains on an anchor. None of this was possible but I had to accept it as truth. If I didn't, it would mean I was going crazy. And which one of those scenarios was better? I'd either end up in a mental institute or in some brutal fate here, which could be worse.

I wondered if that's what Creepy Clown Lady had been talking about. She had said something about people coming to take me away. Take me in away in straightjackets? Take me away to the loony bin? I had been treating Dex like the enemy in this regard but maybe he had the total right to worry about me. He couldn't see the things I could. Not all of them anyway.

If only I could actually see Creepy Clown Lady here, then maybe I could get some real answers. It's funny how she brought an utmost sense of fear in the base of my being, yet if I saw her creeping around in the trees, in her ridiculous taffeta gown, I'd almost be comforted. It would be another tie to that world I knew before this place. This place was taking over day by day, hour by hour. Even Dex was becoming something else to me. Someone foreign.

I thought about that long and hard as I made my way through the brush back to the tent, hoping that maybe she would materialize if I thought about her long enough. She didn't.

Dex did though. The minute I stepped on to the path, he came booking it out of the campsite towards me.

"Where the fuck did you go!?" he yelled at me. He looked like hell. He almost had a full–on beard going, his eyes were bloodshot and the space under his eyes looked like half–moon plums.

"I went for a walk," I said and tried to walk past him.

He grabbed my arm sharply and yanked me towards him. His eyes were crazy. "Bullshit!"

I looked down at his rough grasp, trying to stifle my own anger and avoid a massive blowout.

"It's none of your business," I snapped. I knew that was going to set him off. I probably should have said something else.

He was taken aback, and for a moment, speechless.

"Where were you when I woke up?" I asked.

"In the bathroom," he said through gritted teeth.

"What's wrong with you?" I questioned.

He cocked his head and loosened his grip on me. He smiled sarcastically. "What's wrong with me? Shit, Perry. That's rich. You're the one who flips out whenever I leave you alone. What about all that bullshit about you needing me then? You don't think it's not the other way around?"

I snorted. "No! I don't. And maybe it was just bullshit anyway. You should know all about that, you're an expert at it."

"Now you're just being a bitch."

I glared at him. "We all have to be experts at something."

He rolled his eyes and took in a deep breath. He was trying to keep his temper in check. I could see it strained across his face.

He put his other hand on my shoulder and gave it a lighter, nicer squeeze. In my head I had the image and feel of Mary's bones shattering under my own grasp. The disgust showed up on my face.

Dex noticed my expression and looked correspondingly uneasy. "What's happening to us?"

"What happened? Well, we ended up getting stuck on this god damn island first of all. You know what this is? It's purgatory."

"Come on now–"

"I am serious. This place is death!"

"And that's why we're going to see if maybe we can get the Zodiac going. I have some ideas."

"What if it doesn't work? Why hasn't anyone come for us? I mean, we were supposed to be back yesterday. There's this storm. Why hasn't the Coast Guard shown up? Doesn't Zach want his boat back? Wouldn't he have reported us?" I started blathering on like a woman on a verge of a nervous breakdown.

Dex abruptly pulled away from me, suddenly apprehensive.

"What?" I asked.

"I…" he took in a deep breath again. I knew I was not going to like what I was about to hear. "I told Zach we were staying an extra couple of days. They won't expect us back until tomorrow."

I was floored. Stunned. Unable to process. Did not compute.

"Tomorrow?" I managed to say. "But…tomorrow is my birthday."

"I know it is. I figured since you don't have a job, it wouldn't matter if we stayed here a while longer. You know, to get some real good shots and–"

"Tomorrow is my birthday!" I shrieked, my arms flying out to my sides. "Why the fuck would you think I'd want to spend my birthday on an island with you!"

"I didn't think you'd care. I didn't think your family would notice."

There was no warning or premeditation over what happened next. I felt myself making a tight, hot fist, felt my arm winding up and felt the animosity powering my arm through.

I punched Dex right in the nose. Felt it give under my knuckles as my knuckles themselves erupted in a flurry of fiery pain.

Dex screamed and stumbled backward, grabbing his nose in agony, looking at me with wild animal eyes, half afraid, half livid. I grasped my throbbing hand and held onto it tightly, trying not to feel the pain. I had to admit, punching Dex felt better than I thought it would. If I broke my knuckles on his nose, it would have been totally worth it.

"You bitch!" he cried out, taking his hand away from his nose and looking at it. It was bleeding lightly, a tiny trickle coming out of his nostril and gathering in his moustache. "Jesus fucking Christ, I think you broke my nose!"

"Good," I challenged, still feeling the impulse to hit him again. An absent thought, the one that this island really was changing me, snaked across my brain and then faded into the thud and whir of my pounding heart and pulsing veins.

Dex shook his head. His eyes were watering, from the shock and impact, not because of any emotion, and his nose was looking more swollen by the moment. The teeniest tinge of guilt tugged at my heart strings. OK, I was glad I hit him but maybe he didn't quite deserve a broken nose.

We didn't know what else to say to each other. Whatever intimacy we exchanged last night was gone and buried. This was the new us: A sucker punch and a broken nose.

Before I could feel bad, I turned on my heel and walked off in the direction of the bathroom. I needed to clear my head and be alone. I was sure Dex would be busy plotting his revenge against me.

~~

I sat down on the rocks just north of the outhouse for at least an hour. Just stewing over what had happened, trying to make sense of everything. It was a futile exercise. Dex had left me alone, which I figured he would. I knew he was probably thinking of some way to "handle" me or calm me down. Some way to deal with me so I would learn like a good little girl, and do what he said. He always had me by the scruff of the neck, and I had always done everything he asked of me. He used me, frequently, like he did last night. All part of his sick little game. That's probably why he picked me in the beginning. He knew I would be easy to twist under his thumb.

I was hoping that by distancing myself from Dex and the campsite that Mary would show up again. I wanted to talk to her. She seemed like she understood what I was going through. She felt like an ally, another woman to take my side against the men. But she never came.

Finally I decided it was time to go elsewhere. Maybe if I went to the dead heart of the island, she would show up there. She did say she always had to keep moving.

I got up and made my way to the center. Only problem was having to walk on the path for a bit, just past the outhouse. I hoped Dex wasn't milling about. And if he was, I hoped he wasn't too angry. Mary had said something about there being trouble when he was enraged.

I almost made it to the trail without being seen, but Dex came out of the tent at the last minute and spotted me. He yelled, "Where are you going!?"

I glared at him, and spat out, "Don't you dare follow me." I kept going. To his credit, he seemed to stay at the tent. I couldn't feel or hear anything behind me.

The first ten minutes of the hike were fine. The trees were providing their shelter from the wind and cold and the rain only came in fat sporadic drops that fell from the canopy above. But the closer I got to the center, the darker it got. It was only early afternoon (I think, anyway; time seemed to be weird around here), but it was acting like it was near sunset.

I wondered how long I had been walking for when I felt a sharp pain at the back of my head and a cracking noise that filled the recesses of my brain and seemed to explode outward in stars and swirls.

I fell over and collapsed in a heap. The world went ink–black.

CHAPTER SIXTEEN

I came to with a throbbing, pounding head and in the most uncomfortable position. My legs were spread out in front of me, my back was propped up at an unnatural angle against a rugged, scratchy pine tree. My arms were pulled back behind the trunk and tied together. The rope went around my shoulders and waist a few times too. I couldn't move if I wanted to.

I didn't know where I was. There was nothing distinctive around me, just tall, overbearing trees with spindly limbs that swayed from the wind at the upper reaches of the canopy. The wind whistled around in here at an unrelenting pitch, the soundtrack of madness if I've ever heard one.

I couldn't tell where north was, what end of the island I was at or what time it was. It was much darker than it had been earlier. Not quite dusk, but then again, it was hard to tell in a forest that did its best to block out what meager light there was from the dense clouds above them.

What had happened? My head ached at the thought. I was hit on the back of the head by someone. Or something. And then tied alone to a tree in the woods.

It was the same thing the Reverend had done to Mary whenever the supply ships would come in. Could it have been Reverend John who dragged me out here and left me for who knows how long? Or was it Dex?

No, I thought wildly. It couldn't have been Dex. I know I thought he was plotting his revenge against me, but Dex's revenge would always be more spiteful or ironic. Even humorous. He wouldn't club me over the head and tie me to a tree. What would be the point of that?

Unless this was his way of "handling" me. I did bop him in the nose after all. And Mary did say he would be trouble for me. Maybe he thought this was the only way he could control me, to ensure I didn't go running around the island causing trouble for both of us.

I just didn't know. And sadly, I had all the time in the world to think about it. Part of me wanted to call out for him, for him to come running and save me. But then again, I didn't know what side he was on.

I decided to call out for Mary. Maybe she could find me and untie me.

I called out her name. It sounded weird in the forest. The words sounded hopeless and dull like there was no echo at all. I also felt silly, calling out the name of a dead woman, hoping she would come by and help me. Is this what I'd become?

I called again and again. I tried not to show any worry or panic in my voice but that was hard to hide near the end. My throat was getting raw and I was really starting to lose it. What if it was John Barrett? What was he planning to do to me? How the hell was I going to get out of this one?

A strange sound rang out from behind a patch of tall ferns a few yards in front of me. The ferns shook lightly, back and forth. There was something in them. And I was powerless to do anything about it.

The sound came again. It was weirdly familiar. But not in a good way.

It almost sounded like…the coo of a baby. The wet gurgles and nonsensical noises that blabbering infants make.

In the dark murk of the forest air and the shadowy gulfs between the rampant ferns and nearby trees, a baby's gurgle was probably one of the most disturbing things to hear. I hoped that whatever was shaking the ferns back and forth was a wayward bird or curious squirrel. Squirrels were smart, right? Maybe they'd be like a dolphin and save me.

I kept my eyes locked on the ferns. My body was poised and ready to run. If only I could.

The ferns shook again. The gurgle.

A baby appeared among the long green fronds, poking its head out like tiger cub and looking at me. I was right and for once I hated it. There was an actual fucking baby in front of me. I had to blink a few times to make sure I was seeing what I was seeing.

It crawled out of the ferns, slowly but with an unnatural sense of self–assurance. I didn't know kids enough to know how old it was however it was too young to walk but old enough to crawl with agility. Just not with *that* much agility.

It stopped a few feet away and cocked its head at me. I couldn't breathe. This wasn't about a lack of maternal instinct. This was the most terrifying thing I had ever seen in my life.

The baby was completely naked. Not even a diaper on her bottom. It had a schlock of ashy hair and wide blue eyes. The eyes looked at me with the curious intensity of a stranger. All my senses were wound up. I couldn't look away.

Under any other circumstances, I probably would have felt motherly towards it. Where was the mother? The poor thing, all alone. A neglected, helpless, defenseless child. But I knew this wasn't the case. In this place, nothing was innocent and the only thing helpless was me.

The baby sat back on its butt with an almost comical thunk and put its hands to its mouth. It seemed to smile at the dirt it was eating. It kept staring at me with those unnerving eyes, the eyes of someone older, knowing more than a baby ever should, thinking thoughts that I wouldn't dare touch.

It let out a laugh of some sort and patted the ground like it was the top of a bongo. It seemed to enjoy itself. It was almost playing. A happy baby. That's what every mother wants, right? Maybe it would just stay there. Maybe the mother would come by soon. Perhaps it was Madeleine at a younger age, and Mary was looking for her.

"Are you Maddy?" I managed to say ask, my voice sounding hollow.

The baby giggled a bit and smacked her knee with her hand. Maybe it really was Maddy. That thought brought a bit of calm to my nerves, helped settle the ill feeling I had at the pit of my stomach.

The baby cooed and smiled again, a big toothless, awestruck grin directed at me. She reached up to her face and wiped the area beside her eye.

A rectangular piece of her skin came away in her hands, a solid chunk that fell to the pine–needled floor, leaving a patch of a red, veiny wound on her face.

I was dumbfounded. Repulsed.

I wanted to vomit.

The baby picked up the piece of skin, oblivious to the gaping hole on her cheek, and threw the piece into the forest. Then she touched her forehead with the other hand.

Without much prodding by her tiny, chubby fingers, half of her forehead came loose like a dead, sticky shell and slid to her lap with a loud, messy splat. I could see fresh white bone beneath the bloody mess of her head.

I promptly threw up on myself. I heaved and heaved. The vomit lay on my chest and steamed up in the air. I couldn't help it. The terror and unbelievable disgust was overpowering me to the point of no control.

The baby laughed at the piece of her forehead and started playing with it like it was a Tonka truck. Without prompting from her, the rest of her face began to peel like layers in an onion. First it was the other half of the forehead. Then it was the area beneath the nose. That part just hung above her lip like a red, pulsating moustache. Finally the lips and jaw went, leaving behind a miniature skeletal jaw that gaped and jostled with her wet gurgles.

I closed my eyes tight, trying to keep the sickness down, trying to keep the sight out of my head. I didn't need to see any more. But for as long as my eyes were shut, my body tensed in my unrelenting prayer for this to be over with, the baby still cooed and laughed. I couldn't unhear that.

And it was just as scary with my eyes closed than with them open. I peeked and saw the baby back on all fours, crawling towards me. Her face was still half on, the other half was on the ground behind her. The skin on her arms and legs began to slide off of her with each jerky movement, coming off like raw, sliced butcher meat.

This can't be happening, I chanted to myself. *This can't be real. This can't be happening. This can't be real.*

I shut my eyes again and hoped that it was a dream. Maybe it was a dream. Maybe I was crazy. If I opened my eyes again, maybe it would be gone. The cooing and noises had stopped.

I counted up to ten.

One. Two. Three. Four. Five. Six. Seven. Eight.

Nine.

Ten.

I opened my eyes. The baby was right there, paused at my leg. Smiling at me. It gingerly touched my calf with its hand and then proceeded to climb up me like I was a jungle gym. Its rotting, putrid, oozing body coming up my leg, half skeleton face grinning, those wide, socket–rimmed eyes peering into mine with an indescribable intensity.

I screamed. I screamed and screamed and screamed until my scream was all I was, coming up through my throat and shooting to the trees. It hurt my own ears, it made my lungs burn, it made my body shake with an otherworldly terror, it made my throat bleed from the inside. I screamed and screamed and screamed inhuman sounds as this inhuman infant placed its bloody, dead baby hands on my arm, trying to ease itself up.

It was too much. My eyes rolled back in my head and everything started to fade away. I was so thankful. I could still feel the baby's grip on my arm though, the little feet that tried to get footing on my waist like I was a climbing wall. Death couldn't come soon enough for me.

"Perry!"

That was my name. It was coming from the outside. From somewhere.

I felt the tiny extremities let go and the weight of the child was gone.

I raised my head up in time to see the baby scampering off into the bushes on all fours, like it was an able–bodied gazelle. A human gazelle, after the lion's feast.

"Perry!"

The voice again. I looked up and saw a tall, foreboding man standing in front of me. He had on a long black jacket, white–collared shirt and black vest. His face was in shadows but I was able to make out a blonde beard.

"Who are you?" I asked. My head slumped to the side. I had no desire to keep it up anymore. My eyes closed.

"What the hell?"

Hands were shaking my shoulders. They weren't baby hands. They touched my face and pulled it in the opposite direction.

"Perry!" the voice was in my face now. I opened my eyes and saw Dex kneeling in front of me. Where did the other man go?

Dex looked at me, at the tree, at the vomit on my chest. I didn't care. I just wanted to sleep. I just wanted to go very far away, away from thoughts and images and feelings and sounds. I was so tired. My brain was done.

My head slumped again, chin tucked against my collarbone. Dex muttered some things I didn't understand and began untying my hands from behind my back. Once he was done, he lifted me up and with a groan, hoisted me over his shoulder. He was talking excitedly about something. Maybe it was more worry than excitement. Panic. It didn't matter. I didn't hear it. I went in and out of a delirious consciousness.

I think I passed right out for a while, because when I came too, I was looking down at the dark floor and Dex's butt. I felt raindrops falling on my back, felt his shoulder digging into my ribcage, his arms around the backs of my legs.

"What happened?" The words came out slowly in a thick soup.

Dex slowed and then stopped. "Can you walk? Because I can still carry you."

"Uhh, I think so," I groaned. He gently lowered me to the ground and grabbed my arms before I fell over.

My head felt like it did after a bottle of red wine. Too heavy to keep up on its own.

"We can talk later. I just want to get us back to the campsite now," he said. He didn't sound good. I raised my head and looked at him. It was almost nightfall but I could still make out dull shapes and shadows in shades of grey. He didn't look good either. His nose was purple and blue and twice the width as normal.

And that's when it all came back to me. This morning. Mary. The punch. Being hit in the head. Being tied to the tree. The baby. Oh God, the baby.

"Did you hit me on the head?" I asked uneasily.

He looked shocked. "What…why? Who hit you on the head?"

"I don't know, someone. You?"

He didn't know what to make of that. He looked around him. I did too. We were in the glade, the dead heart with the dead trees and the suffocating moss.

"How did you know where to find me?" I asked, trying to cover up the suspicion.

"I was looking for you and heard you screaming."

I narrowed my eyes at him. He ignored it.

"We have to get back, Perry," he said determinedly. "We can't do this here, now."

I didn't see why being at the campsite was any different, especially since he might be the person I should be afraid of. But the creepy, creaking noises of the dead limbs and the overgrown tangles, which that could hide many deformed and rotted babies, was overkill.

I nodded. He kept his hand firmly around my elbow and led me through the glade as quickly as he could. We were almost out of it, where the moss gave way to clean bark and the ferns turned into sprightly, berried salal bushes, when a hissing sound penetrated our eardrums.

The family of raccoons appeared suddenly. They headed down the path towards us, their figures dark, ominous lumps against the impending dusk.

We both stopped, statues in our tracks. The raccoons kept hissing and kept creeping forward. Though neither of us had a flashlight, their eyes glowed in the dark like luminescent ping pong balls.

I started to calculate how much space was between us and whether we could make a run for it around them when the two biggest raccoons lunged at Dex in a rabid manner, one leaping for his thigh, the other for his chest and face.

We both screamed in unison. Dex fell backward from the weight and shock. I could barely see it but from his cries and their slobbering, violent growls and the sounds of clothes tearing and liquids being expulsed, I knew their intent was to eat him alive.

I looked at the other raccoons. They were eyeing me, the glow in my direction. I had a second to react. I turned to the right and made a grab for the nearest tree. I yanked and pulled and twisted the biggest most accessible branch all while Dex was screaming and writhing on the ground, trying to fend them off.

I pulled until the bark cut my hands and until it gave way with a satisfying snap.

I brought it in front of me just in time to see two raccoons making a frantic scramble for me. I whacked it across both of their heads, sending them flying a few feet, landing with a thunk like furry, ravaged golf balls.

I bellowed something like a battle cry and ran towards Dex, holding the branch high above my head like some demented warrior and brought it down on the crazy beasts. They yelped in pain, as did Dex, since I was hitting him too, but they didn't let go. The sound of their teeth furiously making a meal out of his clothing, or him, caused the sickest, deepest panic within my heart.

I stepped back and took a proper swing as I had before, like a golf club, just another day on the driving range. It cracked against the jaw of the raccoon on Dex's leg and within seconds I brought it across the body of the one on his chest. I might have been yelling the whole time, I wasn't sure. It was just pure instinct.

The raccoons were still alive. I hadn't killed them. I'm sure I would have cared in some other life but right now it didn't mean anything to me. They were just as good as dead. But they did stagger off into the forest, all of them disappearing as fast as they had appeared.

I threw the branch to the ground and stood over Dex triumphantly, my chest heaving. He stirred, a good sign, and looked up at me.

"Can you make it?" I asked, holding out my hand for him.

He nodded and cried out as he took my hand and I pulled him up. I still felt oddly detached from him but I was glad to see he was still alive. Obviously, or I wouldn't have gone so literally "to bat" for him.

We hobbled back together to the campsite, one mentally and one physically crippled camper coming right up.

~~

Things back at camp weren't any better. The wind was gusting more than ever, the kind that knocked over our coffee cups and made the picnic table creak uneasily. The sound of the surf was monstrously loud and within seconds of our arrival, the tarp above the picnic table came loose and was whipped away into the forest, crashing against the trees.

We made a dive for the tent. I ushered Dex inside, snapped up the lantern that was knocked over by the door and quickly went around to all the tent pegs, pushing them deeper into the ground with my boot. I hoped the tent would hold, I could almost see it wriggling out of the ground, desperate to come free. I picked up the heaviest pebbles I could find and started piling them on top of the pegs for safe measure. The wind came at my back like a battering ram.

I had done what I could. I removed my puke–stained jacket and threw it on the picnic table, hoping that any future rain would clean it. It took five seconds before the wind picked it up and tossed it away. I leaped into the tent before the wind could take me too, zipping it up behind me.

I put the lantern on the ground and looked over at Dex. He was sitting on top of the sleeping bag, shirt off and pant leg rolled up to expose the fresh wounds. The first aid kit was out and he was fumbling with it awkwardly.

"Hold on, let me," I said, scooching over as the wind rattled the tent walls furiously. The noise was deafening.

I told him to lie down and try to relax. I looked down at the chest wound. It was on his left pec, a nasty looking slash that bled profusely. I looked away and focused on the shaking blue tent side. I took a deep breath and pushed down the waves of nausea that were still hovering around the surface of my stomach. I had dealt with a peeling leper baby, even though I dealt with it by passing out. I had to deal with this.

Dex was shivering, either due to shock or from being shirtless in the icy wind that managed to trail inside through the tent's pores. I had to act quickly. I poured out a whole bunch of antiseptic onto a clean cloth and pressed it against his chest. He winced from the sting.

"Easy there, kiddo" he said through gritted teeth, his eyes closed, head back.

"Tables turned, hey?" I asked. He had to do something very similar to me in Red Fox. Now it was my turn to play nurse. "Maybe we should avoid all animals from now on."

"Agreed," he whimpered as I dabbed the wound clean. I applied some sticky yellow iodine and clean gauze and pad, securing it with a medical bandage.

"Do you have any clean shirts?" I asked.

He nodded, still in pain. "One. In my pack. It's red."

I went over and found it and slipped it over his head, careful not to touch the wound. He sat up and looked down at his leg.

"What are the symptoms of rabies?" he asked in a dull voice.

"It would be hard to tell with you," I joked quietly and got to work on his leg. It wasn't as bad as the chest, which was a relief, but it still looked pretty dirty and nasty. "I'd be more worried about tetanus. You'll have to get a shot when we get back."

Our eyes met at that. The thought of getting back home seemed almost impossible at this point.

"How are we going to do that?" he said.

I shrugged helplessly and finished up. "Anything else I can do for you?"

"Jack and a cigarette."

I found the nearly empty bottle at the side of the tent and handed it to him while he brought out his cigarettes and tried to light one with his gold lighter. His fingers were shaking too much to catch a spark, so I took the lighter from him. I flicked it on and leaned over to light the cigarette that dangled from his twitching lips.

He kept his eyes on me while he sucked back and blew the smoke off to the side of him. Normally I would have objected to him smoking inside the tent but seeing the state he was in, I didn't care. I was finding it hard to care about anything, really.

I took a sip of Jack myself, enjoying the heat it produced in my throat, and lay down on the sleeping bag, staring up at the ceiling.

After he had a few drags and my view was started starting to cloud over with smoke, he cleared his throat and began tapping his fingers nervously.

"What is it?" I asked sleepily.

"I don't know where to begin," he answered.

It was all going to come out. I knew it. I didn't have the strength to keep things from him anymore. I didn't even know if I could trust him but it wouldn't make a difference. I knew he already thought I was nuts. I had nothing to lose.

"We need to get out of here," he said, skirting the issue.

"That's an understatement."

"I tried to use my phone while you were gone. I think a text to Zach went through."

I perked up and rolled my head over to look up at him. "And?"

"I didn't hear back. Now the phone is dead. Charger is on the boat."

Of course.

"So back to the plan," I muttered. "Which is nothing."

"I would have made a swim for it. But you kind of went missing."

"Oh, so it's my fault."

"Jesus Perry," he swore bitterly, flicking ash across the tent. He glared at me. "What is happening to you?"

"You tell me. Why was I tied up to a tree?"

"I don't know. You tell me."

"Well I don't fucking know! I told you that! I got hit in the back of the head. I don't know who did it. They hit me and tied me up to the tree. I thought it was you."

His shoulders slumped slightly and his eyes fell, looking soft in the flickering light of the lantern.

"Why would you think I would do that? How could you think that? You know I'd never hurt you in a million years," his voice wavered a bit.

"Just mentally," I mumbled.

"What?"

"Nevermind. So you didn't club me on the head."

"No I fucking did not." He shook his head to himself, looking pained and confused. His hands started to shake again, the dull glow of the cigarette tip buzzing like a spastic star. He closed his eyes.

After a moment of silence, he opened them and looked at me. "I know you hate me now after last night. Maybe you hate me for a lot of other reasons. That's OK. You can hate me all you want. But I don't hate you. I care about you. I'm on your side. We're in this together now. I need, I beg you, please be honest with me. Please just tell me what's been happening to you. You've been seeing ghosts. I know you have. You're hiding it from me. Please, Perry, just tell me."

As weirdly distant as I felt from him, as much as there was a current of distrust running beneath my skin, as much as I feared what he thought of me, there was still an ache in my heart that longed to keep on loving him. It was hard to pretend my chest didn't hurt seeing him there, twitching, smoking, out of the loop, and wounded.

And so I told him everything. Starting from seeing Mary running through the woods, all the way up to when he found me tied up to the tree. He didn't say anything the entire time and was watching me so intently that his hands started to shake again.

"That's the truth," I finished, out of breath from talking so much. It actually felt good to get it all out, even though I didn't know what he thought or what he was going to do with it. "And now you really think I'm crazy."

"You're not," he said quickly. "You didn't tie yourself up to a tree. I didn't do it. Someone else did it."

"Random people on the island?"

"Maybe. Does it matter?"

"Why do you have such a hard time believing they are ghosts? After all you've seen, Dex, why is this so hard for you? You're a damn ghost hunter!"

He laughed bitterly. "We may hunt them. But I haven't found them yet. Only you have."

"Then take my word for it!"

"I am! But I still think there is a more rational explanation."

"There are no rational explanations! You won't find them here. Nothing about what has happened to us is rational."

"That's because you aren't rational."

What? Once again, I was utterly flabbergasted by his choice of words and the sneakiness of his attacks on my personal character.

"OK Dex. I'm going to ask you now, what you think is going on. Tell me. I'd love to know what your mighty opinion is."

"It'll just make you mad," he said, putting the cigarette out on the carton, burning a hole through it. He took out another cigarette, lifted it up to his lips. I tried to formulate what I was going to say without blowing a gasket.

CLUNK.

A solid whacking sound from outside the tent. We eyed each other suspiciously.

"What is–" I started.

CLUNK. CLUNK. CLUNK.

I grabbed the lantern. Dex scooped up the Super 8 and a flashlight. I looked at the camera with disdain as I undid the tent.

"Are you seriously still bothering to film this now?"

He looked at me as if I had two heads. "Yeah. I am. Missed an opportunity last night."

Ouch. I pretended I didn't hear that and climbed out of the tent and into the face of a minor hurricane.

The sound was still audible despite the howling, whistling wind and groaning forest. The clunks continued sporadically, coming from the beach area. Out here it was a loud, hollow sound, like someone knocking slowly on a heavy wood door.

I raised the lantern in the direction of the beach, the wind pushing into my chest and flinging my hair wildly around my face. It was too dark to see, the light didn't reach that far. Dex walked past me, the camera rolling, the flashlight lighting his way. I had no choice but to follow.

We walked down the path and onto the beach. His flashlight searched the waves, an eerie beacon against the darkness. The waves were so large and angry that they would have been a crazy surfer's dream, had they not crashed unevenly against each other and wiped out on the shore.

"What is that?" I heard Dex yell above the noise.

I came down beside him and looked in the direction of his light. It was focused on the rocky outcrop. There was something dark bumping up against the rocks, pushed into them by each incoming swell, producing the clunking noise. I squinted, trying to recognize the shape but couldn't quite make it out.

A scraping noise to the right of us.

Dex whipped the flashlight in the direction just in time to illuminate a heavy block of wood that had been dumped on the shore by the waves, the scraping sound coming from the pebbles as they raked against the bottom.

We walked towards the object, slowly, uneasily.

It was at least seven feet long, solid wood, maybe a few feet high.

It was a coffin. A coffin washed up on shore.

Another scraping sound from in front of us. Dex brought the light over, the beam shaking in his hands. Another coffin plowed forward onto the beach, the stones spraying out towards us as the edge of the coffin caught the ground.

He brought his flashlight over the rest of the waves. I raised my lantern.

There were coffins everywhere we looked. At least eight, maybe ten coffins riding the waves, coming in towards us like the Grim Reaper's surfboard.

Dex aimed the camera around frantically, not knowing where to focus his shot, until a flicking sound was heard. He lowered the camera. Film had run out. But the coffins kept coming.

He turned around and looked at me. There were no words to describe what we were seeing. But as scared as I was that one of the coffins may start to slowly creak open and a waterlogged body might rise from the grave, it was a relief to know that Dex was seeing this too.

He walked over to me and grabbed my hand.

I was still annoyed but it wasn't worth it anymore. Not with coffins that came crashing to shore.

"What do we do?" I whispered. He shined the light on the nearest coffin, the dark, wet wood gleaming under the light.

"We open them," he said, wild–eyed. He let go of my hand and walked toward it. I was too terrified to move. I don't know why I asked. Of course Dex thought opening the freaking coffins was the best course of action.

He tried to push the lid of the first coffin off. With his hands placed down, his body straining, legs out, trying to move the object against the weak lantern glow, it was almost a comical sight, like an exaggerated cartoon.

He managed to dislodge it after a couple of well-placed kicks to the edge. The lid splintered into two and went clattering off onto the pebbles.

He paused after noticing what he'd done. We made eye contact. And then he peered over the edge into the coffin. My breath froze in my throat, pure anticipation.

"Empty," he sighed, putting his hand to his chest in relief, then wincing at the pain from the fresh wound there.

I took a step forward and held out my hand. I didn't want to spend the evening turning over all the lids on every coffin that came ashore during the night.

He glanced at it, then faced the storming surf and the rest of the floating graves that were making their way toward us. I know he wanted more than anything to go back to the tent and get more film and record the rest of the night away. The filmmaker in Dex was never too far.

But I couldn't handle it. We were done with this. It was time to put it to bed.

He looked back at my hand, saw my face, and relented. He reached out and I grasped his cold and clammy hand and pulled it along with me as we turned our backs to the coffins. We went to bed cold, wet and miserable, to the faint clunks and scrapes as the wayward coffins were delivered overnight by some unseen and menacing force.

CHAPTER SEVENTEEN

"Happy birthday, kiddo."

My eyes fluttered open. After a night of listening to the coffins, followed by restless tossing and turning due to over–exhaustion and nightmares, I must have fallen asleep during the wee hours of the morning. Now that it was brighter in the tent and Dex was gently shaking me awake, I wanted nothing more than to keep on sleeping.

But, as he said, happy birthday. I was now 23 years old. My birthday had totally slipped my mind last night.

I groaned and rolled over. Dex was kneeling in front of me with a goofy–looking grin on his bruised face. In one outstretched hand he held a paper plate with a Twinkie on top. There was a lit cigarette sticking out of it.

I burst out laughing. "That is the most ghetto birthday cake I have ever seen."

"Well, I didn't have cake and I didn't have a candle but I thought this might do. Just don't blow out the cigarette or you'll get ash everywhere."

He plucked the cigarette out of the Twinkie and stuck it in his mouth.

"Mmm, Twinkieliscious," he said with a smile. I sat up, still giggling, and he handed me the plate. I couldn't remember the last time I had a good laugh.

I picked up the Twinkie and took a bite. Dex blew the smoke away from my face.

"How is it?"

"It's a Twinkie," I told him. "Where did you get this, anyway?"

"I took a few from Zach when we left. I already had one this morning. Was saving it for a special occasion. Oh right, that reminds me."

He disappeared out of the tent for a second. It was then when I noticed that aside from being 23-years old now, something else was different. The wind had eased up to a steady but less–ravaging gale and the rain was nowhere to be found. It was a few degrees warmer as well, which wasn't saying much.

He came back inside and handed me a hot cup of coffee. "Spiked with the last bit of Jack D."

I took a sip and coughed. "This is sad. This is probably the most American birthday meal you could have."

He smiled at that and sat down in front of me, puffing away. He was in better spirits than he was yesterday, or even the day before. He still looked tired and washed out, though, and his nose where I had hit him was swollen and tinged with yellow and purple that was reaching up for his eye. His beard was getting pretty impressive. He was starting to resemble a ragged mountain man. Maybe he could have his own outdoor adventure show where he wrestled raccoons.

"How are you feeling? I'll need to change your bandages," I reminded him. He rolled up his pant leg to show me. The dressing was soaked through with blood. Ew.

"I'll live," he said nonchalantly, ignoring the seriousness of the wound. "You just eat your birthday breakfast first. How are you feeling? Do you feel any older?"

"Yes. I feel disgustingly older." Not only was my head still a bit achy from the hit yesterday, my limbs and bones throbbed mercilessly. On top of that, I felt absolutely gross, having not showered for days. Last night I even forgot to brush my teeth or wash my face. I guess in the grand scheme of things it didn't matter, but in the ugly light of morning things were always a bit different.

I finished the Twinkie, not knowing what it was going to do to my stomach. We had barely eaten anything yesterday.

"Oh," he spoke up, pointing at me. "I have something else for you."

He reached into his pants pocket and pulled out a purple Silly Band. It was in the shape of...well, actually it looked quite phallic.

"Um," I stammered, trying not to laugh. "Cock and balls?"

"What? No!" he cried out and did a double take. "It's an anchor."

I took it from him and slipped it on my wrist, "Sure it is, Dex. What were you trying to say with this, huh?"

"Well, I thought I was being poetic by saying I could be your anchor. But if you want to make this perverted, you know I'm game."

I chuckled at that but didn't forget what he meant by it. He could be my anchor. I hoped he would be. I didn't plan on taking the bracelet off, ever.

I wanted for us to stay in the tent and continue joking about things and pretend we were having fun on a camping trip and that everything was going to be OK. But from the way his brow furrowed as he put his cigarette out on top of his black combat boots, I knew things were going to get serious.

"Do we have a plan yet?" I asked quietly.

He nodded. "It's a long shot. But after we get me all cleaned up, I think I might be able to patch together the tear on one pontoon by sticking all the remaining bandages across it."

"How would that help? Isn't it deflated?"

"Not all the way. It would be enough to prevent some water from seeping inside. Then we lose the motor. Leave it on the beach. We take only what we need from here. Just one bag between the both of us. You might have to lose some clothes, I don't know. Go as light as possible. We're going to get wet. It's going to suck. But if we can use the Zodiac as a raft, we should be able to make it to be the boat. Use it like a boogie board and kick our way over. The wind has died. The swells aren't too high. There's only fog. I think we can make it."

I pondered over what he was saying. His voice was optimistic but it still sounded like an extremely desperate attempt. I guess things were getting desperate. I didn't want to spend another minute on this island and each second I was awake and past the frivolity of my birthday "festivities," the reality of what was going on was sinking in fast. Just because everything was fine at the moment didn't mean it would be fine in five minutes. Whatever tied me to the tree, whatever was out there and after us, they would come back.

"What about the coffins? They floated. Couldn't we carry one across the island and–"

"Coffins are gone," he said flatly.

"What?"

"Go and see for yourself," he nodded at the tent flap. "There isn't a trace of them. Vanished. Like we never saw them last night."

"But," I said cautiously, "you know we saw them, right?"

"I know." He sighed, scratching at his beard. "Really wish I could shave this thing right off."

"You could always do it *Crocodile Dundee* style with the hunting knife," I suggested lightly.

He smiled. For just a wonderful second. It slowly faded from his lips, turning sad like his eyes. I wanted to apologize to him for the way I had been acting but I couldn't find the nerve or the words. Maybe he was thinking the same thing. I wanted to crawl over to him and kiss him, scratchy beard and all, and have him make me feel like everything was going to be all right.

He picked up my backpack that was behind him and tossed it at me.

"I'll give you ten minutes. Get ready and fill half of it with only what you really need to bring. Nothing heavy if you can help it. I'll go clean myself up."

He took the first aid kit and exited the tent, leaving me to wonder which clothes and items I was going to have to leave behind. My boots were heavy, but I wasn't going to part with them. I'd be wearing them anyway. My beloved Chucks wouldn't make the cut but I had more pairs at home. Neither would my yellow peacoat, my pajamas or my two other pair of jeans. I slid into my cargos (they were somewhat expensive), put on my favorite Alice in Chains tank top, my hoodie and a light leather jacket. I put some of my makeup in the backpack, thankful for the waterproof plastic bag it was in, and my own underused point and shoot camera and I was good to go. It was a shame to leave everything else but the sacrifice would be worth it if we could get off the godforsaken hellhole of an island. Hell, Dex would have to leave his tent and camping equipment and that wasn't exactly cheap.

When I was done I brought the bag out of the tent and did a quick inspection of Dex's wounds to make sure he wasn't cheating himself.

"I much prefer it when you're the nurse," he said, wiggling one brow as I made him lift up his shirt. I did my best to ignore him. His self–bandaging job looked fine and he still had a lot of bandages and adhesive tape left over in the kit for the Zodiac repair job.

I quickly brushed my teeth and combed back my greasy, dirty hair into a tight bun and was good to go. The old Perry would have been wincing at being makeup free around a guy, but if this weekend taught me anything, it was that vanity was no longer ruling my life. And that raccoons were evil.

Dex filled the remainder of the backpack with the library books ("don't want Zach to deal with overdue fines") and the Super 8. I observed the campsite to make sure we weren't missing anything.

He was right about the coffins being gone without a trace. The curve of the beach looked unblemished except for a few new pieces of driftwood and washed–up clumps of kelp. The fog looked like it had settled in even closer, like it was giving the island a frothy hug, but the color was light and airy and the wind was down to manageable gusts. It really was the perfect window to try and to leave through. We might not have another chance.

"Ready to go?" he called out from behind me as I stared at the beach.

I turned and nodded. I had a funny feeling it wasn't going to work out quite as he hoped. It's almost as if we couldn't say goodbye to this place, despite how desperately we wanted to.

We walked as quickly as possible across the island. Despite the change in weather, the forest looked extra foreboding. The dead branches reached into the sky like skeleton arms, the shadows seemed to quiver out of the corner of my eye, and the moss looked less like vegetation and more like the green guts from an impaled monster. The last few days of rain had done a number on the ground, turning the trail into an obstacle course of limbs and mud that sucked at our feet. It got worse as we approached the glade.

At one point my foot went through the ground and the mud sucked me in all the way to my knee. Well, there went my expensive pants.

"Dex!" I cried out. I put my hands on the firmest part of the mud and tried to push myself off. "Little help?"

He stopped and came over, trying to pick up my hands while not getting stuck himself. He pulled at me but it only made my arms feel like they were going to pop out of the socket.

"Ow!' I whimpered.

He bent over, wrapped his arms around my leg and started to pull me up that way. If I wasn't starting to feel panicky, I probably would have laughed at the way we looked. He grunted and with a powerful tug, my leg came free with a huge suction sound. I almost fell face first into the mud but his arm shot out and brought me upright.

"I gotcha," he said. We looked down at my muddy leg with interest. I could feel the cold sludge seeping down into my socks. Ugh.

It was an uncomfortable, uneasy walk the rest of the way. Adding to the discomfort of mud squishing between my toes was the horrible feeling that the Mary Contrary might not even be there. If it was somehow still afloat after yesterday's storm, that would be a miracle indeed.

I watched Dex's face as we got close to the coast. Between nervous chewing and the intensity of his pupils, he was probably thinking it too. If the boat was gone, we were pretty much dead.

I pushed the thought out of my head and told myself I would deal with it when I had to deal with it. It kept the terror in check.

As soon as we reached the coastal path, Dex sprinted forward a few steps to the treeline and peeked through the branches.

"Hallelujah," he yelled.

I ran up and joined him. He put his hand on my back as I leaned over and peered through the spaces in the trees. The boat was there. It was a miracle.

We went back on the path and hurried along until we were on the beach and sprinting towards the Zodiac joyously. The Zodiac looked the same as we had left it, no further damage done, and though it seemed that the Mary Contrary's anchor was no longer working and the boat was wriggling back and forth with the waves, the rope's tether to the shore was still intact.

We looked at each other, both shining jubilant smiles.

"I think we can do this," Dex exclaimed.

"Me too." And I meant it. Maybe it was possible to say goodbye to this nightmare after all.

"We're going to make it after all, kiddo," he said as he reached forward and tipped up my chin. His fingers felt warm. I thought maybe he was going to say something else but we just stared at each other for a few beats, all smiles and unsaid words.

"OK, I'll get started on the Zodiac," he said, letting go of my chin and kneeling down to snap open the first aid kit. "Can you go check on the rope, making sure it's not about to give? If you can tighten it or do another loop around the tree, then do it. We don't want it floating away while we are making a go for it."

I told him I could, bringing my eyes up to the cliff top. It didn't seem like it would be that hard to get to and Dex had done it with ease the other day.

"You might want to wash off your leg first," he said, eyeing the mud. "You don't want to slip."

That was true. Even though I didn't want my calf and boots to be soaking wet, it was better than the mud.

I walked over to the water and tried to catch my muddied leg in the incoming tide. The waves on this side of the island were almost nonexistent compared to the east side, which made it seem even more likely that we were going to get our asses out of there.

I undid my boot and slipped it off. I reached over into the water to use it as a scooper. As I did so, I saw the reflection of a tall, menacing form standing over me from behind.

I gasped and spun around, almost losing my balance in the numbing surf. There was no one there. Dex was busy emptying out the kit and wasn't even paying attention to me.

I looked back at the water and cautiously dipped in my boot. I carefully sloshed the water around, making sure the mud was coming out before I splashed some of the water on my leg. It was as cold as anything. I hoped when we launched the Zodiac, we would reach the boat quickly because being in the water for more than five minutes meant certain hypothermia. It was amazing I didn't catch anything the other day and I was only in the water for a minute, tops.

I scooped up water once more and was about to re–douse myself when I saw the reflection again. My lungs seized in fright but I didn't turn around and I didn't make a noise. I slowly splashed the icy ocean on my calf while keeping my eyes focused on the reflection. Because of the waves, I couldn't see it clearly but it was the same person I had seen briefly in the forest. Blonde beard, large frame, black jacket and white shirt. He raised his arms behind me and had a piece of roped rope spun tightly between his hands.

I screamed and whirled around, expecting for the rope to come down around me, but just as it happened before, there was no one there. Now I had Dex's attention and he was looking at me quizzically.

"Cold water?" he asked, though from his tone I knew he thought it was more than that.

"Sure is," I squeaked out. I pulled myself away from the water and sat back on the pebbles, quickly jamming my cold boot back on. My foot was sufficiently frozen now but I just had to deal with it. I tied the laces up as fast as my cold fingers would allow and got back to my feet.

Dex was still staring at me.

"How's it coming?" I asked, trying to sound breezy.

He frowned. "It's coming. You better go check on the rope."

I smiled in response and started sprinting down the beach towards the cliff. I felt like we were running out of time and seeing that man's reflection in the water just added to that feeling.

The cliff wasn't as challenging as it looked from far away. It wasn't that steep and was a gradual climb, save for a few places where I had to haul myself up onto the rocks and boulders. It didn't take long for me to get to the top, where the yellow rope was clinging onto the arbutus tree for dear life, and the tree in turn was clinging on to the soil.

I looked down at the view, the spread of beach beneath me, Dex busy patching up the half–deflated Zodiac, the boat attached to the land only through a single twisting rope. The backdrop of the scene was the fathomless fog that seemed to lick at the sides of the boat from time to time.

I inspected the rope along its length and the way it was wrapped around the tree. Dex had done an amazing job the first time around because I couldn't see a single weak point or fraying anywhere. As long as the whole tree didn't give way, I think we were going to be OK.

"You've seen him."

I jumped, my heart almost coming out of my throat, and looked behind me. There was a strange, murky shimmer in the air and Mary stood between the view of Dex and the beach, hands on her hips, looking strangely authoritative despite her wispy figure.

It gave me the creeps. It always should have given me the creeps but now that we were so close to leaving, I wanted to forget about Mary and everything else. Yesterday, talking with her, the whole thing seemed like some weird sort of trance I was sucked into, just like my leg was inhaled by the mud. Now I felt more in control, mentally, and ready to move on. I didn't want to lose that again.

So I didn't say anything to her. I just went back to looking at the rope, hoping that by ignoring her she would disappear.

She didn't.

She took a step closer. "You're not going anywhere, Perry."

Just hearing her say my name was chilling, maybe even threatening. It didn't really sound like a threat but I had to look at her to make sure. Her one visible eye through the glasses seemed innocent enough.

"Dex and I are leaving soon," I said to her. "As soon as he is done patching up the Zodiac."

"That's what you think," said Mary.

"That's what I know," I replied on the defensive, feeling anger rising through me.

"You're starting to see John now. Soon your Dex will too."

"The tall guy with the blonde beard?"

"Yes. That is John. The lepers will be next. Then Dex will believe you but alas, it will be too late."

"How do you know all this?" I asked, not sure of not wanting to believe her myself.

She pursed her cracked lips and thought that over. "I know things. I've been here a long time. This is how it always works."

Always works? There were others like us? I didn't want to think about that; it was too much of a mindfuck.

"Well. I don't see anyone else here. Who is going to stop me, you?" I said, taking a step toward her. With her tiny, frail body, I knew I could hurt her easily. But then again, she was already dead so, really, what harm could I do?

Mary laughed; it was shrill and worrisome. "Not me. Dex will."

I cocked my head and looked over her shoulder at the beach. Dex had stopped what he was doing and was kneeling on the pebbles, head turned in my direction and watching me. I wondered if he could see Mary.

"How...why...why on earth would Dex stop me, stop us, from leaving?"

"He's going to think of a reason. He may not know the reason right now but it will come up, and you'll have to go back to the campsite."

I shook my head and then stopped, suddenly self-conscious that it might be a one-way show that Dex was witnessing from far away. I decided to play Devil's Advocate.

"All right then, Mary. Say we go back to the campsite. Then what?"

"You both will become sufficiently paranoid of each other. He's going to accuse you of being ill and you're going to accuse him of being ill. That's when John will appear. Maybe San too. When you are both alone and at your weakest. If not them, then the rest of the lepers."

"Why? What did we do to them?" My voice was becoming higher by the second.

"It's about responsibility, my dear. No one has ever claimed real responsibility for what happened here. I tried to fix it but look what happened. They turned on me. They killed me."

"I thought John killed you."

"This place killed me. There are wrongs that need to be righted and these souls won't rest until that is done. This place is too close to the black and white world. It's the responsibility of humankind. It's a shame it got passed on to both of us. It's a shame for two 23-year olds. We were so young."

That caught me off guard. How did she know it was my birthday? And what did she mean "were"? I swallowed hard and tried to concentrate on something else. The sopping wet sock inside my boot. The feel of the smooth arbutus tree bark that I had one hand against. The smell of rain, even though there was no rain.

"I'll be seeing you on the other side," she said with a quick smile that slid easily over her missing teeth. "One more time. I'll have something you'll want to know."

Not if I can help it, I thought.

She looked down at her dress, tugged at the skirt of it, straightening out her bodice and walked timidly into the trees that led up the rest of the cliff, as if she was strolling off to church. I had no urge to stop her. I did have the urge to get the hell out of there as quickly as possible.

With Dex still watching me (seriously, OK, I'm talking to myself, get over it and get back to work), I scrambled down the cliff as quickly and carefully as I could. As soon as my feet hit the stones on the beach, I was off and running toward Dex at full speed.

"How's it coming!? Let's go now, shall we!" I yelled, coming to a stop in front of him, pebbles skidding everywhere.

He blinked hard a few times. He had been in the middle of removing the engine from the back. The tear on the left pontoon had been patched up and a million bandage wrappers littered the bottom of the Zodiac.

His lips formed to make words but nothing came out.

"What? You need help?" I asked, and bent over in front of the engine, working the vice back and forth, loosening it. As I did so, I kept my head down and said, "Yeah, I was talking to Mary. Not myself. Though I can tell you still don't believe me."

With a few yanks, the engine came loose and Dex was there, helping me lift it off the back of the boat and onto the beach.

"That's fine. Thanks," he said monotonously. I eyed him quickly. I could see he was having a battle in his head of what to think and what to say. Obviously he didn't see Mary. It didn't matter. We could deal with my apparent psychosis later.

"Are you ready?" I straightened up and tried to get the urgency across.

"Yeah, I think so," he said. He lightly kicked the left pontoon. "Are you ready?"

"Fuck yes. Let's get the hell out of here."

Dex gave me a quick (but noticeably wary) smile. "I'll pull from the front if you push from the end."

I moved into position behind the Zodiac, my hand placed firmly on where the engine used to be. He picked up the backpack and put it on his shoulder.

"Are you sure the Super 8 will stay dry in there?" I asked. I wasn't sure if he had a special bag around it or if he was going to wear the backpack on his head so it didn't get wet.

"It should be OK, as long as the pontoon holds out," he said as he started to pull the front of the boat along. It moved awkwardly, like we were dragging a dead body. "The only thing I'm worried about is the film if…"

He trailed off and stopped pulling. He let go of the boat's front. His face was awash with panic. For a second I thought he saw something in the trees behind me but after a quick look, that wasn't it.

"What's wrong?" I asked slowly. A sickly feeling started to creep throughout my veins.

"We have to go back."

My eyes widened. No. No, no, no. This wasn't happening.

"We are not going anywhere," I said, half inhaling my words.

He looked terrified, to say the least, but he stood his ground. "No, we have to go back, Perry."

"We have to go back? What the fuck, this isn't an episode of *Lost*, Dex!"

"The film! I left the film cartridges in my other bag. I changed them over this morning. Without that film we don't have a show."

I let go of the Zodiac and stood up. Shocked. Enraged. "Screw the show!"

"Sorry, kiddo," he said, coming around the boat and heading off toward the trees. Toward the rest of the island and all the horrors I knew were hiding there.

I couldn't believe it. I really couldn't. It really was a nightmare I couldn't wake up from. I had to do something.

This time, instead of thinking about doing it, I did pick up a rock. I flung it at him. It hit him square in the back.

"OW!" he cried out and spun around like a cornered animal. "What the…did you just throw a fucking rock at me!?"

"I had to! Please, forget the film. We have to leave now. We have to leave right now!" My voice was reaching epic dog whistle proportions.

"You stay here," he said angrily, feeling for his back where I had hit him. "Please, just stay here and stay out of my way. I'll be back."

I shook my head violently and ran after him. He started running too, to get away from me, but I grabbed his arm roughly and pulled on him hard. I hoped he could see the pure panic in my eyes.

"Mary said this would happen, Mary said…," I stammered.

"Now you're just babbling," he admonished me, trying to swat away my arm like I was some sort of fly or pest.

I pulled on him harder. "Please Dex, please don't do this, we have to forget it, we have to leave now! Right now! Right now! Right now!" I started screaming it. His eyes went wide, unsure of what to do with me, but he quickly composed himself and put my face in his hands. He looked deep in my eyes.

"I'll be right back. You can't stop me. We need that film. We are fucked without it. Without it, this whole thing would be for nothing."

It didn't matter to me. Nothing else mattered except getting off the island alive. Oh, if only he had seen Mary, seen what I had seen, then he'd know.

I started crying. It was really the only thing I could do. He took his hands off and rolled his eyes.

"Not going to work. Now please let go, or I'm dragging you along with me," he threatened, the niceness gone from his eyes. He wasn't going to let up. I began to think about all the things I could do to get him to stay. I could pick up the nearest heavy rock and hit him over the head with it but then what? I couldn't paddle both of us to the boat.

"Are you shitting me? Are you seriously thinking about bashing me over the head?" he asked incredulously. He had followed my eyeline to a barnacle–covered stone that was just large enough to do the job.

I bit my lip.

"Unbelievable," he spat out. "You need to get a fucking hold of yourself."

And at that he flung his arms out of my hands with whip-like ferocity. "Now you can come with me or stay here. Your choice. But those are your only two choices."

He adjusted the backpack angrily, then turned on his heel and marched off into the woods. I looked at the Zodiac and Mary Contrary and prayed both of them would be there when we returned. *If* we returned.

CHAPTER EIGHTEEN

To Dex's credit, he did know that we were pushing our luck by going back for the God damn film cartridges. Considering the wound on his leg, we jogged all the way back to the campsite, not even stopping once to catch our breath. This time we were aware of the mud pits too, so we were able to sidestep them without getting bogged down.

All the running left my chest wheezing painfully and my stomach doing topsy-turvy things with the Twinkie. By the time we saw the stupid campsite, one more time, I had to head off to use the outhouse. I did not want to. I did not want to leave Dex's side. But some things can't be ignored and this was one of them.

"I'm going to use the bathroom," I told him as we came to the junction near the campsites.

"Seriously?"

"Yeah, seriously. Can you come and get me after you find the film?"

"Sure," he agreed, giving me an uneasy look. Maybe he was afraid I was going to sneak around and club him over the head.

He headed off to the tent and I ran as quickly as I could over to the outhouse. My stomach often gave me trouble. It figured that it would happen at a time like this.

On the way over, as I passed across the mossy, rocky outcrop that the outhouse stood on, I noticed a charred ring around some logs. I saw it before, but it never clicked. It had been a campfire at one point.

It got me thinking. Maybe if we took all the toilet paper out of the outhouse and stuffed it under the logs (turning it over so we got the dry side) and lit it, we could create a signal fire. That might cause some attention. Not that anyone would see it through the fog, but you never know. Dark, thick smoke might stand out against the gauzy fog and a nearby ship that plowed the international shipping lanes that were only two miles off shore, or a low–flying seaplane, might see it and investigate.

I sat down on the outhouse hole and looked at the stack of toilet paper beside it. There were enough rolls to do some sort of damage. It sounded pretty naïve, I know, but in case things didn't work out, if we could light it and then maybe the flare as well, there was at least a chance of rescue.

After I was done in the bathroom and felt a million times better (well, my insides did), I stepped out, my arms full of the toilet paper rolls. I began lifting up the pieces of burnt firewood and sticking the rolls in at various angles. The only problem was with how damp the logs were.

Then I remembered the fire pits they had up by the other campsites that were further inland. There was coal and stuff like that, I thought anyway. I got excited and started off for them.

I ran to our campsite first and saw Dex sorting frantically through the bags he had laid out on the picnic table.

"Did you find the damn thing?" I asked.

He glared at me and kept looking.

"Anyway," I continued. "I have an idea. I'm going to light a signal fire, just in case. There's some coal or kindling up at the other campsite. Can I have your lighter?"

He didn't say anything. I expected him to applaud me for my idea. But maybe he was still mad that I threw that rock at him. He did reach into his front pocket and pulled out his gold lighter. He thrust it into my hand and went back to searching.

I gave him a weird look and took off for the campsite, my boot still squishing with each step. I wanted to do this as fast as I could as each second away from Dex was an invitation to disaster.

I went straight to the fire pit/BBQ in the grassy campsite and pried the metal grill away from it. I dipped my hands into the coal but most of it was either wet or pure ash. I couldn't use any of it.

"Shit!" I swore out loud. Now what? Some great idea.

I felt sickly defeated. My shoulder slumped automatically and I turned around, ready to make my way back to Dex. Then I remembered where I had seen kindling before. There had been stacks of cut orchard trees by Mary's rose garden. Some of them were even underneath the stone bench she had been sitting on, which meant they had to be at least partly dry.

Still…it would mean I would have to go a bit further inland, and go to her garden. Her territory, which was even further away from Dex. I would just have to chance it. She always had to keep moving, there was a huge possibility that she wouldn't be there.

I headed off at a trot through the wild brush and within a couple of minutes I was running up along the graying orchard trees, all bent over like a row of forgotten old people. The wet grass brushed up against my legs and I nearly slid a few times before I reached the roses. I moved through the grabby bushes as carefully as I could and came out the other side.

She was already there.

Mary was sitting on the stone bench. Her hands were clasped on her lap as if she was praying. Praying with her eyes open, staring right at me. Was she praying for me to show up?

I stopped between the bushes and the bench, not wanting to go any closer to her. A quick glance to the bottom of the bench showed that there were indeed some logs underneath. The question was, would Mary let me get them? She seemed to be on my side. But then again, I didn't know who I could trust anymore.

She took her hands out of the prayer position and patted the space beside her. "I told you you'd see me again. Sit down, please."

"I'm good. I'm just here to get some logs."

"Ah. A signal fire. No ships would stop for us. Why would they stop for you?"

"Because it's not 1880 anymore," I pointed out. "This is a national park now. The world has moved on, Mary. People have taken responsibility."

"Your friend hasn't."

"For what?" I asked, throwing my hands up in the air. I refused to get dragged into another pointless, aggravating conversation with this loony ghost. I had had enough.

"He won't take responsibility for being a father. I didn't take responsibility for being a mother. Nothing good can come out of that."

"That's…none of my business," I managed to say.

"It will be. He won't let you leave. Did I not tell you?"

I chewed on my lip, trying to take in proper breaths through my nose. If I shoved Mary off the bench and grabbed the logs, could she do anything to stop me?

"He's hiding so much from you. Always will. He refuses to take responsibility for his actions and instead blames everything on you."

"Blames things on me!?" I was taking the bait. I couldn't help it.

"Why do you think he is so afraid to believe you? He thinks he'll go down that path again. Part of him is jealous because you are seeing things he is not, and part of him thinks if he did see the same things, that they'd put him away again."

"I'm sorry...what?" I asked, my heart stopping cold. Put him away...again? She was talking about Dex, right? Put him away where?

"He was in a mental institution for two years," Mary said, her eyes gleaming, obviously taking some sick pleasure in telling me that.

I went numb inside. I shook my head. "I don't think so..."

"It is true. You can ask him. It may push him over the edge again, though. To know that you know. One of his deepest, darkest secrets. Just one of them, but it's enough."

I couldn't breathe. My hands flew up to my hoodie and I frantically tried to loosen the cord at the top, feeling like it was choking me. "How...how do you possibly know this?"

"I told you, I just know. I don't know how. I've stopped asking the Lord. He's stopped listening. We are both accustomed to this by now." She rolled her eyes back, looking up to the heavens.

Abruptly, she brought her head back to me, eyes focused on me like a hawk. She removed her glasses and put them on the top of her hair. I could now see that she was slightly cross–eyed, at least the other eye was. It pulsated strangely.

"You need to dispose of him. Before he harms you."

"Dispose?"

"You need to kill him."

I laughed. It was nervous, raw and frightened. My mind was having too much trouble comprehending any of this. All I needed was the logs. That is why I was there. I needed to start a fire. Start a fire, get help, and go back to the Zodiac with Dex. Dex and his stupid film that he couldn't even find. How convenient. Maybe there was no film. Maybe he was going to try and to stop me from starting the fire...

"You know you can," she said, her tongue sneaking out of her mouth for a second like a curious snake. My lip curled in response.

"I can't kill Dex. I don't want to kill him. This is ridiculous. I mean...I love him," I said truthfully, realizing how absurd that string of sentences was.

A twinge of sympathy passed through Mary's face. "I know you do. San loved me. John did too, in his own way. Yet, they killed me. And Maddy. I loved her. You won't believe it, but I really did. But I still killed her."

"*You* did?"

"I had to. It was too much. I couldn't handle the responsibility. I had to look after the lepers. The real victims. I had to look after myself. And they loved her too much. I drowned her in the water, right over there." She pointed in the direction of the cove north of the outhouse. She did it so casually, I wasn't sure whether to believe her. But the strange menace behind her eyes...it said something else. Each time her left eye twitched, it was like the beep of a ticking time bomb.

"When San found out, he got the rest of them to come after me. I didn't think they could. The poor souls were walking around on rotted limbs. But they hunted me down like hounds through the forest. John caught me first. They put me in the coffin with Maddy's body and pushed me out to sea. That's where we rotted together, with rats in the coffin."

I was speechless. Paralyzed with fear, wrought with disbelief. How could she kill her own daughter? I felt a passing sense of guilt for my own misdoings in the past, but this wasn't the same at all. This wasn't an abortion, I told myself, this was a three–year–old helpless child. She drowned her own kid. She deserved the death she got.

Mary knew what I was thinking. The twitchy eye got worse. Her hands started to wring nervously against each other, the movements growing rougher and more vigorous with time. Her skin started to stretch underneath her fingers as they pressed and rubbed against each other until it was too much. Something had to give.

And it did. She pushed so hard her index finger came right off and fell to the ground like a discarded twig.

Not again, I thought absently, growing numb to the horror.

I had to get out of there.

I tried to move, to look away, but even without ropes holding me in place, it was hard to escape the sight. Her fingers all began to spring off their joints. The sound was like popping champagne bottles and they plopped to the ground in a small, bloody heap. Kindling made of body parts.

Her eyes watched me, blank and in another world. She was from another world. Her left eye began to pulse forward like something was hatching underneath the eyeball, pushing it out. With a wet, popping sound, her eyeball sprung out of the socket. It dangled by the slimy red cord. There was a movement in her skull. Almost like if she had fur lining her eye socket.

The head of a small rat poked out of her empty eye hole.

I screamed bloody murder and despite the extreme rigidness of terror, I somehow managed to move myself. I turned on a dime and made a mad, panicking dash back through the rose bushes.

I almost made it out. I was halfway through and the branches caught me. I screamed again and fell to the ground. I turned on my back and looked back at Mary. She was still sitting on the bench, motionless, the rat emerging from the eye socket and climbing up her face.

At my feet the rose branches made a move for me. They had come alive and were trying to wrap themselves around my legs and waist. Soon I couldn't see Mary at all; they had blocked the way. I tried to turn around and get up but it was impossible. The branches were coming in closer, shooting out for my arms like some thorny assaulter. I was stuck, feeling the hundreds of thorns enter my body from head to toe.

One of the branches snaked around my left wrist and dug itself into the underside. Blood spilled. I followed the red streams as they ran down into my sleeve and dripped onto the wet grass below, spots of scarlet against the dull blades.

I reached into my pocket with my one free hand and brought out the lighter I took from Dex. It was the only defense I had. I tried lighting it but in my panic I couldn't get a grip on the turn. I was going to die here. Death by a demonic rose bush. I couldn't believe it if I tried.

Then my thumb caught and the flame flew up with a flash. I held my thumb down as hard as I could and aimed the flame at the branches. The nearest branch made a go for that hand, wrapping around my wrist the same way, digging and slicing away in the same spot until it was leaking blood from there too. The cut was above the silly band and it began to pool against the purple edge.

I took the deepest breath I could and yanked that hand over to the other. The motion slashed up my wrist even more and I quickly was enveloped in the purest agony possible, the kind that made you throw up and see stars. But the flame was closer now to the other branch, and I was able to hold it there until the leaves began to curl and the branch began to singe and smoke.

Then the branch abruptly let go and my bloody hand was free. I switched the lighter over and proceeded to do the same to the other branch until that was burnt as well and it let me go. I kicked and kicked with my legs, trying not to look beyond the roses at Mary who was shimmering, and amazingly they let go as well and retreated quickly into the depths of the bushes, like frightened dogs.

I scampered to my feet, slipping here and there on the grass and took off out of the bushes and away from the orchard. I don't think I've ever run so fast. I didn't look back once.

CHAPTER NINETEEN

Dex was filming with the Super 8, spanning it across the empty campsite by the time I came staggering in. I was growing fainter with each step I took; the corners of my eyes were sprinkled by tiny spots, my legs were feeling like jelly and barely able to hold my body upright. I knew tears were streaming down my face in dirty streams and my communication was whittled down to animalistic sobs as I tried to link my hands to hold the profuse bleeding that spewed from my wrists.

Dex turned and brought the camera's focus on me. Then it fell out of his hands and clanked to his feet. His mouth dropped in abhorrence at the sight of me.

"Oh, Perry," he cried out softly, bringing his hands up to his face. I stumbled up to him and crashed against his chest. He grabbed me and held me up. I was shaking like a leaf and now he was too. I sobbed into him for a few minutes, knowing I was getting blood all over his front, unable to express a single thought or feeling except the seemingly limitless surge of dread that pushed through my every crevice.

He pushed me back a bit and eyed my wrists strangely. "What did you do?"

I shook my head. It wasn't me. I didn't do anything. But everything came out in sobs.

He quickly sat me down on the picnic table and disappeared into the tent. He came out with a t-shirt of his and began ripping it in half and then into long strips of cloth.

I continued to cry but managed to slow my heart rate and breathing down enough so that the dots in my vision started to fade, and the possibility of fainting grew less and less.

"Why did you do this?" he asked. His voice was soft but the accusation was menacing. How could he think I did this to myself? Couldn't he see what was happening?

"No," I managed to mumble out through spit. "It wasn't me. It was the bushes. The rose bushes."

He shook his head angrily. I sounded like a loon.

"Really!" I cried. "It was the bushes. It was Mary–"

"There is no Mary!" he screamed at me, a vein sticking out on his wrought forehead. His ferocity sucked the tears back into my face.

"Dex," I began, feeling the shakes coming over me again. Tremors of frustration, shivers of fear.

"You're crazy, you know that? You've lost it," he said, taking one of my forearms in his hand and wrapping the cloth around my wrist as tightly as possible.

Indignation sparked inside of my chest, threatening to come up in a furious pile of word vomit.

"I'm not crazy," I said as steadily as I could, looking him in the eye, begging for him to see the truth. "Mary is real. She was up by her rose garden, she–"

He raised his hand briefly. "I don't want to hear it anymore. What you're doing now, Perry, is you're hurting me as well as yourself. You're 23-years old now. You're too old to do this kind of shit anymore. You need to...you need to just stop. And think. I don't know if this is a cry for help or what the fuck, but whatever it is, you need to stop it right now and think about me. This isn't fair."

Now it was my time for my jaw to drop. "I swear. I didn't do this to myself," my voice choked with disbelief at what I was hearing.

He tightened the cloth around my wrist and fastened it with a bunch of tiny knots. "You need help, Perry. More help than I can give right now. You aren't well."

That did it. Word vomit was coming up.

"You," I sneered, "you're the one who needs help. You were in a fucking mental institution! When the fuck were you going to fill me in on that, huh?"

He looked like I had just struck him across the face with a plank of wood. His face lost all color, his eyes sank into his head like frightened shadows. I had hit his soft spot. Mary was right after all.

"How did you know that?" he breathed in a heavy spasm.

"I'd tell you but you'd just call me crazy. Funny how all this time you're the one I should be worried about. Acting all high and mighty while you're the fucking nutcase." I spat the words out at him, hoping they'd inflict the same damage that the roses had done to me.

His jaw clenched but he didn't say anything. I think he was speechless. Good. Because I wasn't done.

"Oh, poor Perry, let's look out for her; oh she must have been such a pain to her parents with all these shrinks and panic attacks and teenage hi–jinks. Poor little Perry, with her mental problems and her seeing things. Let's ignore Dex, the real problem here. Yeah, he makes light about having some fucking bipolar thing, but that's it, he takes pills here and there, it's no big deal. Sure he might be a bit of asshole and a fucking weirdo but it's not like he was ever institutionalized. Oh wait, yes he was. And no, of course he wasn't going to tell poor little Perry about it; how dare his partner think for one minute she might be his equal or even better than him!"

I was yelling now, on my feet and in his stony face, venom flying everywhere.

"What did it, huh? What made them put you away, huh? Oh, your ex–girlfriend dies in a drunk driving accident. Was that it? Was that enough, you felt like wallowing in your pain and feeling sorry for yourself, Declan Foray, so adept at being a martyr, a composer of nothing but self–pity. Or was it something else? Daddy issues maybe? Your daddy leaves you when you're young and you think the event is so special, so tragic and unique to you, never mind the fact that everyone has fucking family problem problems. And now, 32-years later you can't get over the lack of daddy love. Or maybe it's that your mom died. Is that what did it? Fuck, now that you have a baby on the way, they better start making room for you in your padded cell again!"

I had gone too far. I knew it. I was panting from the viciousness of my words, watching his face sink, his breath sucked in one sharp inhale.

First hurt appeared in his brow, like I had slapped him with it, but he nursed it for a split second before his eyes turned into the most vile orbs of pure hatred I had ever seen. He loathed me. He was pure viper. And so was I.

"Fuck. You," he said through clenched teeth.

He took the remaining cloth, rolled it up into an angry ball and threw it far into the forest. "You can look after your fucking self. I'm done."

He picked up the camera from the ground, shoved it into backpack, and strode off into the forest.

I was alone. My one wrist continued to bleed, though it was slowing down a bit. I struggled to catch my breath and watched the beads of blood roll back and forth, depending on what way I turned my arm. A lot of the blood was starting to clot in sticky black balls.

I don't know how long I stared at my wrist and my arm. It was much easier to think about that than it was to think about what had just happened. What I had just said. I had just ripped Dex's heart and pride out of his body and stomped on it. It felt shamefully good at the time, the way the words just flew out of me like volcanic fire, wanting nothing more than to burn him with them, burn him slowly, so he could feel all of it.

Now I just felt ashamed. I had hurt the man I loved in the most poignant way possible. There was no way we could recover from that. Even though he was partially guilty, I had a feeling that this wound was impossible to blot.

Don't forget, he thinks you're the crazy one, I thought to myself in an effort to cover up the remorse that was taking over. I didn't want to feel guilty about this. I needed to remember that he wasn't innocent. Even though he should know better, he would rather think I was crazy than think I could actually be seeing ghosts. That said a lot about how he felt about me.

I let out a long, shaky breath and tried to get my bearings. Regardless of what happened, I still needed to cover up my other wrist.

I walked unsteadily through the salal bushes to where the strips of shirt had fallen like oversized confetti. Even vegetation was scary now.

I picked up a strip and quickly wound it around my wrist as tight as I could without cutting off the circulation. I really was going to have start getting ghost hunters insurance or something like that.

If I was even going to be a ghost hunter after everything that had happened. I wouldn't be surprised if Dex decided he didn't want to work with me anymore. Hell, I didn't even know if by the time I showed up at the other beach, the boat would even be there. If he sailed away without me, it would be tantamount to homicide. But that look in his eyes had been murderous.

I'd just have to hope for the best. And I'd have to act on it soon. The longer I was here, alone, the more vulnerable I was.

I finished tying up the wound and threw the rest of the cloth back into the trees. As soon as I did so, a familiar scraping sound came from behind me.

I slowly turned around to see but there was nothing there except for the picnic table, our cooking gear and the tent.

The scraping sound again. Pebbles on the beach. The sound that the coffins had made the night before.

I didn't want to look, but I knew I had to. I gingerly crept to the edge of the tent and poked my head around the side of it.

The coffins had washed up on the beach again. Eight of them; old, decaying wood crates, sitting there in the surf like dead whales. It was still terrifying, even in the daylight.

They were all lined up in a row, perfectly placed, waiting for...

The lids of the coffins popped off simultaneously, clattering on the stones.

The Chinese lepers with their poor bulbous faces and missing hands and feet, lurched out of the coffins and, catching sight of my head peeking out beside the tent, started heading my way in jerky, awkward movements.

Just like zombies, I thought mildly. Then it sank in. Whatever the fuck they were, they were coming for me, and considering they were walking around on stumps, some even on all fours like disfigured hounds, they were coming fast. The reality hit me like a sledgehammer. This was real. This was it.

I had to run and I had to run fast.

I turned and sprinted up the path, turning into the woods. I moved my legs as fast as they would go. I didn't know if they could catch up to me and I didn't want to waste time looking behind me, so I just kept going, leaping over logs, sprinting across dead twigs, launching myself over the mud puddles. The only advantage I had was that I had walked across this stupid, godforsaken path so many times, it was like I knew it like the back of my hand, knew each turn and twist and obstacle that was waiting to trip me up.

Then again, this island was their home. My knowledge was nothing compared to theirs.

I could only hear the blood from my heart pounding at a techno rate in my head, my breath as it wheezed with each painful inhale, the sound of my boots hitting the ground, kicking up sticks and sending dirt flying.

I rounded a slight bend, knowing that the dead glade was coming up ahead and the real mud pits that were waiting to try and swallow me whole again. I was making good time, at least I thought I was, but I hadn't come across Dex yet. He must have run the whole way too. Smart boy.

I entered the glade seemingly at the speed of light, not looking around, just concentrating on the fast–approaching ground as it rushed at my feet. For some reason I had "More Human Than Human" as my mental soundtrack. It worked to keep me moving, to keep me going, to keep me from turning around seeing what was behind me. I was grateful and amazed at the adrenaline I had rushing through my muscles and that I was able to keep running without collapsing in a heap in the mud.

The mud was now upon me on either side, new puddles and depressions that weren't there earlier. I had to leap quickly across them, narrowly going in a few times. I kept my eyes at my feet and up ahead on the trail. There was a huge puddle in the way.

I leaped to the left side of it, nearly colliding with an ancient mossy stump. I pushed myself off of it in time to see Reverend John Barrett leap out from behind it, rope stretched across his hands.

Before I had time to scream or react, his slimy, foul–smelling hand was at my mouth and the rope was going around my arms. I kicked out with my legs, squirming violently, trying desperately to break free, but it was useless.

He held me above the ground, choking away my breath, and turned me around in time to see the pack of lepers slinking towards me with vengeful curiosity, their fingerless hands extended and reaching for me. They didn't stop coming.

CHAPTER TWENTY

My mind reeled awake like the slow wind of undeveloped film. Everything was black. Very black. A shade of coal darker than anything behind closed eyes. And then I realized my eyes weren't closed at all. They were open, squinting against a light mist that burned them like salt.

Where was I?

I couldn't bring my mind around fast enough to remember anything concrete. But there were thoughtless flashes. The reel in my head spun wildly, more shady images skittering past the spokes. There was a forest. I was running. I was hunted down by hounds. Or humans on four legs. Their grotesque, disfigured shapes flicked flickered in the woods like a pilot light. Then nothing.

My watery grave. The phrase floated around in my head for no reason.

I lay still. I was on my back, on top of something awkward and bony. I told my limbs to move but nothing happened. I concentrated, desperately finding some light my retinas could latch o to, to give some meaning to where I was and what was happening.

There were sounds, suddenly, like ear plugs were plucked out of my head. I heard muffled cries, like someone was yelling very far away and the sloshing sounds of water encompassing the space around me. The distinct feeling that I was floating was apparent and my inner ear rolled and swayed back and forth inside my heavy head.

All my senses were coming to me now. I could smell seawater and a putrid, decaying smell like rotted fruit and mold. I felt dampness at my back and bit by bit, the sensation that my hands were emerged in ice-cold water.

I moved my arms and this time they responded sluggishly. They had been in water, though the rest of me was dry. I moved them out to the sides and they struck hard barriers with a force I barely felt through my numbed nerves. The sound of the impact echoed around me. It told me I was in some sort of box or…or…

Panic began to sweep through me. I moved again, feeling like I was balanced precipitously on top of something very peculiar yet very familiar. Whatever it was, it was smaller than the length of my body and I noticed my legs dropped off below at an angle. I kicked them up. A spray of ice water fell up on top of my shins and my waterlogged boots met with the bottom of something.

I felt all around me, wildly placing my hands and feet on whichever surface they could reach. I was in a box after all. The space above my head was only about half a foot before a damp wooden ceiling cut me off from the rest of the world.

I tried to catch my breath but the fright inside my chest was overpowering it. I was trapped, trapped in a box. A mime's worst nightmare.

Not only that, but the box was filling with water. I could feel the liquid fingers crawling up my legs and arms and saturating my back.

I started writhing and fighting. I couldn't keep it together any longer. I was in a box and I was going to drown in here.

I started pounding my hands against the top, hoping to break through. They were tired and without much feeling and soon I felt a gush of warmth flowing from them. My blood. More blood. It seemed oozed freely from the wounds at my wrist. I didn't care. I had to get out. If I didn't I was certain I would die.

The water came faster now and it wasn't long before I was floating slightly above whatever had been below me. In seconds it would come over the tops of my pants. My pants, where my front pocket felt tighter than usual.

I quickly slipped my hand into my front pocket on a hunch. There was the lighter in my pocket from earlier.

I pulled it out and started to flicker flick it. My fingers were cold and clumsy and I almost dropped it but after a few awkward attempts, the flame came alive, the spark catching hold. I held it up and away from me. The weak, orange light illuminated the space around me.

I was right. I was in a box. It wasn't just a box though. No, it wasn't. I knew with sick, absolute certainty what it was.

My watery grave.

I swallowed hard, feeling my world jar wildly with the incoming waves. I was in a coffin, set adrift in the sea.

"Your ship has come in." A man's voice echoed inside my head.

Amidst all the commotion in my head, among all the confusion over what had happened – I knew where I was and why I was here. I wished I was alone. But I knew that wasn't true either. I knew that awkward, protruding, lumpy shape beneath me spared me of that luxury.

I felt my left hand slip into the water and gingerly feel felt for the bottom of the casket. Maybe the only way out was through. It met with the ragged wood bottom and felt around. I was careful to avoid what was directly beneath me.

The water was up to my chest now, heaving and wet. I was running out of time and fast.

I placed my hand on the bottom and tried to stabilize one part of me while I prepared to kick out with my legs, hoping that the splintery walls would give way.

Tiny, slimy fingers made their way around my submerged wrist.

I screamed but it escaped through my lips like a wordless gasp. The fingers tightened like a tiny clamp and held my wrist down, drowning it.

Something shot out from the water beside me and knocked the lighter out of my hands, enveloping the casket in darkness again. My arm was seized by another miniature grasp. It pulled it roughly down into the water.

I tried to move, to yell, to fight but the water's chill seized me like poison. I was being held down, the water was rising and almost to my face.

Something moved beneath my head. It came close to my submerged ear. Someone whispered into it.

The voice was distorted and muffled underwater. But it was unmistakable.

"Mother!" it cried out, cold, child lips brushing my earlobe.

I opened my mouth to scream again but only found water. I took it in instead of air and let the liquid saturate the life out of me.

"Mother" it said again and again until we were floating together and the world closed its eyes.

I felt my body losing consciousness. I had been captured just like Mary had, on my 23rd birthday, and set off to sea with the remains of Madeleine. I was going to drown with her. I was going to drown. Drown.

Drown.

Nothing.

A flash of celestial light.

A brightness coming from inside my head.

Nerves misfiring.

Water.

Peace.

"Breathe, baby, breathe."

I was cold. The light began to retreat and everything was black again. Multicolored planets twirled in my head.

"Please, baby. Don't leave me. Don't leave me."

A rush of air entered my lungs. It met at the bottom, creating a whirlpool in my chest. The water was rising.

It rushed out of me in one monstrous convulsion. I turned over and let the water flow out of my lungs and stomach and onto the space beside me. I gasped wildly for air. My eyes flew open to see black sky and waving tree tops.

I felt a hand at my face, gently resting on my cheek. After my lungs were clear enough and I felt icy air replacing them, I gingerly moved my head up and looked.

Dex was kneeling over me, soaking wet from head to toe, water dripping off of his hair. He was holding one of my hands very tightly, the other hand on my face. He was smiling painfully through tears, or maybe it was just salt water.

He stroked my head and brought my hand up to his chest, holding it there tightly.

"I thought I lost you," he croaked. "I thought I lost you."

It all came rushing back to me, the feelings of guilt flooding my head.

"I'm sorry," I said weakly. The words pushed me into a coughing fit.

"No," he said, cradling the back of my head with his hand and propping me up, helping me get it all out. "Don't say anything. I'm sorry. I am so sorry. I should have believed you."

I slowly eased myself up to a sitting position. We were on the beach, just a few feet from the waves that overturned the stones with each passing. We were both soaking wet. I knew the intense cold would set in at any minute but for now I was numb. It was pitch black outside, nighttime already.

"What happened?" I managed to say. I remembered John coming at me with the rope, the lepers and that was it.

He shook his head. "I was at the beach. Waiting for you. I was worried sick. I started heading back into the woods to get you when I heard this ripping sound. I saw...I saw a small woman. I thought she was a child at first. She had the hunting knife. She cut open the Zodiac."

"Mary," I whispered.

"Yes. It was her, all right. I knew it. And then suddenly...it all made sense. And I knew you were right. I didn't say anything to her, I didn't need to. The damage was done. I ran off into the woods to find you. I guess I tripped up on a log and knocked myself out. When I came to it was dark. I went to the campsite and saw...I saw the lepers. They were standing right here. Pushing the coffin out to sea. I don't know how, but I knew you were in it."

"What did you do?" Feeling was coming back into my hands and feet like pins and needles. Or maybe that was the fear.

"I just...ignored them. I ran out past them and into the water to get you. I almost couldn't; the lid was too strong and the water too deep. But something gave. And I saw you in there, blue, floating. And I...I really thought you were dead."

He closed his eyes and took in a deep breath.

"But I'm not dead. Dex, you saved my life," I wished I was strong enough to properly express how I was feeling. Weak words were not enough. "After everything I said to you–"

He put his finger to my lips and pressed it gently. His eyes searched mine earnestly. "No. You had every right. The thought of losing you…I've been a terrible partner and a terrible friend."

Now I wanted to shut him up. "You haven't been. I don't blame you for not believing me. Most people don't."

"But I, of all people in this world, should," he finished. He squeezed my hand again.

A snap was heard amongst the trees behind us. Suddenly I was filled with panic.

I sat up straighter and looked around me wildly. "The lepers, where did they go?"

"I don't know," he said grimly, eyeing the forest. "They were gone when I came out of the water."

"I don't think we have much time left," I sniffed. We were both soaking wet. If they didn't get us, the hypothermia would.

"I know. Can you walk?" he asked, getting to his feet and gently pulling me up.

I nodded, feeling numb and useless. The shivers were starting to build up. I could see them running through Dex too.

"What do we do? You said she slashed the Zodiac," I mumbled hopelessly.

He squeezed my hand again and said in the most confident voice he could muster, "There's still one more way off this place. Come on."

He led me away from the beach. It was painful to move but we kept going. We got to the turnoff to the trail across the island but he kept leading me towards the bog and other campsites.

"Where are we going?' I whispered, all too aware that things could be watching us from among the trees. The shadows all seemed to move.

He leaned to my ear and said roughly, "There is no way we are going down that path anymore. The mud has a mind of its own. There's a weak trail up by the other campsites. I don't know how far inland it goes, but at least there won't be anyone waiting there for us."

I nodded. An unmarked bush hike through the dark haunted island was just as disturbing as going through the middle, but he was right. Maybe they wouldn't expect it.

We walked as quickly as we could up the path and through the campsites. The ground here was like a small lake of grass, and covered the tops of our shoes. For once, being wet didn't matter. We were already soaked to the bone.

We were almost out of the grassy lawn, looking for a sign of a small trail out of there, when Dex cried out. I spun around and saw him fall to the ground with a splash. The earth was opening, the rocky grave markers were moving aside and graying, peeling arms were reaching out from the dark chasms below, holding onto Dex's leg and trying to pull him down.

I screamed but luckily my reaction time wasn't as numb as the rest of me. I grabbed Dex around the chest, not able to avoid his chest wound, and tried to yank him out. He was swearing, screaming, kicking out with his legs but unable to get free of them.

I let go, picked up one of the small boulders and bashed it against one of the ghostly arms, the sound of bones splintering reverberated through the air. Their grasp loosened for long enough for Dex to get to his feet.

He grabbed my arm and we scampered off into the forest, forgetting about the path; the only instinct was to run for our lives. I could hear the ground still being unearthed behind us, their maddening moans, the sloppy, thumping sound of their bodies flopping out of their graves and coming after us, wanting to exact their revenge, their justice for the horrible lives they were forced to live.

We ran in silence and as fast as we could while trying to avoid the tangles of bushes at our feet, darting in and out between the trees, ducking beneath the branches, our hands the only thing keeping us together in this blind marathon. Foot in front of foot, stride by stride, leap by leap, stumble by stumble, we kept going, ignoring the cramping in our legs, the tightness of the dark and the feeling that we were being chased by things too terrible to imagine.

Somehow, I don't know how, we reached the other side of the island, our feet flying out of the brush and landing on the dirt coastal path. We hurried down to the left and galloped along it. The urgency never left us.

Finally the trees opened up and we could see the beach, the deflated, defiled lump of a Zodiac and the sailboat swinging out at sea.

We piled down through the brush until we hit the stones. Dex ran straight for the Zodiac, picking up his backpack he had left there and swinging it on his back. He ran back up to me and began pulling me along with him in the direction of the cliff.

"Where are we going?" I yelled, unable to catch my breath for even a second.

"The rope!" he yelled back. We leaped over a piece of driftwood in unison. We heard the sound of the beach stones scattering from behind us. It was the lepers, they were still on our trail. I knew better than to look. I couldn't afford to lose it now.

We got to the start of the cliff and proceeded to climb up it as quickly as possible. My hands burned from the sharp edges and slicing barnacles but I pushed the pain out of my head and kept going. I eyed the rope at the top when I could, just to make sure it was still there, and understood what Dex's plan was.

We were going to slide down the rope and onto the boat. It was ridiculous but our only choice.

We were almost at the top, only a few more feet of scraggly ground and crusty boulders to go, when Dex stopped in his tracks. I pulled up beside him and followed his gaze.

Mary was standing at the arbutus tree, her dress blowing billowing out to the side of her like a black cape. She was as grotesque as the last time I saw her. The rat was gone from her face, but her eye was still missing and all her fingers were still gone except for the thumbs and ring fingers. In her disfigured hands she held the hunting knife in her hand, waving it front of the rope, taunting us with it.

"Mary," I yelled at her, raising my hands in surrender. "Please don't do this, Mary. You need to let us go. We don't belong here."

"I didn't belong here either," she said. Her voice sounded distant, robotic even, and buzzing with a metallic edge. "They want you to stay. Stay here or in the black and white world. You've seen it before. They'll take you there."

She nodded at the distance behind us. Dex and I turned and looked. The lepers were climbing up the cliff like reverse lemmings, with John marching behind them all, a mad herder.

We didn't have much time before they were upon us. I looked back at Mary. She had taken a step closer to the rope and was wiping the blade up and down the yellow length of it with a scaling sound. "I want you to stay too. We are both the same, you and I. We have no one else but ourselves."

"That's not true," Dex said angrily. "She has me. You're the one who has nothing."

"Not anymore!" she cried out and raised the knife. She brought it down with the first hack, the rope frayed, twirled, began to split.

Dex screamed. I had seconds to act. I remembered he had put the flare gun into his bag earlier. I could only hope it was still there, that she hadn't taken it along with the knife.

I reached into his open backpack, reached around wildly until my fingers found the shape. I grabbed the flare gun from out of it.

Mary raised the knife again.

I raised the gun, aimed it at Mary and pulled the trigger.

The gun exploded in my hands, the flare shooting out in a storm of red light, smoke, sparks and the most heart–stopping bang that shook my ear canals loose.

The flare shot straight below the rope, missing it only by a foot, and hit Mary square in the stomach. She erupted in a sizzling firework of guts and fire and fell backward off the cliff, landing on the rocks below.

I didn't have much time to think about what I just did. Dex and I exchanged a quick look. He was as surprised as I was.

"You *are* a good shot," he said. Then noticing the ghouls were only a few feet away, he grabbed my arm and we made a made a mad dash up the cliff for the tree.

Once at the crest, I got up and inspected the rope. I touched it gingerly. It didn't look good. It would probably snap under our weight. But it was our only way to live.

The lepers were now coming up beside the tree, their scabby arms reaching over the sides of the rocks and swiping at our ankles. Dex quickly whipped off his backpack and flung it over the rope, sliding it down to the very edge of the cliff. He squatted, facing the direction of the boat, holding on to the straps of the backpack and wrapping his hands around them a few times. He looked over his shoulder at me.

"Hold on to me as tight as you can. Don't look down. Don't let go."

I was too afraid to move. This was going to be the world's most terrifying zipline ever.

But I felt a random hand tug at the back of my cargo pants, and I knew it was zero hour. One more hesitation and I would be dead.

I wrapped my arms around one of the backpack straps, linked my hands across Dex's chest and squeezed him for dear life.

A growl and moan from behind me, someone's hot breath filled with death and decay, floated up the back of my neck. I pushed away with my legs and we were gone.

As we dropped away from the cliff, the backpack sliding forward with an abrasive, high–pitched sound, the rope caved down with our weight. We flew through the air at a startling speed. I couldn't watch, I just concentrated on holding on to Dex as hard as I could, even though I knew I was slipping inch by inch.

Snap.

Before I could process what the noise meant, the tension in the rope gave way and we were suspended in air. Then we were free falling.

I screamed as we both fell, not knowing where we would land.

I hit the water like a brick, the cold seizing my lungs and shaking me awake. I rose up and paddled furiously against the water, searching for Dex.

"Dex!" I screamed, the frigid saltwater splashing against my open mouth. I splashed frantically, trying to stay afloat, to see above the waves. I couldn't see him anywhere. The rope was gone. The lepers watched from the top of the cliff. The boat was free and slowly floating away from me, maybe a couple of yards away.

"Dex!" I yelled again, panic rising, my arms treading water as rapidly as they could. There was no light here in the water, only the vague reflection of the moon through the fog vapors. The water was black, the swells obscuring my vision every other second, and Dex was nowhere to be seen.

I panicked. What could I do? What if he drowned? What would I do?

The thought was too painful to handle. I felt everything start to shut down, including the will to keep living, to make a swim for the boat as the current and riptides led it out to the open oceans.

I screamed one last time. It sounded dull, as if no one was around to hear it.

Then a splash from behind me. I twirled around to see Dex pop his head out of the water.

"Got it!" he cried out through chattering teeth and held up the rope in his hands.

It was the greatest sight I'd ever seen.

He swam over to me and handed me the rope. "Can you do this?" he asked between splashes of waves. "We need to haul ourselves in. Pretend the boat is one big fish. OK?"

I nodded and together we both started to pull at the rope. There was no way we could pull the entire thing towards us, so we moved our hands along it, one on top of the other, steadily going up the length of the rope like we were rock climbing. It was tiring and the water was starting to slow my limbs down to an unfeeling slog. But eventually, we were getting closer to the boat.

I just couldn't go any further. My hands had lost all nerves and my heavy boots were weighing me down, too heavy to lift up and kick.

Dex scooped his arm around me. "Hold on to me, baby. We'll make it."

His face was alabaster, his lips a sick shade of blue. This reminded me of the end of *Titanic*. That was a fate I didn't want for myself.

With what little energy I had left, I wrapped my arms around his shoulders and he continued to pull us both. Where he got the strength to pull us both in, I didn't know.

I must have fallen asleep on his back. The next thing I knew, Dex was yelling at me, telling me to put my feet up on the ladder.

I looked up. I thought my head might roll off. It was that heavy.

We were at the back of the boat. I was face to face with the exhaust pipe. The ladder was down and right beside us in the water. Dex moved my legs over for me. I was supported, even though I couldn't feel my feet.

He took my hand into his shaking one and pressed it against the ladder rung.

"Hold on tight. Hold on as tight as you can, OK? Don't let go," he pleaded loudly. I nodded feebly. He climbed up the ladder, leaving me clinging on to the rung. I was so close to be being saved, and yet closer to letting go.

Dex knew that. Once he was on board, he leaned over and grabbed me by the elbow and began to pulled pull me up like a 130–pound marlin. I felt bad that I couldn't do anything to help him.

But somehow he managed. I was pulled up on deck. I lay on my back, unable to move.

"Stay with me," he said through the clank of his shivering teeth. "We're almost out of the woods."

I closed my eyes. I could hear him fiddling around. Then the roar of the engine, the boat shuddering under its surge. I heard Dex run across the deck and haul up the anchor from the front of the boat and then disappear below deck.

He came back up and I found myself being covered with a million blankets. He tapped me lightly on the cheek until I opened my eyes.

"Hey. You need to stay awake. I can't put you downstairs yet. It's warmer there but you might fall asleep and not wake up. OK? Stay with me."

I nodded slowly. He tucked the blankets around me. He was wet too, shivering uncontrollably. I wanted to tell him to cover himself up but I couldn't form the words.

He got behind the wheel, put the boat in the highest gear and motored it away. The more we picked up speed, the colder I got. The wind was brutal.

Occasionally Dex would check on me, shake my leg, to make sure I was still conscious.

Finally I felt him slow the boat down, heard him flick a switch and come out from behind the wheel. He picked me up, the blankets falling away, and took me downstairs.

The heat was going full blast and the lights were all on. In a dream–like state I noticed my iPhone lying on the table as he took me into the front bedroom. He had shut the door so the room was the warmest.

He lay me down on the bed, brought out another pile of linen and sleeping bags from the closet as well as a bunch of towels.

"I don't care if you think this is inappropriate," I heard him say through shivers. I turned my head and saw him stripping down to his boxer-briefs. His body was shiny and translucent from the cold, every inch covered in automatic convulsions. He came on top of the bed and started to pull my jacket and top off.

"What?" I mustered.

"Trust me," he said. He took off my boots and pants as quickly as he could until I was also just in my underwear. Then he lay down beside me and pulled all the blankets and towels over us. He pulled me right up to him and wrapped his arms and legs around me and held me tight. I was too sluggish to protest and I knew I wouldn't have anyway.

He held me until I started to feel again. At first it was the shivering, then the terrible never–ending cold. Then we both began to calm down. The heat between us was warming us over, trapped beneath the blankets in the warm room.

I was able to think more clearly. I was able to feel my body parts again. I was very aware of his bare skin on mine. I looked up at his face. He looked relaxed, relieved, but didn't loosen his grip around me. Our mouths were close. His breath smelt like saltwater.

"Who is driving the boat?" I whispered carefully.

"Autopilot," he said, looking into my eyes. "I'll go up and check on it in five minutes."

I closed my eyes and brought my face into his neck, burrowing it. He cupped his hand behind my head and held it there.

"We made it," he murmured.

I started to cry. It was all too much for me to take. It always would be. I didn't know how much I could keep going.

"I'm scared, Dex," I mumbled between sobs.

"I know."

"I don't…I can't live like this. Why do I have to see these things? Why do they come after me? What is it about me?"

"We are putting ourselves at risk by doing this…"

"No. It's always been like this. I know it has been. I feel like I can't tell what's a dream. What's real. I'm going crazy. I have to be. What if all the world is inside of my head?"

"It's not, Perry. It's not." He held me tighter.

"What if I really am alone?"

"Baby, you aren't alone. I'm here."

"I'm so scared. I don't want to see these things anymore. It makes me want to tear my brain out. I don't know what's real. How can I tell what's real anymore? What's real, Dex? Tell me what's real."

He put his hand on my face and looked at me with the most magnetic, impassioned spark in his dark eyes. "I'm real. This is real."

I closed my eyes in gratitude, my heart filling up, the warmth radiating out from there and soaking up my nerves. He kissed my forehead and pulled me back into him.

CHAPTER TWENTY-ONE

"Is your phone charged yet?" Dex asked me.

We were sitting in a late–night diner in the outskirts of Victoria. It was 2 a.m. and the place was empty except for an old man who nursed a cup of coffee at the counter.

We must have looked like quite the sight. We were both dressed in Zach's leftover sailing gear; the blue and red vinyl Helly Hansen suits were the only things left on the boat that were dry. It looked like we had come in from an epic, wild sailing race and in some ways, it was kind of true. Luckily, the jackets were so long on me that they covered up the crappy bandaging job we did on my wrists from Dex's car's first aid kit.

After our body temperatures returned to normal, Dex went back up top and steered the boat back into the marina. It didn't take long at all. It was amazing how close the island really was to civilization, yet when we were there, it was like another world altogether. A world made up of humanity's darkest misdoings and the most shameful nightmares of our souls.

As soon as we docked, I ran to the shore and literally kissed the ground. I was so overcome with so many different emotions, but the strongest one was just transcendent relief. We really had made it. We were back in amongst the living and we were alive ourselves.

We packed up our stuff as quickly as we could and brought it up to Dex's black Highlander, another sight I almost cried at. I hugged the car, so grateful to see something from our other life, something solid, real and familiar.

We had driven through the streets looking for some place to gather our strength before the morning came and we would have to explain to Zach what happened. The boat was fine despite everything, but Dex would probably have to replace the Zodiac, which wasn't going to be inexpensive. The money didn't seem like a big deal after everything we had gone through, but it was nothing to sneeze at either.

The other issue was that not only had Dex's iPhone drowned when he went to rescue me from the coffin, but we lost the backpack with the Super 8 camera to the depths of the sea. The only concrete footage we had, the only footage that was really spectacular and proved we weren't full of shit, was now resting at the bottom of the ocean, alongside the library books about the island. They were probably the only books in publication too. Maybe that's where they all belonged. Their watery grave.

Dex wasn't sure what to say to Jimmy about the loss. He was going to see what he could salvage from the other cameras before he brought them on the boat. There was the scene with the deer in the night, and a few other instances that might be compelling enough to make an episode out of them. We would have to wait and see. And of course the intro we shot, my red low-cut shirt, the setting sun over the beach. My goodness, that seemed like another lifetime.

I got up from my seat and looked at the iPhone, which was charging at the wall outlet beneath the counter across from us. It was powered and the texts from Ada and my family were coming in one after another. I just didn't have the energy to deal with them.

I sat back down and took a sip of my hot peppermint tea. "Give it a few minutes. Too many texts coming in."

"You should tell your parents you're alive," he said. "I have a feeling they've put an APB out for me."

"It's the facial hair, I'm telling ya." I smiled, even though his beard was taking away the rapist qualities of his moustache.

"I'm serious," he said and I could see he was. "They must be worried sick about you. Go call them now."

"It's 2 a.m."

"They aren't sleeping."

I sighed and unplugged the phone. It had enough juice for a quick call. I went into the women's washroom for privacy and dialed.

My dad answered right away.

There was a lot of yelling and crying and screaming and sobbing and lecturing. Not only from my dad, but from my mother and from Ada as well, who was also up and worried sick. I couldn't tell them the truth. Well, I could tell them the truth but I knew it was pointless. So I told them an abbreviated version of the truth. Zodiac deflated (mysteriously), phones had died, storm came in, yadda yadda.

I knew that once I arrived at the house tomorrow, I would get the same lecture, yelling, crying all over again, and I'd once more have to explain my whole story. But I would be home and that was the most important thing of all.

"By the way. Happy Birthday," my dad said before he hung up. "We love you."

"Thanks, Dad," I said, feeling teary. "I love you guys too."

I staggered out of the bathroom, a weight lifted from my shoulders, and handed the phone to Dex, pressing it into his hand.

"Now it's your turn. You have a family now. Call your baby mama and let her know you're dandy, capiche?"

He sucked on his lip, probably thinking of excuses why he shouldn't. But he nodded and got up. The responsibility must have started to sink in.

He left the diner at the front door and stood outside, lighting up a cigarette and putting the phone to his ear. I couldn't read his face from the fluorescent glare inside.

He was on the phone for only a few minutes. He puffed on the cigarette, the smoke rising around him and floating away into the night. He stared across the parking lot, transfixed by nothing in particular, thinking about who knows what. Then he stubbed out the cigarette and came back inside.

He hooked the iPhone back up to the charger and sat back down at his seat.

"I think I'm going to quit smoking," he said brightly.

I cocked my head at him. "OK. Well, good. What brought that on?"

He shrugged. "I don't know. I had started thinking about how I would have to change if I was going to be a dad. Smoking just didn't seem…appropriate."

"Fair enough," I said, my heart still lurching about at the mention of his impending fatherhood. I tried to hide the feeling but it was there whether I liked it or not.

"How is Jennifer?" I asked, trying to sound breezy.

"She's great, actually," he said taking a slurp of his coffee and grimacing. He waved over the waitress, pointing at his cup for another refill. "She's not pregnant."

"Uh…" It was the only word I could form in response to that bombshell.

"Yeah, she's not pregnant," he said quickly and with a smile as the waitress refilled his cup. She caught the tail end of that and was giving him an unimpressed look. He noticed, grinned at her and winked.

She shook her head and went back behind the counter to read her *Hello! Canada* magazine. Dex looked at me. "I'm telling you. Waitresses find me adorable."

I raised my eyebrow. "Let's go back to what you just said. Jennifer is not pregnant. Are you sure?"

"Well, I'm taking her word for it but she went to the doctor on over the weekend to get a blood test. It came back today as negative. She took two more pregnancy tests. They were all the same. I guess she got a false positive the other day."

It was sick to admit it but there was a wonderfully giddy feeling rising up inside of me. It made me feel ashamed. I watched him carefully. He seemed fine, but maybe I just wanted him to be fine. I certainly did not expect him to feel like I did.

"Are you OK with it?" I asked.

"Yeah. I'm fine with it."

"And is Jenn OK?"

He frowned. "I think so. Yeah, I think so. We're good."

"So..." *what does it mean now*, I thought. But I didn't dare ask it.

"So..." he mused.

He took a sip of his coffee. I took a sip of my tea. There was nothing left to say about it. I sat back in my chair. We both watched each other for a few beats. The quiet sounds of the diner filled my ears. This weekend had taken our relationship further than I ever thought it would go. The strip club. Finding out Jenn was pregnant. A night of ecstasy (for me, anyway). The mental institute. Jenn not being pregnant in the end. And yet I was just scratching the surface. We had come so far and, for me, it just wasn't enough.

I pulled back my jacket sleeve, inspecting the bandages. They looked fine, though I knew we'd both have to go to the doctor as soon as we got back into the country.

I eyed the anchor silly band on my wrist, happy that the roses hadn't cut it off and smiled. I looked up at him, hoping he hadn't caught me staring at the band with a sappy and mushy expression on my face. He was resting his chin on his hand and staring out the window. He quickly glanced at me out of the corner of his eye and smiled warmly in return. He saw. And it was OK.

~~

We were sitting inside the ferry as it motored its way back to Vancouver, the mainland and the way home. Dex was chewing Nicorette, more properly than normal, still deciding to honor his decision to quit smoking. We both stared out the salt–stained window at the sea. The morning was clear, the sun's streams of light were twinkling brightly on the calm water. Not a hint of red in the sky.

Turn the page for an exclusive peek at Book Four in the Experiment in Terror Series, *Lying Season*...

LYING SEASON

I woke up with an extremely uneasy feeling and for a few seconds I couldn't remember where I was. I wasn't at home. The room was too dark and windowless.

I slowly sat up and tried to get my eyes to adjust. There were a bunch of blinking lights in the corner coming from Dex's computer and other gadgets.

It was the second night in the last week that I was dreaming about the past. I don't know why. Normally if I dreamed about weird things, they had something to do with the spirits we were about to encounter. I had begun to rely on my dreams as being prophetic, or maybe a quick glimpse into the mind of a dead person (as lovely as that sounds). But I was dreaming about high school and things that I had pushed out of my mind with the help of medication, doctors and therapy sessions. I didn't like how they were suddenly coming up now. I hope they didn't mean anything. They couldn't. It was all the drug use, that's all it ever was.

Not that I could remember all that much about the dreams. I knew my friend Tara had been in it, maybe Dr. Freedman, my old shrink. Nothing scary had happened. Yet there was something so disturbingly realistic about the whole thing that my heart was pounding away and I was sweating profusely. I felt the sheets. They were damp. Jenn would probably burn them by the time I left.

Earlier that evening, Dex had cooked Jenn and I dinner (his cooking skills were still surprising) and I had a bit too much wine with it. Just to calm the nerves. Actually, we all had imbibed a tad much, which made the conversation easier. Probably helped that we all ate in the living room, watching TV, and didn't have to stare at each other. I had avoided looking at either of them, the conversation I had with Dex still fresh in my head. We were putting it all past us.

Now my head was spinning from the dream and I was thirsty from the night sweats and the wine. I didn't want to get up for a glass of water, the black room was a bit creepy, and it was always weird being in someone else's place in the middle of the night, but if I didn't, I'd never go back to sleep. I carefully eased myself out of the single bed, unsure if I was going to walk into anything in the blackness. I made it to the door, opened it quietly, and poked my head out into the apartment. Their bedroom door was closed. The bathroom wasn't. Fat Rabbit probably slept with them. I hope he messed up their sex life.

I tiptoed to the kitchen, my socks silent on the floor, careful not to wake them or the dog, and plucked a glass from a high cupboard and filled it up at the kitchen tap. The garish, yellow streetlights from outside came in through the balcony doors, filtered by a gauzy curtain that moved slowly, teased by a draft. Even though the apartment was small and beautiful, there was something so…strange about it. Strange and off-putting.

I finished my drink and filled the cup up again, mulling it over. There was no reason for me to be creeped out and yet I was. I listened hard; I could hear the comforting sound of someone's light snoring in the bedroom, the occasional subdued rumble of a car outside, the tick of a clock on the wall. Everything was normal for a middle of the night Monday but that inkling of the unknown was undeniable. The hairs on my arms were rising with each second I stood there.

I gulped down the rest of the water and quietly placed the empty cup in the sink. If I hung around any longer I would just freak myself out.

I started to walk back to the room, wondering if perhaps I needed to go to the washroom, but something made me pause as I passed through the middle of the apartment.

It was *that* feeling.

That nauseating, lung-seizing feeling that someone, or *something*, was standing behind me. I could feel it, feel this solid presence at my back, watching me.

I wasn't alone.

And I couldn't move even if I wanted to. I felt frozen, my legs locked to the hardwood floors.

Then...

A dripping sound. My ears were so fine-tuned that the sound made my heart jump. A steady, slow drip. Had I turned off the tap properly?

But I knew it wasn't the sink. The splatter didn't echo, it fell in small, thick pats and from a greater distance. If it wasn't the tap, what was dripping?

I looked at my door. It was so close. I could run into the room and lock it. I could prop the bed up against the door for security, pull the covers over my head and pray for sleep. Or I could swallow my pride and run into Dex and Jenn's room like a child who has had a bad dream.

Or I could turn around. And see that there was nothing to be afraid of. Then my fears would be put to bed and I would follow.

I tensed up and very, very slowly, turned around on the spot.

I expected that if anyone was behind me, they would be way back in the kitchen.

This was not true.

There was someone...

Right behind me.

I was face to face with a...*being*...covered in graying skin that puckered in the shadows. Their chest had caved in to a red abyss. Their neck looked like a piece of fraying string cheese and could barely hold up their head, which was gruesomely flattened, wider than it was long, like it was smashed in by something heavy, leaving part of it open and exposed, a mixture of brain matter, blood and bone. The blood flowed freely off this gaping wound and fell onto the ground in sticky, wet splotches. The sick source of that rhythmic pattering.

The eye closest to the wound was destroyed, only a hole of gray goo remained, and the other eye fixed itself on me sharply. It was a female eye, puffy, with running makeup underneath. She almost looked like she could be crying, but...

She smiled at me. And it sounded like wasps buzzing.

I finally screamed.

Despite taking self-defense classes, Karate, bootcamp, my instinct wasn't to stay and fight. It was to get the fuck away from it. With nothing in my head but absolute horror, I turned and tried to run back to my room. My socks lost traction and slipped out from under me and I was down on the floor with a frightening thud, lying at the feet of a buzzing dead girl.

ACKNOWLEDGEMENTS

Special thanks to my editor Bob Helle (you'll get on Team Dex one day), to my friends, family and "my book club" for their support and to all the book bloggers who have taken the time to read and review the Experiment in Terror Series. I love you all and your encouragement keeps my chin up and my best foot forward.

For more information about the series, please visit:
www.experimentinterror.com

Follow the author on Twitter at
@MetalBlonde

Become a fan of the EIT Facebook Page by liking us at
www.facebook.com/experimentinterror

Made in the USA
San Bernardino, CA
17 June 2013